"**M**att!" Malcolm's voic
Matt fumbled
down," was all he could say.

His eyes felt heavy. He was dead if he didn't get to demon's blood. The shooters had them pinned in. Luiza, Allan, Malcolm. They'd all die.

Dämoren would die.

Clay's voice echoed in his mind. "Dämoren chose you. She wanted you to live. I want you to live."

He couldn't let her die. He had to live. The weapons had to survive.

Matt opened his eyes. Shots echoed from the direction of the building. Carefully, he looked over the side of the hole. The shooters were hunkered down behind a line of metal crates, firing down on Luiza and Allan. He could see their barrels, but didn't have a shot.

Matt lifted the Ingram and fired, emptying the magazine in a loud burst. The shooters hunkered down, but didn't flee. He needed to get them out. Out where he could kill them.

He had an idea.

He pulled the glass shaker bottle from his belt and stood on his knees, hurling it overhand toward the crates. The bottle flipped end over end, sailing over the truck hiding Malcolm, and out over the ridge above. Matt cocked Dämoren's hammer and fired.

The jar exploded, raining powder over the boxes. Sparks flew and sizzled as two brown werewolves and a pale-skinned vampire leapt out, their skin smoking and blistering as silver and garlic dust ignited at their touch. Matt locked his elbow, gripped Dämoren tight, held down the trigger and fanned the hammer.

DÄMOREN

THE VALDUCAN — BOOK 1

BY SETH SKORKOWSKY

To Kayci. I love our life together.

DÄMOREN

CHAPTER 1

FOURTEEN YEARS AGO

Spencer lay on daisy-yellow linoleum, his cheek against the kitchen cabinets. Slick with sweat, he cradled his arm and clutched the hard lump jutting below his elbow. He knew it was broken, but it didn't hurt. In fact, he didn't feel much of anything except a prickly tingle, as if his leg had fallen asleep in the car.

April's screams echoed from upstairs. How long had she been screaming? Drawing a breath, Spencer rolled his head to see silverware and shards of broken plates strewn across the cabin floor. Grunting slurps came from the other side of the fallen kitchen table, its green tablecloth crumpled beside it. Mom's slender legs stuck out from the other side. One foot still wore a blue flip-flop.

Last year, for his eleventh birthday, Dad had taken Spencer deer hunting. He bagged a six-point on their second time out. Afterward, his dad strung it up by the back legs and showed him how to dress it. When he cut it open, the acrid stink of blood and slimy gray intestines nearly made Spencer throw up. It was the foulest thing he'd ever smelled.

Now, that same stench wafted from his mother's motionless body.

Groaning, he slowly lifted himself to a sitting position. Halos ringed the kitchen lights. He scrunched his eyes, fighting a wave of vertigo. He opened them again and looked around, struggling to recall what had happened. His sister's screams had stopped.

"A ... April?" he croaked.

Bloody fingers, tipped with hooked claws, curled over the lip of the fallen table.

Spencer froze.

A round, leathery head, its ashen skin the color of birch wood, rose up. Blood and slug-like chunks of gore surrounded its lipless mouth. Pale eyes regarded him from deep sockets. The creature gnashed its teeth and gave a growling hiss.

Spencer's mouth opened. He gulped like a fish, his brain struggling to grasp what was happening. Terror and shock took hold, and a wave of calmness rolled up his trembling body, like slipping into a warm bath. The world seemed to go silent, numb, and Spencer's gaze fell away from the monster.

Snarling, the creature cocked its head. But Spencer didn't respond. It sounded faint and distant, as if from a deep tunnel.

Another of the gaunt figures walked down from upstairs. Its head nearly reached the ceiling. Red blood streaked the left half of its face. Its belly was swollen, bulbous like a freshly fed snake. A pink, plastic beaded necklace hung from the creature's neck. It seemed familiar to Spencer, but he didn't know where from. Sniffing the air, the beast strode toward Spencer's mother.

The monsters chuffed and growled with each other, as if talking. It felt as though they were speaking about him, but Spencer didn't care.

Something moved in one of the windows, drawing his gaze, but he saw nothing there.

The necklace-wearing monster gestured toward Spencer, stabbing a long, clawed finger at him. The other gave a short *caw* and crouched back down behind the table. Spencer didn't look up as the monster approached. Hooked talons clacked on the linoleum.

Movement came from the other kitchen window. A man furiously shook one of those red-capped spice jars, like his mother used, with the lid that twists to open all the little holes. Spencer croaked at seeing him, the cry for help lost in his throat. The stranger held out his hand, put his finger to his lips, and was gone.

The monster crouched before Spencer. Its bony hand hovered before him like a cobra gauging where to strike. Its breath came in quick, desperate gasps. The hand snatched Spencer's leg. Sharp claws sank into flesh. He screamed. Squeezing tight, the monster opened its mouth and dove for Spencer's calf.

Wood cracked as the kitchen door burst open. The monster whirled around. The man, wearing an olive green coat, stepped inside, holding some odd mating of a bowie knife and the biggest handgun in the world. Without hesitation, the man swung the pistol toward the necklace-wearing monster. A bright flash erupted from the tip. The thunderous boom shook the walls, snapping Spencer out of his near-catatonia. He found himself staring at the fallen beast before him. A pale finger of orange-blue flame jetted from the hole in its chest.

Cocking the hammer, the man brought his gun around to the monster behind the table. The beast leapt up and scuttled away along the ceiling with blurring speed. The pistol tracked it as if connected by an invisible thread. Another flash and deafening *crack*. Splinters of wood exploded from the brown paneling. Unharmed, the monster jumped to the floor. The hammer clicked again, but the beast sprung up the stairs and out of sight.

"Damn it," the man growled, then ran up after it.

Thick gun smoke filled the room. Spencer let out a breath. His ears rang in a long, steady hum. The wispy flames had spread over the beast's corpse, yet it didn't seem to burn. Slowly, he struggled to stand, but the pain of his broken arm suddenly became very real. Teeth clenched, he held back a scream.

A shot came from upstairs.

He needed to get somewhere safe. He didn't know if his family was even alive, but sitting helplessly on the floor wasn't going to help anyone. A phone hung on the opposite wall behind the kicked-open door. He couldn't see it, but knew it was there. He could call an ambulance, the police, anyone who could help. Setting his jaw, Spencer cradled his arm and stood. Pain shot through the fractured limb as if he were tearing it off. He held his breath and stepped forward, fighting to keep conscious. He passed the table where his mother lay, but didn't look down. Tears streaked his face. An old knife block rested on the counter, black plastic handles jutting from their slotted holes.

Another gunshot boomed above. Ignoring the knives, Spencer hobbled to the phone, slipping behind the door. He started for the receiver when another of the hairless, gray monsters appeared from the back room. It ran to the open kitchen door that hid Spencer from view, and then stopped. Peering through the crack between frame and hinges, Spencer watched the thing crouch and sniff the ground outside the threshold. A hiss rose from its lipless mouth.

Too terrified to move, Spencer held his breath, his eyes locked on the beast just two feet from him. *Please don't see me. Please don't see me. Please don't see me.*

Footsteps echoed on the wooden floor upstairs. The beast turned. Claws open and out at its side, the creature started back toward the stairs. It had taken only three or four steps past Spencer's hiding place when he remembered the knives.

Pushing aside the pain and fear, he yanked the butcher knife from the block and lunged, driving the rust-flecked blade into the monster's back as high as he could. The steel buried beneath the beast's jutting shoulder blade.

Howling, it wheeled around, ripping the knife from Spencer's grasp. Its long hand caught him by the neck and yanked him off his feet. Stabbing pain shot through his broken arm. Blindly, Spencer dug his fingers under the monster's claws, trying to pry them free. The beast twisted its thumb, bending Spencer's head to the side, then bit into his shoulder.

A choked scream gurgled in Spencer's throat. His skin ripped under the jagged teeth. Hot blood sprayed his neck and ran down his chest. Spencer hammered his fist against the creature's head, but to no effect.

A shock jolted his neck, numbing the pain. The prickly numbness spread through his body, taking with it his fear, but bringing a sense of hopelessness. His clenched fist loosened and fell limp to his side. He felt the monster not just on him, but inside him, pulsing through his veins, filling them with blackness.

A gunshot boomed. Something punched him just below the chest and Spencer fell to the floor.

Struggling to catch his breath, he raised his head to see

the beast lying before him. Faint blue flames jetted from a hole through its chest and out its back. In the room beyond, the man in the green coat crouched at the top of the stairs behind a cloud of smoke, his massive revolver held before him, and an expression of bitter disappointment on his face. Following the stranger's gaze, Spencer looked down to see the monster's blood and bits of flesh splattered over him. In the center of the gore, just right of his sternum, blood belched out from a finger-sized bullet hole.

"Don't move!" the man yelled, racing down the rest of the steps. He turned down the short hall behind him and entered one of the two bedroom doors.

Spencer clutched the wound. Slick, wetness oozed between his fingers. Turning his head, he saw his mother's body for the first time. Her blood-soaked shirt lay open in tatters, one breast exposed, the other gone. Slick pink loops of entrails spilled out her side. White bone shone through the gnawed holes in her chest and face. He screamed. Hot blood gushed from the wound and down his arm. He continued screaming. Blackness worked at the edges of his vision.

Booted footsteps hurried up from the back rooms and Spencer found himself looking into the face of the gun-wielding stranger. Streaks of gray tinged his whiskers.

"They're gone," the man assured, sliding the crumpled tablecloth beneath Spencer's neck. "You're going to be okay." Flicking open a knife, he slit open Spencer's T-shirt and scooped it into a ball toward the bleeding hole.

He lifted Spencer's hand and pressed the wad of torn shirt over the wound. "My name's Clay. I've fixed up a lot worse than this."

Spencer couldn't help but wonder if Clay had shot those people, too. A knot, like a hot coal, formed in his chest. *The bullet*. The burning spread, coursing through his veins like he'd been injected with lit gasoline. He thought of the monsters, the orange-blue fire that spilled from their wounds. A wave of blazing pain surged through him, twisting his body like a leaf on a flame.

"Hold still!" Clay said, fighting Spencer's thrashing. His

large hands pressed against the bloodied rag, pinning him to the floor.

The heat inside Spencer's body spiraled to the bite in his neck. He expected fire to burst from him like a geyser, but instead, the pain vanished. And not just the burning heat, but the bullet hole, the bite, even his broken arm. It was suddenly quiet, and he realized he'd been screaming. He sucked a deep breath and opened his tear-soaked eyes.

Clay stared at the wound in Spencer's neck, his dark eyes narrowing. The pressure on the blood-soaked shirt loosened, then vanished. Reaching for the revolver on his belt, the old man rose to his feet and backed away.

Spencer clawed for the rag and pressed it back over his wound.

Eyes on Spencer, Clay lowered himself into one of the wooden dining chairs. He gnawed his lip, then spoke. "What's your name, boy?"

He stared at the black barrel pointed at him. "S ... Spencer. Spencer Mallory."

Clay nodded as if he'd just learned some obscure piece of trivia. "Well, Spencer, that was a pretty brave thing you did." He nodded to the monster lying dead inches from Spencer's legs. Ethereal flames flickered over the body, seeming to almost hover above it. A thick pool of dark, burning blood spread out beneath it, soaking Spencer's Levi's.

"'Course a knife like that won't do anything against a wendigo," the old man continued. "Just piss it off. Now a staghorn blade, that'd kill it. But just the body. The spirit, the demon itself, now that's a lot harder to kill. Killing a demon needs a special weapon." He raised the gun up higher, turning it over for Spencer to see. Swirls of gold etched the blackened metal. A gleaming edge ran the length of the ten-inch blade mounted below its octagonal barrel. "A holy weapon."

Spencer swallowed as the gun barrel seemed to click back into place, aimed at his heart.

With his left hand, Clay flipped a latch on the back of the gun's cylinder. "You can stake a vampire, pump a hundred silver bullets into a werewolf ..." His gaze didn't waver as he pushed an empty shell out of the cylinder and dropped it into a canvas bag slung over his shoulder. "But its spirit will just move to a new host." The old man's fingers, as if independent of the rest of him, pulled a fresh bullet from his leather belt and loaded it into the gun.

"You see, when a demon bites you, it marks you. Not physically, you see. It marks your soul. It can possess you anytime it wants after that. No matter how much time passes, or how far away ... it'll take you." He reloaded a second round into the revolver. "When that wendigo bit you, it bound you."

A cold dread wormed in Spencer's brain as he remembered the numbing darkness when the monster had bitten down. It had entered him. He looked to the creature's corpse, then back to the gun in Clay's hand, pointed straight at him.

"Your wound's stopped bleeding, Spencer." He dropped another spent shell into his bag and pulled a fresh one from his belt. "Don't think I need to tell you that ain't normal."

Spencer loosened his grip on the rag to his chest. No blood surged out. Carefully, he lifted the red-soaked wad to see purple skin, like a fresh scar, where the hole had been. Sliding his fingers to his shoulder, he felt no wound. Was he becoming a monster? A wendigo, the man called it?

"You're not a wendigo," Clay said, reading Spencer's obvious panic. "That fire, you see, is its soul burnin' up. Only happens when the demon itself dies. If I'd just killed the body, it'd transform back into the corpse of whomever it possessed. But now it's burnin' up. In half an hour or so, it'll change back to the host. Thing is, Spencer, if the demon's dead, why are you healing?"

"I ... I ... don't know," Spencer mumbled, shaking his head.

Clay loaded another bullet. "How do you feel? Physically, I mean."

"Fine ... I guess."

The old man nodded, as if to himself. "I owe you an apology. See, I've been followin' this pack up the Appalachians for the last month. Thought I had 'em in Warren couple days ago, but they got away. My mistake. They'd been posing as an Indian family. Four of 'em. Parents and two teenage kids, but they transferred into a group of college students. Made it past me. Just didn't get here in time."

Spencer remembered the beaded necklace. He'd seen it on a pretty brunette girl that day out on the lake. She and her friends said they'd rented a summer cabin a mile or so up the road from theirs.

"You hungry?" Clay asked while loading a last bullet and snapping the little latch closed. There felt more to the question than just idle chat.

"No."

Pursing his lips, the old man seemed to study Spencer. Ponder him like one might ponder one of those puzzle questions his teacher Mrs. Metcalf asked every Friday, like, "Is stealing in order to save yourself wrong?" or, "Would you rather be blind or deaf?"

"Close your eyes, Spencer."

"Why?"

"Humor me."

Spencer did as he was asked. He heard Clay shuffling, maybe digging in his bag. A sharp pain shot up his arm as the broken bone fully crunched itself back into place.

"You all right?" the old man asked.

"Yeah." He nodded, his eyes scrunched from the now fading pain. "My arm." He rubbed it. A warm knot melted below the skin.

"Still hurtin'?"

He shook his head. "Just a bit. But it's going away." He realized his mistake as he said it. The mere fact his arm was healing was why there was a man holding a gun on him. Not that it was somehow weirder than his other mending wounds.

"Do you know any other languages, Spence?" His voice sounded a bit muffled, like when the phone would sometimes pick up an echo or other conversation in the background. "French, Latin, any of that?"

"No."

"Nothing in school?"

"No. I'll be taking Spanish in high school." The sudden thought that he probably wouldn't go back to school again flickered in his mind. It didn't seem real. An hour ago, he was eating with his family and bickering with his sister. Now they were gone. Eaten by monsters. Demons.

Something soft hit his chest, snapping him back to the present. He touched his skin and it felt gritty like sand. Rubbing it between his fingers, he sniffed the coarse powder. It smelled spicy, like his dad's roasted game hen. "What is this?"

No answer.

Spencer touched his finger to his tongue. It tasted more like salty dirt than anything.

He heard Clay's grunt. "Aren't you a mystery. Got a third-ounce blessed silver in you. Powder doesn't do anything, but you heal like one of 'em and speak French."

"What?" Spencer's eyes opened catching the last bit.

Clay's hand tensed on the gun.

He scrunched his eyes. "I'm sorry. I ... I ... didn't mean to ..."

"It's all right. Go ahead and open 'em."

Slowly, Spencer did so. The scruffy man sat in the chair watching him, the bladed revolver still trained on him, but somehow relaxed.

"What did you mean I speak French?"

"I mean you understand it," Clay said, his voice again muddled. "You didn't even notice I wasn't speaking English." His lips moved out of sync with the words, like in a Kung Fu movie. Instead, they mouthed the voice in the background, which Spencer now recognized as another language.

The old man grinned, seemingly amused at Spencer's obvious bewilderment.

"How?"

Clay shrugged. "Demons aren't hindered by human languages."

He glanced to the dead wendigo now blanketed in ghostly flames. "Are you going to kill me?"

The question hung in the air.

"Don't know," Clay said, finally. He lifted the revolver up. Its gold etching glinted. "This is Dämoren. She's going to tell me." Opening the latch, he pushed out a single shell and held it up. Tiny swirls and writing covered the silver bullet and golden brown casing. "She holds seven rounds." He slid the shell into one of the empty loops on his belt.

Keeping his gaze on Spencer, Clay lowered the hammer slightly, then spun the gun's cylinder. It whirred with rapid little clicks.

"What are you doing?"

The clicks slowed then stopped. Clay cocked the hammer back. "If Dämoren thinks you're safe, she won't fire." His brow rose, finishing the explanation.

"No! No, please." Spencer held out his hands, as if he could somehow push the barrel away with mind-power. "Don't kill me."

"It's not up to me, son," his voice regretful.

"Please!"

Clay raised the gun and pulled the trigger.

CHAPTER 2

PRESENT DAY

Blue hands glided across the polished wood box, rubbing a cloth disk around the seam. The officer looked at the swab in his hand and lifted the box lid. The fluorescents gleamed off the nameplate as it swung open. "Dämoren" etched in brass. A long low breath escaped the border agent's lips, like he'd tried to whistle, but maybe didn't know how. The other CBSA officer beside him looked down from his clipboard at the elaborate black and gilt gun resting inside amongst an assortment of intricate tools. The man in blue gloves removed a new swab from a plastic jar and ran it over the barrel. Tiny red gemstones glistened as the moist disk passed over them.

"That isn't going to hurt the finish, is it?" Matt asked from the other side of the table.

"No sir," Blue Hands answered without looking up.

"It's not going to leave any residue or anything?"

"No sir. It evaporates very quickly."

"What is it you're looking for?"

"It's a standard check for explosives and other chemicals," Blue Hands replied patiently.

"Explosives?" Matt said. "That pistol hasn't been fired in at least fifty years."

The officer holding the clipboard gave a short cough. His nametag read, "M. Johnston." "We need to ask you a few questions, Mr. Hollis."

"Sure."

"Your name is Matthew Aaron Hollis?"

"Yes." It wasn't a lie. Not anymore. He'd lived longer as Matt

Hollis than he ever had as Spencer Mallory.

Johnston's pen ticked the clipboard. "Country of origin?"

"United States."

Another tick. "And what is your destination?"

"Calgary. There's an antique showing there and I'm hoping to exhibit some of my goods."

"Are you aware of the laws about bringing guns, specifically handguns, into Canada, Mr. Hollis?"

Matt nodded. "Yes, I am. And this piece falls into the category of antique firearm."

Officer Johnston looked down from his clipboard to Dämoren resting in its case. He flipped to another page. "Year of manufacture?"

"1873, by Dumonthier of Paris."

"Black powder or cartridge-fired?"

"It's a black powder cartridge," Matt answered. "One of the first. Just a few months younger than Colt's Single Action. Mechanically, they're very similar, but notice the loading gate is on the left side. Very unusual."

The officer gave no more than a moment's glance. "Caliber?"

"Eleven millimeter, but the only shells made for it, you see, are those in the box." He motioned to the two triangular wedges set in the case's front corners. Gold-lined holes dotted the wedges, fifteen per side. Etched bronze disks, with brass centers, covered a little over half the holes. "Out of the thirty, those are the last eighteen shells in the world that can fit in it."

Blue Hands wedged his gloved thumbnail into one of the tiny grooves below the disks and drew out a long, empty bronze casing. He slid it back in and drew another, then another.

"They're not loaded, I assure you," Matt said calmly.

Officer Johnston's brow creased. "So they made a gun with only thirty shots?" the official tone to his voice waning into conversational.

"Those other tools," motioning to the little clamps and rods nestled in their velvet-lined compartments, all etched with intricate scrollwork and foreign words, "are for molding bullets and reloading."

The officer jotted something on his sheet.

Matt glanced out the window to the little parking lot behind the building. He couldn't see his car but knew it was out there somewhere. Probably getting a good once-over by more CBSA agents. Not that they'd find anything. He'd made sure of that.

"It is a very unusual pistol, Mr. Hollis," Officer Johnston said as his partner lifted Dämoren from its niche. Decades of gun oil had stained the velvet beneath to near black. "The blade under the barrel ... Very different."

"It was a sword blade," Matt said, trying to hide his discomfort as the agent handled the revolver.

"A sword?"

"Thirteenth century from what's modern-day Switzerland. The blade was broken and the owner had a gunsmith craft it into this." Matt pointed to the straight handle angling down from behind the trigger. A bronze knob, resembling a two-headed wolf, capped the end. "That's the original ivory sword handle."

"What's it worth?" Johnston asked.

"Oh, I've no intention of selling it. I just use it to draw people to my other goods."

"No." He tapped the clipboard with his pen. "The value?"

"Ah," Matt said with a chuckle. "It's appraised at eighty-four thousand. I, um, already put all that on the forms, sir. This won't be its first trip up here for one of these shows." He smiled, running his fingers through his sandy hair. "I'm getting used to the drill."

The officer smiled back. "Routine questions. I just have a few more."

The agent ran down his list, asking Matt each question, which Matt answered. Blue Hands placed Dämoren back into her box and closed the lid before moving his attention to the two sets of Victorian-era silverware, various jewelry, a dozen gold coins, and a yellowed diary once belonging to a Lieutenant James Whitmore of the North-West Mounted Police.

A door opened and a blonde woman stepped inside the small Customs office. The sharp creases of her dark uniform were so pronounced, Matt wondered if she did anything in her off-time but iron. She handed Johnston a pair of forms and a passport, gave Matt an emotionless glance, turned, and left. Through the open door, Matt caught a glimpse of a TV in the other room. A picture of a teenage girl smiling with her family. The name beneath it read, "Rachel Fidell." The fourth victim. Next, a grainy picture from a parking lot camera showed an old woman talking to Rachel. Then an artist's rendition of the woman: high forehead, round cheeks, gray-white hair. Matt only saw it for a moment before the pneumatics silently pinched the door closed. It didn't matter. The face meant nothing. The old woman was a mask. He knew the face under the mask, under the flesh.

"These are yours, sir," Johnston said, offering Matt his passport and a laminated blue card. "Welcome to Canada, Mr. Hollis."

Matt took them. The picture staring at him from the open passport was his, although the hair was noticeably shorter and it was taken during one of Matt's occasional, and always unsuccessful attempts, at growing facial hair. He closed it and slid them both into his shirt pocket. "Thank you." He followed the officer out of the office and toward the door.

"One last thing," Officer Johnston said.

"Yes?"

"That card you gave us, the one saying you have a bullet in you."

Matt nodded. "It sets off metal detectors sometimes."

Johnston gave an understanding smile. "How did that happen?"

"Hunting accident when I was a kid." He touched his lower chest, just right of his sternum. "Doctors said it'd be worse to cut it out than to leave it in."

"But the lead?" He looked like he was about to say more, but thought better of it.

"Copper jacketed. Doctors said I'm safe." Like his name, the lie had been told so many times it might as well be true. Unlike his name, however, the silver slug was never forgotten.

The officer bid him goodbye and Matt carefully loaded his belongings back into his car. Once in the driver seat, he pulled out his phone and sent a text to a number from memory, "*On my way."*

Twenty-three miles later, he pulled into the parking lot of an abandoned grocery store. Circling around back, Matt steered the car past bits of trash and dingy potholes to where a powder blue box truck sat in an old loading dock. A dark Hispanic man stood near the rear, smoking a cigarette.

Matt scanned the area. A cinderblock wall ran down one side of the alley, the building blocked the other. A subtle bend in the lot gave the benefit of being able to see a ways either direction, but not be seen by anyone on the street. There was no one around. He pulled his car up beside the truck and stepped out.

The man sucked a hard drag, and then flicked the butt into a grease-sheened puddle. "I was beginning to wonder. Everything go all right?"

"Fine, Cesar. You?"

Cesar grinned, flashing golden teeth. "Just waitin' on your slow ass." He laughed and motioned Matt around to the rear of the truck.

There, the Colombian removed a battered disk-shaped padlock from the latch and pulled the door open. Matt climbed in behind him and, after adjusting a mountain of shipping crates, cardboard boxes, and other debris, they withdrew a gray plastic footlocker and hauled it out.

Matt looked around, making sure they were still alone, then drew a key from his pocket and unlocked it. Cracking the lid, he saw an old army blanket. He pulled it aside, unleashing a waft of leather and oil. He spied the black steel of his Ingram machine pistol, a half-dozen 30-round magazines loaded with silver, one mag of gold, a gallon jug of grayish powder, and a wide array of various jars, tools, hooks, books, blades, and other trinkets. It was all there. He closed the lid. "Good."

"I said you got nothing to worry about, my friend." Cesar lit another cigarette.

Matt opened his trunk and heaved the awkward box inside. They needed to go before someone saw them. "I know I can always count on you, man." He pulled a thick fold of bills from his jacket and offered it out. "Three grand."

"I said you ain't gotta pay me," he said, taking the money. "Least not this much. Not after ..." His gaze averted. "You know."

"Yeah, but I want to keep this strictly business. I don't want to be burning any favors because sometime I might really need one. And that's when I'll call you."

The Colombian grinned. "You better."

The men gave their farewells and left; Cesar, west toward Vancouver, and Matt, north.

Thick trees grew along the winding road, hanging overhead and forming a tunnel through the forest. Matt, wanting to enjoy the cool air, rolled down the window and cocked his elbow out as he drove. Hours passed, and the number of little towns began to dwindle. Intersecting roads became fewer and fewer and less paved. His GPS showed him as a cartoon blue convertible ticking along a red line over a green background of nothingness.

Red and orange streaked the sky as he pulled into the little town of Milton Hill. A sign outside of town boasted it as the Winner of the Red Leaf Award, whatever that was. He wondered if maybe little towns like this made up these awards just to put them on their signs. Milton Hill consisted of maybe six intersections, three blocks of quaint storefronts, two working gas stations, another that had been converted to a used car lot, a pizza joint that claimed to serve real Italian sausage, and a school. On the far side of town, Matt pulled into a gravel drive motel and rented a unit under the name Walter Franks.

A few more of the cinderblock units were also occupied. One looked like vacationers, with kayaks and bikes strapped to their truck like escape pods. Two units over sat a gray Range Rover, its rear door open. A man with bushy, brown hair stood at the back of the SUV, his eyes seeming to study Matt. Matt looked at him, and the man's gaze instantly fell away as he removed a flat, black case from the vehicle and closed the door. Matt's attention moved to the black, and very obvious, unmarked police car sitting in front of another unit. Probably RCMP investigators for little Rachel Fidell and the high-foreheaded woman pictured with her not twenty miles from here. Hopefully, Matt would be done with his business, and Rachel and all the other victims avenged, before the Mounties even noticed he was there. Once in his room, it was straight to work. He flipped on the TV and his computer to see if the news had any updates on the investigation. Her family had announced that Rachel had been three months pregnant at the time of her death, a fact Matt had already guessed. Victims One and Three had been pregnant as well, although Victim Three, Anna Kurner, was the only one showing it. Of course, in none of the cases was the baby's body recovered. Those were assumed to have been eaten by whatever scavengers had torn apart the bodies before their discovery. Same ones that ate their livers.

To his relief, no new women had gone missing in the last four weeks, but that didn't mean much. There's always the hitchhiker, the lone traveler. Maybe no one had noticed it yet. Besides, aswangs didn't have to feed every single month. Maybe its escapades had brought too much attention and it was laying low. Maybe it had left. Maybe it had hopped bodies and was now possessing some poor bastard whose soul it had marked thirty years ago and now living on the other side of the world. Matt could only pray that wasn't the case.

As the news blathered on about wars abroad, sports predictions, and some puff piece about a family of adorable raccoons living in an apartment complex, Matt retrieved several jars from his locker, then opened Dämoren's case. One by one, he removed the spent primers from the eighteen shells, and using the intricate tools, set fresh ones in their place. He'd prepared the black powder back in Utah two weeks prior. Like everything with the sacred gun, each process was ceremonial. Flecks of his own dried blood had to be added to the mix, making each shot part of the shooter, part of him. Clay had always wondered if Matt's unusual blood might cause issue with Dämoren, but the pistol handled it fine. The gun demanded the sacrifice, corrupted or not.

From inside a red plastic box, Matt retrieved a gleaming silver slug. Intricate scrollwork covered the entire surface.

A single word, written in tiny script, spiraled up the bullet. *"Amen."* The closing line to the gold-inlaid prayer etched up the revolver's barrel. Like the powder, he'd cast the slugs down in Utah. Had Cesar not been able to get the trunk through the border, the Victorian silver in Matt's possession would have been melted down to make new blessed bullets.

The news show ended and Matt half-listened to an old Mel Gibson movie as he carefully measured and filled the shells with powder, slipped them one at a time into the plier-like tools, etched with scripted blessings, and squeezed a silver slug into place. By the time Mel had busted a ring of coke-dealers, leapt off the roof of a downtown building, and survived an exploding house, Matt had reloaded all eighteen rounds. The last eighteen in the world.

He loaded seven in Dämoren, then pulled on a nylon shoulder rig. Clay never liked the holster Matt designed. Said Dämoren preferred leather. Said dressing her in nylon was like putting her in a cheap dress.

"She ain't no whore," the old man had grumbled. "She's a lady. And the lady likes leather."

Clay insisted leather held the oil better, and that kept her slick. Matt didn't know about all that, but in the six years Dämoren had been his, he never once felt the gun didn't like his shoulder rig, leather or not. He pulled his jacket on, covering the gun as best could be expected, and headed out. Maybe he'd try some of that real Italian sausage. Tomorrow, he'd go to work.

The GPS didn't even acknowledge the dirt road as Matt rumbled the car up the primitive, rock-strewn trail. Once, thirty years before, the road withstood trucks and heavy equipment. Now, between washouts and fir trees, some places barely let him through. The crumbling bricks of a ruined building, a house at Matt's guess, peeked through the undergrowth. After nearly a mile the road widened into a white, gravel clearing. A sagging and broken chain link stretched end to end, venturing into the green forest on either side. Beyond it, angular sheet metal buildings, the color of rust and sand, jutted from the earth like the hulking remains of some half-buried battleship. Swirls of colorful graffiti covered every wall below eight feet. Faded black letters spelled "Bullard Mining" across the top of the main building.

Matt pulled the car around, its nose facing the entrance road, and parked. He popped the trunk, grabbed a bottle of water from the console, and stepped out. A chirping bird hopped between the branches above, obviously angry at Matt's presence. Circling around to the back of the car, Matt pulled off his leather jacket. Dämoren hung snugly beneath his left armpit. The bulletproof vest beneath his shirt made his lean frame appear stockier.

He opened the trunk and removed the Ingram. Its can-like suppressor was longer than the gun itself. He shoved one of the long magazines up the hollow handle, cocked a round, then pulled its green sling strap over his arm. Matt then removed an old policeman belt from the footlocker and put it on. Dämoren's bronze-cased slugs filled most of the bullet loops. Matt slid two of the Ingram's magazines, one gold and one silver, into the mag pouches. Automatically, his hands verified and adjusted his pepper spray, light, knife, a padded pouch for spent shells, and another for the powder.

Setting his foot on the car bumper, Matt pulled up the leg of his jeans and velcroed a knife sheath to his ankle. The staghorn blade was more of a good luck charm than anything. He prayed the day would never come when it was his only defense.

The bird above continued its tirade as Matt removed a red-capped spice shaker from the trunk. He popped the lid and sprinkled a ring of gray powder around the car. If the demon tried to run, the last place Matt wanted it was hiding in his back seat, or worse, destroying his car. Once done, he closed the lid and slid the glass jar into its belt pouch. He pulled his jacket back on, concealing the weapons, then closed the trunk.

Matt picked up the plastic water bottle from the roof of the car and opened it, breaking the white tamper-proof ring. He took a tiny swallow, then set the bottle back down and removed a flat blue tube from his pocket; about the size of a pen cap. Carefully, he pressed against his left index finger and pushed its oval button. It clicked with a short moment of pain. A crimson bead of blood welled from his fingertip. Holding his finger just above the mouth of the bottle, Matt forced a few drops inside. The red droplets plumed and swirled as they hit the water. Once he'd squeezed seven or eight drops, Matt screwed the cap back on and shook the bottle hard, then held it up. The pink water swirled, but did nothing. Holding it out beside him, Matt slowly walked toward the abandoned mine.

Warning signs clung to the old chain link, their original messages lost beneath rust and layers of spray paint. Not needing to pick the padlocked gate, Matt ducked through one of the several openings and continued toward the buildings. He navigated the rusted and decayed remains of equipment, searching for signs of the monster. Aswangs, like many demons, preferred to live in places with dark pasts. Places of great suffering. Mines were always popular. Most, especially the older ones, had their share of accidents and death. This one was no exception, but what had caught Matt's attention over any of the other possible locations was not the history during its operation, but its more recent tragedies.

After the mine had closed, it became a popular site for teenage parties. In the last twenty years, three teens had died here of drugs and alcohol. Two more were shot by a jealous ex-boyfriend. One, the girl, somehow survived a bullet to the head and spent several hours crawling down the gravel road to the highway where she eventually died. A sordid past like that would be irresistible for a demon seeking a lair.

Matt neared the first building, a one-story shed with a sagging metal roof. He checked the bottle again. Nothing. He removed the spice shaker from his hip, flipped the lid, and sprinkled a line across the doorway before stepping inside. Broken bits of debris crunched beneath his feet as he made his way through the building. Someone had left an old mattress inside. Grungy stuffing and grass lined an animal nest chewed in through the side. His hand near Dämoren's grip, he searched everywhere, even a small closet near the back, then left.

Matt checked the bottle again. The pink water was unchanged. He pursed his lips. The demon had to be here. Nowhere else met all the requirements. What had he missed?

Bypassing a blackened mound of burned tree limbs and charred bits of lumber, he made his way to the main building. Again, he shook out a strip of powder across the threshold before stepping through the open doorway.

Dread permeated the dim building. Matt checked the water again. Still nothing, but the creeping tingle up his spine assured him that something terribly wrong had happened here. He drew the pistol from its holster.

Light shone through several cracked and dusty windows into what he figured was once a cafeteria by the size of it. A glint of bright pink and white shone from a pile of refuse near the corner, its distinct lack of dust making it stand out. As he approached, he realized that it was a woman's sneaker lying atop a torn and filthy pair of jeans. Brown smears, the color of dried blood, stained the light blue denim.

Carefully, he pulled them aside to find a small figure of a young woman woven from bundled leaves and strips of grass. The hair, made of yellow, finer grass than the rest of her, was pulled back in a ponytail, except for short bangs in the front, which hung just above her eyes.

Rachel Fidell. She had died here. The monster had devoured her unborn baby, killed her, then ate its fill of her before dumping the body for animals to fight over. Afterward, it had made the doll. Matt didn't know why, it was just something aswangs did.

The bottled water was still unchanged. Matt scooped up the grass figure and jammed it into his jacket pocket. Later, he'd burn it along with any others he might find.

Keeping Dämoren out front, he searched the rest of the cafeteria, but found nothing. He checked a few more rooms, sprinkling the gray powder across their doors once he was done, then moved on. Aswangs favored higher points to make their nests, but Matt wanted to be sure before turning his back to the first floor.

Grimy metal stairs led to a catwalk above. Slowly, he followed them up, his footsteps making metallic *pings* on each step. Once at the top, he followed the walkway past several large bins rising from the floor below. Rusted chains hung from the ceiling like hideous vines. The walkway ended at a steel ladder leading further up. The rust-flecked bolts appeared secure. Matt holstered his pistol, pocketed the water bottle, and climbed.

An alcove opened up to the right, near the top. Heaps of what looked like crumpled canvas covered the floor. The stink of rot came from somewhere behind the filthy folds. Matt looked up. Light peeked through the gaps in the trapdoor above. He checked the bottle again. Still pink. Holding tight to the cold bars with one hand, he stretched out until his foot found enough purchase on the landing. The concrete floor was thirty feet below. In one quick move, he swung over the gap and into the alcove.

Bird feathers and bits of fur littered the lumpy canvas nest. Other objects lay strewn about as well. A silver watch. A few rings. A pair of green plastic-framed glasses. Anna Kurner had been wearing a pair just like them when she vanished.

Matt spied a gray rectangle of corrugated tin, lying a little too intentionally placed among the chaos. Drawing Dämoren, he crossed the uneven floor and slowly lifted the flimsy metal. A red plastic file envelope. Blocky letters written across the front in black marker read "Matthew Hollis."

A knot of fear balled in his gut. He looked around, half-expecting to see the barrel of a gun pointed at him, maybe a red laser beam, but no one was there. Matt turned back to the package and read his name again. Of all the things that could have been under that scrap of tin, this was the one that he hadn't prepared for. He holstered his weapon and picked up the envelope. Licking his lips, he unwound the white string from the plastic button holding the flap closed. Inside, he found a bundle of papers held together with black binder clips. A typed letter on thick paper rested on top.

Dear Mr. Hollis,

As you can see, we've been aware of you for some time. While we have always made it a point to not interfere with your activities, developments have arisen that have forced our hand into contacting you.

Matt stopped reading and flipped the pages. The first page was a printout of a web article from three years ago, detailing a multiple homicide and arson outside of Atlanta. The bodies of nine young women, possibly prostitutes, living in an old farmhouse had been discovered. The remains of nearly a dozen more terribly mutilated victims had been found beneath the house. The story had made national headlines.

Memories of Atlanta flashed through his mind. He turned the page to see copies of police photographs of the scene. Charred bodies, their limbs contorted into dance-like poses, lay sprawled out across a tarp. Close-ups of bullet holes, still visible in their crinkled skin or punched through their blackened skulls. Matt's fingers flipped faster. It was the biggest pack of werewolves he'd ever found. They operated a brothel outside the city. The things he saw, the bodies, the torture. He'd seen many horrors, but that house was seared into his mind forever, branded by the nightmares within. He'd sent those bitches to hell, even taking the last one down with the blade affixed beneath Dämoren's barrel. Once finished, and whatever evidence of his presence removed, he'd burned it down. Police, the FBI, even private bounty hunters, hired by the girl's families, all worked the case. Many, no doubt, still did. And now, one had found him.

Without making it even a quarter through the packet, he jammed the pages back into the file. His finger fumbling, he tied it shut, then swung back to the ladder and hurried back down. Maybe they didn't know he was here yet. Maybe they thought that he had killed Rachel Fidell and the other women. And where was the aswang? In his rush, he didn't see the little curl of rusted metal peeling out from the ladder rung. It bit into his palm and Matt winced, clenching his teeth. Blood oozed freely, but it didn't appear to be serious. Cursing, he continued down, leaving wet smudges on every other bar. *No time to clean them now.*

Matt reached the catwalk and ran. He shot down the clanging stairs two at a time. *How did they find me? No. That doesn't matter now.* He'd get back to the States, change his name, change his face. Right now, he just needed to get away.

He glanced through the broken windows, but didn't see anyone outside. No helicopters circled above, with men sliding down ropes beneath them. Gravel and shards of broken bottles crunched under foot as he hurried out of the building and across the yard toward the fence. He'd ducked through the torn chain link and started toward his car when he saw movement through the woods ahead.

A gray vehicle rumbled up the gravel road. Matt recognized it as the Range Rover from the motel. Through the tinted glass, he made out two figures inside. The vehicle pulled up and stopped in the forty feet remaining between Matt and his car.

Matt took a step back. There was nowhere to run. His thoughts automatically moved to the machinegun slung under his long jacket.

The driver side door opened and an older man in a dark suit with no tie stepped out, his hands lifted, palms outward. "Don't worry, Mr. Hollis." His accent sounded German. "We don't mean you any harm."

The passenger side door opened and the brown-haired man from the motel emerged, loosely holding a black and gold sword, its blade extending a hand-length before bowing forward in a long curve.

"I am Max Schmidt," the German said. "This is Allan Havlock and his sword, Ibenus. We are with the Valducans and only wish to talk with you."

Matt looked to the old man, then to his companion. The machinegun still pressed in his mind as a viable option. His gaze then moved to the strange sword. He'd seen one like that in a museum once. Egyptian; likely ancient. It was pristine. He'd never seen another holy weapon before.

"Are you familiar with the Valducans, Mr. Hollis?" Schmidt asked. "Did Clay Mercer tell you about us?"

Matt nodded. "Demon hunters. Kind of like Templars or something."

The German and his swordsman companion both gave pursed smiles, like they thought it was funny, but kind of offensive at the same time.

"Something like that," Schmidt said. "Descended from a

holy order. Is that all he told you?"

"No." Matt drew Dämoren out from under his jacket. The men's eyes locked onto the weapon. The hammer clicked three times as he cocked it back. He held the gun down at his side, just like Allan with his Egyptian sword. "He said you were dangerous and to stay the hell away from you."

The German nodded. His gaze moved from Dämoren and back to Matt. "I can't say I blame him for telling you that. Under the circumstances at the time, it was true. Did Clay tell you that he was a member?"

Matt's eyes narrowed. "Never said anything about that."

"Clay was a brother for over twenty years before our disagreement. He was among the best."

"What disagreement?"

Schmidt's tall stature straightened a little higher. "He took in a boy, who not only was bitten by a fiend but showed multiple signs of demonic corruption."

"And you told him to kill me?"

"Yes."

"And he refused, so you threw him out?"

The old man shook his head. "He left of his own volition."

Matt chewed his lip, studying the two men. Their stone faces said nothing. "And now that Clay is gone, you still want me dead?"

"No."

"Why not?"

"Dämoren." He nodded to the massive revolver. "It's bonded to you."

"Bonded to me?"

"Don't pretend you don't understand, Mr. Hollis," Schmidt said with a knowing smile. "The bond with a holy weapon is unlike anything else. A love deeper, more selfless than anything."

Even as the old German spoke, Matt knew what he meant. Clay said he'd loved Dämoren more than his late wife, even more than himself. Matt's infatuation with the weapon had started early. Even then, he'd known to keep that a secret from the old man as to not arouse jealousy. Only after Clay had died, and Matt inherited the widowed gun, did he fully understand the love of which Clay had spoken. "So what do the Valducan Knights want with me?" he asked, finally.

"Only to talk. Recent events have made contacting you necessary. We'd hoped to catch you in Boulder, but you'd killed the lamia and left before we had arrived. Once we heard of the killings here, we came hoping to catch you. Mr. Havlock found and neutralized the demon two weeks ago. We'd begun to worry you weren't coming."

"I was in Utah." He pulled the red folder out from under his arm. "And if your group knows enough about me to fill this, why didn't you just contact me instead of making me drive all the way up here?"

Schmidt nodded and ran a finger over his neat moustache. "We have far more than that information about you, Mr. Hollis. Our duty is to protect the weapons."

"Then why the game?" Matt's patience was running low. He'd driven a thousand miles and paid Cesar three grand to get over the border for nothing. Getting back to the States would cost the same, if not more, and he didn't have that much. He'd have to liquidate antiques, maybe even sell some of Clay's gold coins. Just the idea of that pissed him off even more.

"Ah," Schmidt said, as if somehow embarrassed. "Some of us wanted to see how you operated. How fast, and how quietly, before you were contacted."

"So you didn't know? Wasn't the fact I was in and out of Boulder before you even got your little game started, enough? If what you want is so important, shouldn't that have been your test?"

The German sighed and brought his hands together as if about to start a prayer. "I believe this meeting is starting very poorly, and I do apologize. Perhaps we can let emotions cool and go somewhere else to discuss this?"

"Hell with you. Just tell me what you want and get it over with. Not unless you're going to pay me back for how much your little test has cost me."

"Maybe a peace offering, then." He slid a hand inside his suit jacket.

Matt raised Dämoren, aiming at the German's chest. The old man gave an assuring smile. "Relax, Mr. Hollis, this is an offering of trust."

Matt kept the pistol locked on Schmidt, his gaze watching both he and the swordsman for any sign of attack. "Slowly." Schmidt withdrew his hand, careful and deliberate. Rolling his fingers upward, he held a small brown tube.

"Where did you get that?" Matt asked, instantly recognizing the bronze shell.

"Amsterdam," he said, admiring the etched casing. "One of your predecessors lost it in 1938 before fleeing to America." His cold blue eyes turned back to Matt, still aiming the revolver. "You may have it. All we ask in return is to talk."

Matt regarded the old man and the priceless shell. He lowered Dämoren's hammer and holstered the revolver. "Then let's talk."

CHAPTER 3

Matt gazed out of the window beside him, watching a logging truck drive past as the waitress set drinks onto the graffiti-coated table. Neon from the various beer signs covering the walls reflected up from the patches of lacquer still clinging to the worn tabletop.

Schmidt had suggested the roadside restaurant as a location to continue their talk. "Public enough, so you won't need to worry, but private enough to speak freely."

Matt followed them for forty-five minutes before coming to the Moose House, a quaint little roadhouse that served as the area's gas station, eatery, and late-night bar. The two men had evidently become regulars in the weeks they had been waiting. One of the waitresses seemed real happy to see Allan, whose accent was British, Matt guessed, once the man finally spoke. As Schmidt had predicted, Matt's temper had cooled significantly during the drive. The return of the long-lost shell, now safely nestled in one of the cutouts in Dämoren's case, had been the greatest contributor to that. The fact the old man had freely offered the treasure before the conversation did a lot to calm Matt's nerves. Now that it was with him, he felt it only fair to hear their story.

"What's in the shaker?" Allan asked, breaking the silence.

"Huh?" Taken aback by the sudden question, Matt looked to the salt and pepper shakers on the table.

"The powder. I saw you sprinkling it on your motel doorstep last night."

"Ah." Matt gave a half smile. "Magic powder."

The Englishman's brow furrowed.

"Kosher salt, garlic, silver shavings, white oak, bone dust, ash, tobacco ..." He recalled the ingredient list he'd read on the side of the plastic jug a thousand times. "Sulfur, dried wolfsbane, soil from the shores of Galilee, marble from a saint's tomb, mandrake ... Little bit of everything, really."

Allan nodded approvingly. "So a sort of catch-all ward?"

"Pretty much. Clay made the first batch back in the 80s. Been adding to it ever since. Once I find something new that works, it gets added to the mix."

"I like it," Allan said with a grin.

Schmidt didn't seem as amused. "That does bring up a point." He poured what looked like a cup of sugar into his coffee. "Whatever happened between us, Clay Mercer was a brother. How did he die?"

"Cancer," Matt answered, the smile melting from his face. "Stomach cancer."

The German frowned. "I'm sorry to hear that. We found the insurance claims for medications, but—"

"Wait, you read his insurance claims?"

"Never found any word of his death," Schmidt continued as if Matt hadn't spoken. "Just one day, he was gone. Where is he buried? The Valducans have ... traditions to honor our fallen."

Matt chewed his lip. "Vacaville, near San Francisco. Unmarked grave."

"Why hide him if it was cancer?" the old man asked, his voice bordering on accusation.

"He was bitten." Matt snorted, shaking his head. "Vampire. One of those bald kind with the extra-long fingers. Clay dropped Dämoren in the fight. I nailed it with a forty-five. I had these silver hollow points. Killed the body." He met Schmidt's blue eyes. "By the time I got to him he was too far gone. He told me to take Dämoren, put a slug in him, burn him, and bury him at a crossroads. So I did."

The German's gaze softened. "But you said cancer?"

"If he hadn't been sick," Matt spat, his anger rising. "All doped up on that shit they gave him, that vamp wouldn't have stood a chance. I'd seen him fight his way past four times what that thing could do. It was the cancer."

Swallowing, Schmidt ran a finger along his thin moustache.

"I understand." Sadness crept into his face. "He was a good man."

No one spoke for several long seconds. Matt replayed that terrible night again and again through his mind.

"Did you ever kill it?" Allan asked. "The vampire?"

Matt shook his head. "Never saw it again. Coulda jumped to a body it marked, now living in Australia, or something. Maybe it went to England and you got it with Ibenus, there." He motioned to the black flat case, like for a keyboard or other instrument, sitting beside Allan's chair. Matt understood. Even after stripping off all his weapons to come into the roadhouse, he still kept Dämoren holstered under his jacket. A real hunter never leaves his weapon.

The waitress returned, a welcome distraction for Matt. He ordered a sausage and egg platter. Even though it was after three o'clock, the Moose House was one of those places that served breakfast up until dinnertime. The German ordered a salad and a beer. He hadn't even touched his sugar-drowned coffee.

"Well, love," Allan said, looking up from the paper menu. "I'll have the roast beef sandwich, chips, and if it wouldn't be a bother, horseradish sauce." He smiled up at her.

"No," the waitress answered with a warm grin, jotting his order with a bit more care than the others. "No bother at all. That it for you?"

While Allan was attractive, with his dark hair and athletic build, Matt couldn't help but wonder how much of the Englishman's appeal was in the accent.

Allan shook his head and gave her a little smile. "I think I'll have a beer. Same as my friend here." He gestured to Schmidt beside him.

The dye-job blonde nodded, her gaze lingering on Allan for a brief moment before scooping up the menus. "I'll bring them right out."

Schmidt waited for the girl to leave before speaking. "Tell me, what did Clay say about the Valducans?"

"Not much. You're a group of demon-hunting knights. You find and keep track of all holy weapons. Your library on demon species and lore is massive." Matt ran his tongue along the back of his teeth, his eyes meeting the two men's. "And that you wanted me dead."

Allan's eyes shied away at the last part. Schmidt gave no reaction at all.

The old man rubbed his narrow chin and sighed. Clay had often done the same when teaching Matt math or introducing a new lesson.

"Holy weapons," Schmidt began, "have always existed. Whether it's Perseus's sword which killed the gorgon, Medusa, or Saint George's lance, Ascalon, these weapons are legendary. During the Middle Ages, there were several of these artifacts known across Christendom.

"When the Pope summoned thousands of men to the First Crusade, there were, of course, many whose souls had been marked by demons. So, as the crusaders invaded the Holy Lands, they brought with them vampires, werewolves, and other creatures that were virtually unknown to that region. Then, as soldiers returned home, they not only carried back the spoils of war, but ifrit and ghouls – monsters that, until that time, were alien to Europe. In response, the Order of Valducan was formed in 1142. It consisted of eight knights and their holy weapons. When the Pope announced the Second Crusade, the Valducans, whose ranks had grown to ten, answered his call.

"The knights were not invaders, but came to protect the crusaders and rid Christian lands of these Saracen demons. However, once they arrived, they found that the Muslims had their own holy weapons." Schmidt smiled to the returning waitress and took his glass of beer.

As the German returned his untouched coffee to the blonde, desperately hovering around Allan, Matt found himself staring at a deer's head mounted to the wall. The taxidermist had somehow captured a quizzical expression on its face. Maybe it had looked that way the moment the animal had died. Maybe it, like Matt, was wondering where the German's history lesson was headed, and why the Valducans had spent the past several weeks chasing him down so they could tell it to him. Had they wanted him dead, they could have done it at the motel, or hidden at the mine with a high-powered rifle, like the one that probably killed the puzzled deer there, and taken him down without Matt even knowing they had found him.

Schmidt took a long swallow and set the glass down on the worn tabletop with a soft clack. "Now," he continued. "The Valducan Knights learned of Muslim weapons that worked against demons the same as theirs. They captured Khirzoor, a holy scimitar. Because of its Muslim markings, they were ordered to destroy the blasphemous sword. But the knights couldn't bring themselves to destroy it. They said that the power of the weapons came from God, and if God chose for the Saracens and Turks to have them, destroying them was a sin. They swore instead, to protect them."

Matt swallowed his coffee. "The Church must have loved that."

Allan snorted.

If the old German was amused by the joke, he hid it behind another sip of beer. "Excommunication. They were *vitandus*; banished. They were proclaimed traitors to the Church and God, Muslim supporters, and thieves of the ten sacred weapons of Christ."

"So what did they do?"

"Went into hiding," the old man answered. "While not exactly pleased with the invaders, the Muslims did appreciate the Valducans for killing any and all demons. There were many ifrit in the Middle East back then, before they spread out across the world, and they called them Al Afareet Qatilla, the Ifrit Killers."

Matt suppressed a grin at Schmidt's needless translation for his benefit.

"As a measure of good faith, they returned Khirzoor to its people, and even helped in the training of its new owner, Faisal Ibn Sabbah, the first non-Christian inducted into the Order. The Valducans stayed in the Holy Lands for the next twenty years before finally fleeing up the old Silk Road into India."

"Is that where you're based now?" Matt asked. "India?"

Schmidt shook his head. "No, as wars and political climates have changed during the centuries, we've had many locations. Our current base of operations is in France, although we do have properties in various parts of the world."

The waitress came, carrying their food. Matt eased his caution enough to order a beer as well. She brought a pitcher, filled his glass, then topped off Allan's and Schmidt's. As Matt reached for his drink, he felt an unexpected weight in his jacket. Moving his hand down, he felt the plastic bottle jutting out from his pocket. He'd tucked it there when fleeing the mine and forgotten about it. He noticed Schmidt watching him. Casually, Matt picked up his fork and began to eat.

"I've enjoyed this little history lesson," he said between mouthfuls. "But why are you here? I mean, what's prompted this little truce?"

The old man drew a long breath, seeming to roll around Matt's question. He traced his moustache again. "The first duty of the Valducans has always been to protect the blessed weapons. Whether we are in control of them or not, we make sure that they are safe."

Matt felt Schmidt's pale gaze where Dämoren hid beneath his leather jacket.

"In the last four months, eighteen holy weapons have disappeared. Fifteen of which we know have been destroyed."

Matt froze, a bite of sausage still in his mouth.

"At first, their losses seemed unrelated. A team of three hunters disappeared in Hungary. A Roman gladius was stolen from a museum in Naples. It wasn't until the mauled corpse of a hunter was found in Florida, everything on him but his weapon, that we began to see the pattern."

Matt gulped down his food. "What pattern?"

"The weapons were the target," Allan answered. "The gladius, you see, was in a case beside a gilded helmet. The helm was untouched. The thieves knew what the sword was."

"But you said fifteen were destroyed?"

Schmidt nodded. "Two months ago, the blessed weapons of the men lost in Hungary were found in an abandoned house in Plevin, Bulgaria, along with an Ottoman saber last seen forty years ago. The mutilated remains of five people were there as well. The weapons had been smashed. Some were used on their former owners. A similar scene was discovered a few weeks later in China and again in Mexico. At all of them." He tapped the tabletop with a hard *thunk*. "The weapons were broken, then desecrated. Demonic glyphs and other symbols were found as well."

"How bad is this? I mean, how many holy weapons are there?"

The old man looked to Allan.

"Forty-six."

"That's it?" Matt asked, his eyes wide. "That's all that's left?"

Allan sheepishly nodded. "We think the Vatican might control at least four more, but they don't ... speak to us about that."

"They still can't be mad about the Crusades?"

"No. They just don't share anything with outsiders. Especially regarding the validity of holy relics. We've tried many times over the years to open communication, but they refuse."

Matt wondered just how hard they might have asked. Blaming the Church was an easy excuse. No telling how many years of animosity might have existed. Maybe thefts. Maybe murders. A lot of bad blood can happen over eight centuries.

"However," Allan continued, "many of the remaining holy weapons are in the possession of individuals, and that's why we've come."

"To warn me?"

"And to ask for your help."

"Mine?"

"A third of all the known weapons are gone," Schmidt said. "We can't afford for any more to be lost. This threat must be stopped."

Matt's eyes narrowed. "So what do you want?"

"We want you to come back with us," Schmidt said.

"What?" Matt asked with a shocked laugh.

"We want you to accompany us back to France. We are gathering as many hunters as we can for protection and to find whatever is destroying the relics."

"Look, I understand the desire to circle the wagons," he shook his head, "but I don't feel the need to follow you half way around the world."

The German opened his mouth to speak, but Matt cut him off.

Leaning forward, he spoke, his voice low and deliberate. "I've lived my entire life with monsters and people wanting to kill me. I've looked over my shoulder every day since Clay told me about the Valducans, the bogeymen who hunted me the way we hunted demons. So this is nothing new. This is what you've put me through ever since my family was killed and I was bitten."

Schmidt straightened, his lips tight. "Yes, Mr. Hollis, you were bitten. Clay told us about the wendigo. He said he'd seen its essence burn, yet you still exhibited signs of corruption."

Matt leaned back, withdrawing his arms from the table, suddenly very uncomfortable with where the conversation had turned. He felt the old man's cold, blue gaze drilling into him.

"He told us that your wounds healed before his eyes, bringing you back from the edge of death. He said you could speak any tongue, just like a demon. Yet he didn't kill you. He adopted you." Schmidt drew a long breath, giving Matt another dose of his piercing stare. "At first, I thought maybe you had bitten him, rendering him your familiar."

"I'm not a demon," Matt growled, his jaw tight.

"Then what are you?"

"Wendigos can't make slaves."

"Humans can't heal their wounds. So what are you?" Hatred tinged the old man's voice.

Matt glanced to Allan. A tension vibrated through the hunter's body, like every muscle was primed, ready to spring at any moment. He looked back to Schmidt. The old man gave no sign of fear that he sat unarmed, not three feet from a suspected demon. Balls like that could only come from one of two places. Either the old man was insanely confident Matt wouldn't be able to reach across and harm him, meaning he or Allan had a weapon other than the one locked in the Englishman's black case, or that there was a third Valducan. Maybe one of the dozen or so other customers in the near-empty roadhouse. Maybe a sharpshooter trained on him from outside the window. However, Matt somehow doubted that. Even with a hidden weapon or sniper, three feet was too close to be fearless. An incubus once knocked him across a room, even after taking two blessed slugs to the chest and a disemboweling gash from Dämoren's blade.

The other source, Matt guessed, was that Schmidt wasn't just some messenger or minion of the Valducans, like Alfred from Batman. Guts like his could only be had from a man who'd seen Hell. Seen it and lived. "You're a hunter."

Schmidt nodded tersely. "Retired."

Matt let out a long sigh, releasing a bit of tension. He hoped the two hunters would follow his lead before things escalated. "I can't just heal myself. Not exactly." He peeled the stained Band Aid off the side of his left palm, showing them the fresh cut from the mine ladder. "But when I touch demon blood, I can heal myself."

"Demons don't have blood," Schmidt said. "Their victims, the humans they possess, have blood."

"No," Matt replied, the tension returning. "It's demon blood. The burning blood that comes from a demon after its soul has died, but before it returns to human form."

The old man sat silent, his pale eyes studying Matt's face. "What's in that bottle you're always carrying?" His gaze darting briefly down to Matt's jacket pocket.

Matt's jaw tightened. There was no telling what the old bastard already knew. What had Clay told them? What had they learned while spying on him? *You're testing me, you son of a bitch.* "It's water mixed with my blood." He pulled the bottle out and set it on the scarred tabletop. "The blood will gather in the direction of a nearby demon. Clay called it my blood compass."

Allan leaned in a little toward the bottle of pink fluid, his expression like some zoologist discovering a new type of toad. "Amazing."

"It loses potency after a few hours," Matt added, just in case the two hunters developed some plan to bleed him dry and pass out blood compasses as standard equipment.

"Demons can sense one another," Schmidt said. "That's evidently how they can."

"Maybe, but you just said they don't have blood."

The German gave a tight smile, making him appear like he had no lips. "Perhaps I was wrong."

"Fine." Matt stood. "I thank you both for returning the shell." He pulled his wallet out of his pocket. "But I'm not interested in joining you."

"Mr. Hollis, please," Allan pleaded. "There's more."

"Better make it fast," Matt said, drawing a ten-dollar note.

"The demons are teaming together."

"So?"

"This isn't like a vampire nest or a pack of skin walkers. Different species are joining ranks, species that normally avoid one another. They're grouping."

Matt paused. "Joining ranks how?"

"I mean rakshasas actually mingling with one another," he whispered, "and also working with werebeasts and yokai."

Rakshasas forming packs? A knot of dread formed in Matt's chest.

Allan gestured to Matt's empty seat, which Matt took. "One of our teams found a pack outside Krakow. The beasts had raided the estate of a former hunter and taken his sword. At least eight demons. Among them: two rakshasas, two werewolves, a vampire, and a yokai."

Matt let out a long breath, trying to imagine the speed, cunning, and raw power of a pack like that. "Did they save the sword?"

The Englishman nodded. "One of the hunters was maimed. The demon that bit him escaped." His lips tightened. "They had to finish him."

"Jesus."

"That's not the worst," Schmidt said, his voice calm like a doctor delivering bad news. "We've begun encountering new species. Things we've either never seen before or breeds that haven't been reported in centuries. Monsters we'd thought extinct are reappearing."

"New species?" Matt said, mostly to himself. He leaned back into the chair.

"Yeah," Allan answered. "Which means that aside from holy weapons, we don't know what else affects them. Learning that a silver blade works on one species, while another needs glass or iron, took centuries and untold lives. We're blind."

"But how?" Matt asked. "If a demon can only enter a body that it marked, how are new ones appearing?"

"We don't know. We have theories, but nothing—" Allan's gaze moved to the table beside Matt.

The pink water in the plastic bottle cleared as a crimson bead of blood formed against the side facing the window.

Matt turned to Allan. "You said you killed the aswang."

"I did."

Flipping the snap open on Dämoren's holster, Matt peered out the roadhouse window. About fifteen cars littered the parking lot. He knew more were around the corner at the gas station. He leaned further, trying to follow the blood compass's direction, but didn't see anything. The red sphere elongated and split like a dividing cell. *Two demons.*

He barely heard the door behind him creak open.

"Get down!" Allan yelled. He pulled the old man to the ground and threw the table over, slinging beer and shattering plates across the floor. A woman screamed.

Matt whirled around to see a pair of men in the doorway with shotguns, raised in his direction. He dropped behind the table just as the gun blasted. The wall behind him, where Schmidt's head had been a moment before, exploded. Splinters of paneling and shards of glass from a framed photograph rained down around him. Matt drew Dämoren as another blast blew apart the table edge beside him.

The distinct *cha-chunk* of the shotgun's pump came from the other side, followed by another blast. The heavy table jarred back. Four holes, big enough for Matt's little finger, suddenly appeared before him. Hunkering back, he cocked Dämoren's hammer.

Allan lunged with his arm out, grabbing Ibenus's black case, and pulled it beside him before another loud shot blew the floor to shreds.

A gun clicked behind Matt. He looked back to see Schmidt huddled behind him, clutching a .357. Blood tricked down from a cut atop his balding head. Shards of glass and wood clung to his thin white hair like tinsel.

Another blast took off the table's top corner. He stole a quick glance through the buckshot holes. The two men closed in. Their eyes held a yellow sheen.

"Take the one on the left," Allan said, pulling the black and gold khopesh from its case. "I'll get the other."

"Wait, you ca—" Matt started.

Clutching the sword, the Englishman swung upward and vanished. Another shotgun blast vaporized the right half of the table where Allan had hidden.

Matt peered through the holes to see Allan standing eight feet from the table. One of the gunmen swung his weapon toward him, but the hunter stepped forward, swiping his sword and suddenly appeared three feet away from where he'd been. Allan swung again, and again seemed to blink another step with impossible speed.

"Shoot!" Schmidt yelled behind him.

Raising his head above the table, Matt leveled Dämoren and fired. Blue smoke plumed out from the holy revolver and the yellow-eyed shooter's chest exploded in a burst of crimson. Cocking the hammer, Matt brought Dämoren around toward the second attacker, but stopped as Allan suddenly appeared between them. The Englishman opened the gunman from his shoulder to his opposite hip in one horrific swipe, spraying a fan of blood across the room and onto the screaming waitress hunkered behind a barstool.

Dämoren out, Matt stepped around the table and approached the bodies. They didn't burn.

Allan moved toward the door, clutching Ibenus. Matt followed, hurrying through a haze of gun smoke.

Crouching to one side of the wood door, Matt held the revolver in both hands and nodded to Allan. Allan threw the door open and Matt leaned out. A shot fired. The bullet whizzed past Matt's head, hitting somewhere behind him. The shooter, a redhead in a dark blue van, adjusted her aim as Matt jerked himself back to the safety of the wall. Two more shots. The doorframe splintered with a hard crack.

An engine revved and tires screeched on pavement. Braving

a peek, Matt leaned out to see the van tear out the lot, turning left onto the road.

He jumped up and raced out of the door. Scrambling for the keys in his pocket, he yanked them out and pressed the unlock button several times. His car's lights flashed with every click. Once he reached it, he opened the door and dove inside. He had the keys in the ignition when the passenger door flew open.

Matt blinked as Allan scrambled into the seat.

Allan slammed the door shut. "They're heading south!"

Matt opened his mouth to tell the knight to get the hell out of his car when Allan slapped the dashboard. "Go! They're getting away."

Fuck it. Matt cranked the key, popped the car in reverse, and squealed out of the parking space. "Hold on!" He shifted to drive, hit the gas, and shot out onto on the street after the van.

Trees blurred past as they sped down the narrow county road, engine roaring. Matt yanked the car around a sharp bend. Momentum slammed his shoulder against the door.

"I don't see them," Allan yelled, struggling with his seatbelt.

"Nowhere else to go," Matt said. "Just hope we can get there before a crossroad."

"The compass?"

"Back at the bar." Matt veered around another corner. A rust-red truck ahead swerved out of the way, its horn blaring. "Sorry," he said to the rearview.

"Why didn't it detect the gunmen?"

"Familiars. It only points to the demon itself."

An electronic beat began playing, followed by a guitar. Diving a hand into his pocket, Allan withdrew a phone as a second rift blasted.

"Yes?" Allan said, pressing the phone to one ear and his hand over the other. "We're following them now." He nodded. "Okay." Nodded again. "All right. I will."

"Schmidt?" Matt asked as Allan jammed the phone back into his jeans.

"Yeah. Said he's left the bar. Wants to meet back at a fueling station outside of Milton Hill when we're done."

"He's not going back to the motel, is he?"

"No. Packed this morning." The car jolted on a pothole, knocking the Englishman's head against the ceiling. He grunted. "You need anything out of your room?"

Matt jammed a thumb behind him. "In the back. Never leave stuff in case I have to make a quick exit."

Allan nodded. "So, I take it the German doesn't like me," Matt joked.

"Who?"

"Schmidt."

"No. But don't call him German. He'll kick your ass."

"Why?"

"He's Austrian."

The road forked ahead. With no time to think, Matt kept to the right on the main highway.

Allan clutched the handle by his head in one hand and steadied Ibenus between his legs with the other. "This the right way?"

"Sure hope so."

Cresting a hill, they turned, running parallel to a river. A blue van sped along the road below. Matt hit the accelerator, seizing advantage of the straightaway and hurdled down after it.

"What's the plan?" Allan asked.

Matt tightened his grip on the wheel. His Ingram and Dämoren's extra ammo were in the trunk, which might as well be on the moon. He still had six shots in the revolver. "Don't know."

They drew closer. The road turned and the van vanished again behind the forest. Matt touched the heavy pistol in his lap. *Almost there.*

They were close enough now to see it through the blurring trees. A glimpse of blue as they rounded a corner, only to lose it again around the next curve. Setting his jaw, Matt hugged the bends. Tires squealed. Red lights framed the van's back door ahead as it took a steep turn. Gunning the engine, Matt shot around the tight corner, coming out less than twenty feet behind the bouncing van.

Matt hit the window button. Wind roared, whipping his shaggy hair. He took Dämoren's ivory handle in his left hand. "I'm gonna hit the tire."

Allan looked at the gun and back to the van, his eyes wide. "You're fucking kidding!"

"Get ready." Holding Dämoren out of the window, Matt leaned his head out. Wind hit Dämoren's blade like a rudder, and shot up his jacket sleeve. Fighting the resistance, he aimed at the van's back tire and fired.

Missed.

He cocked the hammer and aimed again. The van turned into a slight bend, offering Matt a glimpse of the tire's profile. He took the shot, striking the chromed bumper.

Damn it. He cocked the hammer again.

"Turn!" Allan yelled.

Looking up, Matt saw a tight curve ahead, just as the van hurled around it, its bulk leaning out with momentum. Pulling back into the car, Matt fought the wheel around the hard bend, the car's outer wheels grinding against the asphalt's edge. The road straightened, and he let out a breath. "Thanks."

"Pay attention to your surroundings," Clay had lectured. "Tunnel-vision'll kill ya dead as anything."

Matt started out the window, but Allan stopped him.

"Hold on."

"What?"

"Wait for the next turn. Just stay on its arse."

Matt nodded. Holding the pistol out the window, he hit the gas and closed in. The van sped faster. Matt leaned out, aiming at the tires. The van swerved serpentine, back and forth, each time leaning out with its weight. They crested a low hill.

"There's a left ahead," Allan yelled. "Bottom of the hill."

Matt kept on the gas, pressing the van faster. He wished he had the Ingram. Hell, he wished he had any gun. Dämoren's bullets were too precious for this. Steadying his arm on the side mirror, he aimed at the back left tire.

"Almost there," Allan said. "Slow down."

Matt let off the gas. The van hurtled away toward the bend, still weaving back and forth. Brake lights flared as it started the turn. Just a little late. The van turned, giving Matt a second's window. He led the tire a few inches and fired. The rear of the van jolted, like a kicked toy. Smoking tires shrieked and the blue van spun off the road and into the woods. Matt hit the brakes, stopping the car twenty feet past where the van had stopped. It sat motionless behind a cloud of black rubber smoke, facing the other way a few feet off the pavement. Chunks of broken tire lay scattered around it.

Allan hit the seatbelt release and opened the door, swinging the sword out in front of him. Matt jumped out, holding the pistol up, and circled around the car. Allan neared the van when the back door burst open. Something big and red moved inside.

Allan sprang back, directly into Matt's line of fire, as a pair of tall creatures emerged. Short horns ran the length of their bony jaw lines, up to a pair of curved white ones, no thicker than a pencil. Turning its golden eyes to Allan, one opened its mouth. An impossibly long tongue slithered out, then split open, revealing a writhing mass of pink tendrils. They shot out toward him, but the Englishman swung his khopesh and appeared four feet to the side.

Seizing the opening, Matt fired, hitting the beast between its knotty pectorals. Black blood exploded from the wound, followed by a geyser of purple flame. Matt swung Dämoren to the second beast when something moved inside the van.

The red-haired driver stumbled out clutching her pistol. *Pop. Pop. Pop.*

The bullets slammed into Matt's chest. Pain exploded through his senses, blinding him. He fell back and hit the leaf-covered ground.

Someone screamed. A man.

Allan!

Matt gasped, regaining consciousness. Dämoren lay beside him. Allan screamed again.

Matt reached for the gun, and pain shot through his arm. Blood poured from a hole in his left arm, filling his jacket sleeve. Gritting his teeth, he picked up the revolver. His chest felt like he'd been beaten with a hammer. The Kevlar had saved his life, but his ribs were broken.

Pushing himself up onto his knees, he saw the redheaded shooter. She stood still, her Beretta at her side, watching her master. The crimson demon hissed; its long tongue was peeled open like a banana from a hundred tendrils. Allan stood writhing, tangled in the pink ribbons, his face contorted in agony. Red welts covered his neck and hands where the strands touched.

The monster turned its long head, locking its gold-and-black-slitted eyes onto Matt. The woman turned and aimed her pistol.

Bypassing the familiar, Matt raised the heavy revolver and fired. The monster's head knocked back, blood and brains exploding out into the woods. It fell, its tentacles sliding from Allan as it went. The gun fell from the familiar's hand, her arms limp at her sides.

"Oh God!" Allan shrieked, his hands grabbing his face as he collapsed.

"Hang in there," Matt shouted. Clutching his wounded arm, he staggered to his feet. Blood poured from his sleeve. He scrunched his eyes, fighting a wave of dizziness. Purple and orange flames danced over the first demon, its black blood running down its sides. Matt dropped to his knees and thrust his hands into the warm, sticky blood. Tingles spread up his arm, soothing the gushing wound. He smeared his fingers deeper into the ooze. Ribs crunched into place beneath his vest. He gasped at the moment's pain, and then rose to his feet.

The woman still stood there, her face slack. The golden sheen faded from her eyes.

Allan lay on the ground. Tears streaked his pained face.

"You're going to be okay." Matt crouched beside him. Bright welts crisscrossed the man's hands and neck, like he'd been lashed with a cat o' nines. A few of the lines marked his face, but those didn't appear as severe. Many of the red welts on his neck and hands had blistered.

"It burns," Allan hissed.

"I don't know what that thing was. What do I do?"

"Don't know."

"It's like a jellyfish sting. Do you want me to piss on it or something?"

"No!" Allan's eyes flashed open. He gulped several deep breaths. "Vinegar. Water. Wash off the venom!"

"I don't have any!" Matt mentally ran through the contents of his car. "Vodka?"

"Yes," Allan winced. "The alcohol."

Matt raced back to the car and popped open the trunk. He pulled out the footlocker and dug through the bags behind it, pulling out a mostly-full bottle of Polish vodka. 120 proof. He grabbed a wadded shirt from the bag then ran back to where Allan lay.

"Here you go, man." He unscrewed the top and splashed some of the clear liquor onto Allan's hand.

Hissing, the Englishman balled his fist. "Fuck, that hurts!"

Matt stopped. "I'm sorry. I thought—"

"No." He motioned toward himself frantically. "More."

He splashed more onto Allan's hand and poured some over his blistered neck. The slime on the Englishman's wounds congealed into strips of clear jelly as the alcohol ran over the wounds. "This helping?" Matt asked, dabbing them with the wadded shirt.

Allan nodded. "Thanks." He pushed himself up into a sitting position, took the vodka-soaked cloth, and wiped the back of his neck.

A piercing scream erupted behind them. Grabbing Dämoren in her holster, Matt whirled around to see the red-haired woman screaming, her hands up by her face, and eyes frozen onto the burning monsters before her.

"Ma'am," Matt said, holding out a hand.

The woman looked down at herself, then to the gun at her feet, the van, and back to the demons.

"Miss, it's okay. No one's going to harm you." He stood.

The shrieking woman looked up at them, her eyes crazed and wide. Her gaze locked onto Matt's blood-smeared hands. She stepped back.

"Miss, you're okay." Matt kept his voice calm and low. "You're safe."

Without a word, the woman turned and ran away screaming.

"Hmm," Allan said. "She took that well."

Despite himself, Matt chuckled, then burst into laughter. He turned back to the hunter, sitting upright and wincing with every laugh.

"Poor thing. I wonder what all she'll even remember."

"If she's lucky, nothing."

Allan swigged the half-empty bottle and coughed. "Thanks. Thought you were a goner when she plugged you."

Matt rapped the vest under his shirt. "Worth the investment."

Allan swigged the bottle again and offered it up. "Good shot."

Matt took the bottle and knocked it back. The vodka burned his throat, taking his breath. The first demon had shrunk, its horns slowly retracting. He guessed it might take another half-hour before it had fully returned to human form. "Gotta dig that slug out before the Mounties get here. Ballistics."

"What about that guy you shot in the bar?" Allan asked, crawling to his feet.

Matt shrugged. "Can only hope it shattered. Can't have too many deaths linked to me. Caliber is pretty unique. No telling how many unsolved murders I'd be charged with if they ever caught me. Besides, by the time anyone might get it out, I hope we're halfway across the ocean."

"What?"

"They hit us, Allan. Must have watched you and Schmidt visit that place, then waited for me to arrive." He shook his head. "Never heard of a demon like those, either. I'm convinced. I'll join you."

CHAPTER 4

Matt sat in one of the worn blue and red pleather seats, reading his laptop screen while trying to ignore the endless drone of the plane's propellers. He scrolled through police photos of the grisly crime scene in Bulgaria. The bodies weren't just mutilated, they'd been torn to pieces. While stray dogs were responsible for some, the dismembered limb and crushed skulls were caused by something more. He examined a picture of the blood-inscribed walls. Curved symbols, like alien hieroglyphs, decorated the dingy sheetrock.

The plane shuddered and Matt tensed, letting out a sigh once the turbulence ended. It wasn't that he didn't like flying. He just hadn't been on an airplane since his dad took him to Colorado when he was ten. A lifetime ago. Airlines frowned on bringing handguns aboard. True, he could always check Dämoren. But trusting a baggage handler with her, even locked in a case, was out of the question.

When Schmidt said the Valducans owned a plane, and sneaking the weapons through customs wouldn't be a problem, Matt had envisioned a private jet. Fast and smooth, just like in the movies. Instead, he found himself on an old prop plane they'd picked up from some defunct airline. Fokker, they called it. It was loud, rickety, and felt like it might come apart around them with each jolt of turbulence.

When they stopped in Winnipeg to refuel, he had hoped he'd have a chance to get out. Maybe take a few minutes to enjoy fresh air. Schmidt said they didn't have time, and that the air on a tarmac wasn't the least bit fresh at all. So Matt had stayed on board, and watched the world through the little window beside him, his fingers fidgeting with the ancient and grimy ashtray built into his armrest.

The cockpit door opened and Allan made his way down the center aisle. The pink lines on his face had nearly faded. Gauze bandages wrapped his neck and wrists like some sort of mummy. A few red welts, covered in yellowed scabs and slick with antibiotic cream, peeked out, running down his fingers. He nodded to the screen in Matt's lap. "Pretty gruesome stuff."

"Yeah." Matt glanced back to the closed door. "He all right alone up there?"

"Schmidt?" Allan snorted, taking the seat beside him, across the aisle. "He'll call me if he needs me. I'll take the controls once we hop through Quebec."

Matt nodded, trying not to imagine the old man having a heart attack or something while manning the controls. He clicked back to one of the images, a close-up of what appeared to be sharp-edged letters within a nine-pointed star and half-circle. "You know what these mean?"

"Nope. We think it might be some sort of ward, possibly a summoning."

"I found a cult in Louisiana once. Crazy fuckers." Matt tapped the screen. "Looks similar to some things they'd written inside a barn."

"Demon worshipers?"

Matt nodded. "They'd kidnapped a girl. Sacrificed her while trying to invoke some monster. Don't think they really knew what they were doing."

"I never really understood demon worshipers."

"Why?"

"A demon has to possess a host. Who would willingly allow that?"

Matt shrugged. "They might not understand what it is. Maybe they think they're getting the power and not the entity. Maybe they just don't care. Either way, if they do it right, it lets one into our world."

"You think that's where the new monsters are coming from?" Allan asked.

"Sure."

Allan made a see-saw motion with his head and grunted.

"Maybe, but there's a lot of new breeds. These killings have happened all over the world. That's a lot of people giving themselves to possession. A lot of very organized people for it to be worldwide."

"So where do you think they're coming from?"

Allan gave an embarrassed smile and glanced away. "I think they're forcing their way into our world."

Matt's brow rose. "How?"

"Well, used to be, people believed that a person didn't become a demon because one bit them. They saw it as a scourge on the wicked. Like a murderer became a vampire, or someone who was just so full of sin, the entity entered them. Wendigos, for example ..." He paused, looking like he wished he could suck the words back.

"What about them?"

"They were people that were usually kicked out of their tribe. Starving, angry, they transformed into these emaciated monsters with insatiable appetites."

"Clay told me about spontaneous possession. Said if you killed the body of a demon that didn't have any other souls they'd marked, they just kinda floated around, waiting for the right moment."

"Exactly." Allan nodded, running his fingers through his dark hair. "So what if there's all these demons just floating around, been there for God knows how long, waiting for the right time and it's now? What if these cult markings aren't human worshipers, but demons calling even more demons?

"Like the moon and stars are lined up right and they're just forcing themselves through, then widening the door for their friends to follow?"

"Something like that."

Pursing his lips, Matt glanced out the window. Blue nothingness. Clouds. He could just make out green at the bottom. "Personally I like the idea of demon worshipers better. I can't shoot the planets and stars."

Allan chuckled. "Just a theory." He touched his gauze-wrapped neck.

"I'm not saying it's wrong. I just hope to shit it is."

The plane hopped twice more through Canada, before finally beginning its Atlantic crossing. Relinquishing the controls, Schmidt headed to the back for some rest, and insisted Matt join Allan in the cockpit to keep him company for the long stretch.

Matt sat in the padded seat, his hands in his lap, afraid he might bump the stick up between his knees, or one of the dizzying number of controls. Huge gray headphones covered his ears, muting the plane's drone. Outside was dark. Blackness. He tried not to think of the endless ocean beneath them. Yet the horrible fantasy that something would happen, something rendering Allan incapable of piloting, and leaving him to somehow man the controls, kept playing through his mind. The jolting turbulence was worse at the front, and each bump and shimmy fueled his imagination.

"That's a pretty cool trick you do with Ibenus," he said, breaking the latest mental scenario. This one involved freezing in the North Atlantic with a severed leg. "How does it work?"

Allan shrugged. His voice came in through the headphones. "I just swing and step. Nothing to it."

"How far can you go like that?"

"Just a couple steps. Not far, but enough to keep a demon off me."

"Or a shooter."

The Englishman chuckled. "That, too."

"I'd like to check it out sometime, if you don't mind. I've never seen another holy weapon before."

Allan's face tensed. He licked his lips, and grinned, turning his head toward Matt. "No problem. Mind if I shoot Dämoren?"

A sharp pang shot through Matt's gut. Anger mixed with insult. His jaw tightened.

Allan laughed. "Not that easy is it? It's like admiring another man's wife. Innocent enough until he says he'd like to shag yours."

"Yeah." Matt grinned, his jealousy melting. "Never mind. Sorry about that."

"Don't worry. I did the same thing when I first hooked up with the Order. Thought Marcus was going to take my head off when I'd asked him."

"Marcus?"

Allan nodded, running a hand over the bandages at his neck. "One of the knights who showed me the ropes. Big guy. Had this Norse axe." He paused. "He was among the ones killed in Bulgaria."

Matt remembered the crime photos, wondering which of the mangled bodies was Allan's friend. His blood had made the streaked glyphs, and dogs had chewed his corpse. "I'm sorry."

Allan only nodded.

Minutes passed.

"So," Matt said, breaking the silence. "How did you get into this line of work?"

Allan smiled. "Still nervous about flying?"

"Just answer the question."

"Fine." He lifted a water bottle from a holder beside his seat and took a swig. "My great-great-grandfather was an Egyptologist, which is really just a polite term for grave-robber."

"Huh?"

"Well, at the time Egyptian artifacts were very popular, and the prospect of pharaohs' hoards buried under the sand was very enticing. So he made several expeditions down, and became quite wealthy stocking museums and private collections with the treasures." He tipped the plastic bottle to his lips again, then put it back into the holder.

"During his last expedition, in 1903, they discovered a hidden temple near Thebes. It was dedicated to Horus, a hawk-headed god." Allan made a beak-like gesture in front of his face. "Inside they found a trove of artifacts. Priceless. They split the treasure up and took it back to England. He sold some, but kept several of the more impressive pieces for his collection, including Ibenus.

"Years later my father's uncle inherited the estate. We used to go out to the country to visit every summer. And as early as I can remember, I was fascinated with the sword. It was weathered. Hadn't slain a demon in three thousand years, but I was entranced." Allan gave a toothy smile. "When I was twelve I picked the lock to its case. Uncle caught me playing, swinging Ibenus around. Wonder I didn't break anything. I thought he was going to kill me. Really did. That was the last time I was allowed near the antique room. Then, when I was seventeen, my uncle passed away. His estate was split amongst the family, but he willed me Ibenus. That, and the cost of an Egyptology degree at Liverpool."

Matt shrugged. "Doesn't sound too bad."

"I took fencing. Specialized in saber. I tried to dedicate myself to my studies, but became more and more distracted."

"With what?"

"Vampires. Werebeasts. The occult. I started courses on folklore. Spent more and more time practicing my swordsmanship. It began dominating my dreams. I was obsessed."

Matt gave an understanding nod. "She bonded with you."

"Yeah." Allan let out a long sigh. The sound of it whooshed in Matt's headphones. "It was like puberty, but instead of discovering my cock and girls, all I wanted to do was kill a monster with Ibenus."

Matt laughed. "Dämoren did the same thing with me. She was Clay's, but I was completely enthralled with her. Learned pretty quick not to let him catch on. Like you said, it'd be like cheating on him with his wife."

The Englishman turned his head, his brow creased. "She bonded with you while still with Clay?"

"Uh-huh. Why?"

"Just never heard of that before. The weapons are very committed to their owners."

"Nothing happened," Matt said with a dismissive wave. "Maybe she was just flirting me up, letting me see what my future held. Kinda like the bright spot ahead. One day, she'd be mine, and I'd kill every damn demon there was with her." He licked his lips. "So you telling me my gun's got a wandering eye?"

"No," he laughed, turning back to the controls. "Every weapon is unique. Not just their form, or powers they might have, but … personalities. I just find it fascinating."

"So you think they're alive?"

"Well, alive-ish maybe. I mean, why not? You refer to

Dämoren as a she. You know they can bond with people. That's intelligence isn't it? I think, therefore I am."

"I've called my car a she before, too."

"True but ..." Allan bit his lip. "But with Dämoren you mean it."

Matt nodded. "Yeah. Clay used to say she had a soul. An angel that lived within her. That true?"

"Don't know. There's a lot of different theories."

"Like what?"

"Well, some believe that the power comes from pure faith. Like when they made the weapon, they had so much faith in it, that the blacksmith maybe put some of himself in there. Or maybe the power of God. But not all weapons that were intended to be holy weapons are. It isn't that easy. There's a lot of gilded and jeweled blades which were utter disappointments."

The plane shuddered and Matt gripped the armrest. "Have you tried?" he asked, his lips barely moving.

"Not me personally, but Valducans have tried several times over the years. I've found record of over seventy attempts. In all those times, we've made two. Two in eight hundred years. However, other people have made holy blades in that time, people that didn't know any of the prayers and techniques that had worked before. They just made them. And if asked to do it again, they couldn't."

"Any ideas why it doesn't work?"

Allan shook his head.

They flew in silence for several minutes. The engines' drone wormed back into Matt's consciousness. He looked out the window again. A few stars glinted through the darkness, not as many as he'd hoped. Matt leaned closer to the glass, looking down. A path of silver moonlight reflected off the black ocean below, stretched out like some endless marble floor.

"You never finished your story," Matt said, settling back into his seat. "So how'd you get involved with the Valducans?"

"When I was twenty, farmers had reported a monster lurking outside Greasby, killing their sheep. They described a huge black dog, like the Black Shuck or something. Press called it the Beast of the Wirral, but no one paid it much mind. Then the body of a girl was found in a bog. Some animal had attacked her. Of course some blamed the Beast of the Wirral, but not many."

"So you went looking for it?"

Allan nodded. "Yeah. Armed with a flashlight, a motorcycle jacket, and Ibenus in a beat-up DJ case I found in pawn, I spent two weeks creeping around farms and moorland. I started missing lectures, my marks were plummeting. I thought I might be going mad. Then one night it found me."

"What was it?" Matt asked

"Hellhound; a kind of werewolf, really. I had just crossed a farmer's fence onto a dirt road, when I heard it howl." He gave an exaggerated shiver. "Like an idiot, I pulled Ibenus out and headed toward it. I'd passed a hillock when I saw its red eyes in the shadows. It was huge. Massive. Like a small horse. I don't think I've ever been so scared in my life. It charged at me and leapt. I swung, trying to block it, and bam, I was a meter away. Ibenus had never done that before. It came again, and this time I blinked to its other side and brought my sword down right into its flank. Legends had said a hellhound's wail could sour milk and cause a miscarriage." He nodded. "I'd believe it. Unholy sound. It staggered back, then turned toward me. I blinked closer, and split its head in one blow.

"I hadn't been ready for the fire. Brilliant blue flames. Then Ibenus changed. The corroded metal mended. It became as new. The leather I'd wrapped around her handle split open as the ancient wood beneath grew back. Bloody amazing." He paused. "Then I saw the burning dog was becoming a woman. Naked, face cleaved open, and there I was, holding a fucking sword above a corpse."

Matt sighed. It had taken him years before he could handle seeing the body after a demon kill. Sometimes, it still got to him. "What'd you do?"

"I freaked. Killing a monster is one thing, but murder, prison. Thought about burying her, but what then? I just got the hell out of there. Went home. Police found the body the next day. I swore I'd never do anything like that again. But Ibenus had me. Month later, I'm in Chinatown looking for a succubus."

"You find it?"

"No, but Marcus found me. Valducans recruited me, and I've been with them since. That was four years ago."

"You finish school?"

Allan shook his head. "No, but I've been leading the project to convert the Valducan library to digital. Learned a lot. Lot more than anything school could have done."

"Like what?"

"Everything. Lore, demon-types, histories. There's a lot of stuff they've packed away. Like, do you know why silver hurts some like vampires and werewolves?"

Matt shook his head. "Why?"

"They're deceptive creatures. That's essentially their power. Silver is the metal of mirrors, so it hurts them. It reflects what they really are. That's why vampires abhor mirrors."

"Why don't werewolves, then?" Matt asked, his brow furrowed. "They don't give a damn about them."

Allan rubbed his bandaged neck. "Well … maybe because werewolves are more physical. Vampires are more spirits. It's why a vampire can continue inhabiting a body even after it has died. They aren't as tied to the flesh as a werebeast."

"OK, then. What about gold or iron. Rakshasas are masters of deception. Silver just pisses them off."

"It's a different kind of deception. Gold is highly reflective. It doesn't corrode. They need something more powerful than silver."

"But gold won't kill a vampire."

The Englishman shrugged. "It's just a theory," he said, his tone surrendering.

"Well," Matt said. "Best one I've heard so far."

They landed late the next day at a tiny airport in Southern France.

A tall man with hair so blond that it bordered on white picked them up in a sedan the color of oiled leather.

"Jean, this is Matthew Hollis," Schmidt said to the driver in French. "Clay Mercer's student. Matthew, this is Jean."

"Good to meet you," Matt said, holding a heavy duffle over

one shoulder and clutching Dämoren's wooden case under his other arm.

Jean gave a terse smile. His dark sunglasses stared back with cold indifference.

"Jean is protector of Lukrasus, and is one of our finest knights," Schmidt said proudly.

Matt smiled back at the white-haired hunter, then loaded his gear into the car. Not all of their baggage could fit in the trunk, and he and Allan constructed a makeshift wall of bags and suitcases in the backseat. They held it up between them as Jean drove. Matt held Dämoren's case in his lap, his shoulder pressing against the precariously stacked luggage as he stared out at the rolling hills. Picturesque houses of wood and stone sat perched above the lush farmland and vineyards. Ancient low stone walls draped in moss divided the farms. After forty minutes they turned up deeper into the hills and came to a large chateau nestled in a valley.

Passing through an arched gate they entered a wide courtyard. Large gray blocks formed the corners of the imposing brick building, three stories high. An Asian man in gold and white stood in the courtyard twirling a long pole with a curved blade on one end. Jean pulled into a red brick off-building, likely a barn in a previous life, but now a garage with nearly a dozen other vehicles housed inside, and parked in a vaulted alcove.

"If you want to wear Dämoren in here," Schmidt said stepping out of the sedan, "you may. We are holy knights, protectors of God's weapons. We wear them with pride and to ensure their security. However," his blue eyes hardened, "if it is ever unholstered outside your room, it will be considered a threat. Understood?"

"Understood."

"Allan will show you around and to your room. I hope you find our home to your liking." He turned and walked toward the manor, Jean in tow, carrying the old man's bags.

Matt looked up and around, admiring the ornate stonework of the garage. He could make out what appeared to be boxes and stacked furniture stored in the old hay lofts above. "Nice place."

Allan opened Ibenus's case and put on a dark clamshell sheath. The stitching was open along the top two-thirds of one side, allowing Allan to draw the curved khopesh. Following his lead, Matt opened his locker and removed his shoulder rig. He kind of wished he had Clay's old holster of tooled leather and brass that hung low off his belt, rather than the plain black nylon.

"*She's a lady. And the lady likes leather.*" Clay's voice echoed in his head.

Their weapons in place, the two men shouldered their bags and headed out into the courtyard. As they neared the man twirling and swinging the bladed pole in mock combat, Matt recognized his gold and white attire as some form of gi. A younger man, maybe seventeen, stood nearby. His sharp features appeared to be Japanese.

"That is Takaira Susumu, and Riku his apprentice," Allan said. "The naginata is Shi no Kaze. Theirs is the last existing samurai clan. Their sole existence is to protect Shi no Kaze, a duty they have performed for four hundred years, even after the official abolishment of the clans in the Nineteenth Century."

"Are they Valducans?" Matt asked, watching the samurai deftly swing the long blade back and forth in a series of rapid steps.

"No. But the Takaira clan has been on good terms with us since after the Second World War when we helped smuggle out many of their relics during the American Occupation." His voice lowered. "They are very proud and undoubtedly view joining us here as more of a favor than actual need for protection."

They followed short stone steps up to a pair of large doors. Inside, Matt found himself staring into a massive floor to ceiling mirror. Pale green masks looked out from glass cases hanging on either side.

Matt stepped closer to one of the jade masks. Tingles of discomfort rippled through him as he drew near. While at first they seemed identical, with their bulging eyes and scowling mouths filled with fangs, they were different. One's teeth curved outward, its short horns straight up. The other's teeth jutted forward before a rippled tongue. "What are these?"

"Chinese mask demons," Allan replied, stepping beside him. "They were bound to these masks in the Eighth or Ninth Century. They repel demons."

"So they're possessed? With demons inside them?" Matt took a step back. He felt their jade eyes boring into him. There was intelligence to them. Burning hatred.

"Yes. Nothing to worry about. Not unless you put one on. Their cases are alarmed and bulletproof."

Matt nodded, trying to suppress the unease the masks gave him. "Do they work?"

"The alarms?"

"No, man, the masks. Do they repel demons?"

"Evidently. Never seen them face to face with one myself, but there are multiple accounts in the archives. Unfortunately the technique of binding one to these masks was lost long ago. They're just amazing."

"Fucking creepy is what they are," Matt said, turning away. "We're supposed to be killing those things not decorating with them."

Allan shrugged. "Still, I'd like to try one of your blood compasses on one, just to know there's something in there." He motioned Matt to follow and they headed left, deeper into the manor. The passages smelled of wood and old smoke. More mirrors lined the halls, one before every barred window.

"So tell me," Matt asked, eyeing one of the small cameras mounted near the ceiling. "Were you wondering if the masks would repel me?"

The Englishman hesitated, his hand resting on a jeweled, silver doorknob to another room. "No. I won't deny there's something unsettling about your abilities, but I don't think you're a demon."

Matt smiled. "Thanks."

"But I'm not exactly in the majority here. So just watch yourself." He pushed open the door into a green-painted room. Old paintings stared down from the walls, overlooking several cushioned chairs, and carved wooden tables. A man with a two-day beard and tattoos running up his olive-tanned arms played billiards with a Latina woman, while a blonde woman sat nearby, reading a computer tablet. The haze of cigarette smoke hung in the air.

The blonde looked up from her tablet. "Allan, nice to see you again." Her accent sounded Slavic, maybe Russian. "So this him, huh?" Her gaze moved to Matt, partially hidden behind the Englishman.

Allan stepped aside. "Everyone, this is Matt Hollis from America and his gun, Dämoren."

Matt, suddenly feeling a bit awkward at center-stage, just smiled. "Hello."

"Matt." Allan motioned to the pale blonde. A jeweled-studded sword hung at her side, a yellow tassel dangling from the tip of its curved scabbard. "This is Anya Jeliazkova protector of Baroovda."

She extended a delicate hand. "A pleasure."

"Good to meet you," said Matt, shaking her hand.

"Anya joined shortly after I did," Allan said, smiling. "Baroovda has been in the family since the fourteenth century." He pointed to a painting of a bearded man in a turban holding the same curved sword.

Allan led him further into the room, closer to the dark pool table. "This is Luiza Moreira and that," he gestured to the gilded saber at the dark-skinned woman's hip, "is Feinluna."

Luiza brushed a lock of black hair from her eyes and gave a hard smile. Her full lips were painted burgundy. "So you're the famous gunslinger?"

"That's me."

She nodded as if to herself. "Welcome."

"Finally, we have Doctor Malcolm Romero protector of Hounacier." A horn-handled blade hung from the man's belt, its short, wide scabbard of carved wood. It appeared more like a machete than a sword.

"Good to meet you," Matt said, extending his hand.

The man stepped closer, his hand out to meet Matt's, then stopped. Rolling his arm over, he looked to a cobalt beetle tattooed on the back of his wrist. The image moved, seeming to crawl up his arm. Dropping his hand to the weapon at his side, Malcolm stepped back. "This man is possessed."

Matt's gut tightened. Three hunters in the room, four counting Allan. Anya, the blonde, was behind him. He caught her reflection in a mirrored case along the wall. She still sat fifteen feet away, but her posture had straightened. Tense. Luiza inched back, her expression calm, but cautious. Her hand rested on the golden saber hilt. Matt's fingers itched for Dämoren's ivory grip.

"He's all right," Allan said, his hand out between them. "Master Schmidt is aware of Matt's condition. It's okay."

"The fuck it's okay!" Malcolm took another step back, his dark eyes locked on Matt, sizing him up. "He's corrupted."

"He's safe, Mal," Allan said, his tone steady. "He's passed every test, even the masks. I've watched him kill two demons. He saved my life. I trust him. *Schmidt* trusts him."

"Tat doesn't lie. He's demon-marked."

"The masks don't lie either. A holy weapon has bonded to him. None of us can argue when a weapon has made its choice."

Matt wondered what would have happened if he had mentioned how unsettled the masks had made him. Still watching the three hunters, including Anya in the mirror, he opened his hands out to his sides. If anyone made a move it wouldn't be him. If they did, he could draw Dämoren from the rig and fire in under half a second.

Malcolm's jaw tensed.

"Don't trust me?" Allan asked. "Think the old man and I are his familiars? Give me the test then. Make sure he isn't controlling us."

The hunter gave a moment's glance to Luiza, then Anya. With his right hand still on his weapon, Mal opened his left hand wide, revealing a heavy-lidded eye tattooed in red on his palm. He thrust the open palm toward Matt and Allan.

Matt stood frozen, wondering what was supposed to happen.

Allan gave a dramatic shrug. "Well?"

Malcolm stepped forward, his arm extended straight, tattoo firmly before him.

Nothing happened.

"We're not your enemies, Mal," Allan said.

Malcolm's lips tightened. He lowered his hand. "You're demonbound," he said to Matt. "I know it. You so much as give me half a reason and I'll end you."

Matt's lips curled into a small half-smile. At least he knew where the scruffy hunter stood. "Noted."

"Come on," Allan said motioning him to follow.

Matt looked to the two women and gave a short nod. "It was good to meet you." Then he followed the Englishman up a staircase and into a long room filled with cases and old books.

"The hell was that about?" he asked, closing the door behind him.

Allan shook his head. "Sorry. Kinda hoped that would have gone better."

"What was up with those tattoos?"

"Mal spent several years down in Jamaica, Haiti, that area. Received his Doctorate of Anthropology studying voodoo and mysticism. Said he got the first one from a witchdoctor. Won't say where the others came from. He just picks them up here and there somehow. I understand his predecessor was the same way."

"What about the others?"

"Luiza's Brazilian. Sword of hers came over with the Conquistadores." Allan led him past the shelves of leather-bound tomes and cases of dusty relics. "Been in her family forever. She's a third generation Valducan. Tough as shit." He bent at a small cabinet and opened a squeaky door. He removed a green bottle of Scotch and a pair of glasses. "Anya's Romanian. Schooled in Florence. Good artist and outstanding programmer. We found her hunting in Rome. We'd thought Baroovda lost for the last two-hundred years, but it evidently had made it into her family." Allan unstoppered the bottle and poured a healthy shot into each glass. "She's been helping me scan, translate, and organize all the old books. She's been wonderful. Practically lives in here." He offered a glass, which Matt took.

The smooth whiskey tingled as it went down, warming Matt's throat. He looked around at the narrow room, resembling both a museum and a library and smelling that mixture of dust and age found in both. Paintings of men, presumably members long passed, covered the walls. Turning around, a picture on the wall caught his eye. A man dressed in a flat hat and a long, tan coat stood, his hand resting on a wide-bladed sword before him. Tiny red stones ran down the blade. Its white pommel capped with a pair of bronze wolf's heads shone beneath his gloved fingers.

"Holy God," Matt uttered. "Dämoren."

"That's right." The Englishman sipped his drink.

Matt suddenly realized several of the other portraits on the wall also featured the same sword, each from a different time and in other men's hands. Other men who'd loved the weapon as he did. "I'd never seen what she looked like before. She's bigger than I'd imagined."

"Look there, then." Allan pointed to a narrow case below the paintings. Framed sketches on brown paper, featuring various angles and cutaways of the holy revolver covered the back of the top shelf. Little scribbles and numbers noting measurements and notes surrounded the drawings. "That's the original designs from after she was broken."

Matt peered at the old drawings, then to the modest collection of mushroomed silver slugs circled before it. Little yellowed tabs with hand written dates indicated the year each bullet was fired. A tiny circle, absent of dust, denoted where the shell Schmidt had given him had once sat.

"Dämoren's the only holy weapon to be rebuilt after being broken," Allan said. "None of the others could be saved."

"My baby's got a will to live," Matt said, stooping to see the photos on the lower shelf. One showed a man with slick-parted hair and a hideous striped sweater holding the revolver beside a younger man with curly hair and sideburns. He grinned, recognizing Clay before seeing the little name card verifying his old mentor's identity. Beside it stood another picture, this one showing Clay older, maybe mid-thirties. Two men stood posing proudly beside him, one with a broadsword, the other with a mace. Matt peered at the slender man with the sword. "Is that Schmidt?"

"They were once close."

"I had no idea," Matt said, staring at the younger, clean-faced

Austrian smiling beside Clay. *He blames me for taking his friend away.*

"Dämoren's been with the Valducans since the fourteenth century." Allan took another sip. "That makes her more of a senior member than any of us and most of the surviving weapons."

"So what does that make me?"

The Englishman grunted. "It makes you alive. As long as she remains yours, the Order has no choice but to honor her decision."

Matt chuckled. "I can live with that."

"If you're interested," he said, almost shyly. "I can show the records we have on Dämoren's exploits."

Standing, Matt gazed back up at the painted images of Dämoren's former owners. Her lovers. He couldn't help but feel a kinship with them. "I'd love to."

FROM THE JOURNAL
OF SIR ERNEST BURROWS
1873

19 April - *It has now been three weeks since Dämoren, my sacred charge, was broken, smashed by a vampire's axe. I have wished the fiend's blow had struck me dead in her place, saving me the torment and humiliation of failure.*

I would be a liar to say that I have not considered taking my own life. Surely damnation awaits me for my sin, and I accept it. I have held my pistol to my head and prayed for the courage to end it, but in that, too, I have failed. The sword is broken.

I have gathered her shards, unsure what to do with them. I may be mad—no sacred blade has ever survived such destruction— but I still feel my maiden's life within her. If Dämoren still lives, I must protect her. I must atone for what I have done. I must find a way to mend her.

23 April - *I have just experienced a marvelous and most curious dream. In it, I stood again on that stone wall, the vampire charging me. I raised Dämoren to defend myself, but instead of a sword, Dämoren had assumed the form of a pistol. I shot, unleashing the fiend's Hellfire in a blast of smoke. I know this was no dream, but a vision, a message from my maiden telling me what I must do.*

9 May - *I have arrived in Birmingham and booked stay in the Bemore Hotel. Despite the rain, I immediately ventured to the*

Gun Quarter. While I found several impressive pistols, none felt as the one in my dream. There are many smiths here, the finest in the Empire. I have but to find the right one.

11 May - While visiting the Proof House today I examined several displays. There I beheld the most incredible of inventions, a revolving pistol with a sturdy twelve-inch cutlass blade affixed below the barrel. The eleven-inch blade section that had been Dämoren's tip would be ideal for this. The balance itself was front-heavy, but I imagine a pommel counterweight might solve this. This pistol is so akin to the one in my vision, it must be from the same man.

I inquired as to the weapon's creator and was told it came from a William Watson, a most reputable smith and inventor from London.

CHAPTER 5

Matt sat upright in bed, the laptop propped up on his legs, memories of past lives filling his head. Dim light peeked through the shuttered windows. The faint sounds of footsteps and voices echoed through the waking house. The time in the bottom corner of the screen read 6:32. His body, however, told him it was closer to midnight. After going to bed early the day before, he had awakened at two o'clock with a stopped-up nose and unable to coerce himself back to sleep.

After his cold reception from Jean and deathly warning from Malcolm, Matt figured wandering the house alone at that hour probably wasn't the best of ideas. He had spent the last few hours reading some of Dämoren's exploits that Allan and Anya had transcribed. While most were dry accounts of monster attacks and methods used to track and exterminate them, one hunter, a seventeenth century swordsman named Sir Victor Kluge, was a true storyteller. Kluge's flair for dramatic prose read more like an action novel documenting his adventures across Europe. Once finished with an especially exciting story of Kluge battling a nest of vampires in Greece, Matt closed the laptop, pulled on Dämoren's shoulder rig, and ventured out into the house.

Outside, fiery hues of orange and red streaked the morning sky as the sun peeked over the hills, casting long shadows through the valley. Matt stared out one of the windows overlooking the eastern vineyards when he noticed Luiza, the Brazilian huntress, jogging down a narrow road between vine rows. Some real exercise after the past few days of travel sounded like a good idea, but the pressure clogging his sinuses told him otherwise. Maybe after a hot shower and some breakfast, he'd feel up to it. First, he needed to figure out where in the hell the kitchen was.

He explored deeper into the house, past several dark doors he assumed were more bedrooms. Paintings and old photographs decorated the walls, and Matt found himself wondering where Victor Kluge's portrait might be. He'd have to ask Allan whenever he found him. Voices came from outside one of the tall windows, and Matt looked down into the courtyard where several people buzzed around a white van. A black woman with tight braids, and a lanky man who could double as a scarecrow in his off-time, talked to Anya and a gray-haired man with a cane. A hulking guy with the type of long blond hair most often seen on a romance novel loaded boxes into the back of the vehicle.

"They're leaving for Barcelona," said a soft voice.

Jumping, Matt spun to see a dark-skinned man with a neatly trimmed, black beard standing beside him.

"Sorry," he said, hiding his surprise. "I didn't hear you come up."

The man grinned, revealing a mouth of white teeth. "I get that a lot." His voice sounded British. "I'm Behrang." He offered his hand. "You may call me Ben."

"Matt Hollis." They shook hands.

Ben turned, showing a curved sword at his hip. A golden crescent moon formed the sword's pommel. "This is Khirzoor."

Matt's brow creased. "Khirzoor. That's the Arabian blade from the crusades?"

"Turkish," he said with a smile. "But, yes."

Matt couldn't help but feel a sense of wonder at seeing the ancient weapon. It was true history and also, in a way, a celebrity. "This." He lifted his arm to show Dämoren's ivory and bronze grip jutting from its holster. "Is Dä—"

"Dämoren," Ben said, finishing the sentence. "I have heard of it. And of you. Your reputation is well known."

A tinge of apprehension slithered in Matt's stomach. "Well, I hope it's a good one."

Ben stood silent for a moment. His lips tightened, as if trying to choose his words. "You are a very accomplished hunter."

"Thank you." Eager to break the sudden tension, Matt nodded back toward the window. "What's in Barcelona?"

"There's been reports of monsters. The older gentleman is Master Alex Turgen, one of the elders. The black woman is Natuche. She protects Krayaf and is leading the team. Anya, the blonde woman, and Ramón, the skinny man, are Librarians. Ramón isn't the most experienced knight, but he's the authority on demonic rites. They're hoping he might find some clues about the murders."

"Does Turgen lead the Valducans?" Matt sniffed his clogged nose.

"No. Not ... officially. He's a senior knight, and his word carries a lot of weight."

Matt eyed the old man. His right hand, the one without the cane, moved quick, animated, as he spoke to Natuche. "So he's like Schmidt, a former hunter?"

"Ah, similar. But more ... diplomatic."

Less of an ass, you mean. "And the Librarians, they're the ones in charge of the archives? Like Allan?"

"Yes, but also much more than that. They search old stories and records, finding long lost holy weapons. They also keep track of, um ... independent hunters."

Matt nodded. "Like me."

"Like you." Ben looked out at the knights loading the van and sighed, his gaze lingering on Natuche. "Have you eaten?"

"Not yet. Haven't found the kitchen."

"Well, then," he gestured down the hallway, "let me show you."

Matt followed him down a flight of stairs and into a blue-plastered room with several tables, two of which stretched the length of the right side. A pitcher of milk and another of some red juice rested atop a bar on the back wall beside some fruit and various condiments. It reminded Matt of something he'd see in a hotel or bed and breakfast.

A big man in a bright orange shirt and a gray flat cap, like newsies wore in old movies, leaned his head out an open doorway. "Mornin', Ben." His accent sounded like a mixture of Australian and Irish. "Whose yer friend?" It sounded like he said *freend.*

"Tom," Ben said. "This is Matt, protector of Dämoren."

Tom's mouth opened into almost a shocked smile. "Ah, the shootah!" He extended a large hand. White scars crisscrossed part of his palm and across onto the back, like thick spiderwebs. His pinky finger was nothing more than a wrinkled nub.

Trying not to react to the gruesome wound, Matt shook it. "Good to meet you."

"Right. You got any allergies, any of that?"

Matt gave a sniffle, then shook his head. "Nothing food-wise."

Tom nodded and motioned to one of the tables. "Right. Just have a seat. Ye want coffee?"

"Coffee sounds good."

"Ben?" he asked the dark-skinned hunter.

"Please, and I'll just have some fruit, thank you."

The two men helped themselves to the bar. Matt made a plate with some cheese and sliced meats, while Ben picked toast and some yogurt. A few minutes later Tom came back with a pair of coffees. Matt couldn't help but notice a slight limp in the man's walk. He sipped his coffee, which was really just a cup of espresso and milk, but it was the best Matt had ever tasted.

"So tell me," Matt said, folding a thin circle of meat onto a cheese slice. "Are all the Librarians also hunters, or are there any that are just full time?"

Ben sipped his coffee. "They are all knights. Some are former. Sonu, my old mentor, is in India. He's looking after some of our interests there while helping with research. Mikhail is still a student. Although," he added, his voice regretful, "his mentor, Julius, was killed not long ago and his weapon destroyed. But soon, when Mikhail is ready, a weapon will choose him."

"What about you? Are you a full-time hunter?"

"No," Ben chuckled. "No one is what you would call a full-time hunter. We all have other duties. I, for instance, am an accountant. I handle the Order's books for the vineyard here, as well as our other properties and income."

"Like what?"

Ben ran a finger across his bearded chin. "We have different properties across the EU, some in Africa, even in the Americas. Some is used for farms, or leased to tenants. We're planning to build a wind farm in Chile. The income from that should help us a great deal. My job is to keep the Valducans' anonymity. Mask where the money goes. With it, we can afford this house, fuel for the autos and airplane, stock the hospital. Even a bit of pay for ourselves."

Matt ate another bite of cheese and meat, visualizing the Valducans' web. Money in his profession was a rarity. His only real job had been antiques. Clay had taught him the tricks. How to find them, what to look for, how to buy and sell. It wasn't much. Not for his expenses. The rest of his income had come from demons or their victims. Jewelry, petty cash, anything he could move quickly. He didn't see it as stealing. Not really, anyway.

"Think of it as a service charge," Clay had told him. "You freed their souls. Avenged 'em."

Tom stepped out of the kitchen and set a plate down before Matt. "Ere ya go."

Matt stared at the golden, triangular omelet steaming before him. He'd expected something more like scrambled eggs and soggy bacon. "Wow. Thank you."

"Try it."

Even through his stuffed nose, Matt could smell the buttery aroma.

He cut off a corner and slipped into his mouth. "Delicious."

The burly cook gave a proud nod. "Right. You just let me know if you need anything." He sauntered back through the kitchen door. The cuff of his pant leg lifted slightly with each limped step, revealing a dull silver rod jutting from Tom's shoe.

Ben peeled the foil lid off his yogurt and began to eat.

"Tom," Matt said, his voice low. "What happened to him?"

The hunter's dark eyes darted back toward the kitchen. "He was a knight. Two years ago, he was mauled by an itwan." He seemed to read Matt's blank face. "They have a corrosive venom, like acid. He managed to kill the beast, but ..."

"Jesus."

"Yes. So now he stays here. His sword, Eslarin, is now bonded with Yev, another knight."

Matt sighed. The man's injuries were tragic enough but

imagining how it must feel for him to see his sword, his holy weapon in another man's hands, that it had chosen another over him because he was no longer capable, that was somehow worse. "I couldn't do it."

"Nor I."

After a few minutes, Malcolm walked into the dining room, accompanied by a man with short, coppery hair. A thick-bladed sword hung on his hip. Malcolm glanced at Matt then away. "Good morning, Ben."

"Good morning," Ben replied. "And to you as well, Colin."

Colin only grunted.

Matt finished his omelet, as the two men talked to Tom. "You said you have a hospital?"

Ben gave a little shrug. "More of a clinic, really. Colin oversees it. No big surgeries or operations. Mostly stitching wounds, removing spines, or claws, or the occasional bullet. You can probably understand that we avoid hospitals as much as we can. It leads to … questions."

"I understand," Matt said through a grin. "Would there be any allergy medicine there."

"There should be. Would you like me to take you?"

"Please."

Two hours later, Matt found his way to the library. Anya sat at a desk nestled in an alcove of wooden bookshelves typing at a little gray laptop. A blue coil of smoke rose from her ashtray and out the narrow window before her desk. A dark-haired teen poked his head out from behind a shelf. He regarded Matt with a short, curious glance, then tucked back out of sight. Across the room, Allan sat at a computer clicking his mouse with hard, rapid taps.

"Hell with this bollocksed piece of shit!" He jabbed his finger hard into the mouse button.

"Everything all right?" Matt asked.

Allan threw his hand up in frustration. "This damned system. It's old and buggy. We've asked for new equipment but Turgen keeps insisting we don't need it." He let out a long breath. "Week's worth of work lost. Have to start again."

"That's why they pay you the big bucks," Matt said.

"Yeah," Allan forcefully laughed. "So, how's your morning?"

"Fine. Been reading about Victor Kluge, one of the old hunters. Good stuff."

"Kluge," Allan mumbled, his eyes moving upward. "The one who killed two vampires in one blow?"

"That's him."

The Englishman gave a half-grimace. "I'll tell you, Matt, Kluge's stories, while fun, don't always coincide with reports of those with him. It seems he was prone to a bit of exaggeration."

"So he didn't kill two vampires in one swipe?"

"Actually, that part is true. At least according to other knights with him at the time. However other things like the size of the nest and the role of the three other men with him in Budapest, are disputed."

"Three? I hadn't thought there were that many with him."

"Precisely."

"Still," Matt said, "Two in one swing is pretty impressive, especially if that one is confirmed." He looked in the direction of the wall with Dämoren's former owners. Three cases packed with leather-bound books stood between them. "I didn't see his painting over there."

Allan touched his neck lightly. The bandages were gone, but the pink, scabbed wounds were still there. "I think it's downstairs."

"Do you know where?"

"By the gym." He looked back at the computer screen and shook his head. "Come on." He stood. "This thing is just pissing me off. I'll help you find it."

Matt followed him through the old house down to the first floor.

"So that kid in the library," Matt said. "Is that Mikhail?"

Allan nodded. "That's him. Why?"

"Ben told me about him. Real sad losing his mentor like that."

"He's a good bloke, but probably not the most fit for Librarian."

"Why's that?"

"He spends more time fluttering around Anya than anything

else. Bloody annoying."

"Sounds like a teenager."

The hall turned. The walls in this portion were wood-paneled and much simpler than in the rest of the home. Allan explained they were in the old servants' side. They turned down a little hallway, and then stopped before a wall of paintings. Muffled metallic clacks came through one of the wooden doors behind them

"He should be right here," Allan said, scanning the portraits.

Searching the paintings, Matt spied the image of a man holding the sword Dämoren to his side. Brown curls spilled out from under his wide hat onto the shoulders of a black and tan doublet. The sprawled body of a blue devil lay at his feet, sheathed in green flame. A small plaque on the bottom read, "V. Kluge." "There he is."

"Good eye," Allan said. "There you go. Look at him. Arrogant twat. The painter must have thought him mad to add that little beastie at his feet."

Ignoring the jabs at his predecessor, Matt admired the dashing image. Regardless what the painter might have thought, the portrait was one of the better ones in the house. Almost life-like. Kluge must have paid a fortune for it.

The door behind him creaked as Allan peeked inside. "Hey, once you're done, come here. There's something I want you to see."

Matt gave a little nod to the painted man and followed Allan into a modest gym. The smell of old sweat permeated the room. Various weights and workout equipment packed one side, leaving the other half-open. A pair of men sparred before a mirrored wall. Wooden weapons filled little racks on the far side.

Allan gestured to a stout black man. "Matt, I'd like you to meet Luc Renault, protector of Velnepo."

Luc transferred a flanged iron mace to his left hand and offered his right to Matt. "Good to meet you." His voice was surprisingly deep.

Matt shook the hunter's strong hand. "Good to meet you, too."

"Velnepo is one of the original eight Valducan weapons," Allan said. "She can smash just about anything."

Luc gave a proud smile and swung the ancient mace once in a downward sweep.

Allan turned to a small Asian man holding a katana. Four long, pale scars ran from his left ear down to his jaw. "And this is Kazuo Miyagi and his sword Akumanokira, the youngest of the known holy blades. This is what I want you to see."

Kazuo held the sword out flat before him. Its copper handle was cast with a woven diamond pattern, mimicking the look of silk-wrapped katana grips.

Leaning in closer, Matt noticed a series of numbers stamped neatly at the base of the blade. "Is that an army sword?"

"Yes," Kazuo answered with a short nod. "My grandfather was in the Great Pacific War, stationed in the Philippines. One night, many demons came out of the jungle and attacked his squad. My grandfather emptied his rifle into one to no effect. When the demons came for him, he picked up his commander's fallen sword and slew them."

Matt peered at the Japanese sword. The lights above reflected off the polished steel. No blemishes, not even a scratch. It looked as though it had just come off the factory line. Almost expecting a joke, he turned to Allan, his brows raised.

"I know." The Englishman shrugged. "It defies every theory on how holy blades are made, but there it is. In the 50s, the Valducans heard stories of a demon-killer travelling the islands, ridding them of monsters. Became bit of a folk hero, really."

"But how?" Matt asked. "It's a machined blade."

"How did Dämoren survive being broken, then turned into a handgun?"

"Faith," Kazuo answered. "It's all from faith."

Thick clouds lumbered across the morning skies, their edges pink and red at where the rising sunlight penetrated the canopy. A soft breeze rushed down into the valley, rustling the grape leaves. Matt jogged along a dirt road between the vine rows, fighting to keep his breath steady. In the three days since his arrival, his sinuses had yet to let up. He hadn't had many issues with allergies back home, but thankfully the jet lag was about gone. Matt hoped he'd get summoned on the next expedition. Maybe find a demon. One good touch of demon blood could heal anything from poison to a punctured lung. Something as simple as allergies wouldn't be a problem.

He followed the path up a long slope until he came to the chest-high wall circling the property. Succumbing to his clogged sinuses, he stopped to fish a tissue from the wad he'd jammed in his pocket. A quick gust swept through the vineyard, bringing a sudden coolness to Matt's sweat-slicked skin.

Footsteps crunched up from behind. Matt turned to see Luiza jogging up the road toward him. He couldn't help but appreciate her red sports bra bouncing in sync with her black ponytail.

"If you ran any slower, you'd be walking," she said, stopping beside him.

"Allergies," he said. "They're kicking my ass."

"Have you taken anything?"

Matt nodded. "I raided the clinic. Found something there, but they're not working too well."

Her brow arched. "In a yellow box?"

"Yeah."

"There's a reason no one's taken them."

"Oh."

"I have some better ones back at the house you can have."

"Thanks, I'd really appreciate it."

Luiza gave a small smile. "So," she said, looking out over the valley, "what do think?"

"About what?"

"About all of this. The Valducans, the house, everything."

Matt gazed out across the property. Straight lines of green vine rows cut across the smooth landscape. The huge chateau and outbuildings overlooked it all from a hillside like in a painting or travel brochure. "Not quite what I was expecting," he said, finally.

"And what was that?"

"I don't know. Some Medieval tower with battlements, bearded men in tabards and hoods, maybe."

She laughed. "Well we only wear those for special occasions, the beards, that is."

Matt chuckled. "Good to know."

"So have you had a chance to try out the range yet?"

"Not yet. I figure the last thing my sinuses need right now is a room full of powder smoke."

"After you get your medicine you should be fine."

"Should be."

Luiza gave a toothy grin. "I'll tell you what, if you can keep up with me, I'll give you the medicine, and then give you a chance to show off your shooting. Think you can beat me?"

Matt pursed a smile. He'd expected a shooting challenge eventually, but from someone like Mal or his buddy Colin. "Okay," he said. "You're on."

"This is it," Luiza said, flipping on the lights. Fluorescents flickered to life, illuminating the long, cinderblock building. Five metal tracks spaced along the ceiling ran the length. Red painted lines marked ranges out to fifty meters. A wide window looked into a darkened room behind the range. The familiar smell of powder hung in the air.

"Very nice," Matt said, noting the silver panel that controlled the target tracks. He set his duffel onto one of the tables along the back wall and stepped over to it. "So you can time them all differently?"

"One at a time, all at once. You can also do random patterns." She set her cube-like canvas bag down beside his and zipped it open, then removed a black plastic holster and clipped it to her belt. "Help me set up the targets."

She pulled several paper targets out from a rack on the wall and Matt stapled them to the hole-ridden cardboard squares hanging from the tracks. Once done, they stood in a row before him like five black-silhouetted men. Their only features being the concentric oval rings blossoming from their chests, each printed with a number, decreasing with each larger ring.

Unzipping a side pouch, Luiza removed a blued nine millimeter.

She popped in a fresh magazine, cocked the action, and slid

it into her holster. "Muffs are on the wall."

Matt took a pair of the olive-colored earmuffs off one of the pegs and put them on. "Ladies first," he said, gesturing toward the range.

The Brazilian smiled. She showed Matt how to operate the targeting tracks, then once she was ready, stepped up to the middle of the firing line, her hand by her side. Matt selected the correct program, pressed the green start button, and all five targets flipped sideways and raced away down their tracks. At ten meters they stopped, then began slowly moving back. The second target to the right turned, facing forward. Luiza ripped her pistol from the holder, bracing it in both hands, and fired two quick shots. The target rotated back. Another target flipped to face her; she fired again, nailing it twice before it reset. One by one the targets flipped, allowing no more than three seconds for her to fire.

Once all five targets had flipped, she holstered the gun, and removed the large muffs.

Pulling off his own earmuffs, Matt walked up to the line of targets. All but three rounds had hit within two inches of the center mark. "Good shooting. Little practice you might even get them all in the center ring."

Luiza's brow arched sharply. "You can do better?"

"Well, yeah," he answered like it was the easiest question in the world. "I'll tell you what," he said, walking back to his duffel. "Winner gets to shoot this first." He removed the black Ingram machinegun and set it on the table.

The Brazilian's face brightened. "Now we're talking."

"Now I only had fifty practice rounds for it. Not shooting the silver ones. So that's one full magazine and the other will just be twenty. So you're not going to get a full mag after I shoot the first one."

"Stop stalling and get up there." Luiza placed black stickers over the holes she'd shot in the targets, then took her place by the controls.

"Dämoren only holds seven," Matt said, unbuttoning his holster. "So I'm just going to fire once at the first, third and fifth targets."

"Wait, so I shoot ten and you shoot seven, that isn't fair."

"Consider it a three-shot handicap for you." He smiled.

Luiza's lips pursed. "All right, then" She turned to the controls. "Get ready."

Matt turned toward the range, his hand resting on his belt. The targets flipped sideways and raced away. He drew a breath. They stopped as they hit the red ten-meter line.

The lights went out.

Bright yellow and red spinning lights on the walls sprung to life, filling the room with dizzying patterns. The target on the far right, barely discernible through the confusing light, flipped toward him. Matt pulled Dämoren from the rig, cocked the hammer, and fired. A plume of dense smoke erupted downrange. It caught the spinning light, obscuring the targets even more. The target turned away. It had seemed longer before they reset when she shot. The approaching middle target clicked and rotated toward him. Matt fired, cocked, then fired again. The target reset no more than a second after it had activated. *She shortened the times!* Gritting his teeth, he finished the course. Once all the targets had activated, the ceiling lights flicked back on, and the spinning lights ceased.

"What was that about?" he asked, holstering Dämoren.

Luiza's chocolate eyes widened like a child's. "I was just making it even since you're such a good shooter and all," her voice overly innocent.

Matt chuckled.

Fanning her hand in attempt to disperse the thick cloud, Luiza approached the targets. "And this is what you do for a living?"

Matt looked at the man-shaped silhouettes. Two hits were perfect bull's-eyes. The rest were scattered around the centers, but no further than three finger-widths from their mark. "I'd call that pretty good."

She shrugged. "I saw a trick-shooter once. He could quick draw and hit aspirin glued to a board."

"Aspirin?"

She nodded. "From the hip, even. I figure since you're a professional gunslinger and all, hitting a bull's eye wouldn't be a problem."

A bitter pang needled Matt's gut. He knew the trick. He'd seen an exhibition shooter once when he and Clay were in New Mexico. The showman had reduced four tablets, suspended by stings, into puffs of white powder in just over a second. For six months after that Matt had egged Clay mercilessly, telling him he should be better than some Wild West reenactor. Now it was his turn. He could almost hear the old man laughing at him.

"Marksmanship and trick shooting aren't the same," he said, his words mimicking Clay's.

"Uh huh."

"I'm serious. Those guys are impressive, but it's all muscle memory. They're not really aiming. They shoot at the same target every day at the same distance. It's not a real comparison."

Her tongue ran behind her lower lip. "Not buying it."

"It's true."

"So you're wanting a rematch?"

"Just a fair game."

"No such thing," she said through a mischievous smile. "Loser goes first. I'll reset your targets."

Matt emptied Dämoren's cylinder, dropping the spent shells into a canvas bag as she covered his last shots with more round black stickers. Once she'd finished, and he'd loaded fresh rounds into the pistol, Matt approached the firing line.

The musical tone of a cell phone came from Luiza's bag, barely audible through the sturdy earmuffs.

She pulled it out and answered. "Yes? What is it?" She nodded and her face went slack. "When?"

Matt stepped closer toward her. Her grim expression told him that their game was over.

"I'll be there right away." She paused. "Yes, he's here with me now. Okay, we'll be right up."

"What?" Matt asked, as she hung up the phone.

"The team in Spain hasn't reported in and isn't answering calls. They're meeting right now to discuss a search and rescue."

"You're here," Schmidt said as Matt and Luiza entered the meeting room. A dozen people sat in chairs along one side. Almost twice that many seats remained empty. Matt could almost taste the bitter tension.

Mal, seated beside Jean, rolled his eyes and looked away. He touched the scarab tattoo at his wrist.

"That should be everyone," Turgen said, his voice husky like a life-long smoker's. He stood, leaning on his cane beside where Allan sat before a computer. He cleared his throat. "To catch everyone up, our expedition team in Spain has not reported in since last night. Their last communication was at nine o'clock. We have been unable to contact them since."

Turgen waited while Riku translated the old man's words into Japanese to Susumu. The samurai, holding his wood-sheathed naginata, nodded.

"The tracking units they carried last showed them all here."

Allan clicked on his computer and a map flashed up onto a large TV screen against the wall. A blue dot ringed in red appeared in the center. A white cursor moved to a vertical bar along the side and slid upward, zooming the image. The dot, which now appeared as multiple spots stacked nearly on top of one another, rested half a mile off a snake-like road, judging by the map scale in the lower corner.

"It's on a farm an hour and a half outside Barcelona. Local reports in the area drew our attention. Anya," he said, gesturing to the blonde woman, "discovered the location as the site of a resistance massacred under Franco's regime."

Matt studied the map, now transposed with a satellite image of the farm, as Riku relayed the information to his master. It appeared as a small clump of buildings surrounded by only a few trees.

"Their GPS trackers simultaneously stopped working at 2:17 this morning. Prior to that, they arrived at the house at ten o'clock."

A window on the screen beside him dropped open, and the cursor selected 9:45 pm from a list of fifteen minute intervals, then *Play*. The map showed the clump of dots quickly move up the road toward the house, stopping about a mile away. Then two of the dots broke off and circled around. A green clock in the corner of the screen read the time in thirty-second flashes.

"You can see them circle around the property in two groups."

"Who's that?" Jean asked, pointing to the two dots that broke off first.

Pausing the video, Allan moved the cursor over the indicators, their names, in red, appeared up beside them. "Ramón, and Anthony." He started the recording again, but the names stayed floating beside them.

"Here you see Natuche, Daniel, and Yev, head up the other side toward the house, circling the buildings one by one. At 10:49 something happens." He gestured up to the screen, showing the two groups suddenly break apart. The dots moved erratically, weaving and circling. One, Ramón, suddenly charged up around one of the buildings, then stopped. The others continued their agitated movement, staying close together, but one by one, they each ceased. The time read, 10:56. Seven minutes after the action had begun.

"Then," Turgen said, holding a finger in the air, "they all moved inside the house."

Matt watched the blue dots, each with a name beside it, pulse toward the house. Once inside they shuffled a bit, and then stopped in the pile that he'd seen at the very beginning. The video continued, nothing moving until 2:17 when all the dots and names suddenly disappeared.

Turgen waited until the signal stopped. "We need a team to find our missing knights and retrieve them and their blades. Malcolm, I want you to lead them."

The tattooed hunter nodded.

"Also, Takaira Susumu, Luc, Kazuo, Anya, and Matt Hollis."

"Master Turgen," Anya blurted. "I have my research. I've almost found the meaning for those symbols."

"The records are centuries old, Anya. A few more days won't make a difference."

"But I'm so close. Maybe Allan could be Librarian."

Allan looked up, dutifully.

"Sir Havlock just returned from a three-week expedition," Schmidt said. "He was injured and nearly died. His own research has waited for his return. We need knights that are healthy and ready for combat. No, he's to stay here until he's healed."

The pretty hunter nodded in defeat. "Yes, sir."

Riku raised his hand. "Master Turgen, am I to go as well?"

"No, Riku. This mission is too dangerous to risk an apprentice."

The young man relayed the order to his mentor.

"Preposterous!" Susumu said in Japanese. "I must have my student. I cannot speak without him."

Leaning on his cane, Turgen listened calmly, nodding, his face emotionless as Riku translated the samurai's words. "I understand your concern," he said. "However there are five knights that are missing. We can only send our very best on a mission of such importance. Both Kazuo and Matt speak Japanese and can assist you."

"That half-breed's accent is so bad, he can barely speak my language while the other is possessed with a demon. A demon that I should kill, not use as my ears and mouth."

"He says that Kazuo's Filipino accent makes it difficult to understand," Riku explained. "And he does not trust the demon."

Matt's jaw tightened as he felt every eye in the room fall over him.

"Mister Hollis is an accomplished hunter," Turgen said, gesturing his pale hand toward Matt. "And while I admit apprehension in working with him, no one can deny that his holy weapon Dämoren has chosen him. He has saved the life of one of our knights who also personally witnessed him slay two demons. For this, we trust him. If Takaira Susumu does not wish to help find what happened to our brave knights, he may decline this mission. We will choose a replacement for him. However, unless he says otherwise, Mister Hollis is going." The old man gave Matt a tiny smile as Riku relayed Turgen's words.

The samurai said nothing for several seconds. He curtly nodded. "I accept."

"Good." He turned to Malcolm. "You'll need to leave within the hour."

"Master Turgen," Malcolm said. "I need to voice my concern about this."

Schmidt looked up at the ceiling, then lowered his gaze onto the hunter. "If this concern is about the team we have selected, Master Turgen has made our stance very clear."

Malcolm's lip moved, as if about to say more. He shot a bitter glance toward Matt. "Understood. We'll leave in the hour."

Matt drew a breath, trying to quell the excited dread. He had his wish. He was going hunting. He only hoped it wouldn't lead to a knife in the back.

A COMPARISON
OF DEMONIC TERRITORIES
IN THE OLD AND NEW WORLDS

In contrast to Europe, Africa, and Asia, whose histories span millennia of wars, plagues, and innumerable incidents of human misery, the New World continents of Antarctica, Australia, and both Americas have experienced significantly less suffering.

Comparing Europe and North America, for example, the European continent boasts 39% more population than North America, while occupying only 41% of the geographical area. Furthermore, the sheer number of atrocities in the last three-thousand years is incomparable. The total sum of dead and wounded in all North American wars is less than 8% of those lost and wounded in the First World War alone. While historical records of North American wars prior to the European migration are unknown, scholars agree that even the worst-case estimates would be incomparable to Europe. Even the Native American Genocide, whose total numbers will never be known, is at most half of the fatalities caused by the Black Death of the 14th Century. The summation of this comparison is not to demean the loss and suffering experienced in North America, but merely to illustrate the difference.

The result is that Europe, as a physical continent, contains a substantially higher density of sites tainted with human suffering. Each of these sites acts as a magnet that draws demonic energies closer until capturing them. This creates a bowl effect with multiple demonic entities held in each of these sites. The more lurid a particular site's past, the greater the demonic gravity.

To illustrate, compare this attraction to the rubber-sheet model of gravity. Imagine a physical region as a sheet of smooth rubber tautly stretched. Every site tainted by death and suffering affixes a weight corresponding to the degree of negative energy. Now imagine demonic entities as smooth, yet irregular beads poured over the sheet. The beads will roll across, but frequently become trapped in the divots caused by the weights.

With this illustration in mind, now picture the continents of North America and Europe. North America has relatively few weights that mar its smooth texture. Meanwhile, the sheet of the European continent is densely pockmarked with divots, leaving virtually no portion flat. Beads poured over the North American sheet will roll freely but become heavily clustered in the major gravity wells. The European sheet will have wide disbursement of beads as they are caught in the various pits, with only a slightly higher density in the location of heavier weights.

This study does not explore sites that have a natural attraction or repulsion to demonic energies. Natural "holy" or "unholy" geographic anomalies of course affect the rubber sheet, but for purposes of this exercise, consider them neutral.

Once every few centuries, natural disasters have eradicated certain sites, causing a sudden migration of demons into the surrounding regions. Some Valducans have theorized that these disasters themselves, be it Pompeii or Port Royal, were in some way caused by the abnormally high concentration of demonic powers. I however, disagree with that theory on the grounds that many hundreds of other corrupted sites have never experienced cataclysmic ends.

One recent example was in the city of New Orleans. New Orleans, a city deeply scarred by suffering and well known for its substantial demonic population, was evacuated in 2005 in the wake of Hurricane Katrina. In that evacuation, thousands of refugees were scattered up to 2,500 kilometers away. Repopulation of the region took six years before reaching its pre-hurricane size. However, estimates show that demons and practitioners of demonic rites returned far faster than the general population, achieving full repopulation in only three years. This example only supports the theory that North America, as a continent, has far fewer demonic gravity wells, thus causing each one to affect a far greater range than their Old World counterparts.

Hunters operating in Old World regions, therefore, must employ different tracking strategies than those operating in the New World. Old World hunters are more likely to find demonic entities grounded to their particular territories unable to migrate far before being caught in a new well. This also leads to major sites or corruption being less densely populated with demons, as they are more spread out among the wells. New World hunters often have large areas where demons can migrate freely, unhindered by wells. Also, those fewer wells can be more easily monitored. However, in deeply tainted regions, the high demonic saturation makes them far more dangerous.

Adjusting to these differences is not a simple task, and the Valducan Masters must weigh an individual hunter's regional specialization before assigning them on various missions. Sending a New World hunter to track and locate demons in Old World territories, or vice versa, can result in disaster.

Sir Malcolm Romero Ph. D, 2013

CHAPTER 6

"Are you sure that's safe?" Anya asked. She sat as far away as the van's bench seat would allow.

Matt tapped black powder into an etched metal vial, measuring the proper load. "Nothing to worry about. Just try not to open any windows or light a cigarette until I'm done." He smiled.

No one in the rumbling van seemed amused.

In the hour before leaving, Matt had only enough time to clean the bronze shells. Reloading in a car was tricky. Clay had never let him reload Dämoren, but Matt had spent many hours loading silver .45's in the backseat.

Once measured, he poured the powder into an empty casing, then inserted it into the hand press with a silver bullet. He only had a dozen of Dämoren's slugs left. Hopefully, he'd get a chance to cast more soon. Matt gripped the ornate press in both hands and squeezed until the bullet was fully seated.

Luc's deep voice rumbled from the back seat. "Seems wasteful to shoot silver bullets for practicing."

Matt slipped the round into a belt loop. "That's all she'll fire. She won't shoot lead. So if I want to practice with her, I have to use silver."

"Won't shoot?" Luc asked. "It jams?"

"No. She just won't fire." He measured the powder for the next round. "Pull the trigger, nothing happens. Never tried lead, myself, but Clay warned how picky she was. Won't even shoot if it's mixed alloy."

Anya's blue eyes lit. "So she can choose not to shoot?"

"Oh yeah."

Luc laughed. "Your gun is most definitely a woman."

Matt grinned. "Won't argue with that."

"You need to hurry that up," Malcolm said, watching Matt through the driver's rear-view. "Any police or passerby on the road see that, they're going to pull us over. It won't be hard for them to find all the other weapons."

"I doubt any officer would even recognize a century-old hand press." Matt squeezed the bullet into place.

"You can't say that they won't," Malcolm chided. "You can risk that on your own. But you have five knights you're endangering. Now hurry up."

Matt swallowed his anger and continued working in silence.

Outside, steep hills gave way to rolling fields. An hour later they rose up into sharp, mountains. Snow capped the distant jagged peaks.

On their fourth hour, they came to the Spanish border. Expecting something similar to what he'd encountered in the States, Matt sat astonished as the van crossed over without even having to stop.

Dark clouds greeted them in Spain, threatening rain. After an hour or so, Malcolm exited the highway and headed up into the winding roads. The lingering tension in the van swelled with each passing mile, though no one mentioned it. Kazuo strummed two fingers on his thigh, looked at his watch, then out the window. A minute later, he did it again. Luc stared out his side, his elbow on the windowsill and fist below his chin. His thick, curled fingers kneaded in succession. Through the rear-view, Matt could see Malcolm's eyes repeatedly glance to the GPS screen, watching the countdown until their destination. Susumu seemed unaffected by the foreboding dread. The samurai calmly sat in the front passenger seat, hands on his lap, watching the road as if nothing important waited at the end.

Matt leaned over to Anya, peering intently at brown images of pages on her tablet. "What are you looking at?"

She brushed a lock of hair from her ear. "I've been working on the symbols we've found, trying to find them in any of the old texts."

"Any luck?"

Anya shrugged. "Very little." She tilted the screen to where he could see it. A faded black picture resembling three circles joined by a swooping line against a dun background dominated the screen. A column of smaller images ran down the right side. Matt recognized them as photos from the gruesome murder scenes. "I've found maybe a third of the symbols, but can't tell you what most of those mean."

"Well, what can you tell?"

"It's definitely a summoning." She paused. "You can understand all languages. Can't you read it?"

"No." He shook his head. "I don't understand the words as much as I can understand voices. I can hear their intention. Can speak it the same way. I just can't read it."

She frowned. "That's disappointing."

"Sorry."

She cocked her head quizzically. "So does that mean you can hear lies?"

"Not any better than anyone else, I guess."

"But if you hear their intention and not their words ..." Her brow raised, finishing the question.

"It's not really like that. I understand what they are intending me to hear. For example, let's say you spoke ... Greek."

"I can."

"Oh. Well, do you speak Russian?"

She nodded.

"All right. What's a language you can't speak at all?"

Anya pursed her lips, seeming to think for a moment. "Mandarin."

"Okay. So let's say you read a little book on Mandarin, then went to China and tried to speak it. However, you don't know enough to fully express yourself and what little you do know, you're mispronouncing so bad that no one can understand you."

"But you could?"

"Exactly. Even if what they're speaking is so poor, that no one can understand a word they're saying, I can understand them."

"Can you understand dogs or horses," Luc asked, his deep voice grinding behind him like a tectonic plate.

"Well ... sort of," Matt said, turning. "I mean I can understand the emotions they project. They don't really communicate in words, so I don't hear the words, but I get a feeling."

"Babies?" he asked.

"Infants, no, but once they begin using words and beginning to think with more tangible ideas, then yes. When a little child is trying to speak, and no one has any idea what they're saying, I understand it just fine."

The black man smiled. White teeth, save a missing one near the corner. "You should have been a psychologist. Get rich talking to people's babies and dogs."

Matt laughed. "If demon hunting doesn't work out, I'll think about it."

They continued up the sinuous road. Occasional droplets struck the glass then rippled back along the side windows like wind-blown tears.

"Anya," Malcolm said. "How are we looking?"

She tapped her screen, and the image changed to the map with the farm house. She zoomed out until a cluster of white-ringed red dots appeared along the snaking road. "Three kilometers."

"Everyone get ready."

Bags shuffled. Matt passed packs back over the seat behind him. Zippers whirred and Velcro tore open, as the hunters prepared in the tight confines.

"Sorry," Matt said, nearly jabbing Anya as he wiggled into his gray Kevlar vest. He had to lean forward, almost putting his head between his knees to get it on. The van bumped suddenly and Matt's head smacked into the back of Malcolm's seat.

They turned onto a narrow drive, walled in by bushy trees. A dirt path led off to the left and Malcolm steered the van off and turned it around before pulling to a stop.

Matt gripped the door handle and pulled. The sliding door squeaked back, and he swung out. Gravel crunched beneath his feet. A moist breeze rushed down the road, channeled through the canyon of trees. He circled around to where Malcolm was already opening the rear door and helped unload the larger bags. Luc and Kazuo stood nearby, their eyes scanning the area.

Matt pulled on Dämoren's rig and ammo belt. He sort of

wished he had a jacket to cover everything, but his last one had been left in a Canadian dumpster filled with blood and holes. He pulled the thin metal chain around his neck and looked at the little box of white plastic hanging off the end. The LED was green. Right now, hundreds of miles away, the Valducans watched a red dot with his name outside the farm. He hooked the radio they'd given him onto his belt and pushed the clear bud into his ear.

After checking that everything was in place, Matt drew the Ingram out from his bag, loaded a magazine of silver hollow points, and racked one in.

Susumu stepped around the van wearing a golden yellow band across his forehead, Shi no Kaze over his shoulder. He eyed Matt's bulletproof vest. "Are you expecting a gunfight?"

"I'm not sure what to expect," Matt said in Japanese, slinging the machinegun over his arm. "But I want to be ready for it."

"I have never seen a demon shoot a gun. Do you think one of *us* will shoot you?"

"There might not be as many guns where you come from, but I've seen an ifrit with a shotgun, and a vampire with twin pistols like in some bad action movie. Demons might favor teeth and claws, but if they possess someone who knows how to shoot, they know how to shoot. And they'll never forget."

Matt reached into the van and removed a water bottle he'd picked up when they'd stopped for fuel. He took the flat pricker from his pocket and clicked it against his finger. He squeezed five fat, red drops into the bottle, screwed the lid and shook it to a dim pink.

"You ready?" Malcolm asked, stepping around the van. Three tight stands of jagged seashell hung from his neck, ending in a crescent-shaped bone. The oiled wood grip of a sawed-off protruded sideways from a holster at his back. His gaze tensely moved to the bottle in Matt's hand.

"Almost." Matt removed the shaker of powder from his belt and started sprinkling a ring circling the van.

"What are you doing?" Kazuo asked. His katana hung from one side of his belt. A holstered Colt on the other.

"It's a ward," he answered. "Don't want anything getting

into our ride out of here."

"What's in it?" Malcolm demanded, blocking his path.

"Everything I can think of."

"Such as?"

Matt's ground his teeth. "Silver, acacia, shit demons don't like."

Malcolm snorted. "You know that doesn't work, right? Wouldn't a demon-hunter know that?"

"It does work. I've seen it."

"When?" Anya stepped closer, hand on Baroovda's grip.

"Yokai," Matt answered. "Wendigos."

"Wendigos," Malcolm said, his lips curling into a nasty smile. "You know a lot about those, don't you?"

Matt's hand tightened around the shaker, fighting back the urge to smash it into the hunter's face. *Five knights. Allan's not here to stop them.*

"If that worked, don't you think we'd already be doing it?" Malcolm asked.

Matt didn't answer.

"A demon has to either touch or be pierced by those for them to work," Malcolm continued. "They could just step over that."

"Maybe," Matt said "But you forgot the secret ingredient."

"And what's that?"

Matt glanced to Kazuo, then back at Malcolm. "Faith."

Malcolm's arrogant smile melted.

"So does anyone have a problem with me doing this?" Matt asked.

No one answered.

Finally, Luc said, "I don't."

Sighing, Malcolm stepped aside and motioned Matt to continue.

Thanks, asshole. Matt finished the circle and snapped the shaker lid closed. A cold raindrop hit his ear. He turned to the hunters. "Ready."

Keeping to the tree line they followed the little road over a low hill. A white van rested along the side of the path ahead, its doors gaping wide. Matt checked the water bottle. Nothing. Cautiously, they approached, weapons drawn.

Luc and Kazuo circled around the far side, peeking through the windows. The passenger door glass was gone, reduced to little glistening cubes. A bullet hole curled outward from the open door. Nylon bags and bits of smashed electronics littered the area. Matt crept closer and looked inside. More debris. Yellow foam bulged from parallel slashes deep in the upholstery, like claw-trails. Empty brass shells lay on the floor and seat. Matt leaned in closer. Three dark spots of dried blood stained the beige carpet.

"They must have gotten Selene," Anya said.

"Who's that?" Matt asked.

"Anthony's student. She probably stayed here to protect the vehicle."

"I didn't see her name on the video."

"She didn't have a tracker." Anya shook her head regretfully. "We only gave them to the knights with holy blades. She would have stayed here and monitored the camera feeds as backup."

"Feeds?"

"Knights place cameras before raids," Malcolm said, sifting through the broken electronics. "Apprentices relay anything they see to the team, in case they miss something."

"Why aren't we doing that?" Matt asked.

"Turgen said no students."

"How many other students were there? Maybe one escaped."

"Just Selene," Malcolm answered. "And we can assume she didn't escape." He shook his head. "Computers are gone. The cameras have internal memory. Maybe we can find them."

Kazuo motioned to the road. Chunks of safety glass lay scattered about. "The vehicle was here when they took her. They moved it after."

Luc knelt beside the broken glass. In the air, he traced a little trail of cubes smeared down a tire groove worn into the dirt road. "They drove away. They must have moved the van to make room."

Malcolm nodded off to the right. "Then let's look at what they left behind."

They slipped between the trees and climbed over a rusty pipe fence. A brown barn stood across the field, nearly blocking out the farmhouse behind it. The sun peeked on the horizon, shining beneath the dark clouds above. In two hours it would be dark.

"Look there." Susumu pointed his bladed staff toward a dingy green cattle feeder. A hay bale rested inside the metal bars, bulging over the top like some giant grass cupcake. A small black tube, the size of a flashlight, rested atop a bale, aimed at the buildings.

"Looks like one of our cameras," Malcolm said.

Swinging wide, they approached the little camera. A plastic antenna jutted straight out the back. From its angle it could see the entire barn and a quarter of the house.

Malcolm reached up and plucked it off the bale. "Keep your eyes out for any more of them."

They continued toward the house, attempting to follow the path the hunters had taken the night before. Luc spotted another camera near the barn, its plastic crab-like legs wrapped around a fencepost.

They circled the building until it opened up into a wide gravel area. A tiny white car sat off to one side. Five fresh, bloodied corpses lay scattered around the open area. Severed limbs lay beside some of them, many also sported deep gashes, showing bone and spilt organs. It smelled of blood and that acrid stink of guts that always reminded Matt of his mother's body. Two of them were naked. Black flies scuttled across their bare skin.

Kazuo knelt and picked up a spent ammo casing. Matt counted several more sprinkled across the white gravel.

More bodies lay on the other side of the house and two more beside a stone well house. Nine in all. None were the missing knights.

Inside the barn they discovered four mutilated corpses piled on the floor. Their withered eyes and shriveled skin didn't look like any of the others. Two were children, the youngest no more than six. All wore pajamas or minimal clothes. Deep bites and missing scoops of flesh pitted their thighs and torsos.

"The demons killed these," Matt said. "Bled them out. Ate part of them."

Luc nodded. "They must have lived here. Do you know what did it?"

He shook his head. "Never seen bodies drained and eaten. Usually one or the other, but if there's multiple breeds maybe they all took a piece."

"Maybe."

Anya and Kazuo found another two bled and gnawed bodies in a nearby shed.

The door to the house was unlocked. The overpowering stench of death hit them like a wall. Covering his nose and mouth with one hand, Matt shook a line of gray powder across the threshold before he entered. The drained corpse of a black-moustached man lay in the first room, his throat torn out. Hideous bites covered the left side of his chest, exposing the ribs beneath. Then in the next room, a body of a teenage girl slumped in a cushioned chair, her face half-eaten. Brown, dried blood stained her baby blue shirt. She wore nothing else.

Up three steps they found what had once been a wide living area with a red brick fireplace. Toppled furniture rested against the walls, blocking the windows. Burned candles of various sizes and color blanketed every surface. Bloody symbols and designs covered the white walls. In the middle of the floor, five naked corpses were laid, arms and legs splayed out. Carved designs and mutilations decorated their skin. Broken shards of metal and wood jutted grotesquely from their bodies. Joined only by the toes, they formed a ring, leaving a star-shaped opening between their open legs.

The overpowering stink of burned rot hung so thick Matt could taste it. Suddenly hating the effectiveness of Luiza's medicine, he covered his nose.

"My God," Malcolm uttered.

Luc shook his head. "God is not in this place."

They were all there. The scarecrow-looking Ramón, his nose no more than a triangular hole. Blood-stained teeth grinned out from where his lips should have been. Natuche's slender long braids spilled out from atop a smashed and faceless head. The romance cover guy, Anthony, split cock to throat, peeled open like a dissected frog. Matt recognized Daniel and Yev from their photos. Yev, the man who had carried Tom's sword when Tom was maimed. Now jagged slivers of blade protruded from his hands like nails. A bent and broken hilt jutted from his belly. Their skin that had faced inside the open star was burned away from the soles of their feet up to their mutilated genitals. Whatever had done it hadn't affected the pink flesh beneath, only the skin. Unlike the rest of the floor around them, the tile inside the star was clean. Pristine.

Luc stood above Anthony, staring down, his lips tight. He swallowed and looked away. Malcolm shut his eyes and mumbled what sounded like a prayer.

Averting his gaze from the blood-drenched bodies, Matt circled the room. "These symbols, they're different."

Anya wiped her eyes and studied the gruesome writing across the plaster. "You're right."

"Any idea what it means?"

She shook her head. "It's obviously a summoning, like the others, but more … more elaborate."

Malcolm circled the swirling script painted between each of the dead knight's heads, forming two rings of writing. "Don't know what this says, but I can tell you what it is." He pointed to a row of larger symbols, partially smudged. "That's its name. They weren't just calling a certain type of demon, they called a specific one."

Luc pursed his lips and growled.

"What are they saying?" Susumu asked.

"That they summoned a specific monster by its name," Matt answered.

The samurai gave a solemn nod. "This is not good."

"How do you mean?"

"Because," Kazuo said, sifting through a pile of torn and bloody clothes. "When the laws of the universe are called and powers are invoked or bound by their true names, waves are felt everywhere. That's when prophecies come true. Things change."

"Like what?"

"Everything. All worlds feel the ripples." He pulled a metal chain out from the bundle. A red-smeared white box dangled from the end. "I found the trackers," he announced.

"Gather them up," Malcolm said. He knelt beside the symbols, the back of his hand across his mouth. "Look at this."

Luc stepped up beside him and gazed down at the smudged writing. "What is that from?"

Matt stepped up between them. "Is that a …" he turned his head, trying to get a better angle without having to step inside the circle, "footprint?"

Malcolm measured it with his hands. It was long, slender at the back, but wide at the toes. It had to be eighteen inches, at least. "I've never seen anything this huge. Make sure we get some good shots of it and any more it might have tracked."

"I do not see the student," Susumu said.

Kazuo scanned the room. "He's right. Selene isn't here."

"Spread out," Malcolm said. "And keep your radios handy. This … feels off."

They searched the house. Dark patches of dried blood stained many of the tattered beds where the sleeping owners had met their end. The digital clocks beside the beds all blinked, 12:00. In the kitchen, the green oven light read 17:23. The two dots inside the time blinked.

Matt checked his watch. 7:40.

"You notice the time it says?" Luc asked.

"Yeah, it's off by two hours seventeen minutes. Same time the trackers flipped off."

"Have you seen that before?"

"No. You?"

Luc frowned. "I have not."

Matt opened a washroom door when the pink fluid in the bottle suddenly cleared up, forming a crimson bead toward the outer wall.

He thumbed the radio. "There's one outside!" There was a door beside him with a window. Matt pulled the curtain back. The rear yard was empty. Dämoren in hand, he stepped out.

Matt looked in the direction the blood compass pointed. Fiery hues tinged the sky around the lowering sun. A tin shed rested twenty feet away. Beyond it, there was a dense cluster of trees across a field.

The compass pointed toward them.

"Look!" Luc yelled.

Three men moved through the grassy field toward the house. One carried a wood club, like a sledge handle or some other tool. Another clutched a metal pipe. The third, a bald guy, held an old varmint rifle.

A sharp cry came from somewhere inside the house.

The shed door groaned open and two gray corpses shambled out, their skin drawn and wrinkled. Their dead eyes turned toward Matt and Luc. A gurgling groan resonated from their torn throats.

The four desiccated bodies emerged from the barn and shuffled toward the house.

The compass didn't indicate they were demons, and Dämoren's ammo was too limited. Matt holstered the revolver and raised the slung Ingram. Holding the thick suppressor in one hand, he aimed at a black-haired teen and fired. A short burst of rapid, metallic *tinks* and the boy's face erupted into jagged chunks. The creature didn't seem to notice. It opened what was left of its mouth. Broken bits of teeth and tongue tumbled out.

Matt fired again. Silver hollow points tore its head nearly off.

It kept coming.

He stepped back. "Luc?"

The hulking hunter charged forward, mace in hand. He hit the first one, a young girl, in the head. It burst like a melon hit with a shotgun. Luc whirled Velnepo around and struck the side of the teen Matt had shot. Its body flew back twenty feet as if hit by a bus. Bits of brown gore stained the flanged mace.

Holy shit, Matt thought, awed by the mace's power.

The bodies rose back up.

Matt glanced at the bottle. Two red beads. The men were halfway across the field now.

One of the other dead creatures neared the front of the house. Susumu's naginata shot out from the open doorway. The blade drove through the corpse's chest and out the back. The blade jerked free and the limp corpse dropped. The samurai stepped out.

Malcolm came out behind him. Chunky blood coated his machete. "The heart! Stab the heart!" He thrust his left hand out toward the nearest monster, the crimson eye tattooed inside his palm opened wide. The creature stopped, as if frozen. "They're stronger than they look."

Susumu lunged, skewering it. He pulled the naginata out and whirled the long blade around, clipping the legs off another walking corpse. He twirled the weapon up, over, then stabbed down into the creature's chest.

Following their lead, Matt aimed at the headless girl and fired. Her chest burst with gelatinous holes and she fell. He turned toward the one Luc had knocked back. Splintered bone jutted from its smashed ribs, its head little more than a malformed bag of hair and bloody skin. It limped toward Kazuo. The short hunter sidestepped and stabbed his katana down into the creature's long shadow. A triangular hole opened up in the corpse's chest and it went slack like a marionette held by only one string. Kazuo pulled the blade out from the shadow and the monster crumpled.

Matt looked back at the bottle. Four beads. Two toward the trees, one toward the barn, another behind them. "We're surrounded!"

"Where?" Anya asked.

"Two demons there. One up there," he said, pointing the machinegun. "Another down the drive." Matt checked the bottle again. One of the beads elongated, like the goop in a lava lamp, then split into two smaller beads. "There's another up there." He pointed across the yard.

Anya motioned to the approaching men. "And them?"

"Familiars, I think."

"Everyone stay together," Malcolm said.

Kazuo lifted his blade before him with both hands. "This was a trap."

"We're ready for it." Malcolm turned toward the last direction Matt had pointed. "Send those fuckers to hell for what they did."

Matt stepped up beside the dilapidated shed. A shot fired,

punching a hole in the corrugated tin by his arm. "Stay down!" Crouching, he spotted the bald man with the rifle about twenty yards away aiming his direction. Matt popped the Ingram up and fired.

Blood burst from Baldy's gut. He staggered back, the gun going off in the air. He dropped to a knee and brought the rifle up.

Matt shot another burst. Red plumes erupted, stitching a jagged line up the shooter's body and he fell. Matt ejected the spent magazine and slapped another one in.

Four quick pistol shots fired behind him. He glanced back to see Kazuo, katana in one hand, Colt in the other, firing up the other hill.

Matt couldn't see the two other men in the field. Squinting, he scanned the area, trying to find them. Near the tree line, maybe sixty yards away, a dark shape moved.

He drew Dämoren.

Green eyes ignited. It stepped out. Orange embers crackled over a red, muscled body. *An ifrit.* The machinegun wouldn't work on it and Dämoren's ammo was too precious to try at that range.

Another beast moved behind it, towering and broad with black-brown fur. Werewolf. A big one.

"I see one," Susumu called from beside the barn. "A pale woman with wings."

Kazuo relayed the samurai's words, then added, "Succubus."

"Get ready," Malcolm called.

The ifrit moved forward, then stopped. It looked at Matt, its eyes pupil-less emerald fire. Orange flames flickered across its shoulders.

"What's it doing?" Anya hissed, behind him. "Why are they waiting?"

Matt kept watching them. "I don't know."

The ifrit stepped back, the flames dimming. Green eyes narrowed. It turned and vanished into the shadows. The werewolf threw its head back toward the sky. A wailing howl pierced the air. Then it, too, ran into the cover of trees.

"Where'd it go?" she asked, stepping beside him.

Instinctively Matt put his hand out, keeping her from going further. The man with the wooden club jumped up from the grass thirty feet away and sprinted away. The other man fled out from behind a rusted pile of metal pipes.

Matt checked the bottle. Six blobs, then five. Three. "They're leaving."

"What's going on? Malcolm called.

"They're leaving," Anya yelled back.

"What?" Malcolm marched closer, keeping his gaze out on the surrounding property. "Why?"

Matt shook his head. "I don't know." The last sphere of blood burst and swirled apart.

"Do you feel them?" Luc asked Malcolm.

"I can only tell if one is close, a feeling I've had ever since *he* showed up," Malcolm said, shooting a hateful glare Matt's direction.

"They're gone," Matt said, lifting the bottle.

"Did you see the way it looked at you?" Anya asked him.

Malcolm turned to her. "What do you mean?"

She shrugged. "There was an ifrit and werewolf. The ifrit looked at him, stopped, then left. Then the wolf howled."

"And then they all fled." He looked at Matt. "Why would they do that?"

Matt shrugged.

The hunter seemed to chew on that for a second, then turned to the others. "We have an hour until dark. They could come back, and I don't want to be here when the sun goes down. Anya, you and Kazuo photograph everything. Start with the bodies, then the walls. I want every detail recorded. Luc," he turned to the huge man, "there were some fuel cans in the shed. You and Susumu take those. We'll pile the bodies out here into the barn and light it. Once the others are done, we'll give rites to our brothers and sister and burn the house. No evidence."

"What about Selene?" Anya asked. "We never found her."

Malcolm slid Hounacier back into its wood sheath. "If her body isn't here we can only assume the worst. If this was a summoning, the demon they called needed a body."

"No." Anya covered her mouth.

"There were six of them. Five made the ring, the sixth became the vessel. Once we're done we'll head out the other way, see if we can find any cameras Ramón and Anthony might have left on their approach. Let's move."

"What do you want me to do?" Matt asked.

"You? I want you by my side."

"What?"

"They laid a trap for us," Malcolm said, his jaw tight. "They waited. Then the moment they see *you* they just leave. And until you can explain why they'd do that, I don't want you out of my sight."

GHOUL

DAEMO CADAVERDEGULO

The ghoul is a cowardly fiend frequently nesting in burial sites and sewers. Its diet consists primarily of corpses and refuse, but given safe opportunity it will kill humans and animals, especially children or the ill. Ghouls are often mistaken for undead demons, such as vampires. However, a ghoul's spirit will not survive in a host that dies. The demon's association with corpses and their unique ability to enslave dead bodies as servants perpetuates this confusion, even with Valducan knights.

Physical characteristics:

Ghouls have two forms, depending on what type of host they possess. In a human body, the creature appears as a thin man with long arms and wild hair. Their skin is dry and varies in color between gray and green. Human ghouls walk on hands and feet in a manner akin to chimpanzees. Ghouls can also possess the bodies of hyenas. In these bodies they appear as a man with a dog's head. Their color ranges from brown to black. ––Ghouls cannot change their form to appear as a normal human or hyena. They maintain the sex of their host's body. ––When killed, a ghoul's soul burns with a brilliant yellow flame.

Weaknesses:

Ghouls are among the weakest of demonkind, and their bodies can withstand only a little more grievous harm than what would kill a normal man.

Obsidian blades kill them quite easily.

Sakaran and Quaysoum herbs repulse ghouls.

Behavior:

Ghouls prefer digging up graves for food rather than risk direct confrontation. They will attack when cornered or if they judge the victim as helpless, often the very old or very young. They are opportunistic in combats, seeking ambush over frontal assault.

Ghouls are pack-minded and will gather in groups of four or five. They also will serve stronger demonkind as slaves. Ghoul packs are extremely brutal, led by the most powerful member, who is frequently overthrown and killed by the rest of the pack every few years. Because demons can permanently kill other demons, this means few ghouls reach the astounding ages that other, more powerful demons can achieve.

They are most frequently found in dry, arid regions.

Corpses:

While unable to create familiars, older ghouls possess the unique ability to infuse a piece of their essence into a corpse, animating it as a mindless servant. These walking cadavers, while slow, are extremely strong. Destroying these abominations requires piercing the heart.

In a pack, only the pack leader will be allowed to control corpses, even if other ghouls possess the ability. Those ghouls may, however, kill their leader, taking the pack for themselves, or leave the pack entirely.

The number of corpses a ghoul can control is a strong indicator of how many centuries it has existed.

History:

The oldest accounts of ghouls originate in Arabic and Mesopotamian texts. It is believed that ghouls may also have inspired Egyptian lore of Anubis, the jackal-headed god of the dead.

Sir Gudmund Linblad, 1823
Translated and amended by Lady Helen Meadows, 1958

CHAPTER 7

"**O**h lord God, no," Tom blurted. He turned away from gruesome image on the screen. Eslarin, his once-bonded sword smashed and driven through his former student.

Ben put a hand on the big man's shoulder, but Tom brushed it aside.

Matt wished he could say something, anything.

More pictures flashed, graphic close-ups of the symbols and carnage. The hunters all watched in grim silence as Anya scrolled past images of their dead.

Matt drank the last of his coffee. He'd been awake for twenty-one hours, thirteen trapped inside a van. He wanted one of those big twenty-four-ounce coffees from back home, maybe two. These tiny porcelain cups they served here just didn't cut it.

"There it is," Malcolm said. An image of the giant bloody footprint filled the wall screen.

Seats creaked in unison, creating an almost musical groan as everyone leaned forward followed by a chorus of mumbles and whispers.

"What in the hell is that?" Luiza asked, seemingly to herself. She sat in the seat beside Matt.

"Something big," Jean said.

"Have you ever seen anything like that?" Malcolm asked Turgen.

The old man leaned closer, studying it for several seconds. Finally, "No." He looked to Schmidt who only shook his head.

Anya took a drag off her cigarette and flipped to the next photo. It was a wide shot, showing the large scrawled glyphs. On the left, Natuche, her head nothing more than a crushed and bloody lump. On the right, Yev, his face contorted in some hideous expression left by a broken jaw. The thick rivulets of congealed blood down the sides told he'd still been alive when his eyes had been torn out.

Tom stood abruptly and limped out.

Luiza started for the door after him, but Turgen raised a hand to stop her.

"Let him go. I'll go speak with him in a bit."

She hesitated, then reluctantly returned to her seat beside Matt.

"I feel so terrible for him," she muttered.

Matt nodded. "Me too."

They sat silent as more bloody images flashed past. Several times Matt caught sidelong glances from the others in the room. Malcolm was the only one who didn't shy away.

Once the photos had finished, Schmidt asked, "Allan, are you ready with the videos, yet?"

Allan clicked through keys on the desktop near the screen. A yellow cable ran from the computer to the last of the four recovered cameras. "Almost. Five minutes."

Turgen slid his fingers beneath his wire-frame glasses and rubbed his eyes. "Fine. While Mister Havlock is finishing, I suggest we take a break. We'll reconvene in fifteen minutes." He pushed himself up from the seat with his cane and left.

Matt looked in the bottom of his empty cup. With a sigh, he rose from his uncomfortable chair and headed toward the door.

"And where are you going?" Malcolm asked.

Matt lifted the little cup, shaking it. "Coffee." He turned to Allan, peering intently at his screen. "You need a refill?"

"No thank you. Haven't touched the last cup."

Malcolm shook his head. "I don't think it's a good idea to let you go alone."

Everyone went quiet.

"I appreciate your concern," Matt said, fighting down his anger, "but I think I can find the kitchen by myself."

"I'm not worried about you getting lost. I'm worried about a demon creeping around our house."

"Demon?" Matt snapped. "Look, I didn't ask to join this

little party. You found me. I'm very sorry you lost your friends. I really am. But I didn't fly halfway around the world for you to treat me like some God-damned monster."

Malcolm chewed his lip, staring Matt down as he rose to his feet. "Doesn't change what you are. Why did those demons run when they saw you? What aren't you telling us?"

"I'm not hiding anything. Maybe they left because we killed their familiars before they could get close enough."

"Bullshit. They had us surrounded. They could have kept us pinned in."

"They were trying to close in while we were inside. If I hadn't alerted everyone they'd have been on us before you knew it."

"And how again did you know they were coming?" Malcolm asked. "Blood? Not exactly human."

"You saw me kill one of those dead things and the guy with the rifle. The one trying to *shoot me*. If I was against you, why would I kill them?"

"Familiars. They're expendable. Maybe trying to gain our trust. I don't know. Maybe they didn't expect you to be there, then once they saw you they were gone." His fingers inched toward Hounacier's white horn handle.

Matt grabbed Dämoren's grip and thumbed the snap open. "Just try it."

Schmidt slammed his fist down on his chair's arm. "Gentlemen!"

He glared up at Matt, his blue eyes cold. "Mister Hollis, I warned you."

"You warned me never to draw it, and I haven't, but if this asshole pulls so much as an inch of steel from that sheath, I'll consider it a challenge. I read enough about the Valducans to know challenges have happened before."

Malcolm grinned. "That rule only applies to Valducans."

"You're right. I might not be one, but Dämoren is."

"Mister Hollis," Schmidt growled. "Stand down."

"I will right after he does."

Schmidt's jaw tightened. "Fine. Sit down, Malcolm."

"Master Schmidt, I don't—"

"I promised Mister Hollis he would be safe here," Schmidt

said, his stern voice rising. "I gave him my word. Now sit."

Malcolm released the machete handle, holding his hands out to the side. His eyes narrowed, but never left Matt as he lowered back into his seat. "I still don't want him wandering around by himself. Demon or not, he's not one of us."

Others murmured their agreement: Colin, Jean, Ben, Luc, Anya.

Schmidt nodded. "I tend to concur. Mister Hollis, you are welcome to stay in this house, but outside your room you need to be accompanied."

Matt chewed on the old man's words. *I suppose I'll be calling you every night when I need to go take a piss.* "Fine." Matt forced a smile.

"Would someone please accompany me to the kitchen?"

"I will," Luiza said. She marched straight toward the door and opened it, seemingly blind to the others' stares. She turned. "Coming?"

"Yes, thank you." He shot a *fuck you* grin to Malcolm and followed her out.

The door closed behind them, and Matt let out a long sigh. His heart pounded with anger. He could almost feel the silver slug jarring with each beat.

Malcolm. Arrogant shit. Matt wanted to punch that bastard square in the mouth. Knock that cheap-ass attempt at intimidation right off his face. And Schmidt saying they didn't trust him alone. Well, he *was* alone. He'd been alone since Clay died. Hell, he'd been alone since that wendigo killed his family and turned him into ... into whatever he was.

"Don't talk like that," Clay had once said when Matt was seventeen and feeling particularly sorry for himself one day. "You ain't no monster. Dämoren chose you. She *wanted* you to live. *I* want you to live. We're family." By that time the tumor inside him had begun its work, though neither of them knew it yet.

"I'm sorry about that," Luiza said, breaking his thoughts. "Everyone is taking this really hard, and I think they just took it out on you."

He didn't say anything.

"I'm not excusing it or anything. I just wanted you to know why.

We've lost a lot of our family. Not just these but over the past several months ... They're angry, and scared, and ..."

Matt gave a small nod. "It's fine. Thanks again, Luiza."

They headed down to the kitchen where Matt found himself face to face with some industrial coffee machine, all chrome and buttons. He stared at it for a few seconds, trying to figure out where to even begin. He turned to Luiza who chuckled at his helpless expression.

"Move over." She took the cup from his hand. "I'll show you."

He stepped back and leaned against a counter as she filled the steel filter with grounds and twisted it in before manipulating the little knob and buttons. "So why do you trust me?" he asked finally.

She turned, her chocolate eyes regarding him. "Because if you were a monster you wouldn't be killing demons. And if you were trying to infiltrate us, you'd have made some attempt to contact us. Instead, we came to you."

Matt thought about that, watching the syrupy liquids pour into their two cups. "And the things I can do, that doesn't scare you?"

Luiza shrugged. "I don't know, but I don't think you're a monster."

He smiled. "I really appreciate that."

She poured milk into his cup, gave it a quick stir and handed it to him. "We need to get back."

Drinks in hand, they made their way up to the meeting room. Passing a window, Matt spied Turgen outside in the courtyard with Tom. They both limped along the far side near the arched drive entrance, Turgen with his cane and Tom his prosthetic.

"One of the men we lost in Mexico was Master Turgen's student, Gabriel," Luiza said, solemnly. "His sword, Rowlind, was broken as well. He took it very hard."

Terrible thing to have in common. Matt touched Dämoren

under his arm. Losing her, seeing her broken and defiled, was probably the single worst thing he could imagine. For them it was real. They'd seen it. Seen their students dead. He watched the two men slowly circle toward the house, then he and Luiza continued up.

Voices poured out from the meeting room as they neared. A few people stood outside the door, alone or in murmuring groups. A noticeable hush fell as Matt and Luiza approached. Matt just ignored it and took his seat.

Three minutes later, Turgen returned. Tom wasn't with him. "Allan, are the videos ready?"

"They are."

The old man settled into his chair. "So let us see what happened to our knights."

Allan tapped the keys, and the satellite image of the farmhouse appeared on the screen. "Malcolm's team found four cameras. Cameras one and two were on the east side approximately here, and here." A white arrow cursor glided across the screen circling the cattle feeder and a fence near the barn. "Cameras three and four were on the western side, here and here." He circled a spot maybe thirty feet from the house where they'd found one of the cameras resting on a cement birdbath. Forty feet beyond that, they'd found the last one atop a stump. The old image on the screen still showed a tree there.

"What's interesting," Allan continued, "is that cameras two and three are both clean. Completely wiped."

"What do you mean?" Malcolm asked.

"I mean their memories are blank. There's nothing on them."

"Erased?"

"No. Erased memories will still hold residual information. Camera three is so clean that even factory settings are gone. Two still has memory, but it's unreadable."

"Do you know what could have done that?" Turgen asked.

Allan brushed his hair and shrugged. "It's like they were exposed to a magnet, but not just a little magnet. More like the type you'd pick up a car with. Really powerful."

"All the clocks in the house were blinking," Luc said, his hand on his chin. "Like they were reset at two-seventeen."

"Same time the trackers went off," Malcolm added. "Ever heard of a summoning that did that, Anya?"

She shook her head. "Never. But lightning and other phenomena have been recorded before. Most summoning records are a lot older than electronics. It's possible there could be a pulse."

"That's my theory, too," Allan said. "Those cameras were the closest. One and four were further away. Whatever scrambled the others got camera one a little, but overall it's okay." He changed the screen from the bird's eye of the house to two black, rectangular windows, side by side. "The one on the left is camera one. Right is camera four."

He clicked a button and the right window turned green. The shuffling image steadied and focused on the farmhouse. White numbers in the lower right read 22:34. Little squares of digital static popped sporadically across the screen. A green face leaned into view. Ramón, his pupils like pale lights in the infrared. His lips moved, but there was no sound. He pulled back out of frame. The camera jostled a hair, focusing back on the farmhouse; then Ramón and Anthony crept past, quick and low, weapons drawn.

Matt watched the two hunters approach the house. There was a good view of the front side, lit clear under the full moon. *Worst night of the month to go on a demon hunt,* Matt thought. While werebeasts could change at will, fighting during the full moon made them even meaner, more confident. Clay always avoided it, if possible. Daylight was always safer, though the chance of witnesses became infinitely higher.

A moment later, the left half of the screen flickered to green life. The image whirled around, then stopped, focusing on the house from the other direction. Blurry straw from the hay bale on which it rested, covered the very bottom of the screen. The clocks both said 22:41. Camera four flickered, the image briefly scrambling into little squares before clearing.

The hunters moved forward, cautious and slow. Matt's eyes moved between the screens, watching the two teams close in. Anthony and Ramón stopped to place a camera in the bird bath, then crept around toward the barn. The others affixed camera two to the fence post.

22:49.

Natuche's team headed around the back of the barn when the doors burst open. Five men rushed out with clubs. A broad form stepped out behind them. The low-light cameras seemed to dim as flared lights crackled across the monster's bare skin.

There's that ifrit.

More people stormed out from the house, and outlying buildings. Daniel hacked one of the club-wielding men to the ground, then slashed a busty, winged woman through the gut. She staggered, and he drove the blade through her. Flames burst from the wounds. She fell, burning.

Some of the knights in the audience gave mumbled cheers at the succubus' death, but not much as Daniel didn't have a chance to turn before one of the clubbers smacked him right across the face. He stumbled. Another club hit his arm, knocking the sword from his grasp.

From the other side of the yard, Ramón ran toward the injured knight. A man stepped around a corner and raised a small automatic. Bright flashes burst from the handgun and Ramón fell. Another man raced across the yard at inhuman speed toward Anthony. *Vampire.* The massive hunter spun to the side and ducked, hacking at his attacker's leg as it passed. Moving as a blur, the vampire leapt, dodging the blade. It landed, stopping instantly as if immune to its own momentum. Anthony sprung toward it, his axe cleaving through the air. The creature dodged to the side, but Anthony whirled the blade around and into the vampire's chest. Bright fire erupted from the wound.

"There you go," Colin said to the screen.

Matt watched the videos in silence, his attention wrested back and forth between the two camera feeds like being at a circus with multiple rings vying for attention. Camera four flickered several more times, once even freezing for several seconds before continuing.

Bright flames from the burning demon souls caused the night vision to wash out, distorting much of the action. Instead, Matt focused on the areas outside the battle. In the right screen, beside the house, he noticed four people standing and watching.

He leaned over to Luiza and pointed at the screen. "Who are those guys?"

She shook her head. "Familiars?"

"Then why aren't they attacking?"

"Don't know."

Two withered corpses shambled from the barn and dragged Yev to the ground. The room was silent as they watched the hunters fall one by one. Natuche was the last. She'd almost made it to where Anthony lay when a lanky, wild-haired creature tackled her from the shadows. She kicked and fought the thing hunkered atop her.

Ben gave a little yelp as the monster tore and ripped her face off, then ate it. She rolled on the gravel, one leg kicking the ground.

"My God, she's still alive," Schmidt muttered.

"They all are," Turgen said flatly.

The people beside the house walked out as several more emerged from inside. Ten in all. With the demons, they carried the wounded knights into the house. The wild-haired fiend that had maimed Natuche snarled at the approaching men, but a hulking werewolf snapped its head, and the beast cowered away.

"That's the only ghoul I've seen there," Malcolm said.

"They're not very common," Schmidt said.

"I know, but there were eight zombies at that house. The most I've ever seen one command was three, and that was a real powerful one."

The old man harrumphed. "Maybe there's more we haven't seen yet."

"Maybe." Malcolm leaned back into his chair. "Eight zombies is unheard of."

"Kluge said he'd encountered one with a half-dozen walkers once," Matt said, remembering the story.

Malcolm turned, his brow raised. "Who?"

"Victor Kluge. One of the hunters I read about."

Schmidt laughed. "Kluge? That charlatan probably never saw a ghoul in his life."

A towering shape moved past camera one. It looked dark in

the night vision. Chiseled muscles with two rows of short white horns running down its back. It carried a limp girl over one shoulder. Another creature followed, stooped in an awkward walk resembling a monkey. It was thin with long, thick hair. A second ghoul.

"Selene," Anya said, confirming Matt's suspicion.

Luc cocked his head to the side. "What is that thing?"

"That's one of those tongue monsters we found in Canada." Allan looked back toward Matt and nodded. "The ones Matt saved me from."

Thanks, Allan.

Everyone watched as the monsters and people entered the house. The walking corpses returned to the barn.

"So, not much happens after this." Allan moved the cursor to a gray bar along the bottom of the screen. The first little bit was red. "At eleven twenty-two, these guys come out." Allan clicked a little yellow arrow tacked further down the bar and the red line jumped to that position.

The timers read 23:22. Two figures emerged from the house. Both wore dark robes and executioner-like cowls. They removed their hoods. One was a man, his hair dark and of no particular length. The distance and green night vision made it difficult to see much detail of the other except there was a feminine quality to her movement.

"What's that pendant on the man," Schmidt said, pointing at the screen. "Can you make it any clearer?"

"I'll need some time to clean it up," Allan said. "But we should get something."

The man talked on a phone as the girl smoked a cigarette. Matt could barely make out the glint of something hanging around his neck. Had Schmidt not pointed it out, Matt doubted he'd have noticed it.

Jean leaned forward in his seat. "Who are you talking to?"

The caller seemed real excited, his own lit cigarette waving around as he talked like one of those light batons the guys on runways carried. After two minutes he hung up. He said something to the girl, and they dropped their butts into a clay jar by the door and headed back inside.

Allan moved the cursor to the next yellow mark on the video. "Once they go inside, there isn't anything until two seventeen when camera four loses everything for three seconds. Camera one only got a little flicker. Five minutes later ..." He clicked the marker and the video jumped ahead.

Three figures left the house, two men and a woman. The woman wore a long braid. One of the men was stocky and bald, the other slender with long, dark hair. Matt recognized Baldy from the farmhouse. They jogged away down the gravel drive. A couple minutes later, lights moved across the buildings and two cars, a van, and a blocky box truck pulled up. The truck blocked camera one's view almost entirely, and camera four still flickered, not fully recovered from whatever had scrambled it.

Figures started leaving the house and getting into the cars. Maybe twenty of them.

"Allan, can you clean that up?" Schmidt asked, running a finger over his moustache.

"It'll take time."

"Do it. See who they are. Get the plates."

A huge form emerged from the house, nearly filling the doorway.

"What in God's name is that?" Colin asked.

The monster straightened as it emerged, standing a full head above the van, broad and naked with plump tits, capped with long nipples. A thick knot of hair jutted from the back of its head and hung down almost like a horsetail. It looked around, then vanished behind the truck.

"Go back," Jean said.

Allan clicked the back arrow a couple times. The video started again, showing the strangers loading into the different cars. The hulking form emerged from the doorway. It stepped out and stood straight.

"Stop it there," Jean ordered. "Get its face."

The video paused. Frame by frame Allan moved it forward until the beast turned its head toward the camera.

Turgen leaned, squinting up at the screen. "Zoom it in, please."

The cursor moved over the images, drawing a dotted square

around the monster's head. It zoomed in, filling the window with the blurred image.

A single curved horn protruded upwards above a thick brow. Its jaw jutted forward. A pair of sharp canines stuck up and out from its lower lip.

A wave of defeat washed across the room.

Luiza shook her head. "No. It can't be."

"Look at the eyes," Jean said. "It's her."

Luc lowered his gaze and sighed. "Selene."

FROM THE JOURNAL OF SIR ERNEST BURROWS

1873

14 May - *I have arrived in London and secured a room at Claridge's. I'd almost forgotten the damnable fog here.*

15 May - *This morning I met with Watson to discuss my plan for Dämoren. I complimented him on his work, which he said was a Dumonthier style. I showed him the pieces of Dämoren, expressing my desire to use the entire sword in the gun's construction. Watson seemed hesitant at first, but after expressing my desire and capability of payment, he has agreed to draft a design based on my specifications.*

19 May - *I visited Mr. Watson this morning, eager to see his ideas. His designs, while aesthetic, lacked the functionality I had desired. Watson apologized for my disappointment, and told me to return to see more designs.*

22 May - *Watson continues to disappoint me. He suggested using only a few select pieces of Dämoren, expressing that her steel would be unsuitable for a functioning pistol. I told him that substituting the steel is impossible.*

26 May - *My confidence in Watson's abilities wanes. He showed me three sketches today. None were acceptable. Why would Dämoren lead me to him?*

28 May - *Watson presented me with a more pleasing design, a five-shot revolving gun, using Dämoren's handle as the grip. It incorporated the LeFaucheaux cartridge system. I told him I would prefer the newer Boxer cartridge, similar to those found on the Enfield rifle. He became very distressed at this, stating the Boxer cartridge would be too difficult to adapt to the design. It has become clear to me that Watson does not share my vision.*

Tomorrow I leave for France to find this Dumonthier, who designed the original gun that inspired Watson.

CHAPTER 8

"I just had a moment to grab Feinluna before it was on me," Luiza said.

Matt opened the dining room door and let her step through. "What happened?"

"Once it saw the sword, it knew better than to just keep charging. So it threw a chair at me. The wood caught fire at its touch. I ducked, and it went straight through this sliding glass door behind me. *Boosh!* Right out into the street."

They made their way to the bar along the back wall.

Luiza poured a glass of juice and dropped a few thin slices of meat onto a little plate. "Now this ifrit is mad, and the carpet, wherever it steps, is melting and smoking. It grabs this little coffee table, holds it up, and then charges. It hits me, and we both go right out the broken door. It's crushing me between the balcony rail and this table, which is now on fire. I'm just trying to keep it off me and, for some reason, I'm more worried about broken glass getting into my bare feet."

"Or other things," Matt added with a grin. He poured himself a glass of water.

Luiza gave a sly smile. "That too. Now don't get ahead of me."

"Sorry." They found an empty table and sat. "Go on."

"I managed to get my shoulder against it," she said, twisting in her chair, miming the movements. "I swung low and cut it right across the front of the ankle. It stumbles back, drops the table, and I swing." Luiza gave a wide gesture as if holding the sword in her hand. "Cut its head clean off. This geyser of white demon fire shoots out of its neck. It stands there for just a moment, then falls. Suddenly, this roaring cheer erupts from everywhere, and I realize there's a crowd of at least five thousand people watching me from the street, other balconies, everywhere."

"And you're still naked?"

"Close enough," she laughed. "It's not like I was planning for it to crash through my hotel door while I was changing. But this crowd thinks it's just some act for Carnival. They have no idea that it's real."

"So what did you do?" Matt asked, chuckling.

Luiza snorted. "I bowed to my audience. Then I ran back inside, got my clothes, stomped out a carpet fire, and got the hell out of there."

"Wow," Matt said, nodding. "That's a good one. I'd loved to have seen that."

Her brow rose playfully. "I'm sure you would have."

Matt felt himself flush.

"Mornin'," Tom said, limping toward the table.

"Good morning," Matt replied, smiling, grateful for the distraction.

Tom didn't smile back. "Coffee?"

"Yes, please." Luiza said. "Black."

"With milk, please," Matt said.

"Eggs?"

They both said yes.

"Right." The big man turned and limped back toward the kitchen.

Matt hid his frown with a drink of water. In the three days since returning from Spain, Tom's friendly demeanor had gone cold. At first, Matt thought it was a general mood after seeing Eslarin broken and Yev dead. But more and more he suspected Tom's anger was directed at him. He'd bet anything Malcolm was behind it. His shit had already led to Matt living like a prisoner, never alone outside his room. He must have said something to Tom. Either him or Schmidt. He eyed Schmidt and Jean, his white-haired protégé, eating at a nearby table with Turgen.

"So," Luiza said. "Your turn."

"Mine?"

She ate a slice of ham and nodded. "What's your funniest story?"

"I don't know. Not sure if I can top yours."

"Try."

Matt chewed his lip and thought. Finally, "I'll tell you the story of the two Bobs."

"Two Bobs?"

"Yeah." He grinned. "Back when I was eighteen Clay and I were down in East Texas on some rumors of missing people around one of the lakes. There's always a lot of drowning and accidents on lakes every summer, but that year the number was abnormally high. After a couple days, we heard some kids had made a fuss about seeing a monster one night and so went to check it out.

"It was this dingy little cove with a couple old houses. Clay was more worried about stumbling on a meth-lab than finding a demon. But near the back of the cove, the blood compass went off, pointing to this real shitty trailer near the water." Matt glanced up. "Thanks, Tom."

Tom set two coffees on the table.

Matt sipped it, and sucked a breath, trying to cool his scalded mouth. He set it aside to cool a bit longer before trying that again.

"So we snuck closer. We sprinkled ma ... warding powder along the windows and across the door to keep it inside. Since we didn't know what it was, Clay told me to stay outside. I had a pistol with silver rounds, but he didn't want to take the chance if they didn't work. So I stood watch.

"Clay creeps up and kicks open the door. I hear a shot, and then an ungodly scream, more like a screech. Then the side of this rusty trailer just explodes as this big bird-headed thing just comes plowing straight out the side right toward me."

"Bird-headed?" Luiza asked.

"Yeah. Had a head like a vulture and these talons." He lifted his hands, fingers splayed and curved, almost like he was about to catch a basketball. "Nasty claws. So I'm running backwards and shooting. It's coming at me, bullets going everywhere. Clay steps through the hole in the trailer, and it's a wonder I didn't hit him. He screams, 'Drop!' and I dive to the side, and he nails it with Dämoren.

"So." He sipped his coffee again. "It falls and the fireworks start up. It's burning this emerald green, and then we hear this man's voice scream, 'God damn. What the hell is that?'" Matt said in his best twang. "This bright beam of light hits me and we see these two good ol' boys sitting in this flat-bottom boat, maybe thirty feet out."

She chuckled. "And you hadn't seen them before?"

"Nope. They'd been sitting on the far side of the cove by some trees. No lights on their boat, so they'd just blended in. One of them has this mega-spotlight and the other is holding a little twenty-two rifle. I'm sure we're fucked. Clay and I are armed, but shooting people is a whole lot different than demons.

"Suddenly, Clay busts out this gold badge. 'FBI. Lower your weapons,'" Matt said, giving his best impression of Clay's gruff voice.

"FBI?" Luiza asked.

"Clay used to carry this badge he'd found somewhere. Said, 'Female Body Inspector' on the bottom. He said no one ever looked too close because people always shy away when they see a badge, at least people who aren't cops. Anyway, the guy with the light says, 'Damn it, Bob. Lower your gun.'

"The guy with the gun goes, 'Well God damn, Bob, I heard him.' He lowers his gun a little, points it at the demon that's now burning on the bank, and is, 'What the hell is that thing?'

"'Gentlemen,' Clay says, all serious. 'That is an extra-terrestrial.'"

Luiza burst into laughter.

Matt kept going. "Hell, you're shitting me," his voice in the higher twang of Bob One.

Bob Two's drawl was deeper. "Look at it."

"Son of a bitch."

"Clay tells them that he and I are part of some secret government mission to find aliens," Matt said, becoming aware that the other tables had gone quiet.

"And they believed it?" she laughed.

He nodded. "Well, the six-foot bird-headed thing was pretty convincing. That, and the dozen or so empty beer cans in the bottom of the boat probably helped. But the best part was that Clay convinced them to help dispose of the body even after it turned human. He said, 'Now the local authorities can't recover the body. Autopsy will show the truth.' And he got them to sink it into the lake for us. They were more worried about poisoning the fish with radiation than they were about sinking a body."

Still laughing, Luiza wiped a tear from her eye. "Why aliens? Why not tell them the truth?"

Matt shrugged. "I asked Clay the same thing, later on, and he couldn't even tell me. Said it was the first thing that came to mind. He used to watch this old show about FBI agents who tracked aliens, and he just went with it. He told them that they had done a great service to their country and to mankind. Got their information in case he ever needed them again, and that was it. One of them went, 'Damn it Bob, I told you I wanted to go to Lake Fork. This one's got damn chicken aliens.'"

She laughed again. Matt liked that.

Tom set two plates down on the table. "That's a fine story, there."

"Thanks." Matt smiled at him.

Tom smiled back. A small victory.

"I'd say that wins," Luiza said.

Matt ate a corner of omelet. "I don't know. I wasn't naked in front of five thousand people."

After they had finished breakfast, Luiza said, "I'll be going into town. You want me to take you back to your room?"

"Allan should be in the library by now."

"Still up for tomorrow?"

He nodded. "We never finished our shoot-off."

They stood. Before following her out, Matt approached Turgen at his table.

The old man looked up from a newspaper. "You're a good storyteller, Matt."

"Thank you." He fished a fold of paper from his pocket. "I'm almost out of reloading supplies for Dämoren. Some of it you have here, but not all of it."

Turgen took the note and read it. "Black powder. Thin felt fabric. Pure silver."

"Dämoren can't shoot smokeless. I asked Luiza, but she's not a citizen here and can't buy it. I also need to cast spare bullets. Ten ounces at least."

"I understand." The old man nodded and handed the list to Schmidt. "We'll have it for you this evening."

Matt shifted a bit uneasily as Schmidt glanced at the list, then slid it into a shirt pocket. "It's very important they're exactly what's on the list. Dämoren's picky."

Turgen smiled assumingly. "Max is familiar with Dämoren's needs."

Matt gave a little sigh. "Thank you."

As expected, they found Allan in the library engrossed in his computer. Mikhail, the orphaned student, sat at a table, his dark hair over his face as he scribbled notes beside a worn book. The lingering smell of Anya's cigarettes still hung in the air, though she wasn't at her desk.

"I might see you this evening," Luiza said. "If not, I'll get you in the morning for our run."

Matt smiled. "Look forward to it."

Once the door closed, Allan looked up from his clicking keyboard. "Got a girlfriend, I see."

"What? No. She's just been keeping me company while I'm under house arrest."

Allan's brow cocked. "Uh huh."

Matt felt his ears redden. "It's nothing like that."

The Englishman nodded. "All right then, 'cause Luiza and I have been shaggin' now and then, and I didn't want that to cause any tension between you and me."

A sudden pang hit Matt in the gut as if Allan had just kicked him. He opened his mouth to speak, but couldn't form the words.

"Oh," he finally said. "No. No problems."

Allan laughed. "I knew you liked her. Don't worry, mate. I'm just fucking with you."

Matt snorted a laugh and shook his head. "Fine. You caught me."

"Not like it was hard." Allan brushed his fingers through his hair. "So did you have a chance to read my notes on the tongue terror?"

"Yeah." Matt, grateful for the subject change, pulled up a rolling chair and sat. "Pretty straightforward. Nothing I could really add."

Allan's eyes narrowed. "But?"

Matt shrugged. "Eh ... Not too big on the name."

"Terriblis lingua? It means tongue terror. We've assigned Latin names to demons since the eighteenth century."

"No. That's fine." He rubbed his chin. "Tongue terror."

Allan gave a puzzled look. "But you said it was fine."

"The scientific name is fine. But actually calling it tongue terror ... I mean, you have the chance to call it anything. It should be punchy."

"How do you mean?"

"Well, a vampire isn't called blood-sucking corpse, and a Lamia isn't a snake-tailed flesh-eater. They have their own name that we use."

"So, what do you suggest?" Allan asked.

Matt smiled. "A strutter."

Allan blinked. "Why?"

"It's a song by Kiss."

He blinked again, then shook his head. "You're joking?"

"No. I wanted to name a demon after them. I mean it's got that big Gene Simmons tongue. They call him The Demon. So it fits."

"Why not call it a Simmons?"

Matt gave a little shrug. "Didn't like the ring as much. Not as punchy as, strutter."

Allan looked at Matt like he was something that just crawled out from under a rock, then laughed. "You're daft, you know that? I thought you were serious."

"I am. I'd like to name it strutter. I mean I'm the one who killed it, right? So I should name it."

The amused smile vanished from Allan's face. "No. You're

not naming a demon breed after a band. No."

"That's why I said you could keep Terriblis lingua, but change th—"

"No," Allan said flatly.

"You're no fun."

"So is this all you did last night," Allan asked, swiveling his seat around toward the monitor, "come up with demon names?"

"Pretty much. I think your computers are still buggy. I was trying to see what you guys had found about that big thing we saw on the video, but I can't access the database."

Allan's shoulders slumped a little. "Oh. *That.*"

"What?"

Allan swung the chair back. "The, um, others think that giving you access to our records isn't a good idea."

"What?" It was more shock than anything.

"I didn't realize they had blocked you yet. I'd assumed Schmidt would have talked with you first."

A hot knot of anger clenched inside Matt's gut. "He blocked me? That son of a bitch!" He brought his hand down onto his armrest a little harder than expected. The resounding thud echoed through the room.

Sighing, Allan nodded. "I know."

"So what in the hell am I supposed to do around here?" he asked, his fingers tightening into a fist. "If he'd told me back in Canada that I'd be treated like some criminal, I'd have told him to kiss my ass. What happened to, *Dämoren trusts you, so we trust you?*"

Allan's gaze darted past Matt, then back. "They're worried about you having access to all of the Valducan records."

"They?" Matt turned to see Mikhail tensely stooped lower over his book, obviously trying not to appear like he was listening. Matt looked back to Allan. "Why don't you just say Schmidt and Malcolm?"

"It's not just them. Others agree, as well."

"Yeah. I'm sure there are." *Anya, for one.* She'd thrown suspicion on Matt the instant that ifrit turned, but he didn't want to say that to Allan. He'd noticed enough sidelong glances to know Mikhail wasn't the only Librarian that liked her.

"But," Allan said, optimistically. "I did get them to agree you can have access as long as it's under my watch. So as long as you're in here, with me, you can go through it."

Matt leaned back into the swivel chair, letting out a long breath. "Thanks, man."

"Don't worry," Allan said through a toothy grin. "I'll be putting you to work."

"Like what?"

"For one, finding out who those people were. We're pretty certain we're dealing with a cult, but don't know anything beyond that." He turned and opened a picture on his computer: A zoomed still of the robed man talking on the phone. A pendant hung from his neck, but was too fuzzy to make out clearly. In the night vision's green monochrome, it was impossible to even tell what it was made of. The light seemed to glint off it. *Metal? Stone?*

"Anya and I have gone through every glyph we know of, but haven't found anything that matches it." He opened a new window. Another picture, this one zoomed in on the pendant itself, filled the screen. Crude digital lines, drawn in black, followed the medallion's pixilated curves. There was clearly a circle of sorts. Inside it a shape.

Matt leaned closer. The little drawn lines gave it almost the appearance of a letter "J" lying on its side.

"I'm thinking a scorpion or maybe a sphinx," Allan said. "Anya is leaning toward a crescent moon or a face. So far we've found nothing that comes close."

"So what do you need me to do?"

"At this point we're checking the old records. The ones that aren't fully scanned in." Allan turned back around. "You said you came across a cult once. Louisiana."

"Shit. There was nothing like any of that stuff there. It was all pentagrams and upside-down crosses."

"But it worked, right? They did summon one?"

Matt nodded. "It was some weird thing. Looked like a horned lizard on two legs. Didn't do much before I got there and put it down. After that, I burned the barn."

"Well," Allan said, the excitement draining from his voice.

"Just look through them. See if anything jumps out at you."

"All right." He nodded toward the cabinet near the wall. "Mind if I pour one?"

"It's nine in the morning."

"And I've already been banned from reading anything without supervision," Matt said. "I'd like a drink."

Allan gave an understanding nod. "Make it two. Oi, Mikhail, you wanna drink?"

The dark-haired boy looked up. He glanced at Matt, then to Allan. "Please."

Matt got up and removed the bottle and three glasses from the little cabinet, and filled them. He handed one to Allan, then walked over to where Mikhail sat. The boy looked no older than seventeen. It felt sort of weird giving whisky to someone so young. Then again, Clay had given Matt alcohol since he was fifteen. Besides, he had no idea if there even was a drinking age in Russia or Slovakia, or where ever the boy was from.

Mikhail took the glass and raised it in thanks.

"So," Matt said returning to his chair. He sipped his drink. "What have you found on that big demon in the video? Any idea what it is?"

Allan nodded. "Sonu thinks it's an oni, and I believe he's right."

Matt gave a little gesture with the whisky glass, telling Allan to explain.

"They have a lot of other names. Ogres. Trolls."

"Trolls? Like, fairy tale trolls?"

Allan knocked back his drink. He winced, exhaled, then set the glass aside. "The folklore is derived from real monsters. Now, we don't know if Beowulf's Grendel was an oni, or even if there was a Grendel, but the monsters responsible for most of the legends were real. Same with dragons."

Matt cocked a brow.

"I'm serious," Allan said. "You have legends of these monstrous, flying serpents from all across the world, spawning from cultures completely independent from one another. China, Greece, India, Europe." He tapped them out on his fingers. "Even Mexico. They were real. Saint George killed a demon, the biggest kind of demon. They're extinct, now. Hopefully, forever."

"Hopefully." Matt finished his drink. "So what do we know about oni."

"Not much." He turned and began clicking on his computer. "We had thought them extinct as well. Last one was reported in 1635, in Ireland." He rolled aside, giving Matt a view of an old wood-engraved picture. A monstrous, single-horned creature with jutting teeth swung a gnarled club, like a tree-trunk, at a trio of swordsmen. Another swordsman lay crumpled at its feet.

"What we do know is that they're incredibly strong, cunning, and very powerful. What exactly they can do is unknown, but some reports say that powerful ones can fly."

"Jesus," Matt said. "Anything work on them?"

"Not much. No known metals or herbs seem to hurt it. Although, one was killed by a jade bullet in fifteenth century Korea."

Matt thought about that. "Don't know how well a stone bullet would work in a modern gun. The pressure and rifling might blow it apart. Shotgun, maybe."

"That's what Malcolm uses. He has his loaded with all kinds of different stuff, similar to your magic powder."

"Smart."

Allan picked up the empty glass. He rolled it in his hand, looking at it as if it might yield some hidden secret. "We've been affixing gems and stones to bullets for several years now. Jade shouldn't be too hard." He stood, took Matt's empty glass and carried them back to the bottle still resting beside the cabinet. "That does bring up a point," he said, refilling them.

"What's that?"

Allan handed him a refreshed glass and sat. "We've had a lot of new or lost breeds come about recently, and we know virtually nothing about them. Their weaknesses. The more we find out about them, the better prepared knights will be in the future."

"I wasn't really planning on letting them live that long."

"We can kill them, yes. But what if more emerge a hundred years from now? If we can tell our successors what can harm a tongue terror or a horned hound or any of the others, we might save lives. I mean, someone, at some point, loaded a silver-tipped quarrel onto a crossbow and shot a werewolf, just to see what would happen. And haven't you benefitted from their risk?"

"What are you suggesting, Allan? That before killing these things we shoot them with several different bullets and throw some herbs in their faces, just to see what works?"

Allan gave a little shrug. "Essentially, yeah."

"And you called me daft."

"I'm just saying that next time we find one, before anyone slays it, you maybe plug it with a silver bullet, also a copper or gold while you're at it. Nothing that'll kill the body. Maybe a leg or arm. If it responds, we can note that. If it doesn't, then we learned what not to use next time. Either way it's valuable knowledge."

Matt thought about that. He remembered that old Colt he used to carry when he was with Clay. It saved his life more than once. Silver for werebeasts and vampires. Gold for rakshasas. Copper for sigbens. Sigbens, or chupacabras as they called them in Central America, lost the demon-metal lottery in Matt's opinion. Most modern bullets were copper-plated, and worked on them just fine. A rancher with a varmint rifle could defend his livestock quite easily. Although the demon never really died, it just lost its body and jumped to the next one, maybe hundreds of miles away. It made hunting them real difficult since most sigbens couldn't stay in a region very long before some lucky shot made it someone else's problem. He sipped his drink. "So why me?"

"What?"

"Why do I have to be the one that shoots it?"

"Because you're a good shot. Me, I can't even shoot a handgun. Wouldn't make much sense for me to be blasting at it."

"You're kidding me?" Matt asked, taken back. "You can't shoot a gun?"

"Well," Allan said, shifting in his seat a little. "I've shot before. Guns really aren't that easy to come by back home so I never really got all that into it."

"So you just carry Ibenus when hunting? What if you drop her? What if *they* have a gun?"

"You've seen me take out a shooter before," Allan said, cocking his brow a little.

"You were lucky, man. It was impressive, but lucky." Matt gestured to the books around them. "How many stories have you read where a knight lost his weapon? You can't just count that you won't and that the partner you're with has a shot. These bastards are using familiars to shoot us. One nearly shot me. I like you, Allan. I really do. But not carrying a gun is just flat fuck crazy."

Allan gave a hurt look, then sipped his drink.

"I'll tell you what," Matt said, feeling a little guilty. "I'll pop a test round or two into one of those demons for you, but only if you do, too."

The Englishman's gaze flicked back, hopeful.

"Luiza and I are going shooting tomorrow after breakfast. Then we're doing some reloading. You should join us."

"I don't know, Matt. I don't want to get in the way."

"No. You want me to help these crazy-ass experiments, you need to help shoot them. That's the deal. You come tomorrow or I don't help you."

Finally, "All right."

They stayed in the library for the next several hours scouring reports of demon glyphs and rites for any clues. Matt couldn't understand the majority of the old writing, so he focused on pictures and scribbles. That afternoon they made their way down for lunch. Allan had plans with Jean and Ben to work out then spar. He'd asked if Matt wanted to join, but Matt said his run with Luiza had been enough for him that day. Allan didn't press him, so after lunch he escorted Matt back to his room.

"I'll be back. Fetch you for dinner," Allan said.

"All right."

Allan looked around the hall, his eyes pausing on the camera in the far corner. "I have something for you." He reached into his red gym duffel and pulled out a thick hardback. The glossy dust jacket had a little tear along the top. A white schooner sailed on the cover over choppy seas. Giant ghostly eyes stared out from the dark sky above the title, *Final Comet*.

Matt took the book. The stiff cover bowed slightly around something inside it.

Allan set his hand over it. "I like my name more than 'strutter.'"

"Okay," Matt said, unsure what was happening. "Thanks."

"Well then," Allan said cheerfully, shouldering his bag. "I'll see you in a couple hours."

Matt stepped into his room and closed the door behind him. He opened the book to find a yellow, 256-gigabyte jump drive nestled between the pages. Setting the book aside he loaded the drive into his laptop.

A password prompt appeared, framed in red.

Matt stared at the blinking cursor, then typed, "Valducan."

Incorrect.

He tried, "Ibenus."

Incorrect.

Matt's sucked his lip, then looked at the novel still resting on the table beside the door. "TongueTerror."

The red box vanished, replaced by a long column of manila file icons. The entire Valducan Archive. *Thanks Allan.*

He clicked "Field Reports: Dämoren" and scrolled down until he found what he wanted. The journals of Sir Clay Mercer. Something he should have started his first night in the house, but somehow intimidated him. He clicked it open and began to read.

To: Alexander Turgen
From: Clay Mercer
Subject: Field Report

I'm sorry it's been so long since my last report. A lot has happened.

After the wendigo pack escaped in Ridgway, I followed their last direction north. They'd been posing as an Indian family driving a green VW bus and I hoped they hadn't ditched it. I spent 2 days searching through little communities until I made it to Warren PA.

I'd stopped for gas just outside of town when I noticed a group of college kids. They had a little sunfish sailboat lashed down on top of this blue Honda. This cute brunette with nice tits kept glancing at me. I figured I might have been staring like some creepy old man, so I didn't think much of it.

2 hours later a call came through the scanner about a bloody scene at a motel. Cops were all over it by the time I got there, but I managed to get myself close enough to find out that an Indian family had stayed there. Never checked out. When the maid came through to clean the room she found it covered in blood. There were claw marks all over the bed and inside. Cops thought the tenants might have snuck a bear in and it got loose, attacked one of them, and the family fled to the reservation before they could get in trouble.

Little after that a new call came in that a burnt-out VW was found outside of town. Cops left to go check it out. I stuck around until they'd gone, then approached the manager. I slipped him $200 to let me look at the security tapes and not tell anyone about it. Cops had the tapes for the lobby and parking lot, but left the pool camera footage. On it I saw one of the Indian boys talking to some teenagers. Looked like he was selling them grass. One of the girls looked familiar. I asked the manager and he told me they'd left that morning. They had a sailboat on top of their Honda.

I figured the wendigos lured the kids somewhere, pretending to sell them dope, transferred bodies, ate their old ones, then ditched their van. All I could do was hope they assumed they'd lost me. I headed east to Kinzua Lake. I worked my way around it, checking all the docks, marinas, and anywhere else they might go. On the third night I found their car parked by a little cabin just across the New York border. I went in, but the place was empty. There were a few other houses in the area, mostly weekend rental places, so I checked those.

A mile up the road, I heard a girl screaming in one of the houses. I checked a window and saw a wendigo eating a woman. There was a boy in there, looked to be in shock, but not bitten. I did a quick dust of powder around the exits so they couldn't get away again. I kicked open the door and plugged one about to eat the boy. I chased another upstairs and shot it and another one. The boy started screaming downstairs and I went down to find the fourth wendigo attacking him. There was a butcher knife sticking out of its back from when the boy had stabbed it. I shot the wendigo, killing it, but Dämoren's slug passed through and hit the boy.

This is when it gets weird.

I checked that the house was clear, then started first aid on him. The wound was bad, but I couldn't let him die. It was my fault the wendigos had gotten away, and I fuckin shot the kid. He started screaming and lashing about. I thought he was done for, but then his wounds healed. Closed right before my eyes.

The wendigo that had bit him was burning, so I knew it couldn't have possessed him. There were only 4 demons and I had killed all of them. Also, Dämoren's slug was still inside him. I've shot enough demons to know that he'd need to dig it out before it could heal. After a short chat (Dämoren trained on him) I learned he could speak French, having never been taught it or even realizing that he could. I threw powder on him, which contains burnt cornmeal, but it didn't do anything.

Finally, I asked Dämoren by removing one round from her cylinder, spinning it, and pulling the trigger. Dämoren said he should live. I know that it wasn't chance. I checked her, and the cylinder she landed on had a bullet. Dämoren chose not to fire.

I don't know what this boy is, but Dämoren wants him alive. His name is Spenser Mallory. He's 12 years old. I'm not sure what we need to do here. I've never heard of anything like this. There's a guy down in Florida that can give him a new name, so we're headed there now.

What do I do?

-Clay

To: Clay Mercer
CC: Max Schmidt; Margaret Lennox; Sonu Rangarajan
From: Alexander Turgen
Subject: Re: Field Report

Sir Clay,

I just finished your report and found it terribly disturbing. If this boy is possessed then he must be dealt with. We understand your guilt for letting the wendigos escape and kill more, but allowing this boy to live is madness.

Your life is in danger. I order you to take care of the situation immediately.

Sincerely,

Alex

CHAPTER 9

Matt awoke in darkness. He rolled and looked at the little green clock beside the bed.

1:42.

With a groan, he adjusted his pillow, crushing it from different sides, punishing it for his sudden and complete consciousness, and tried to go back to sleep.

His bladder ached.

He tried to ignore it.

The pressure grew. Matt shifted and rolled onto his back, hoping that his new position might somehow allow him reprieve until morning. For a short while it worked, but then the pressure came back. Small at first, but growing, until finally he couldn't ignore it any longer.

He looked back at the clock.

1:49.

"To hell with this," he mumbled. Matt rolled out of bed. The bathroom was down the hall, and if Schmidt or anyone tried to make any issue with him leaving his room, Matt planned to just pull it out and piss on the floor. If they were going to treat him like a criminal, he might as well do something to deserve it. He fumbled for the sweatpants folded beside the bed, waiting for his morning run with Luiza in five hours, and pulled them on.

He listened at the door. Nothing. He opened it. The hall was empty.

Matt stepped out, noticing the little red light on the camera in the upper corner flip on once it detected his movement. *That's right, asshole*, he thought to whoever, if anyone, was actually watching the camera. *The demon has left his room. What are you going to do about it?* Matt figured if someone *was* watching the feed, and if they did care, he'd find out soon enough what they planned to do about it.

He turned and started down the dim hall, lit by the moonlight through the windows, and by the glow spilling out from one of the bedroom doors; *Kazuo's*, he thought. Matt had made it probably thirty steps before realizing that his sleepy brain had gotten him turned around and what would have been the closest bathroom had been the other way, but he was committed now. From his current location it would be shorter to just continue on to the one ahead.

He turned down a darkened hallway and had made it only a few steps before freezing in surprise. A dark figure stood in the passage before him, silhouetted by the moonlight.

The dark shape just stood there, staring at one of the doors.

Matt let out a breath, his startled heart still pounding. Slowly he crept forward. In the darkness he could make out a slender form, broad shoulders and scruffy hair. "Mikhail?"

The boy gave no response.

Matt was close enough to touch him now. He put his hand on Mikhail's shoulder. His skin was slick with sweat.

Mikhail jumped and whirled around. Something thudded softly to floor. The boy looked at Matt, then to the door. "I'm ... I'm sorry," he stammered in some language Matt couldn't identify, and then he ran, his bare feet padding softly on the hall carpet.

Matt stood there for several seconds, unsure of what just happened. He looked at the door. Anya's room. A little book lay open at his feet and he picked it up. While it was too dark to see it clearly, Matt recognized the cardboard covers and round cloth spine as a notebook. Matt looked around again. He was alone, save for the little red light beneath the security camera's cold eye. He shrugged, and continued on.

Once he reached the bathroom he emptied his bladder, then looked at the thin book Mikhail had dropped. Tiny black and white splotches filled the cover, like some artist's rendering of static on an old-style television.

Matt opened it. Crisp Cyrillic words filled the narrowly lined pages, their meanings lost on him. He flipped ahead. Occasional doodles began in the margins, starting about a quarter of the way in. They looked to be swords and knives. Matt continued deeper through the book. The doodles became more frequent, cleaner, spilling out from the margins and occupying more and more of the pages. Matt realized that the images were not of random, arbitrary swords, but of one specific sword, with a curved blade and jeweled handle.

He recognized the weapon.

Eventually the writing and notes ceased altogether, replaced by page after page of the same curved sword. Some were highly detailed with shading and soft lines, others were crisp in stark black and white. Some showed fine close-ups, the pommel, the twisting grip, the grooved blade, a tassel. Still others depicted the sword complete.

Matt found himself staring at full-page drawing done in five different colors of pen and pencil. A jeweled scimitar, a tassel hanging from the tip of its scabbard. While Allan and the others all rolled their eyes, believing the young man's distraction was with the busty Romanian, Matt knew the truth. Mikhail was in love. Not with the woman, but with her sword. Baroovda had bonded with him.

Shaking his head and remembering the awkward fear of loving a weapon already bonded to another, Matt closed the book. The boy's drawings were like the ones Matt had doodled in the corners of his study books when Clay was teaching him. If the old man had ever found them it would have been more embarrassing than if he'd caught Matt jerking off.

Allan had considered Matt's early love for a weapon already bonded as unique, a word Matt had grown accustomed to. But Mikhail's drawing proved otherwise.

After checking the hall was clear, he ventured back out into the dark house. His bare feet silent on the thick rugs, he made his way to Mikhail's room. No light peeked from around the door frame. Matt bent and slid the notebook under the door, then crept back to his own room and into bed. The boy's love was an intimate secret, and it would be safe with him. He only hoped Mikhail, in return, wouldn't tell of Matt's late-night wanderings.

"It's not fair to compare yourself to us," Matt said, holding the weave-textured straps of his shooting bag.

"It's embarrassing," Allan grumbled, his lips barely moving. He carried a plastic bucket clinking with their spent brass.

Luiza opened the green metal door along the back of the lane. "He's right. Matt and I have been shooting for years. You'll get the hang of it. Just stop anticipating the recoil."

Allan harrumphed. "I can't help it. It kicks."

"You get used to it."

"I think I want a different gun."

"Ask and you shall receive." Beige foam panels lined the walls of the ten-foot hallway, nearly covering the door set in the far side. A brass lock and handle protruded out through chunky square cutouts in the foam. Luiza unlocked them.

She flicked the fluorescents, and they stepped into a long room, nearly running the width of the gun range. It smelled like a machine shop, that unique combination of metal, grease, and an unidentifiable burned odor.

Matt set his bag down on a thick, scarred table and admired the setup. Two tables met at one corner, creating a neat work cubby. A sturdy vise rested on one side beside an assortment of other clamps. A gray drill press sat on the other end. Various wrenches, mallets, calipers, saws, files, screwdrivers, and many more tools Matt couldn't identify, all hung from a high pegboard backsplash along both walls.

On the other side of the room, past a four-foot double-paned window of bulletproof glass looking out onto the range, was a meticulously organized reloading bench. Two high cabinets, stuffed with wide, shallow drawers, each labeled in ascending calibers, stood as tall as him. Yellow plastic trays lined a trio of shelves against the back wall. Before them, atop a dark and weathered counter, stood a pair of sturdy presses and a bright red tumbler.

"Nice," he said, genuinely impressed. A stainless steel sink rested in a little counter beside him, next to a little black microwave. A battered refrigerator stood nearby, its face speckled with dozens of touristy magnets: an Eifel Tower, a palm tree that said "Costa Rica," a small Venetian mask.

"Welcome to the bunker," Luiza said. "Used to be Nick's little fortress in here."

"Nick?"

"Arms master," Allan said. "He died in Poland some weeks ago."

Matt nodded, remembering the story of the wounded hunter killed in Krakow after the demon that had bit him escaped. A mercy kill.

"He used to hole up in here," Allan continued. He nodded to the three hulking gun safes along the back wall. "It took Jean a couple days before he could open those after Nick was gone. Didn't trust the combination with anyone."

"No one knew how to get in? Sounds odd."

Allan shrugged, slightly. "He'd given the combinations to Turgen, Schmidt, couple others. But then changed 'em without telling them. He was, ah ..." Allan chuckled. "A little paranoid." He pointed to a desk with a pair of black monitors. Each wide screen was divided into four sections, each showing a different video. Hallways, rooms, hilled vine rows.

"Is that the security feed?" Matt asked, stepping closer. He watched Colin lifting weights in the gym while Susumu and Riku sparred.

"One of them. He had a backup installed here. In case something happened, he wanted to know. As I said, paranoid."

Luiza nodded. "I miss him."

"We all do," Allan agreed.

They set their gear out on one of the worktables and Luiza opened one of the safes. Various black handguns hung from little cloth holsters along the inside of the door. She removed a Sig identical to hers and three magazines.

"Here," she said, handing it to Allan.

Allan looked at it like he wasn't entirely sure what it was. "What else is there?"

She made a little face. "Different kinds, calibers. Trust me, you'll like it. Good for beginners, but professional."

"Can I look at some of the others?"

Luiza swept her hand out, offering toward the open safe.

"Feel free. You'll need to test out anything you like. Make sure you can handle it."

Allan made his way to the safe and scoured through it while Matt took the bucket off the table and poured about a quarter of the dirty shells into the tumbler. It took a few seconds before he located the switch and he turned it on. It trembled with a steady hum.

"What's this one?" Allan said, holding up a blocky pistol.

"Glock," Matt answered.

Allan flipped it over. "How big is the clip for it?"

"Magazine," Matt corrected.

"They always call it a clip on the telly."

"So? TV and movies also say that UV hurts vampires like sunlight, too."

Allan frowned. "All right. How much does the *magazine* hold?"

"Seventeen, I think. Never really got into them. Clay used to say anything but a 1911 was a waste of metal."

"Oh." He looked back inside. "We have any of those in here?"

"Doubtful," Luiza said. "Forty-five isn't a common round in Europe."

Matt glanced over at the shelves beside him. Calibers started at 7.65 and worked up. 9mm seemed to dominate the shelves with three drawers for both Luger and Kurtz sizes. .45 had only one. He pulled it open. Eight black trays rested inside, each filled with unloaded bullets, some silver, others copper. A few looked like brass. They were hollow points with six little prongs open above the conical cavity in the tips. He picked one up and noticed that instead of solid silver like the ones he and Clay had always molded, these were silver jacketed with lead cores.

"These are like professional made," he said holding it up to Luiza.

She nodded. "Nick was a genius. They work just as well as solid but weigh more. Penetrates better."

Matt tapped his fingertip on the little prongs. "What are these?"

She smiled wryly, her dark eyes twinkling. "What do you think?"

Matt shrugged.

She pulled open the top drawer and removed a clear plastic box. Tapered brown beads rattled inside. Luiza opened the box and removed a bead, then plucked the bullet from Matt's hand. She slipped the bead into the hollow tip and held it out. "Ta-da."

Matt peered closer. A round-tipped cap of tiger's eye rested perfectly in the bullet's nose. "Oh. Oh wow."

"Like I said, genius."

"So you can put any stone you want in the tips?"

"Or metal. You can make a gold tip, or silver, bronze, anything. Nick locked the valuable ones away, but," she winked. "I know the combinations."

Matt grinned.

Luiza looked down at the drawer of .45 slugs. "Nick never loaded any of the tips on these, so you'll have to. Not enough demand to keep a committed inventory. Once you bend the prongs in, that's it. So choose carefully."

"We have any jade tips?"

She nodded.

"Then let's start with those."

After what had felt like a hundred potentials and a thousand questions ranging from the comically general to the frighteningly specific, Allan had chosen his sidearm: a Walther PPK chambered in the 9mm Kurtz. Allan wasn't sure about it at first, but once he learned it was the same type of gun James Bond used, the deal was set. Luiza took him back to the range just to be sure Allan actually liked shooting it. Through the double-walled Lexan window, Matt watched Allan blast holes through paper silhouettes as he operated Nick's cap setter.

The cap setter, as they called it, was similar to a large stapler made of metal and polished wood. On the lower jaw, Matt slotted a hollow metal post, just the diameter for whichever size bullet he was using. He'd slide a bullet into the ring, where the slug sat tightly, then he'd set whichever type of cap he wanted beneath the prongs in the hollow point. Once in place, he just lowered the jaw, jamming it firmly down, which pressed the claw-like prongs securely around the cap. It reminded Matt of this stupid toy his sister had that attached plastic rhinestones to cloth. She'd spent her fourth-grade year with nothing but sparkly jeans.

"How are you coming?" Luiza asked, once she and Allan had finished.

"Done with the forty-fives. Starting on nine mils." Matt mashed the setter down hard, then rolled his hand a little over the top, trying to get all the prongs perfectly set. He released it, then removed the bullet. A purple amethyst capped the silver slug. He tugged the little claws with a thumbnail. *Good and tight.*

"It took a couple tries to get it down," he said, motioning to the trays of completed slugs. Twelve of the silver bullets and two of the brass had no caps, their broken prongs casualties of Matt's learning curve. "Guess I'll just have to make do with hollow points. Probably better than the ones I've been using for years."

Luiza grinned. "Allan and I can take over from here. We're the ones using them anyway." She nodded toward the corner. "You know how to use one of those?"

Matt looked at the reloading presses bolted securely to the table. The larger one stood over two feet high, grayish green and silver with little rotating plates and topped with a slender clear bottle of gunpowder. A long silver lever, capped with a round knob, jutted up and outward from the front in an almost suggestive manner. "No clue," he said. "Always used a hand press. Easier to carry on the road. You?"

"Nick insisted on it. He said we'd all learn to slow down and shoot better if we knew how long loading them took. A group of us used to all come, watch movies, have a few drinks, and swap turns loading bullets."

Matt showed Allan how he learned to use the cap setter, then set him at it, armed with a list of what stones worked on what demons, then Luiza sat him down and showed him how to operate the press. The press was very simple to use, once he got the hang of it, and Matt wished he'd been able to use one all those years of sitting with Clay or alone squeezing them out at a snail's pace. The solid silver bullets that he molded were also a lot lighter than these lead-core ones. They needed more powder, which the machine properly measured and poured for him.

Reloading Dämoren's special shells however, would always need to be manual, but Matt wouldn't have it any other way. That was something intimate, something special. The Ingram was a tool, a hungry machine that needed feeding. Dämoren was ... well ... like a lover. Matt chuckled at the thought, true as it was.

"What's so funny over there?" Allan asked. He'd almost filled two fifty-round trays with capped slugs.

"Nothing," Matt said. Then, "So Luiza, you mentioned drinks earlier."

She snorted. "Not while you two are still learning how to do this. Beers are reserved for loaders that don't even have to think about what they're doing."

"Ahh, one beer won't hurt," Allan said.

She gave them both a look. "Once we're done. "

"Well, I'm finished with these," Matt said, cranking out the last of his rounds. Eighty in total. Amethyst for succubi, brass for ifrit, obsidian for ghouls, jade for the oni.

"And I'm almost done." Allan pressed the cap setter down. "Four more after this one."

Matt turned to say something when he saw Schmidt walking past the range window. Moments later the door opened and he stepped inside carrying a green cloth bag. His thin lips looked even tighter than normal.

"Here are your supplies, Mister Hollis," Schmidt said tersely, setting the bag down on one of the long tables with a *thunk*. "I trust they are what you need."

Matt rose and looked inside. Four black plastic jars rested inside beside a large square of folded red felt. He picked up one of the jars. Most of the French writing was lost on him, but the little orange warning symbol of an exploding ball was very familiar. He set it back inside and checked the felt. It was the exact same as Clay used to use, even the color, which Matt's list hadn't specified. Had it not looked new, he'd have thought it was from the same bolt.

"These look good." Matt moved the jars aside to find a worn tin box resting at the bottom. Its once-bright paint and picture of what looked like snow-capped mountains was worn and scratched. He picked it up. It weighed more than he'd expected. Matt set the box on the table and carefully opened the tight lid.

Six tapered ingots rested inside, tarnished black with age. Matt picked one up and turned it over. "C.M." it read, scratched deep into the bottom. He looked up at the old man, his mouth opening into a question.

"Clay poured those," Schmidt said. He gave a slight smile, but then it was gone. "I've had them for several years now and decided it was only appropriate they be used for their original intent."

Matt closed his hand, feeling the weight of it. Clay's personal silver. Schmidt had saved it all those years. "Thank you."

Schmidt nodded, then turned to the others. "I've come to fetch you. There was an incident in Limoges last night."

Allan straightened up. "What happened?"

"Attempted break in at the Vedorme-Perrin Museum. Nothing stolen, but a guard is missing. We suspect demons were involved."

"A weapon?" Allan asked, standing.

Schmidt's brow rose. "Possibly. Master Turgen received the call this morning. We have several pieces on loan there and the owner called him personally. We are meeting to discuss the operation and sending a team."

"What about me?" Matt asked. If he wasn't going to the meeting it only meant he was again exiled back to his room.

Schmidt's blue eyes regarded him. "You're going with them. You have an hour to cast your bullets and prepare. We need Dämoren ready. You'll be briefed on the way to Limoges."

SUCCUBI AND INCUBI

A mong the most pervasive and vile of Demonkind is the Succubus, a most awful fiend who desires not the flesh of a man for sustenance, but for carnal dominance. While theologians and scholars believe that Succubi and Incubi are separate species: one female and the other male; they are unquestionably the same entity merely inhabiting the physical body of a human female or male host.

2: Succubi, whom the Germans call *Mara*, the Norwegians *Huldra*, the Arabs *Qarinah*, take the form of comely women; their hair is long and breasts round and full. Succubi possess wings of soft skin that extend from their backs. Through trickery and glamour they can hide these appendages from any physical observation or touch.

Incubi, whom the Italians call *Folletti*, The Spaniards *Duendes*, the French *Follets*, are the male form of Succubi. Their appearance can change, depending on their host. However they all share a beauty that no woman, no matter how chaste and pure, can resist. They are well formed and possess a member whose size and girth rivals a stallion's. Unlike their female counterparts, Incubi do not possess wings and therefore cannot fly, although their physical strength is far superior to that of Succubi.

Succubi can also inhabit the body of a fox, as observed in the Far East.

When slain, the incorporeal body of a Succubus burns with the most unholy of fires whose color alternates from the deepest crimson to rich violet.

3: Several folk remedies exist to ward back the evil of Succubi, though most are in truth merely superstition and possess no power over the Demon. Fearful monks tying crucifixes to their genitals before retiring at night protect themselves no more than ignorant maids relying on phallic-shaped amulets. Succubi do not obey the Exorcist, have no dread of exorcisms, nor reverence for holy things.

In truth, the peony flower does repulse the Demon, as does cold iron and amethysts.

4: Succubi feed through carnal intercourse, sapping the energies of their victims through the deed of Demoniality; a term invented by John Caramuel in his *Fundamental Theology*. While victims can recover in time, repeated attacks over a series of nights frequently results in death. Any victim who tastes of a Succubus's milk or Incubus's seed is damned and becomes a vessel which the Demon may possess at their whim.

Many victims do not understand their attacks, as they are beguiled by the most diabolical illusion. Under the influence of this illusion brought on by the Demon, they fancy that they attend nightly revels, dances, or vigils, where they then partake in carnal intercourse with the Demon, though in truth their bodies are not transferred to those places.

5: A most marvelous and incomprehensible fact: Carnal intercourse between mankind and these Demons on occasion has given birth to human beings. While oft the child is malformed and disfigured, it is not unknown for a child of true quality to spring from this most unholy union. Children thus begotten are naturally tall, very hardy and bold, proud, and also wicked. These Cambions are a most wretched of creatures, for they have never known existence without damnation.

Instead of seeking salvation, they yearn for the total and complete damnation of the world.

Many men have been accused of being Cambions, though most are in fact merely wicked individuals. There are two cases in which the accusations were in fact truthful.

Firstly, the infamous Pope John XII, who invoked pagan gods and hosted foul, incestuous orgies in the Church's sacred halls after his pontification was in truth the child of an Incubus.

Secondly, Marco Barugnano, the Italian lord whose demonic cult was discovered and destroyed by Valducan Knights in 1628, was in actuality a Cambion who very nearly summoned a black Demonic Goddess.

Sir Isidore Vidal, 1765
Translated by Sir Aaron Mulwray, 1884

CHAPTER 10

"Alexander, my old friend," said a pudgy man opening the museum's tall wooden door. The man's pinched face and long nose gave him a raccoon-like appearance, if raccoons wore suits.

"Louis." Turgen stepped inside and gave Louis a small hug. "It has been too long. I came as soon as I could." He turned. "These are the people I told you about. Doctor Malcolm Romero, Allan Havlock, Anya Jeliazkova, Ben Varghese, and Matthew Hollis." Turgen gestured to the pudgy man. "This is my friend, Louis Perrin."

Matt smiled, nodding to the museum owner. His formal attire made him stand straighter than normal. Matt's history in antiques had required him to wear a blazer before. Urban camouflage as Clay had called it, but this full charcoal suit and lead-colored tie they had picked up on the way into Limoges made Matt feel even more … trustworthy. That was the idea. Matt and the other hunters all played the parts of professional security investigators, hired by Turgen.

"Please," Louis said, twisting his hands. "Come inside."

Matt followed the others up the short steps and through the arched doorway. From the outside, the Vedorme-Perrin Museum appeared as an old stone church with high stained-glass windows and a slender bell tower all surrounded by a low wrought-iron fence. Matt hadn't expected the stylish, modern interior of sleek concrete and steel interlaced with gray medieval stonework.

"The police left a few hours ago," Louis explained, leading them past an empty ticket counter.

"Has the guard been found?" Turgen asked, his cane tapping on the polished floor.

Louis shook his head. "Not yet. They advised we change our locks and any passcodes Henri may have known."

"Of course."

"We suspect the burglar was somewhere inside until closing. Possibly a supply closet. We found no sign of forced entry." Louis led them through a hallway past a small room filled with suits of armor behind glass. They turned into a wide room, the former chapel. The spaces between the old stone columns were walled, creating several alcove galleries, each filled with glass cases of art and antiquity. Matt's gaze fluttered between various paintings and cases, wishing he could stop to inspect them.

After turning at a bronze statue of a Napoleonic rider, they entered a large round chamber. A colorful mural of Christ peering down from the clouds covered the inside of the low dome three floors above. Two large rooms broke off to either side, while a smaller door led to a hallway ahead, barely visible through the gaps in a large, art deco sculpture of three dancing women that dominated the center of the room.

"The burglar made it to about here when André spotted him." Louis gestured to the hall ahead. "André yelled out to the man and pressed the alarm button at his belt. The burglar rushed him," Louis said, thrusting his arms forward to emphasize the movement, "with a speed I cannot describe. It was like … a TGV train, just a blur."

Vampire? Matt thought.

"He grabbed André and threw him against the wall. Broke his arm and several ribs. By that time the security doors were closing. The burglar made it into this room before the door shut, but the ones to the wings had both closed by the time he reached them." Louis gestured to the large chambers to either side.

"And then you said the thief began punching the security door?" Turgen asked.

"Yes." Louis nodded quickly. "He began striking it like a madman. Then Henri arrived." He pointed to the balconies above. "He ordered the burglar to stop, or so it appeared on the surveillance video. The man stopped, then ran." Louis turned, pointing back the way they had come. "He charged up the stairs, up to the third floor, where it grabbed Henri, threw him to the floor, then picked him up like he weighed nothing, and jumped through a leaded window."

The museum owner shook his head. "That window is thirteen meters to the ground. No body. The only blood found matched Henri's blood from the floor. I've never heard anything like this, Alex," Louis said to Turgen. "You said you can help."

Turgen set a hand on Louis's shoulder. "Yes, my friend. The people I brought are the very best for this. Now tell me, which room was the thief trying to enter?"

Louis led them through the domed gallery to the entrance to the western side room. Polished silver tracks ran along the top and bottom of the doorway. Lit glass cases covered both walls and ran up the center of the room beyond.

"As I explained on the phone," Louis said, approaching a glossy black keypad beside the doorway. "While you can't see it in the surveillance video, the damage is quite amazing." He removed a key from his pocket and inserted it above the keypad, then punched a six-digit code with a series of electronic beeps.

A massive door slid out from the wall, following the silver tracks. Enormous and clear, it glided shut, sealing off the adjoining room with a heavy click.

Matt's gaze moved to a cluster of white cracks spider-webbing out from impact sites in one of its wide, glass panels.

He stepped closer.

The damage looked like someone had taken an automatic rifle to it, but as he studied it, Matt made out the distinct impression of a fist in at least three of the breaks.

"Christ," Allan whispered.

Matt nodded. He'd seen a vampire punch through an oak door once like it was nothing. But even then, peppering an inch-thick sheet of bulletproof glass was a feat only the strongest could do.

Turgen drew a long breath, regarding the damage. "And you didn't show this to the police?"

"No. You said that ... I shouldn't ..."

"Good," Turgen said warmly. "Now, first I would like to see this video of yours. Meanwhile, may my people inspect this room and hopefully locate whatever this thief was after?"

Louis swallowed, then nodded.

"Very good. If you could also provide Doctor Romero with keys to the cases and disable their alarms for us, they may work while we discuss … business."

Matt stood by while Louis keyed the code into the alarm, and the huge door rolled open, nesting itself into the wall. Louis then handed a small ring of keys to Malcolm, advising him on which ones to use, then left with Turgen.

"Now," Malcolm said, once they were gone. "Let's find what it was after."

The hunters entered the room. It stretched about fifty feet deep and thirty wide. White lights shone down from the rafters high above. When the building had been a church, it was shaped like a cross with the dome at the heart. This room formed the cross's left arm.

Matt and Allan headed to the left side, while Malcolm took the right. Ben and Anya inspected the tall case running up the middle. No one knew exactly what they were looking for, possibly something with the symbols they'd found, maybe even an actual holy weapon. Demons obviously wanted something in here, and that made finding it first that much more important.

The artifacts inside were an odd sampling of antiques from various parts of the world. One featured Native American artifacts: arrowheads, buckskin clothing, stone tools and clubs, even a headdress. Another contained several pieces of Chinese relics and art, though no jade masks. Most items had little teal signs, explaining their contents in French, Italian, and English. Some were only French. Some had no sign at all.

"What is this exhibit?" Matt asked.

"World treasures found by French explorers," Allan said, peering through a case's glass top.

Matt frowned. "Just everything here seems so … random. Like those two statues out there from different eras, different themes."

"Most of the good exhibits go to the more affluent museums," Allan explained. "Private ones like this rely mostly on displaying smaller, personal collections. Master Turgen works with many museums like this one, loaning out many of the Valducans' pieces. A lot of lost or unknown weapons and books end up in these museums, so he maintains close relations. Curators form a rather elaborate circle, and he's well respected."

Matt glanced back to see Malcolm walking slowly along the other cases, his right hand open and gliding along the glass. His eyes were closed. "What's he doing?"

"Mal?" Allan asked, looking across. "He's feeling for a holy weapon."

Matt watched as Malcolm slowly circled the room. When he lifted his hand, moving from a side wall to a display along the back, Matt noticed an orange and blue tattoo on the inside of Malcolm's right palm, very similar to the eye tattoo on his other hand, the one he'd held up when checking to see if Matt had possessed Allan. The same one he'd used to ward back the walking corpse in Spain. "So is that what he does for the Valducans," he whispered. "Finds holy weapons?"

Allan nodded. "He was a Librarian for a few years before being reassigned. To his credit, he's located three in five years."

Malcolm continued his slow search around the room, stopping periodically for a few moments before continuing on. He'd made it almost all the way around when his hand seemed to jump slightly. He stopped, circling his palm slowly above the glass.

"Find something?" Ben asked.

"I'm ... not sure," Malcolm said. "Many of these have ... energies. Deaths. Sadness. But this ..."

Matt leaned to see an elaborately carved pick or axe inside the case beneath Malcolm's circling hand. The lights above glinted off the slender blade of black stone, lashed sideways into the club-like handle. It lay beside several primitive items: grass mats, and carved stone jewelry. Matt remembered reading the small collection as artifacts found on a New Zealand expedition, though none of the items themselves were labeled in English.

Keys jingled and Malcolm unlocked the case and lowered the brass-hinged front pane. He slid his hand inside and held it just above the strange weapon. "This is it." He turned, his smile broad and proud.

"It's a holy weapon."

"This is outstanding," Ben beamed. "A real blessing we located it before they could steal it."

Malcolm wrapped his fingers around the twisted wood grip and carefully, almost reverently, drew it from the case. "It is."

"What is it?" Matt asked, peering closer.

"It's a Maori adze," Malcolm said. "A … toki poutangata, I believe. It's a ceremonial weapon. Though I've never seen one with an obsidian blade."

Allan reached up, his hand almost touching the sacred treasure. "Amazing. I wonder how old it is."

Ben's brow rose. "Old enough the binding looks like it might break. Be careful. We don't wish to destroy the relic for our enemies."

"Once it tastes its first kill that will mend." Allan said, lowering his hand. "Ibenus was the same."

"Then we should take it," Ben said "Maybe it will bond with Mikhail since our other orphans have not."

It won't work, Matt thought, remembering the boy's journal. *He's already spoken for.* "Other orphans?" he asked.

"The holy weapons that no one wields," Anya said. "We protect them until they find an owner. Sometimes, Master Turgen loans one to a museum to see if anyone bonds to it. A … recruitment tool, if you will."

"Wait," Matt said. "We have other weapons in museums right now?"

"Not now," Allan answered. "We gathered them all back once the thefts started."

"So they're at the house?"

Anya snorted. "Probably. Turgen and Schmidt hide them from most of us, in case we're corrupted."

Malcolm's eyes flashed angrily up from the holy weapon. "That's enough." He lowered the toki poutangata cradling it in his other hand, the one with the red eye tattooed inside, its ruby iris peeking just below the half-closed lid. "I'll tell Master Turgen of this. He'll decide what we should do."

"Either purchase it from the owner or … liberate it from captivity," Ben said, a slight smile to his voice.

"It'll be difficult, but we could counterfeit it," Allan said.

"Possible." Malcolm shrugged. "Not as easy now that Daniel is gone."

"There's another option," Anya muttered, almost to herself. "We could leave it here."

Eight puzzled eyes turned toward the Romanian.

"Excuse me?" Ben asked.

She licked her lips. "We could leave it here. Fit it with a miniature tracker, then wait for them to return."

"And let them take it?" Allan asked, his voice rising. "They'll destroy it."

"Maybe not immediately. There were three weeks between Hungary and when the weapons were destroyed in Plevin. Same with Mexico."

"And they were destroyed the same night in Spain," Malcolm said. "We can't take that chance."

"But that was a full moon. They had five weapons then, not one. At none of the sites was just one weapon destroyed. And police reports confirm the other murders occurred during a time window in which there was a full moon. The next one is three weeks away. It's also a lunar eclipse."

"She's right," Allan said thoughtfully. "We had hypothesized that the other ceremonies were during full moons, and, sadly, the last incident confirmed that."

"If the demons took it we could find where they go," Anya said. "Find them, and kill them."

Allan nodded.

"No," Ben said, standing tall. "I am sworn to protect God's weapons. I cannot give it to God's enemy."

"I agree," Matt said. "If we did bait them, I'd rather it be with a copy."

"They'd know if it was a copy," Anya said. "Those only fool humans. Our records show that. The demons know this weapon is here. They will come back for it."

"Then why bother making a copy?"

"The owner," Ben said. "If we simply stole it, then that would reflect badly on the museum, which would come back on Master Turgen."

Malcolm regarded the hunters. "I could never give it to

them. But … Anya has a good idea with the tracker."

Ben's eyes narrowed.

Malcolm shook his head. "I'd rather die than let them have it. But whether Master Turgen offers the owner money, or we make a forgery in its place, that will take time. Weeks for a forgery. The fiends could return tonight, and I want to be here when they do. We can't let them get this weapon, but a tracker is a good contingency in case we fail."

"So we're using it as bait?" Matt said.

"Only until we can get it safely home," Malcolm said defensively. "We know they'll be back. We won't have to go find them. Don't have to guess their moves. And if we can get one of their worshipers, we can make them tell us where the rest of them are."

Thunder boomed, rattling cases and trembling the walls. Matt felt it, even inside the small, windowless security room nestled in the museum's third floor. Matt watched as Luc passed through one of the eight screens before him, two rows of four. The huge, black hunter patrolled through the second floor; his light-blue security uniform seemed natural for him, except for the ancient iron mace at his hip, ruining the disguise. A plastic bottle of pink fluid rested on the table beneath the screens. Beside it, Matt's half-drunk paper cup of coffee, its temperature only slightly higher than the chilly room's.

"One-fifteen, check in," Malcolm's voice blurted in Matt's earbud. "Ben?"

"Here."

"Luc?"

"Here," Luc growled through his radio.

"Anya?"

"Nothing on the second floor."

"Kazuo?"

"I am here."

"Matt, you asleep up there?" Malcolm asked.

Matt thumbed the microphone at his shoulder. "Here. Nothing on camera." He released the transmit button and added, "Asshole." The cameras already fed into Malcolm, Jean, and Anya's computers, making Matt's job to sit and watch them just a pointless excuse to keep him out of the way.

"All right," Malcolm said. "Check in again at one thirty."

It was the third night since the attempted robbery, and so far nothing had happened. Turgen had liked Malcolm and Anya's idea and had persuaded Louis to allow Turgen's *security team* to manage the museum for two weeks, the same amount of time they estimated it would take to construct a perfect counterfeit for the holy toki poutangata. Matt didn't know how Turgen managed the agreement, but after witnessing a few whispered conversations with Ben, the Valducans' accountant, he suspected it was a hefty donation, either money or artifacts.

Per Anya's suggestion, they affixed a tiny transmitter, about the size of a thick sequin, to the weapon. The tracker didn't have much battery life, maybe eight hours of GPS pulses, one every five minutes. It clung to the underside of the toki poutangata, resting flat atop a charging plate that kept its battery full. Anya had also fiddled with the museum's alarm system. Now, when activated, it wouldn't notify the local authorities. In the event the vampire did return, no one wanted the police to arrive and find hacked bodies of it or any of its familiars, let alone any cult member prisoners they hoped to take.

For the plan to work, they had brought a second squad to the city, this one led by Jean, Schmidt's protégé and the most senior hunter. With him came Luc, Susumu, Kazuo, and Luiza. Turgen had returned to the chateau, which was nearly empty, having ten of its eleven hunters gone. Allan had said that combining all the Valducans spread world-wide, mostly in India and South America, the museum team represented almost half of them.

They worked in shifts. Malcolm's team of Luc, Anya, Ben, Kazuo, and Matt, protected it from eight at night until eight in the morning. When not at the museum, they stayed at a dinky hotel a block and a half away. With his background in antiques, Matt had been delegated with counterfeiting the weapon. Not that being able to spot a forgery gave him much expertise in actually creating them, he still had more knowledge than the others. Kazuo was at least helpful. The small hunter was experienced at wood carving, a skill Matt knew almost nothing about.

The schedule however gave Matt zero time with Luiza. Being on separate teams, and his time away from the museum dedicated to sleep and forging a centuries-old adze, reduced seeing her to only during shift-changes, or texting on the pre-paid Jean had issued, since Matt's phone didn't work in Europe. He couldn't help but feel a little foolish with how much he looked forward to those meetings, short and impersonal as they were. It was just that he'd never had a girlfriend before. Not that Luiza was his girlfriend. He just ... liked her. It wasn't sex. A life of growing up and living on the road, constantly moving from town to town, had led to many one-night stands and brief affairs with women who rarely knew his real name, but never a relationship. Luiza made him feel different, somehow relaxed, yet vulnerable and he—

Movement flickered across one of the screens.

Matt leaned closer, staring at an empty hallway, tall cases of fine porcelain lining the walls. He swore he saw something. Curious, Matt leaned the little rubberized joystick to the left. Two floors below camera four turned. There was no one there. Round reflections of light glistened off the floor. He pushed the stick forward, zooming. Wet spots. Footprints?

He glanced up at a map of the building. Red LEDs shone from every window and door, indicating they were shut, locked, and alarmed. Matt looked back at the screen. *Why is the floor wet?*

Sighing, he checked the screens again. Kazuo stood before camera two, staring up at a broken Roman statue. Ben strolled past screen five in the west galleries. A shadow moved past camera six. That was the side entrance. Malcolm had already passed by seven minutes before. He shouldn't be back yet.

Matt moved the camera's joystick, turning it toward the door. His eyes widened. The door was open, wet tracks trailed across the polished marble. Matt turned back to the map. A red light indicated it was closed. But it wasn't closed. It wasn't locked. And for damn sure the alarm wasn't armed. So why the hell did it say so?

Matt pressed the mic button. "Mal?"

"Yes?"

"The side door is open. Did y—"

The pink water in the bottle suddenly swirled, the color condensing into a red bead in the lower corner. *Shit.*

"It's here!" Matt said, his thumb still on the button. "Repeat, demon is here. First floor, side entrance."

"Kazuo," Malcolm, ordered. "Meet me in the dome gallery. Matt, you stay there."

Matt's pulse raced. A red light started flashed on the wall. Malcolm must have hit the alarm. Automatically, it called Jean's team at the hotel. Without moving his eyes from the screen, Matt opened a nylon backpack and drew out the heavy Ingram. The massive glass security doors began sliding closed. Two men in black hurried past camera four. That was the other side of the museum.

"Multiple contacts!" Matt snapped over the radio. He eyed the bottle. The red sphere had split into three separate beads at different points; two quickly glided in the direction of the domed gallery.

A werewolf bounded past camera one, charging toward Ben. The Indian hunter turned, his scimitar in his hand as the beast leapt.

Everything went dark. Blackness. The hum of computers wound down, the rumbling air vents silenced, and Matt sat alone, blind in a windowless room.

Matt stood, one hand on the machinegun. He started toward the door, his other hand stretched out before him. His foot kicked a small trashcan, nearly tripping him as it fell. His fingers found the cold wooden door. He felt for the handle. There was a loud click, and one of the three florescent lights flicked back on. At least the emergency power still worked. Matt yanked open the door and charged into the museum.

Large cases and statues loomed in the dim light. Long shadows crossed the floor, cast from the emergency lights still burning. Shouts echoed from somewhere ahead.

Matt raced through several tiny rooms then emerged out into the domed gallery, his fingers tight around the Ingram's grip he stopped at the balcony rail. Two floors below Kazuo stood before the smaller northern door, katana held before him.

Two figures lay on the floor, a woman and a man. Blue-green flames flicked above the male's body, casting eerie dancing shadows.

Matt could see the cracked security door to the room with the Maori adze. It hadn't fully closed when the power shut off, leaving a seven- or eight-inch gap. Malcolm charged toward the open south entrance, his machete slick with dark blood. He hacked at an emaciated ghoul. The creature leapt back onto all fours and circled to the right. Matt switched the machinegun to his left hand and drew Dämoren. He cocked the hammer.

Malcolm swung again. The ghoul sprung onto a narrow case filled with antique muskets. The case tipped and the creature leapt away before it fell with a terrible crash and shattered glass. Matt aimed Dämoren down, but the ghoul was quick, moving too fast in sporadic directions to lead it.

Someone yelled. Shadows raced toward the glass door Kazuo guarded. Several men ran into view, holding clubs. Kazuo stood still as the men pushed forward, beating on the glass and shouting. One raised a red-handled axe and Kazuo swung his sword down at the floor, through the man's extended shadow. The shadow split and the man screamed as blood sprayed out from the stumps of his uplifted arms. The axe flew into the glass with a thud and Kazuo swung again and again, slicing shadows as redness splattered across the bulletproof shield.

Two more men came in through the south door, past the bronze rider statue. Malcolm turned to face them. The stringy-haired ghoul scuttled up one of the art deco dancers and leapt toward Kazuo's back.

Matt slung Dämoren out and fired. The boom echoed loud off the dome, and a blast of blue smoke erupted downward. Kazuo jumped aside as the demon fell and slid across the floor, trailing yellow flames.

He looked up and gave Matt a *thank you* smile.

No problem.

Footsteps clomped up from behind and Matt whirled to see a man in a wet, gray T-shirt running toward him from a side doorway. Matt swung the Ingram up in his off hand and fired. The heavy machinegun bounced, stitching the man up the stomach, chest, and into the wall behind. The attacker staggered and fell.

Familiar. Where's the master? In his hurry to leave the security room, Matt had forgotten the blood compass.

Matt holstered Dämoren, and held the Ingram in both hands as he approached the fallen man. A growing pool of blood appeared black in the dim light. Movement came from the open doorway and a hulking shape crouched through. Slender long horns curled back from atop its crimson head. The strutter.

It opened its mouth, and its monstrous tongue slithered out. Matt fired a burst from the Ingram into its legs. Silver, amethyst-tipped slugs chewed through the beast's thighs. It stumbled back a step before the holes closed.

You'd better appreciate me, Allan.

The demon's tongue split three ways like some nightmarish flower, revealing a writhing knot of tendrils beneath. Matt dropped the machinegun, its sling yanking on his shoulder as he grabbed Dämoren's ivory handle. The tendrils exploded toward him. Matt yanked the revolver out, hacking at the slimy strands with Dämoren's blade as he spun out of the way and behind a copper statue.

A golden-eyed man came through the far doorway. Lights glinted off his nickel snub-nose as he raised it. Matt shot Dämoren, blowing a gory hole in the would-be killer's chest. Then he turned, stepping out from behind the statue. The strutter was right on top of him. Matt fired, hitting the beast in the bicep. It howled around its enormous tongue and the tendrils lashed out.

They struck Matt like a thousand whips, wrapping his torso and face. Instantly the pain hit, burning him. Screaming, he tried to pull away, but the slender strands held strong, like pulling against red-hot rebar. He cocked Dämoren's hammer, and tried to fire, but the tendrils had his arm, pushing it out and away. The slick worms found his bare wrist and hand, searing into them. It pulled him up, lifting him to his toes then off the floor. The burning continued growing, until all he could see or feel or imagine was pain.

The tendrils jolted, yanking Matt through the air. They

slacked and slid away as he fell to the floor. Dämoren fell from his grip. His skin still burned. He clutched his face, trying to wipe the slime away, but only managed to smear it onto his palm, burning it as well.

"Here!" a voice growled.

A zipper sounded and something cold and wet splashed Matt's face. The thick gel dissolved and the burning lessened. He smelled alcohol. Matt rubbed it over his skin, killing the poison.

"Can you stand?" he heard Luc ask.

Matt opened his eyes. The left one squinted a little, still swelling. The huge man stood over him clutching his mace in one hand and holding a red plastic bottle in the other. Allan had issued everyone the alcohol after seeing the strutter in the video. Matt reached for it and Luc gave it to him. He poured it over his right hand and neck, washing away the remaining venom. "Thanks. And thanks for saving me."

The demon lay crumpled against the far wall. The plaster was cracked where it had evidently slammed into it. Its side was completely crushed, wet guts hemorrhaging from the jagged wound. Purple and orange flames spread across its body. The same fire dripped from Velnepo's iron flanges.

"Can you stand?" Luc repeated.

Matt nodded, but the simple movement stung his inflamed neck. His skin still burned.

The blood. Need to ... heal me, Matt thought, struggling to his feet. Luc helped him up and Matt staggered to the demon's corpse. He knelt, laying his blistering hand into the bloody hole punched into the creature's side.

Nothing happened.

He shoved his hand deeper, spectral flames licking up his wrists and gooey blood running over it. *No! Why isn't it working?* Was it the venom? Demon blood had always worked, broken bones, cuts, gun shots, illness, everything.

"Everyone converge to the main room," Malcolm's voice shouted through the earbud.

"Matt, we need to move," Luc said looking back.

Matt noticed the sounds of shouts still coming from the

gallery below. Frustrated, he clenched his fist, squeezing bits of gore between his tender fingers. He swallowed. Even that hurt. "Okay."

He picked Dämoren off the floor from where he'd dropped it. The hammer was down and he realized he must have pulled the trigger while entangled, though he didn't remember it. He cocked the hammer back with his blistered thumb and squinted up to Luc. Matt's left eye was swollen completely shut now. "You lead."

They hurried through one of the doorways, past a tiny glass elevator and down the stairs. Matt held Dämoren out, looking for movement.

"Malcolm, we'll be there in three minutes," Jean's tense voice said through the radio.

They reached the second floor. A man in dark clothing lay on the floor, his head completely crushed. Blood and chunky bits of brain coated the wall beside him like shotgun splatter. Matt recognized Luc's handiwork.

Two figures moved in the shadows, running toward them, a young man with black hair and another with sandy blond. Matt pushed

Luc aside, knocking them both to the floor as a shot fired. Matt rolled behind a wide island case in the middle of the room. He leaned out, raising Dämoren and fired at the shooter. He missed.

The men split, crouching behind cases in the dim room. *Familiars don't usually seek cover.*

Matt cocked Dämoren's hammer and squinted into the darkness.

A silhouette moved. Matt fired. In the moment of flash he could see the black-haired man frozen like a snapshot, his gun out front. The man stumbled back and fell with a thud.

Footsteps sprinted toward them. Four loud shots fired and the second man fell dead.

Matt looked at Luc, tucked into a tight space behind a half-wall of original church stonework. The hunter still held his tan pistol out, trained on the unmoving corpse. A wisp of smoke trickled out from the barrel.

"Thank you," Luc said.

"Don't mention it." Matt hissed as he picked himself up and approached the nearest black-clad body. Dead eyes stared up at him as Matt patted the body down. No wallet. No ID. He noticed a metal chain around the man's neck, leading down to a round shape beneath his wet, clinging shirt. Matt hooked a finger beneath the twisted chain and drew a flat pendant out from under the cloth. The image of a rearing, winged serpent with a woman's head marked the medallion's face.

Demon worshipers. He'd found their symbol. Matt yanked the chain, breaking it free; then he and Luc continued down the staircase.

Once they reached the first floor, they hurried through the gallery, past the bronze rider and into the main room.

Malcolm stepped out as they entered. He was splattered in blood. Three corpses lay around the entryway. He gave the men a nod, then seemed to grimace as he saw Matt's face. "You see Anya and Ben?"

"No," Luc said.

"They were in the south galleries before the power went out," Matt said, his swollen lips making him slur. "Ben first floor. Anya second."

Malcolm thumbed his radio. "Ben, Anya, do you read?"

No response.

Matt hurried past the corpses to the dead vampire, sheathed in blue-green fire. Kneeling, he laid his hand flat in the bloody puddle spread around it.

Nothing.

Several shots echoed down the hall. Matt looked up, but saw nothing.

"Ben is hurt!" Anya's voice yelled shrilly through the earbud, causing Matt to wince.

"Where are you?" Malcolm asked.

"First floor by the entrance."

"I'll go," Luc said, already running.

Malcolm looked back, seeing Matt's hand in the vampire's blood.

Wariness flickered in his eyes.

Why isn't this working? Matt thought, standing. Unconsciously he wiped his sticky palm on his thigh, then immediately regretted it. He saw Kazuo before the northern door, katana in hand. The light down the passage ahead shone red through the filter of smeared blood. A pile of chopped corpses lay on the other side of the glass. Matt couldn't guess how many. He eyed the dead ghoul lying near the swordsman. "Third time's the charm," he mumbled.

Matt crouched beside the ghoul's corpse and rested his palm against the bloody bullet hole blown through its leathery flesh. *This had better work.*

A soothing wave flowed up his arm, cooling his burning skin. He exhaled a sigh as the wave hit his shoulder and up his neck. Instantly the swelling receded. His pounding heart slowed and the lash-like welts and blisters sank and melted away.

"Amazing," Kazuo said. The short hunter didn't seem afraid or concerned, simply impressed.

Matt stood and glanced down at the still-burning body. Already it had begun transforming back into its human form. *So I guess I have to kill it for the blood to heal me.* Before, when he was the only hunter, they'd just assumed it was demon's blood in general. Being with multiple hunters changed things. *But I was with another hunter,* he realized. *Clay. I could heal off the demons he killed before I inherited Dämoren.* Was it because Clay was his mentor at the time? Or maybe ... Dämoren? *Every demon that healed me had died by her.* Nowhere in the dozens of hunters who had carried and loved her did anyone mention healing. He touched his chest.

A gunshot echoed up the hall.

Worry about it later. Matt opened the latch behind Dämoren's gold-inlaid cylinder and ejected a spent shell. *Six fired. Thirteen bullets remaining,* he mused, loading a fresh round and ejecting the next shell. Matt didn't believe in unlucky numbers, but that didn't stop him from noticing them. He scanned the balconies above for movement as he worked.

"I found Ben" Luc said in the radio. "Arm is broken. No

bites. Anya secured a prisoner."

"Prisoner?" Malcolm asked.

"She had him at gunpoint when I got here. I have him in handcuffs now."

"Are you sure he isn't possessed. He could turn if he is."

"I can't tell," Luc's deep voice made it hard to hear on the radio.

"You'll need to check that."

"I'll check once Jean's team arrives," Malcolm said. "Until then, keep a close eye on him. Jean, what's your ETA?"

"Almost there," Jean said.

"Do you have a med bag?" Malcolm asked.

"We have one."

A dark form moved in the hall, beyond the blood-streaked door.

Kazuo tensed. Matt looked to see orange veins of light worm across the silhouette's body and green eyes ignite. Orange flames erupted, sheathing the ifrit in fire as it stepped forward. A wedge of red light shone through the door as it neared the dim, round gallery. Matt stepped beside Kazuo, Dämoren trained on the bulletproof shield between them and the demon. Its flaming body cast no shadow.

"Mal," Matt yelled stepping back. "We have a problem."

The walls around the ifrit caught fire as did the clothes of the bodies at its feet. Black soot clouded the clear door. The demon's brilliant green eyes stared hatefully from the blaze.

Sprinklers popped and water rained down from the ceiling. Steam and smoke filled the passage, squelching the burning walls, but did nothing but mildly dim the ifrit's fiery body still visible through the clouds.

"Luc!" Mal called into the radio. "We need you."

A terrible crash thundered to the side as a monstrous form burst through the barred stained-glass windows in the back of the west wing. Matt turned as a huge blue creature dressed in banded armor smashed its way through the opening. A single curved horn jutted from its forehead. An oni.

Matt ran for the door, nearly slipping on the slick marble floor.

Malcolm beat him there, drawing his sawed-off and shoving it through the narrow gap between the door and the wall.

He fired.

Most of the shot deflected off the demon's armor, but some found its exposed shoulder and neck. The oni howled. All but two of the wounds instantly closed. Matt guessed those were the jade pellets.

The demon leapt to the side before Malcolm could fire the second barrel. It raised its hands in a double fist and smashed it into one of the island cases in the middle of the room. Glass and wood exploded as the case flew end over end toward them. Matt yanked Malcolm back before the case smashed into the door gap, spraying broken shrapnel through the tight opening.

The oni roared and raced to the case with the toki poutangata inside. Sparks glittered off its skin as it crossed the line of warding powder. It smashed its fist down, shattering the glass top.

"Push it!" Malcolm yelled as he and Matt fought with the broken case leaning endwise against the gap, trying to get their weapons through.

The oni snatched the holy weapon and turned back toward the hole in the wall. Matt jammed Dämoren hard into a broken plank of white particle board and knocked it aside. He fired. The bullet missed by a fraction, blowing out one of the remaining colored panes as the demon jumped into the raining night.

Malcolm screamed in frustration, pounding his fist into the bulletproof glass.

Fighting the urge to join him, Matt looked to the northern doorway. Smoke and steam still billowed behind the blacked security door, but the ifrit was gone.

"Move!" Luc bellowed, charging into the domed gallery. He clomped up to the thirty-foot high door sealing the western wing and raised Velnepo in both hands. Malcolm stepped back, averting his eyes as the massive hunter smashed his mace into the towering bulletproof shield.

The weapon hit with a deafening crash. Matt stumbled backward, stunned as thousands of tiny, white cracks scattered through a ten-foot-wide panel of the glass. Luc hit the door again and it buckled.

Wide-eyed, Matt watched Luc smash the mace into the door again, blasting tiny chunks across the long gallery beyond. The entire broken section collapsed inward, crackling and curling down, its thick laminate holding it mostly together as it fell to the floor.

The men raced through the opening, broken glass crunching beneath their feet. They reached the shattered, stained glass window at the back of the gallery and climbed up onto the stone sill. The black, iron bars that had covered the window now lay in the grass below. Matt peered through the rain down the dark streets. Red tail lights sped away in the distance. They turned sharply around a bend, then vanished. The adze was gone.

CHAPTER 11

They met Jean's team in the museum entrance. Three corpses littered the inlaid church floor. A monstrous werewolf lay among them, red phantasmal flames flickering over its fur. Ben sat against one of the old church columns, clutching his arm. Blood stained a cloth tied to his shoulder. The smell of smoke from fire and shooting still hung in the air.

Across the room Luc held his pistol over a black-clad man lying face down on the floor, hands cuffed behind his back. Anya sat on a carved bench nearby, Baroovda across her lap, and a small revolver pointed at the prisoner.

Allan rushed over and knelt beside Ben. He unzipped a red canvas bag and removed rolls of bandages.

"What happened?" Jean demanded.

"They attacked us," Malcolm answered, his lips barely moving. "At least eight demons, several humans. We killed five of the demons, but they got the toki poutangata."

"How?"

"We held them off in the domed gallery, but then an oni broke in through the back of the western wing and took it," Malcolm said. "The security doors had closed so we couldn't get there to stop it."

"How did they get inside?"

Malcolm's eyes turned to Matt. "That's a good question. How did they make it past the alarms, Matt?" his voice accusing.

Matt shook his head. "The system said all the doors were locked and armed. But one of the doors was open. The one *you* were supposed to be watching."

"Are you saying *I* let them in?" Malcolm snapped.

"You didn't notice the door was open?" Matt shot back.

"You were the one watching the cameras." Malcolm stabbed a finger. "You could have disabled the alarms from the guard room. Maybe you came down after I'd passed and opened the door."

Matt snorted. "Yeah. I came down and opened the door. You're right. Then I radioed a break in, just to warn you. Then I killed a ghoul that was about to get Kazuo right before a strutter nearly tore my fucking face off! That makes a lot of sense."

Eyes moved to Kazuo standing beside them. His army katana hung at his waist.

The small man nodded. "He shot and killed a ghoul attacking me from behind," he said in the quiet, matter of fact way he always spoke. "I saw the flames. He killed it."

"Matt killed three human servants," Luc rumbled. "I trust him."

Malcolm clenched his jaw. He looked at Matt. "They got in *somehow.*"

"They came in expecting us," Matt said, fighting his anger back. "And the side door wasn't the only one they got in through. They might have planned this all along."

Jean's hard eyes moved to Ben. "Are you all right?"

The Indian tensely nodded. "Succubus … flew down and grabbed … me. Anya shot it … before it could mark me. It dropped me. Fall broke my arm."

"He'll be okay," Allan said. The Englishman inserted a syringe into a small bottle and drew out its clear liquid. "We'll need to get him to hospital or back to the chateau."

"Is anyone else hurt?"

Malcolm shook his head. "Anya hurt her ankle in the fight, but nothing serious."

"I'm fine," she said. "Walking hurts."

Jean nodded and pointed to the prisoner at Luc's feet.

"Demon worshiper," Anya said.

"He's not possessed," Malcolm said. He held up a small brass pendant on a medal chain. The image of a winged, human-faced snake, reared to strike, adorned the metal. "He had this on him."

Jean took the pendant. "This is the same symbol from the ones in Spain?"

"It is." Matt fished another pendant from his pocket. "There were other attackers upstairs wearing them as well."

"The tracker?" Jean asked.

Malcolm lifted his phone. The screen showed a map of the city. "It sent a pulse a minute ago."

"We'll have to get to it before they find it or break the weapon," Jean said. "There was shooting and, if anyone heard it, the police might be here soon. We need to lock up and leave immediately. I'll call Turgen and brief him on the situation. He'll start on damage control." He gestured to Ben. "Get him into the car. Load the prisoner and Anya as well. Allan, you take them back to the chateau."

"I can drive," Anya said.

Jean shook his head. "You're hurt."

"But I can drive. No need to lose one more knight. Ben and I can handle taking the prisoner to the chateau."

"Not on morphine he can't." Allan said, tucking the empty syringe back into a plastic case.

"Then dope the prisoner, too," she said. "Jean, they attacked us with eight demons. Three lived, including an oni. And not Selene, a different one. There's no telling how many of them there are and how many of these bastards they have with them," she said, gesturing with her pistol. "We can't afford to lose another knight driving Ben and I back to the chateau. If I could go with you I would, but someone needs to take them back. Make it me."

"She's right," Ben said sleepily, his eyes closed and head against the column.

Jean pursed his lips and nodded. Finally he said, "Fine. Anya drives. Everyone else, load into the van. Gather your things. I want us gone in three minutes."

Rain streaked the window beside Matt as they drove east, out of the city down a winding, two-lane highway. Allan sat beside him, his gaze locked on the screen in his lap. Outside was dark. Trees. Countryside.

"There!" Allan said.

A blue dot flashed on the screen's map. "Seven kilometers. Just stay on the motorway."

The van's tires squealed as Jean took a bend just a little too fast. Matt chewed his lip, watching the little dot pulse on Allan's screen. Where were they going? The demons might be taking the adze to China for all they knew. What if the demons found the tracker? Maybe stuck it on the side of some random car now being followed by a team of pissed off hunters. What if it was too late? They could have broken the weapon already.

No. Matt shook away the doubt and focused on his anger. They were going to find the demons. Find them and kill them.

He looked at his watch. 1:46. The tracker would signal again in five minutes.

Half an hour ago he'd been sitting in the museum's guard room thinking about how much he wanted to see Luiza. Now she sat on the bench directly behind him.

"Careful what you wish for," Clay always said.

Matt turned in his seat to see her. She stared out the window, her eyes hard. Luiza met his gaze and her expression softened for just a moment. She looked away and the hardness returned.

The rain had slowed to a light sprinkle by the time the tracker pulsed again.

"Four kilometers," Allan said.

Everyone in the van seemed to tense. No one spoke. All eyes watched the road ahead, hoping to see tail lights around every turn.

There were none. The tension continued to shuffle through the passengers.

"Hold on," Allan said, zooming in on the map. "We passed it."

"Where?" Jean asked.

"Two kilometers back."

Cursing, Jean slowed to the edge of the road, alongside a flooded ditch, then pulled the van around in a tight U-turn. He hit the gas and they sped back the up the road.

"Take this next left," Allan said.

They turned up a small road into the hills. Matt checked his watch again as they neared the last signal site.

The little dot blipped again, but barely. They were less than a mile away.

"We're right on top of it," Allan said. "Four hundred meters to the left of us."

Jean slowed as everyone peered out the windows. The road eased around a hill and a light came into view, illuminating a tall sign. Beside it, a metal gate sat partially open across a wide entrance drive.

"There," Allan said, leaning in beside Matt. He peered back at his screen. "It's in there."

The vehicle stopped. Jean killed the headlights.

Matt looked back at the sign, trying to read the green French writing. "Asphe?"

"Mining company," Jean said. "It's a kaolin mine."

Another mine, Matt thought with a groan. *Wonderful.*

Allan touched the top corner of his screen and the map changed to a daytime satellite overlay. The mine area appeared like a great white scoop carved out of the surrounding green landscape. It reminded Matt of those chocolate-covered ice cream cones when you took a bite out of them.

"Unless it's changed since this photo was made," Allan said, zooming out. "There's a second entrance three kilometers further down the road."

"We can't let them escape," Malcolm said.

Jean sat quiet for a few seconds before he spoke. "Luc, Susumu, and I will go to the other entrance. Malcolm, you lead the others from here. Keep your radios on. I don't want anyone shooting each other."

Malcolm nodded. "Understood."

Matt swallowed. He couldn't help but notice that once again, Jean kept Susumu separate from Kazuo and himself, even though they were the only two who could fully speak with him. Though he suspected it was more at the samurai's request than bad leadership.

"You heard him," Malcolm said, opening the front passenger door. "On me."

Kazuo yanked open the side door and hopped out, Allan right behind him. Matt flipped his radio back on, touched Dämoren at his side, and followed.

A light mist of rain hit his face. Save the single light above the sloped drive it was dark. Country dark. He held up the blood compass to the light of the sign.

"Got anything?" Allan asked. He gripped his khopesh beside him.

Matt shook his head. "Not yet. Probably won't be able to see it once we get down in there."

Luiza hopped out and drew Feinluna. The saber's blade glinted in the scant light. "Well, Matt. Looks like I'll finally get to see if that reputation of yours is true."

"Looks that way." He winked.

Her brow arched coyly.

"I know I don't need to say this," Jean said through the open door. "But be careful." Luc pulled the door closed from the inside and the van pulled away.

Metal rasped as Kazuo drew Akumanokira. "Killing an oni would be a great honor for Susumu," he said. "I would very much like to get to it before him."

"Understood," Matt said with a grin.

Malcolm nodded as if to himself, then turned to the hunters. "Let's go."

They hurried toward the entrance, circling around the single light pole's glow as much as they could. They passed the pipe metal gate, plastered with warning signs and followed a paved road up and around a low rise.

Matt stopped before cresting the hill and checked the blood compass again. Still pink. He opened the shaker at his belt and sprinkled a line of powder across the road, between a pair of stone retaining walls. *Don't know how much good this'll do. Not like they can't go around it.* But he liked the idea of at least slowing a demon down. The powder melted over the wet asphalt instantly, but Matt knew that did little to diminish its potency. If nothing else, it kept the wind from blowing it away. Once finished he closed the shaker and hurried to where the others crouched.

Beyond the hill, the entire area opened up into a massive, tiered pit. A metal building toward the back overlooked the white quarry. Light shone through several windows but they saw no movement. Several large trucks and hulking pieces of mining equipment rested near the bottom of the basin beside a wide lagoon of dark water.

They hurried to a group of earthen mounds piled off to one side. Behind them, Allan removed the tablet phone from his pocket.

"All right," he said, trying to shield the screen's light. "According to this, the last pulse came from right around that building. He peered over the mound. Right down there."

Matt followed Allan's gaze. A dark box truck sat parked one earthen tier below the structure.

"That looks like the truck from the video," Luiza said quietly. "The one they moved Selene in."

"Yeah," Malcolm said, scanning the area. "But where is everyone?"

"Inside?" Kazuo said.

"Maybe." Malcolm's eyes narrowed. "This doesn't look right to me."

"Last two pulses came from that same spot," Allan said, turning off his screen. "We need to go down there."

"Matt, you got anything in that bottle of yours?" Malcolm asked.

Matt pulled the plastic bottle out and held it against the pale backdrop of the clay mound. He shook his head. "Nothing."

"What's the range on that?"

"Hundred yards in the open. As little as fifty feet if there's a lot of stuff in the way."

"There," Luiza hissed. She pointed to a dark shape moving around the building. It looked like a person, but Matt couldn't tell much more than that in the dark. The figure walked down the earthen slope to the truck and opened the passenger door.

A few seconds later, the figure came back out. A yellow light flared as it lit a cigarette. After a few puffs, it turned and started back up toward the building.

"Do you think they got the adze?" Kazuo asked.

"No," Luiza answered. "If they were going to take it they'd have done that when they got here."

"We'll just hold here until the next signal," Allan said.

Malcolm nodded in agreement.

Allan shuffled on the rocky pile, causing a miniature avalanche of pebbles as he crouched to check his phone. He froze. Matt looked back at the smoker, but it didn't appear to have heard him. Once it reached the building, it took a final drag and then flicked the orange-embered butt out into the basin. Light spilled out as he opened a door. He wore black robes, just like the ones videoed in Spain. The dark-haired man looked human enough, but Matt knew that didn't really mean much.

"I didn't see it on him," Luiza said.

After two very long minutes, Allan said, "There. It's still in the truck." He flipped off the phone's bright screen.

"Good." Malcolm turned to the others. "All right, we don't know if that guy has more friends coming, and I want to secure the adze before they do. Luiza, you and Allan follow me. Once we reach that slope just right of the truck, you two hold there. Matt, you follow behind us. Kazuo, stay with him. Keep your eyes up on that building. Hold position down there." He pointed to a dingy bulldozer parked fifty feet to the left of the truck. "If that compass of yours goes off, signal us."

"What about the others?" Allan asked. He brushed his wet hair back with his hand.

"Once we have the weapon, we'll wait for them before going into that building." He pressed the radio button at his shoulder. "Jean, where are you?"

"We are headed through the employee entrance now," Jean's voice crackled.

"Can you see the main building yet?"

"Yes," Jean answered.

"We believe the weapon is in a truck parked just below it," Malcolm said. "We're going in to investigate, then wait for you to join. The building is occupied, so be careful."

"Affirmative."

"Okay then." Malcolm stood. "Follow me."

Staying low, the hunters hurried along the gravel path. The slung Ingram bounced softly, clacking against Matt's body armor with each step. He paced himself alongside Kazuo, allowing the others to move on ahead. The faint drizzle had soaked his hair, and cold rivulets of water ran down the back of his neck. Matt watched the blocky building but saw nothing. He stopped behind a low berm of white clay and checked the blood compass. Still nothing.

Movement flickered in the corner of his eye. Matt turned toward a towering rock crusher off to one side, silhouetted against the night sky. A sloped conveyer belt ran toward the top. He searched the dark shape but it remained still. He checked the compass again, but there was no movement.

"Come," Kazuo whispered. "We're almost there."

They made their way down the slope, then raced across a short open expanse until they reached the giant dozer. Matt knelt beside the metal tracks. Wetness from the muddy ground wicked up his pant leg.

He leaned out for a better view. The other hunters had almost reached the final slope. He checked the building. It remained still. He turned toward the rock crusher beside them, but saw nothing. *Why leave it in the truck?*

The other hunters reached the slope. Allan and Luiza crouched low into the shadows, their swords drawn. Malcolm looked toward Kazuo and Matt. Matt checked the compass and waved him on.

Hugging the shadows, Malcolm followed the tiered wall around below the mining building. He dashed through an open area to the box truck and pressed against the side. Matt watched, his heart thumping as Malcolm circled around the back of the vehicle and reached for the rear door. He checked the compass again.

Two—no, three beads formed inside the bottle; one ahead and two off to the right. They were closing in fast. A trap.

Matt waved his hand out, trying to signal the hunter. "Malcolm!" he hissed.

Malcolm didn't appear to hear. He reached for the rear door latch.

Matt depressed the radio button. "Ma—"

Malcolm opened the truck's door and an alarm shrieked, piercing the night.

Blinding lights flipped on atop the ridge, shining down into the white basin. Orange flashes of gunfire erupted from beneath the lights, spraying bullets through the box truck below.

Shit! Matt pulled back behind the bulldozer's treads.

A spotlight flicked on atop the crusher to his left, bathing them in light. Metal *tinged* around him as shots rained down. White plumes exploded as bullets hit the rocks, spraying broken dust. "Kazuo, move!" Matt yelled, diving around the corner of the vehicle, between it and a parked power shovel. Clutching Dämoren, he scooted between the vehicles, trying to keep low.

Another burst of *tings* hit near his head and Matt dropped to the ground. He looked back and his eyes widened. Kazuo lay face down on the muddy gravel. Blood streamed from a hole behind his ear.

"No!" Matt dove out, momentarily exposing himself to the shooter above, and grabbed the small knight by the shirt. Bullets whizzed around him, *plinking* off steel and rock. One hit Kazuo in the hip, but the fallen knight didn't react. Matt yanked Kazuo back behind the cover of the vehicle.

"Kazuo!" Matt yelled rolling him over. He recoiled in horror. The bullet had exited under Kazuo's eye, taking half his face with it. There was no question. Kazuo was dead.

Shots rang out behind him. "Mal!" Luiza screamed.

Matt couldn't see them from his position, not while the shooter had him pinned. Kazuo's killer. Anger welling, Matt slithered alongside the vehicle then carefully peeked over the top. Expecting a bullet any second, he searched the crusher, but couldn't see past the bright light atop it. Orange flashed like fiery flowers and Matt jerked down as more shots zinged past. Taking the slung Ingram, he dove to the side of the vehicle and leaned out. He fired a burst up at the light and it exploded. Squinting, he saw movement. A dog-headed man stood atop the conveyer belt holding some kind of assault rifle. Matt fired the Ingram and ducked away as the creature shot back.

Demons with machineguns, he thought. *Great.* He let go of the Ingram, took Dämoren in both hands, then popped back out. The demon hadn't moved. Matt fired.

The demon slumped, nearly losing the rifle, but leaned on the rail and fired back. The shots went far and to the right. Matt fired again and the creature fell. Golden fire quickly consumed it.

More shots echoed behind him. *Luiza and Allan.* Matt started toward them. Kazuo's half-face stared up at him, and Matt tried not to look at it. He noticed a curved shape in the wetted clay beside Kazuo's body.

Akumanokira.

Matt froze for a moment, unsure what to do. He couldn't just leave it there.

Matt holstered Dämoren and knelt beside the dead knight. He picked the katana up by the copper grip and squeezed. "I'm sorry," he whispered, not sure if he was speaking to Kazuo or the sword. He pulled the metal scabbard out from Kazuo's belt and slid the katana inside. A tiny latch clicked, locking it closed. "I'll take care of it, for you."

"Jean!" Malcolm's voice called over the radio. Matt could hear the shots firing behind him through the earbud as well. "It's a trap. We're pinned down."

"We're coming," Jean replied.

Matt crawled out from behind the bulldozer and stole a glance. Allan and Luiza lay flat on the ground behind a low pile of earth, bullet strikes puffing all around them. Matt leaned out further. The box truck's rear door still hung open. Fingers of light shone down from the roof, cast through the dozens of bullet holes riddling the truck. Malcolm lay flat on the ground directly beneath the bed, staring back at him. Shooters fired down from the ridge above hidden behind the blinding light.

Allan gave Matt a nod, then leaned out from his cover, clutching his tiny Walther pistol and fired several shots. The brilliant light atop the ridge burst and faded.

Four shooters, three of them werewolves, returned fire. Allan hunkered down under the onslaught. Matt fired Dämoren at the first one. It fell dead and the others scattered for cover. Red flame ignited over the fallen werewolf's corpse.

A bullet whizzed past. Matt looked back to see more figures running along one of the other slopes. They'd have him trapped for sure. Clutching the katana in one hand and Dämoren in the other, he sprinted out from behind the shovel and headed to a scooped-out pit he could use like a foxhole. He weaved as he ran, trying to elude any shooters, bullets striking around him.

He'd gotten within fifteen feet of the hole then dashed straight for it. In that moment, he knew his mistake.

A round hit him in the side, spinning him about. Stumbling, he kicked his feet, directing his fall into the pit as more shots flew past. Milky water filled the bottom of the hole, and he hit with a splash, dropping the sword but holding Dämoren tight.

His side burned. Keeping low, Matt twisted to see the damage. The bullet had hit his vest, but the armor couldn't stop a rifle round. Blood poured freely from under it. He pressed his hand over the hole in the hard vest but it did little to stanch the flow.

The wound was bad. Very bad.

Somewhere above, a werewolf howled, followed by another. "Matt!"

He swallowed and tried to pull himself deeper into the foxhole. Clouds of red blood swirled around him. They gathered in crimson pools at the water's edges, pointing toward the circling demons.

"Matt!" Malcolm's voice screamed in his ear.

Matt fumbled with the radio button. "Kazuo's down," was all he could say.

Matt's eyes felt heavy. He was dead if he didn't get to demon's blood. The shooters had them pinned in. Luiza, Allan, Malcolm. They'd all die.

Dämoren would die.

Clay's voice echoed in his mind. "Dämoren chose you. She *wanted* you to live. *I* want you to live."

He couldn't let her die. He had to live. The weapons *had* to survive.

Matt opened his eyes. Shots echoed from the direction of the building. Carefully, he looked over the side of the hole. The shooters were hunkered down behind a line of metal crates, firing down on Luiza and Allan. He could see their barrels, but didn't have a shot.

Matt lifted the Ingram and fired, emptying the magazine in a loud burst. The shooters hunkered down, but didn't flee. He needed to get them out. Out where he could kill them.

He had an idea.

He pulled the glass shaker bottle from his belt and stood on his knees, hurling it overhand toward the crates. The bottle flipped end over end, sailing over the truck hiding Malcolm, and out over the ridge above. Matt cocked Dämoren's hammer and fired.

The jar exploded, raining powder over the boxes. Sparks flew and sizzled as two brown werewolves and a pale-skinned vampire leapt out, their skin smoking and blistering as silver and garlic dust ignited at their touch. Matt locked his elbow, gripped Dämoren tight, held down the trigger and fanned the hammer.

All three demons fell dead.

The disks of blood in the water swirled apart, joining with others in the pool. Two were moving to where Allan and Luiza still hid. Matt looked, but saw nothing there. Squinting, he spied odd shapes moving through the light drizzle as if the water was hitting something that wasn't there.

"Rakshasas!" Matt fired Dämoren at one of the invisible creatures.

One jolted back, the bullet striking its shoulder. It materialized, taking the form of a black, featureless man. No light reflected off its body, giving it the look of nothingness, just an empty, humanoid hole of blackness.

Dämoren was empty.

The demons closed in.

Allan rolled out from his position on the ground and swung Ibenus. Instantly he was standing, facing them down. The black monster lunged, but Allan swung the khopesh again, and appeared beside it. He slashed the blade in an upward arc, cleaving through the demon's side. It fell.

The other, still invisible, save the water on its head and shoulders, turned to face Allan. Luiza charged, attacking with her saber.

Figures rushed down the slopes. Demons and familiars swarmed, ready to finish what the shooters started. An emaciated wendigo scuttled over the cliff face and leapt onto the truck as Malcolm crawled out. Matt pulled a new Ingram magazine from its pouch. His numb fingers fumbled, and it fell into the water. He moved for it, but his body just collapsed.

He rolled onto his back. Blood coursed through the milky water, running in little streams and joining the moving pools at the edge. Matt opened Dämoren's loading gate and ejected a spent shell. He lifted his pouch flap to slip it inside when all the blood in the water suddenly gathered around him.

A winged woman slammed on top of him, the succubus straddling his shoulders. She hissed, latching an iron-firm hand over his face and shoved his head beneath the water. Matt fought, gurgling and spitting. Water ran up his nose and into his eyes, but the demon was too strong. Jagged rocks dug into the back of his skull as the monster pressed down.

Still squeezing Dämoren, Matt hacked the gun's blade, blindly trying to hit the demon. Claws tore his arm as she fought to grapple the swinging blade. She caught his bicep, and slapped his arm back into the water. Matt hooked his wrist, slicing down into the succubus's forearm. It let go and Matt thrust his head out of the water as he slashed the blade into the screaming demon's neck. Blood poured from the gaping wound and out her mouth. It ran down her pale breasts and arms and onto Matt. Her violet eyes rolled back and her blood ignited into purple and crimson flames. She crumpled on top of him.

The wave of calming pleasure hit him like drug. Matt gasped as the bullet pushed from his body, wedging itself between him and the inside of his vest as the skin behind it healed. The exhaustion of being awake so long, the weariness from blood-loss washed away.

His eyes focused, and he pushed the succubus's nude corpse off of him. Her flaming blood spread out across the water, flaring as it met his.

Matt rolled onto one knee and saw the chaos around him.

Malcolm hacked Hounacier into the shoulder of an axe-wielding man as he dodged a scaly orange demon's swing. A flaming wendigo lay at his feet. Allan held back a shrieking woman and a bald, pointed-eared vampire, as he blinked around them with sword swings. Luiza still fought the rakshasa, now visible and bleeding from several wounds.

There's so many of them. Matt rose to help his companions.

He loaded a fresh round from his belt into Dämoren's cylinder when a bullet struck him from behind, knocking him down in a jolt of pain.

He hit the water, still saturated with burning blood, and the wound instantly began to mend.

Matt turned to see one of the gunmen coming down the slope behind him, carrying a black rifle. The gunman's eyes widened in surprise, seeing the man he'd just shot rise from the cauldron of violet-red fire. Matt spun Dämoren's cylinder, aligning the single loaded chamber with the barrel, and fired.

The silver slug hit the man in the gut. He staggered, then raised his rifle toward Matt. Orange flashed from the muzzle, and Matt threw himself down into the water-filled pit. A shot grazed his leg, and Matt screamed, more in surprise than pain. The demon blood still burning on him soothed and healed it.

"No!" Luiza cried.

Gunshots popped from behind and Matt's would-be killer fell, dying.

Matt turned to see Luiza racing across the open stretch toward him, saber in one hand, pistol in the other. Her eyes were wide with worry.

She doesn't know the blood is still healing me.

A dark shape flew down from the sky hitting the ground beside her with an earth-shaking thud. A towering, blue oni raised a metal club, resembling a hammered section of railroad track, and swung.

Luiza sprung back, barely dodging the blurring swing. The oni attacked again, swinging the weapon like a bat. Luiza ducked and rolled out of the way.

Matt splashed out of the pit and ran toward them, Dämoren in his hand.

Luiza hacked at the oni, but it jumped back with surprising speed and parried the blade with his steel beam. Feinluna flew from her hand, cast aside like it was nothing at all. Luiza fired her pistol at the monster as she started for her fallen sword, but the bullets, obviously not jade-capped, had no effect. The hulking demon raised its club and smashed it straight down onto the gilded saber, shattering it to pieces.

Luiza froze, her mouth open. She started at the broken sword. The oni roared. Leaving its club imbedded in the ground, it raised its fist to strike her.

Matt leapt, grabbing Luiza and knocking her out of the way. They hit the hard-packed mud, and Matt immediately jumped to his feet, putting himself between Luiza and the demon. "Run," he screamed. Dämoren was empty. He had only her blade.

Luiza didn't move.

The monster charged, and Matt dodged a beefy fist. He hacked Dämoren at the beast's arm, slinging water. Metal rang as he hit the oni's crude armor. It growled.

"Luiza, run!" Matt sprung forward, hoping to take the creature by surprise. He hacked at a sliver of exposed blue skin at its thigh, but the monster sidestepped the attack.

Forming both hands into a single fist, it swung. Matt moved to dodge the blow but the beast was faster. The fist glanced off Matt's vest, sending him sprawling to the ground. He gulped like a fish, the breath completely knocked from him.

A pair of bouncing headlights raced down the long slope across the basin toward them.

The oni roared at the coming lights, then looked down at Matt, lying at its feet. It raised a fist. Still stunned, Matt couldn't move. He met the beast's eyes, readying for the killing blow.

A shot fired and the unarmored back of the creature's left knee exploded. Violet blood splattered the ground and the beast howled. A second gunshot struck again, and the oni tumbled backward onto the gravel.

Malcolm ran up behind it, Hounacier in one hand, smoking sawed-off in the other. The oni struggled to rise, but Malcolm rammed the machete straight into the demon's open mouth. Kicking his foot against the monster's armored chest, he wrenched the blade free as silver and green fire burst from the dead oni's mouth and eyes.

Malcolm looked down at Matt. "You all right?"

"Yeah," Matt croaked, struggling to his feet. "Just in time."

Malcolm motioned to Luiza. "Get her out of here." He turned and ran to where Allan still fought back six opponents, blinking around them while hacking his khopesh.

Luiza had knelt beside the imbedded club gathering pieces of the broken sword.

Matt touched her shoulder. "Luiza?"

She turned. Tears streamed down her face. "He's gone," Luiza mouthed. "I can't feel him."

Matt met her eyes, seeing her pain. "I'm ... We need to move."

She nodded absently.

The hunters' van tore through the basin toward them, jolting over the white rocky ground as it circled the lagoon. Susumu stood in the open door his long naginata at his side, the ends of his yellow headband flapping behind him.

"Come on!" Matt lifted Luiza to her feet. She hesitated, and then followed. They ran to meet the oncoming knights.

The van slid to a stop and Susumu leapt out, carried by his own momentum. The samurai hit the ground running, charging the army of demons and men.

Luc came out of the passenger door, his mace in hand. He saw Matt, covered in mud and blood, running toward him with Luiza. "Come on!" A bullet shattered the window beside his head, showering him with glass, and Luc crouched behind the door.

"Everyone fall back," Jean ordered over the radio. He stepped out of the vehicle, carrying a black bullpup assault rifle. He brought the weapon up and returned fire on the shooters on the far slope.

Matt and Luiza neared the van. Luc jogged out to meet them. "Take her," Matt said.

They helped Luiza up into the seat and Matt looked back at the battle behind them. Allan and Malcolm fought side by side, falling back toward the van. Susumu stood before them, swinging his naginata in fast, graceful strikes, cutting through the demonic ranks with lethal proficiency. Matt ejected a spent shell and reached for his bag. The mud-caked flap was open. It shouldn't be open.

Panicked, he reached inside. Water. *No!* Matt pulled it open with both hands and peered inside. The shells were gone. "I'll be back," he called, running back toward the battle

"Where are you going?" Luc cried, but Matt didn't answer. He hurried to the water-filled pit. Pools of his blood still moved inside, tracking the oncoming demons. Swirls of burning succubus blood still moved over the surface. He splashed inside and felt along the bottom. *Where are they?*

He scooped up handfuls of mud and rocks, checking them only briefly before tossing them aside. *They have to be here.* He checked a fistful of white clay and saw two bronze shells. He shoved the filthy cases into his pouch and searched the same spot with both hands. He found one more. *Come one. Come on. Come on.* Two more. His fingers touched Akumanokira's metal sheath and he pulled the katana out from the muddy water.

"Matt, fall back" Allan yelled. The Englishman ran past, headed toward the van, his shirt stained with blood. Malcolm jogged behind. A deep cut marred his chin.

A brilliant orange light illuminated the basin as a fiery ifrit came down the slope. Susumu still stood at the bottom of the ramp, bodies strewn at his feet. Many burned with demonic flames. Matt ejected a shell from Dämoren and loaded a fresh bullet.

The ifrit was nearly to Susumu. A blonde woman's hair caught fire as the demon came up behind her. Screaming, she continued fighting, and lunged at Susumu with a metal baton. The samurai skewered her on his blade and stepped back onto even ground to face the fiery demon.

Matt loaded a second round and snapped Dämoren's loading latch closed.

The Ifrit charged, and Susumu thrust the bladed staff at its chest. The ifrit dodged to the side just in time and closed the distance. Susumu moved back, swinging the naginata with him, slicing the demon along its side. Its flaming skin flared brighter as the enraged demon staggered, then rushed for the small hunter.

Matt aimed the revolver, but couldn't get a safe shot without risk of hitting Susumu. A shape moved atop the ridge and Matt saw a white-skinned man crouched at the edge above the samurai. Matt brought the gun up and fired. The vampire jolted back and scrambled off into the shadows.

Susumu lurched at the sound, and the ifrit swiped at him. The stunned samurai held his ground, blocking the demon's arms with an upswing, then circled the blade around and drove it into the ifrit's chest. He pushed the impaled demon, and it fell backward. A jet of blinding white fire shot from the wound like a welding torch.

A small grin cracked Susumu's firm face as the demon's soul burned. He turned to Matt when a blur shot from the shadows and smashed into him. The samurai fell, dropping his weapon. The white-skinned man crouched atop him. He yanked a slender knife from Susumu's back. The blade glinted in the light of the ifrit's white fire and the vampire drove it in again.

"No!" Matt yelled, aiming Dämoren toward it. The vampire sprung up on top of the twenty-foot rise and into the shadows as Matt pulled the trigger. The bullet smacked into the clay cliff wall behind where it had been.

Susumu started to rise, then faltered. A red stain spread across his shirt.

Matt ran to the samurai, stooping for his fallen weapon, and helped him up. "Come on."

"I can walk," he said sharply.

"I know." Matt hooked an arm under him and helped the struggling hunter toward the van. They moved slowly. Matt looked over his shoulder, worried the vampire might come back. Dämoren was empty.

Jean raced toward them, his sword at his belt and rifle up, sweeping the area. He fired a burst, followed by another. A half-empty magazine, marked with blue tape, clattered to the ground. Jean loaded a fresh one and continued firing at some unseen opponent. Red tape circled its bottom.

"I am fine," Susumu snapped, but he didn't make any move to remove Matt's arm from under his shoulder.

"Sure you are." A bullet whizzed past, answered by another rapid burst from Jean's bullpup.

Luc ran up to meet them and put his arm under Susumu's other side. The samurai didn't resist.

They lifted him and hurried to the van's open door.

"Jesus, he's bleeding everywhere," Malcolm said as he and

Allan helped the injured hunter inside.

Allan already had his trauma kit out and guided Susumu half-conscious body onto the bench seat.

"Jean," Luc bellowed over the sounds of gunfire. "We need to go."

The white-haired hunter backed up, keeping his weapon trained on the hillside. Luc circled to the driver's side and crawled in. More pops came from the darkness alongside the building, and Jean staggered.

He returned fire, but then the weapon fell from his hands. A red bloodstain spread down the back of the hunter's jeans below his black vest.

"Jean," Malcolm cried, running to him. Matt followed.

The tall hunter turned. More blood ran down the front of his pants. A bullet hole marked his stomach.

"God damn it," Malcolm yelled, catching the hunter before he fell. More shots struck the ground around them.

Matt grabbed the fallen rifle and fired at the shadows. "Move him. I'll cover you!" He peered through the rifle's small, built-in scope. A robed figure fled from the metal building clutching a small duffel bag. Matt squeezed the trigger and the figure fell.

The van's engine roared behind him. Moving backwards, Matt laid a quick stream of fire across the ridge. The gun's bolt clicked. *Empty.*

Turning, he raced to the vehicle. He slammed the side door closed once Malcolm had pulled Jean inside past where Allan desperately worked to stop Susumu's bleeding. Bullets pinged through the open passenger door beside him, blasting out shards of plastic paneling.

"Go!" He jumped into the passenger seat.

Luc floored the accelerator, gravel sprayed the underside of the vehicle and the van took off. Matt yanked his door shut, spilling the cubed remains of its window into his lap.

They tore through the mine pit, circling the wide lagoon. The van rumbled and shook, jostling the hunters inside. Matt grabbed the handle above the window, fighting keep steady.

"He's dying!" Malcolm yelled in the back.

"Give me a minute here," Allan growled hunched over

Susumu. "I can't work any faster."

The rear window exploded, sending more glass inside.

Luc yanked a hard turn and the van leaned dangerously to one side. A straight earthen ramp stretched up before them. He hit the gas and they raced up it.

"Luiza," Allan said. "Can you give me a hand here?"

Matt turned to see the Brazilian sitting in the corner of the van, her teary eyes vacant.

"Luiza!" Allan yelled.

She blinked and looked around as if suddenly realizing where she was. Her eyes widened as she saw Allan, his hands pressing blood-soaked gauze over Susumu's pale back. "Yes. Yes!" She reached over the seat, banging her head against the roof as the van hit another bump. "What do you need?"

Matt twisted to where Malcolm crouched on the floor, fighting to get a wadded cloth under Jean's half open vest. Dark blood soaked the tan carpet around him. "Let me help you."

"Zipper's stuck," Malcolm said, his teeth clenched.

Matt crawled down with him and jerked the heavy-duty zipper. It didn't move. He gripped the coarse cloth in one hand and yanked the metal tap. It peeled open, revealing a red-soaked shirt beneath. Malcolm pressed the wadded shreds of his own shirt against the dying man's wound as the van crested the slope and sped out into the night.

CHAPTER 12

"Keep holding pressure," Malcolm said.

Matt pressed the cloth tight. Jean's blood oozed between his fingers. The van jostled, knocking Matt hard against the driver and passenger seats on either side. "He's not breathing."

Malcolm crouched over Jean's body, pumping his palms into the man's chest. He twisted, fighting his cramped angle on the van's floor and began mouth to mouth.

Tires squealed on wet pavement as the van took another hard turn. Matt leaned closer, trying to keep Jean's body steady. His knees ground into some of the sharp bits of broken safety glass scattered on the floor

"Come on, Jean," Malcolm yelled, starting another set of chest compressions. "Stay with us!"

"Luc," Allan said, from the bench above where he and Luiza worked on Susumu. "Where are we going?"

"Away from here," Luc answered.

Malcolm gave Jean two solid breaths of mouth to mouth. "Jean will die if we don't get him to a doctor."

"And tell them what?" Luiza asked. She held a clear IV bag over the back of Susumu's seat. "Bullet wounds. Stabbings. The police might already know about the shootings."

"Then we'll leave him on the hospital's curb! He'll die if we don't."

Sweat dripped off Matt's face despite the cool wind blowing through the van's broken windows. Beneath Jean's half-lidded eyes, his pupils were wide. Black. Malcolm continued CPR, but the hunter's eyes never changed.

"Come on, Jean!" Malcolm yelled.

"Mal."

Malcolm blew into Jean's mouth.

"I think he's gone," Matt said.

"Shut the fuck up!" He continued compressions. "Stay with us, Jean."

Matt frowned. He loosened pressure on the bandage. The wound didn't bleed.

Malcolm didn't stop. "Come on, Jean. Stay with me." He continued the rhythmic pulses on the dead man's chest, stopping only to give mouth-to-mouth before continuing. "Stay with me. Come on. Come ..." Malcolm's voice cracked. He stopped, crouched over the fallen knight, then looked up to meet Matt's eyes.

Matt saw the pain, the hopelessness and rage. "I'm sorry."

Malcolm chewed his lip. He opened his mouth to say something then looked up to Allan and Luiza. "How's Susumu?"

"I think we got the bleeding," Allan said ruefully. "He's lost a lot."

"Can you save him?"

The van lurched around another turn.

Allan shook his head. "I don't know. He needs fluid, and I'm out of saline. If we got him to hospital they could—"

"Arrest him," Matt said. "Luiza's right. The police probably know about the museum by now, maybe even the quarry."

"They can't prove his involvement," Allan said.

"But they'll investigate," Matt said. "He's obviously foreign, doesn't speak French, and someone clearly attacked him. Besides, we're driving a van covered in bullet holes!"

"He'll die," Allan pleaded.

"They're right," Malcolm said. "We can't take him to the hospital. Not in Limoges."

Allan's eyes widened. "What? So it was fine when it was Jean, but not Susumu?"

Malcolm shook his head. "No. I ... They were right. Do you have the equipment for a transfusion?"

The Englishman snorted. "We need blood."

"Then take ours," Malcolm barked. "What type is he?"

"O positive. No ..." Allan scrunched his eyes. "Negative."

"Sure? O negative?" Malcolm asked.

Allan let out a breath. "Fuck. Check the database. I have it in there."

Luiza retreated to the rear set and removed her phone. The screen's light filled the car. A long smear of Susumu's blood ran the length of her jaw. "I can't get to it."

"It's under Profiles," Allan said.

"I know that," she said, her voice rising in irritation. "I mean, it's not working. I can't get in."

"What?"

"It's just a blank screen." She turned the phone toward him, filling the van in blue light. "See?"

"Fine." Malcolm pointed to the front floorboards. "My bag."

Matt twisted and reached for a black canvas backpack jammed in passenger floorboards. Chunks of broken glass and plastic door paneling gathered in the fabric's folds.

"Middle pocket. My tablet is in a leather cover."

Matt shook the bag, shaking off the debris and unzipped it. He felt inside, finding the smooth leather square and handed it to him.

"Alright," Malcolm said, flipping the computer on. Pale light shone up into his face. Globs of red caked the gash at his chin. He tapped the screen with a bloody finger. "It's frozen. Not letting me in."

"They can't both be down." Allan reached for the tablet.

Malcolm handed it to him. "Seems that they are."

"Virus?" Matt asked.

Allan checked the computer. "Can't be. Different operating systems. Anya's been really diligent about keeping the security tight on them. Did an update right before we left." He tapped the screen and frowned. "Check your laptop."

Malcolm snatched the tablet back. "We don't have time for this! You entered Susumu's medical info. What is he? Think, Allan."

The Englishman pursed his lips. "O positive."

"Are you sure?"

He nodded. "Yes."

"Okay. I'm A positive. Luc?"

"A," Luc said.

"As am I," Allan said.

"I'm O," Matt said. "Positive, I believe."

"Luiza?" Malcolm asked.

"Matt's blood will work," Allan said.

"Luiza?" Malcolm repeated.

She nodded. "I'm B."

"Matt's blood works," Allan said.

"He's possessed," Malcolm snapped.

Matt's jaw tightened. He'd hoped this issue was done. Forgotten.

"For Christ's sake, man," Allan said. "You know Matt's not one of them."

"No." Malcolm turned to Matt. "He's not." He met his glare. "It isn't that you killed them. It's not even that you helped Luiza or Susumu out of there. But you risked your life to save Kazuo's sword."

Matt studied the knight's face. He seemed sincere. "Then what's the problem?"

"I can't trust what's inside you."

"Mal," Allan pleaded. "No known possession has ever come from a blood transfusion. If it were don't you think demons would be lining up at donor clinics?"

"It's still a risk. We don't know what he is."

"We know what he isn't! Matt's saved my ass twice now. He saved you. Those gunmen would have killed us. You said it yourself, he saved Akumanokira. He protected a holy weapon, a Valducan's highest duty."

Luiza closed her eyes and looked away. No one but Matt seemed to notice.

"A demon might kill another demon," Allan continued. "But they'd never do that."

"What do you think Susumu would want?" Malcolm asked. "You know how he feels about Matt. You believe he'd accept Matt's blood?"

"I don't give a damn what he'd want," Allan said flatly. "Matt saved his life. Isn't he honor-bound to him now or something?"

"You know he won't accept that."

Allan drew a breath. "We can't lose another hunter. Not now. Not when we could save him."

Malcolm sat quiet. "Luc, pull over somewhere safe. We're doing the transfusion."

"Let's try this again."

Matt pressed his tongue against the roof of his mouth as Luiza slid the needle up into the vein of his outstretched left arm. Allan's failed attempts had already blown the one in his right. Frustrated, Allan had insisted someone else try it.

Voices crackled from the police scanner resting on the dash. So far no one had reported the shootout at the mine.

"Looks good." Luiza fixed the hypodermic in place with a strip of white tape and loosened the rubber strap from Matt's upper arm. A stream of red flowed down the clear tubing and into an empty plastic water bottle on the floor. Allan had rigged the makeshift bottle, claiming that direct person-to-person transfusion was dangerous. No means to measure the amount, and clearing the air from the line between them was tricky.

Matt let out a breath, feeling the surge of blood drain down his arm. "Good job."

Luiza gave a weak smile, deepened by the shadows of the dome light above her. "I have to be good for something now, right?" Her chocolate eyes looked away.

Matt followed her gaze. Feinluna's gilded hilt rested on the back seat beside them, its broken blade only extending an inch before ending. Jagged shards of steel lay on a rain-soaked cloth beside it.

Luiza ran a finger gently down the handle. "I can't believe he's gone."

"Can it ..." Matt paused. "Can he be mended? Dämoren was broken once."

She shook her head. "Not from this. He's gone, Matt. I can't feel him. That little piece that's always there even when you aren't touching one another. Like a blanket. Comforting. It's gone. I feel ... empty." She drew a long breath and held it.

The tube of blood was on the arm closest to her. Matt reached across his body and placed the other hand on her hers.

"I'm sorry."

"He was a Toledo, forged in 1512. Sailed to the Americas in 1514. He was five hundred years old. My grandfather's blade. My father's. And I let him die." Luiza met Matt's eyes, tears filling her own. "I killed him."

"No. No, you didn't. They killed him."

"I'm not a knight anymore."

Allan turned his head from the front seat in which he sat, fidgeting with a laptop. Concern shadowed his face, but he said nothing.

Matt squeezed her hand. "Yes you are."

"No." She drew back and wiped her teary eyes. "I'm not. I'm just a ... I don't know. I'll be working in the kitchen like Tom, or maintaining the vineyard. And everyone will quietly pity me like they do him and Mikhail."

"You never know," Allan said. "One of the orphan weapons might call you."

"I don't want another weapon!" She clenched her jaw, obviously fighting the tears.

Matt cursed the transfusion hose. He wanted to hold her. Tell her it would be all right. But even if he could hold her, press her against his chest, he couldn't lie to her like that. If things were reversed, and Dämoren lay dead in pieces, he wondered if he could even survive the pain. No. Nothing he or anyone could say could comfort her. Still. "We'll make them pay for this. I promise."

Luiza wiped her eyes. "Well," she said, the stone hardness returning to her voice. She nodded to the near-full bottle on the floor. "That should be enough for now. Allan, we're ready."

Allan set the black laptop down in the seat beside him, and crawled back down the van, stepping over Jean's blanket-covered body. He squeezed around Susumu's seven-foot-long naginata, lying across the aisle, positioned so that it touched the unconscious samurai. "You doing all right there, mate? You look a bit pale," he said, sliding up beside Susumu in the bench before them.

"I'm fine." Matt winced as Luiza untaped and slid the needle from his arm. She held a folded square of gauze over the wound and Matt crooked his arm, holding it in place.

Luiza coiled the hose still attached to the blood-filled bottle and handed it to Allan.

"Well you're down almost a half-liter, so take it easy for a bit, all right?"

Matt sat while Allan worked on Susumu. Outside, Luc circled the van, carrying a roll of silver duct tape. Shaking his head, he stopped at the broken window behind them.

"How is he?" Luc asked.

"Not good," Allan said, fidgeting with the red, coiled tube. "He needs a real doctor. I'm just EMT trained. We need Colin."

"You're doing fine." Luc ripped off a strip of tape and began covering holes shot through the rear door.

Matt noticed Malcolm pacing out in front of the van, phone pressed to his ear.

"We need to get back as soon as possible," Allan grumbled. He took the upturned bottle from Luiza's hand and slid it into a crude harness made from a bent wire hanger and tape. He then hooked it through a beige, plastic loop mounted above the side window.

Luc tore another patch of tape and pressed it to the van. "We'll be there shortly."

Allan smiled sourly as he checked Susumu's pulse.

"You done with me, Allan?" Matt asked, as Luiza taped the gauze bandage down to his arm.

"For now."

Matt crawled out from the back bench, squeezing past the seats and debris, and out the side door. The rain had gone, but dark clouds still sped across the sky. He stretched, then turned back to the van. Long, horizontal strips of silver tape covered the door. Taut round circles, like miniature drum heads, marked the patched holes hidden beneath. *Beats nothing at all, I suppose.* He opened the passenger door, broken glass rattling inside it, and grabbed his discarded shell bag.

Malcolm emerged from the shadows, holding a closed flip-phone.

Dried traces of Jean's blood still stained his tattooed forearms. A hint of blue vanished as the inked scarab scuttled around to the other side, away from Matt. "I can't reach the chateau."

"My phone acting up too?" Matt asked, removing a handful of pebbles and Dämoren's muddy casings from the bag.

"No. Only one still working, but I still can't reach them. Tried Turgen's and Schmidt's phones, as well, but no one is answering."

"What about Anya?" Luc asked. "She should be there by now."

Malcolm shook his head. "Don't remember her number. Colin's either." A tinge of guilt accented his voice. "And Matt doesn't have them in his phone."

"Didn't think I'd need 'em," Matt said as he sifted the grimy, bronze casings. Aside from texts to Allan and Luiza, Matt had never used Jean's pre-paid. No need. He never went anywhere alone and if they needed to call anyone, someone else did. The cheap thing barely had Internet. The fact it survived the succubus's dunking at all was a miracle.

"Anyone remember their numbers?" Malcolm asked. "Tom's? Mikhail's?"

"I had them on my phone, and computer," Allan said. "But they're both out."

"So you think it was a pulse, like in Spain?" Malcolm asked. "EMP or something like that?"

"No."

"No?"

"What happened in Spain drained the batteries and wiped the memories of everything nearby when the oni was summoned. The GPS, the cameras, even the clocks in the house reset. This is different. Our radios still work, Matt's phone, even his computer, they're all fine. Our phones and computers still have battery power, but their memories are completely gone. Even the factory settings."

"So why do Matt's work?" Malcolm asked, turning toward him. The familiar mistrust returned to his eyes.

"Don't ask me," Matt said.

"There's no reason why yours should be working. You were with me when I killed the oni, but your computer was in the van with the rest of ours. Two places. So why would they still work?

"A virus," Luc growled.

Allan shook his head. "Can't be. The phones, the computers, that's three operating systems. They don't work that way."

"What if it did?" Luc said. "Matt was the only one of us who wasn't on the shared drives. Schmidt forbade it."

Malcolm's eyes widened. "That would require we got it *before* we left for Limoges. When we were still all connected."

Allan's face visibly paled. "Impossible. That was almost a week ago."

"I think we need to get back to the manor now," Luc said.

"I can't." Matt closed his shell bag. "I need to go back to the mine."

"What?" Allan asked. "Why?"

"I lost four of Dämoren's shells. I spilled them when the succubus attacked me."

"We can't go back there, Matt," Allan said. "Jean and Kazuo are dead. Susumu's hurt and ..." Allan grimaced, seeming to regret his word.

"And Feinluna is gone," Luiza finished, her gaze cast down to her lap.

Matt nodded. "I know. I understand if you can't go with me, but those shells are part of Dämoren. She can't fire without them. I won't leave them."

Allan looked to Malcolm, his face urging him to say no.

Malcolm pursed his lips. "Then we go back."

Allan's jaw dropped "Mal, Susumu is dying. Can we at least take him to a doctor?"

"I agree with Allan," Luc said.

"They're right." Matt nodded. "This is my fault. You take care of Susumu first. I'll meet you back at the chateau, or you can send someone for me."

Malcolm shook his head. "We'll go back to the chateau, but our oath is binding. Dämoren needs those shells. Kazuo's body is still there. We have to get them."

Allan looked as if he was about to protest, but just shook his head.

"No," Matt said. "You can't go back there. Not for me."

Malcolm met his eyes. "You said yourself Dämoren's a Valducan."

"Dämoren's *my* responsibility."

"Luiza?" Malcolm asked.

She looked up. Cold determination shone in her eyes. "We go back to the mine."

CHAPTER 13

Cool morning air whisked through the van's blown-out windows as they followed the winding road back to the mine. Matt held Dämoren in his lap, wiping off the last of the chalky mud. The tiny red stones glinted along her barrel. Her blade felt keener, refreshed after tasting the succubus's blood. Still, a small notch marred the edge from when he'd hit that oni's armor. No matter. Once she bled her next demon, the wound would mend. He still couldn't believe he'd lost the shells. Carelessness. There was no excuse.

In Dämoren's century and a half since becoming a revolver, twelve of her original thirty shells were lost. Matt never understood how any of her previous guardians could have let that happen. He'd even recovered one of the lost flock, bringing her up to nineteen. Now he'd lost four of them. If any of their enemies found them, they'd be destroyed. *No.* He pushed it from his mind. *That's not going to happen.*

He opened Dämoren's loading gate and rotated her cylinder, seeing the intricate designs etched along its face, only visible when the latch was open. Most of the holes were empty, save two. *Two shots.*

Luiza sat on the bench seat beside him. She held Kazuo's sheathed katana in her lap, cleaning the white mud from its copper handle. *They're both orphans now.*

She seemed to notice his gaze and looked up to meet it. Sadness tinged her smile.

Hesitantly, he touched her leg.

She looked away.

Matt started to withdraw it, but then she took his hand in hers, squeezing it, then let go.

Malcolm pulled the van around a tight turn and started up a hill. "Almost there."

Matt's fingers kneaded Dämoren's ivory handle, fighting back a creeping dread. In just a couple more minutes they would know if the demons were still there. He'd know if they had found the shells. If they had to fight, and anyone died, it would be his fault. What if the police were there and arrested them? What if Susumu died? No excuse. He cursed Malcolm for risking everyone for Matt's stupidity.

"Anyone smell smoke?" Allan asked.

Luc sniffed the air. "I do."

Matt drew a long breath. A faint hint of smoke tickled the back of his throat. It wasn't like leaves or even wood, more like the sharp tang of burning trash. Wisps of it swirled in the van's headlights.

They could see the mining company's sign ahead. Malcolm slowed to a stop and killed the lights. "Matt, anything on that compass?"

Matt removed a half-empty bottle from the cup holder beside him and held it up. He and Allan had split the last of the water between two bottles to make compasses. Allan checked his as well.

"Nothing," Matt said, swirling the pinkish water.

"Keep an eye on it." Malcolm turned to Luc, in the front seat beside him. "Luc."

The big knight raised Jean's bullpup to the open window and cocked the charging handle.

Malcolm turned up the narrow entrance drive and slowly headed inside. Gravel crunched under the tires. They crested the basin's rise and the pit mine seemed to open before them. The large metal building still loomed over the rocky landscape, like some medieval castle above a barren land. Its windows were dark.

Several small fires, maybe half a dozen, burned in seemingly random spots. Not demon fires, but real ones, spewing black smoke and casting an orange glow through the quarry. Some around the main building, a few down in the basin near the shot-up box truck, even one up on the far slope.

Allan nodded toward the darkened building. "The cars are gone."

"Doesn't mean they all left," Malcolm said, guiding the van down the long grade.

Matt peered out the window, searching for movement through the haze. From their height, he saw the round pit where he'd lost the shells. The glow from a nearby fire illuminated the area around it, leaving a black hole of shadow. Strange how small it appeared from a distance. Crumpled bodies still littered the ramp down to the truck. Off to the side, the parked shovel and bulldozer where Kazuo had died sat like a pair of ruined tanks left to rust on a battlefield.

They reached the bottom then circled around the wide pond at the basin's center. Pink and orange streaked the horizon. Dawn.

Matt checked the half-full compass. Nothing.

Malcolm pulled up between the pit and the dozer and parked. "Luiza, you stay here with Susumu. Radio us if you see anything. Let's do this fast." He opened the door and hopped out, leaving the engine running. Allan and Luc hurried out after him.

"Here," Matt said, handing her the compass bottle. "If it beads, call us."

Luiza nodded, still idly cleaning Kazuo's sword. "Be careful," she said as he stepped out of the open door.

Clouds of oily smoke wafted through air. Flames enveloped a black and charred body lying on its back, gnarled hands across its chest.

Matt approached, covering his mouth to block the stench. Empty brass rifle casings glinted in the firelight a few feet away.

"Why did they burn this one?" Luc asked.

"Don't know," Matt said. "He came after me with a rifle. Luiza shot him."

"So he wasn't a demon?"

Matt shook his head. Smoke stung his eyes.

"They didn't burn the demons," Malcolm said. "Just left them there. Familiars, too."

"Cult member," Luc said, making a sour face. "They honor

them. The others are just corpses. Demons have no bodies."

"Burn in Hell, asshole," Matt muttered and started toward the pit.

A figure stumbled from the shadows beside the box truck. Everyone spun, weapons raised.

A wild-eyed man with blond afro hair stepped out. He was naked. "Help me."

Allan moved as if about to approach the man, but then stopped. He checked the bottle in his hand. "He's human."

"Please," the man begged in some weird guttural language. His hands covered his privates. "I don't know where I am."

"What's he saying?" Allan asked.

"He doesn't know where he is," Matt answered. "Could be a familiar whose master died."

"Maybe," Malcolm approached slowly.

The man started toward him, then froze as he saw the weapon. "Wait! Please! Don't hurt me."

Malcolm thrust his left hand before him, palm flat, eye tattoo facing the terrified stranger.

"I don't know where I am. I just woke up here. My name is Pytor. Please, please don't hurt me."

Malcolm stepped forward, palm still raised.

"Please, I just want—" A pained hiss came from the man's lips. He recoiled, as if suddenly struck with a blinding light. "Please!"

Before Matt knew it, Malcolm sprang forward and hacked Hounacier's blade into Pytor's neck. He fell, and Malcolm hacked the machete again, severing the man's head.

"What the fuck!" Matt cried.

Malcolm wheeled back to face him. "He was possessed."

"But the demon wasn't in him," Matt said. "The compass said—"

"Just because it wasn't in him then, didn't mean it won't come back any minute. He was a danger. I freed his soul."

"But the demon who owned him knows we're here now," Allan said.

Malcolm nodded. "If it wasn't watching through his eyes already. It must have leapt bodies after we left. Abandoned this one here."

"He wasn't the only one." Luc motioned toward the building. A pair of disheveled figures, a man in a torn shirt and a woman wrapped in some shiny brown fabric, like a tarp, hurried down the ramp toward them. They waved frantically as they came, evidently not seeing the beheaded corpse at Malcolm's feet.

"Thank God!" the man yelled in what sounded like German. "Please help us!"

"We'll check them," Malcolm muttered. "If they're familiars, freed when their owners died, we'll spare them."

Matt felt ill. He understood the reason, but hated it nonetheless. Clay would have agreed with them. Said their souls needed to be free. But Matt, well, he understood the other side of it. He'd felt a demon's icy grip on his soul. He remembered the fear, so many years ago, lying on a floor, his mother dead beside him, Dämoren in Clay's hand, aimed at him, debating if he should die.

"Please," the man said, drawing near. "Where am I? Where is my wife?"

Matt turned and walked toward the shallow pit, trying not to hear what he knew would come next. The body of a nude girl lay inside, her throat sliced open. She wasn't the succubus, not any more. The dark lines of tattooed knot work on her shoulder stood out against her pale skin. Red blood colored the once milky water.

Matt sloshed down into the hole and knelt in the crimson pool.

The woman screamed behind him, then was cut off.

Slimy mud and jagged rocks covered the bottom. Matt felt in a circular pattern from where he best guessed he dropped the shells, working outward. He touched something smooth and round. A surge of relief bloomed in his chest. Scooping it up, Matt sighed as he saw the etched bronze casing, filled with mud. He dropped it in his bag and searched the area around where he'd found it, quickly finding another.

I know you're here. Come on. Come on. Matt scooped through mud, tossing sticky handfuls aside as he searched. He almost threw one out, but stopped, catching the glint of golden brown metal at the last moment. He slipped it in his bag. One more to go.

The other hunters moved toward the dozer, recovering Kazuo's body, and Matt suddenly felt very alone. Little prickles danced off the back of his neck, like someone was watching him. He wanted to check his compass, but remembered he'd given it to Luiza. His own blood, still in the water, should still be potent, but with all the red of the dead woman's mixed in, he wondered if he'd even be able to see it gather at the edge.

Just paranoia, he thought, still feeling through the clay sludge. His finger brushed the sharp, circular edge of a shell, and he grabbed it, drawing it from the water. Triumph. The weight of worry lifted away. Matt dropped it into his bag and sloshed out from the bloody pit.

Matt approached the railroad track club still jutting up from the ground. Nearby the body of a bearded man, mid-thirties by the look of him, lay inside a suit of piecemeal armor twice his size. Looking down, Matt noticed a small shard of polished metal. He picked it up. Two sides of the diamond-shaped wedge were sharpened. A piece of Feinluna's blade. Matt ran a finger along the keen edge, wondering how many demons had died along it. The joy of finding Dämoren's shells faded. *Five hundred years, now dead.*

He slipped the shard into his pocket and headed back to where Luc and Allan carefully loaded a thick, crinkly brown roll into the back of the van. Matt recognized the tarp. He could easily guess who was inside it.

Malcolm stomped toward him. Blood glistened along the machete's blade in the morning's light. "They took Kazuo's head."

Matt frowned. *Bastards.* He looked at the smoking body nearby. "One of Dämoren's slugs is in that guy's gut. I need to get it out. Ballistics."

"Is that something you need to do yourself, or can we help? Speed things along."

He shrugged. "You can help, if you want." Bullet recovery had always been the more distasteful job. "There's a couple more I'll need to get, too."

Malcolm gave a crooked smile. Vengeful. He squeezed Hounacier's horn grip. "Let me take this one for you."

The hunters worked their way through the field of corpses spread around and up the earthen ramp. Matt dug one of Dämoren's squashed silver bullets from the shoulder of an eviscerated body who had once been a rakshasa. The well-built man looked like he could have been an underwear model, with chiseled muscles and high cheekbones. Matt couldn't help but wonder what had led him here. Who was he? Where did he come from? How did he become possessed?

"Best not think about that," Clay had warned. "You saved 'em. Don't write their eulogy."

At the top of the ramp, they found the corpses of the gunmen still lying where Matt had shot them. Spent rifle and shotgun shells littered the ground around them. Allan checked the compass, but the water was still pink. Matt rolled over the body of an Asian man, checking for an exit wound. Not finding one, he began to cut the slug out. He held his breath as he worked, slimy gore oozing around his fingers. Still, the taste of iron and death permeated through.

"Look at this," Luc said, picking up a battered AK with his gloved hand. He tapped its enormous grip, wrapped in black tape. "They made the handle bigger and cut off the trigger guard."

"Big enough for a werewolf's claws," Malcolm said, scooping a silver slug out of a corpse with his machete blade.

Luc tossed the weapon aside. "They were prepared for us."

"Yeah," Malcolm said. "And we fell for it."

They circled around the side of the building to another smoldering corpse laid out, hands on its chest. Tire tracks scarred the soft ground around it, though all the cars were now gone.

"What's that?" Allan pointed Ibenus to a teal-colored strap peeking out from a pile of rusted machinery.

Shielding his mouth from the dark smoke, Malcolm circled around the fire and pulled out a canvas gym bag. "It's mostly dry. So it wasn't here during the storm."

"He was carrying that when I shot him," Matt said, nodding to Smokey. "He was running to the cars. Must have fallen back there."

"Well then." Malcolm set it down on an empty steel drum. "Let's see what we have." He pulled open the zipper and rifled through a wad of folded clothes. "Hello there." Malcolm removed a burgundy passport, blazoned with gold writing, and flipped it open. "Mister Alessio Brunelli."

Allan's grim expression faded for the first time all night. "Couple hours with that, we can find his friends' names, too."

Malcolm slipped the passport back into the bag and dug behind the ball of clothing. "There's some papers in here, might be helpful." He closed and zipped the bag. "We'll go through it once we're home. Get a few answers out of Anya's prisoner."

"Malcolm," Luiza's voice shouted through Matt's earbud. "The bottle."

Matt spun to see Allan holding his blood compass. A single red bead pressed against the bottle's side, pointed toward the building beside them.

"It just appeared," Luiza said.

"Demon must have leapt back into a host body," Matt said.

Malcolm nodded. "We'll need to take care of it before any more come back. Other possessed might still be hiding around here, or ran off once the demons left." He didn't mention that had he not killed those three people they might be on them right now, which Matt was grateful for.

Malcolm pressed the radio button at his shoulder. "Luiza you stay there. We'll check it out. Tell us if anything happens." He looked at the hunters around him, meeting their eyes, then nodded to the building's green steel door.

Without a word, Allan and Luc took point on either side, weapons ready. Holding his machete out front, Malcolm approached the door. Allan pulled it open, revealing a darkened, cement-floor hallway. Spots of drying blood speckled a trail down the corridor, suggesting that some injured person had passed through.

Cautiously, Malcolm entered, followed by Allan, then Matt. Luc took the rear. Doors lined either side of the passage, some closed. The hunters took their time, checking every room before they passed, just to be sure no one snuck up and attacked them from behind. The first few were basic offices, furnished with desk, computer, cheap upholstered furniture that no one ever had thought looked good, yet seemed to decorate every office in the world, and then the photos and personal knickknacks of whoever's offices they were.

Allan kept a close eye on the red blob inside the bottle. It hadn't moved.

They passed through a rather dingy break-room, its stained linoleum tiles chipped and broken off in places.

"Looks like they opened it up in here," Matt said quietly, noting the stacked chairs and tables along one wall. "Just like Spain."

"So much for Anya's theory about the lunar eclipse," Luc said.

Malcolm grunted in agreement. "I doubt they thought they could keep us alive long enough to wait for it."

"Compass points this way," Allan whispered.

They passed down another short hall, eventually coming to a large hangar-like garage. Beams of morning light shone through the dusty windows, casting rays across the room. A pair of giant rolling steel doors formed one side. Cluttered racks of tools and oiled machinery lined the walls, save a caged section on the back, filled with stacked fuel drums. A boxy, blue-and-rust-colored vehicle dominated one side of the floor. Chunks of cracked, gray mud clung to its giant wheels, which were almost as tall as Matt.

Compass in hand, Allan gestured toward the big earth-mover.

A loud, metallic crash came from the other side of the vehicle.

Malcolm pointed to Matt and Luc, gesturing that they go around the other side.

They made it about three steps before Matt caught the sharp smell of diesel. He came around the edge of the vehicle, Dämoren out front, and saw a tipped fuel drum on its side. Amber fluid glugged out from a hole in the top, spilling across the concrete floor.

A lean, golden-eyed werewolf crawled out on top of the vehicle, its claws clacking on the hollow steel. It was female.

Dual rows of dark nipples ran down her gray-haired torso. She held one arm high, clutching something in her long-fingered hand.

Matt brought Dämoren up and froze, noticing the spring-loaded trigger squeezed in the werewolf's grip. His eyes traced along the twisted red and black wires extending down to a bundle of steel pipes in her other hand.

"It lets go of that," Luc said, flatly, "and we die."

Matt thought about the fuel drums behind him, at least forty of them. More than enough to blow the entire building to Africa. It'd kill the werewolf's body, sure. But what was a body to a demon?

Her upper lip curled back from sharp fangs as she looked at Matt. "So proud. Arrogant," she growled, yet Matt understood it. "Eat us for what we do, yet here you are. Guilty of your own crime, flesh-walker."

"I ... don't understand," Matt said carefully. The growing pool of spilled diesel reached his feet. It ran around his shoes, leaving him an island in a potential lake of fire.

"I don't speak to you, food," she snarled. "By now, they are all dead. Your order is destroyed, Urakael."

Urakael?

"What's it saying?" Allan asked without moving his lips.

"The Great Mother will return, and your kind will perish."

Matt eyed the detonator. If he shot the werewolf, she would release it before he could get close. *Maybe the wire?* He remembered the trick-shooters he'd seen, but severing a wire at fifteen yards—

The werewolf's hand suddenly came off at the forearm. It fell, the spring-switch popping the fingers open. The detonator clattered on the wet concrete, wires severed.

Blood poured from the beast's hairy stump. The werewolf looked past the hunters and roared.

Allan sprang forward, swiping his khopesh, and appeared at the vehicle's side. Stepping, he swiped again, blinking on top of one of the vehicle's tires. Matt raised Dämoren, aiming at the creature's heart, when her head split in half. The top of the werewolf's skull, just above the snout, seemed to pop free, perfectly severed.

The demon fell and hit the ground right as Allan blinked to where she had stood.

Ruby fire burst from her wounds, quickly spreading over the still quivering corpse. Matt flinched, momentarily forgetting demon fire couldn't light the diesel.

What the fuck? Matt turned to see Luiza standing fifty feet behind them. She held Kazuo's katana, its curved blade gleaming in the morning light, light that just moments before would have been shaded by the standing werewolf.

"Luiza!" Malcolm said, his voice a mix of surprise and relief.

She nodded. Her black hair shone in the sunlight. "I ... I thought you might need me."

Luc released a long, steady breath, then laughed.

Malcolm eyed Akumanokira in Luiza's hand, but said nothing.

She swallowed and looked down at it, seeming to sense the question. "He called to me," her voice proud, yet shameful. "He ... missed Kazuo. The pain of losing him. And to heal one another, he called."

"Just in time," Allan said, climbing down off the giant vehicle.

"We need to go," Matt said, spoiling the reunion. "Now."

"Why?" Allan asked. "What did it say, Matt?"

"It said the Order is all dead." He tensed his jaw, meeting the knights' stares. "I think we can't reach the chateau because they attacked it."

CHAPTER 14

Matt sat, strumming his fingers on the armrest as Malcolm raced to the chateau, knuckles white around the steering wheel. French traffic cops were renowned for strictness, and Matt prayed none saw them barreling down the twisting highway. The patched bullet holes might pass a careless glance, but if anyone saw inside, saw the blood-soaked floor, Susumu unconscious on the bench seat, human bodies wrapped in a tarp in the back, one missing his head ... Matt tried not to think what might happen to that policeman.

He glanced over at Luiza, protectively clutching Kazuo's sword ... no ... her sword, as if someone might try to take it from her. She ran her thumb absently over the clover-like hand guard, following the rim's decorative dips and rises.

Luiza said the sword had called her, that it missed Kazuo, and chose her to heal their mutual pain. Feinluna had been gone only four hours. Luiza had been devastated at its loss. But yet ... she accepted the katana's call. Matt wasn't sure how he felt about that.

How could she do it?

If Dämoren died, smashed to pieces before him, he wouldn't want to live. The idea that the single most important thing, something he'd kill for, die for, could be replaced so easily. How?

Luc twisted in his seat to face Matt. "What did the wolf say to you?"

Matt blinked, his line of thought broken. He hadn't liked where it was taking him, anyway. "It said they were all dead by now, that my order was destroyed. But ..."

"But what?" Luc rumbled.

"I don't think it was talking to me ... More like, at me."

Luc's brow rose.

"It called me Urakael." He turned to Allan sitting in the seat behind him with the still-unconscious Susumu. "Have you ever heard that name?"

Allan's lips tightened into to a thin line. He shook his head. "What else did it say?"

"That I was guilty of my own crime and called me a flesh-walker."

"Maybe," Luc said carefully, "it was speaking to the being inside you. You are a demon-killer, but yourself possessed."

"Urakael could be the wendigo's name," Allan offered.

Matt shook his head, fighting a small knot forming in his chest. "The wendigo died. Clay shot it. Its soul burned up."

"Maybe not all of it," Luc said. "There is something inside you, Matt. That much is true."

It's dead, Matt thought. Still, Luc's words troubled him. What if it wasn't? What if some piece was still alive? What if it got free? *No. Its dead. I saw the fire.* "It said the Great Mother will return. Does that mean anything to you?"

"The werewolf said that?" Allan asked.

"Yeah."

Luiza raised her gaze from Akumanokira. "A demon mother?"

"Demons don't have mothers," Matt said. "They don't even have a sex."

"Grendel had a mother," Luc said.

Matt frowned. "Grendel? Like Beowulf?"

Luc nodded.

"He's right," Allan said. "Beowulf kills Grendel, then along comes his mum, who's even worse."

"But you said that there probably wasn't even a Beowulf or Grendel," Matt said.

Allan shrugged. "True. But Grendel was a troll, and we know they've been summoning those. What if the oni are just the precursor to something more. Just building up to it, or maybe need the oni to summon something greater."

"Then thank God I killed that oni," Malcolm said from the front.

"One of them," Luc said. "Selene is still out there."

"Unless the one Malcolm killed was the same one summoned in Spain," Matt said. "Just in a different body."

Luc shrugged. "Maybe."

Matt turned back to Allan. "So, Mister Librarian, are there any records of some demon goddess?"

Allan ran his fingers through his hair. "Stories, yeah. Dozens. But real occurrences, that was Ramón's area. He'd been working on finding all the references before he went to Spain. He was trying to find a pattern to the killings."

"Did you read any of it?"

"Not much. He worked on it mostly while Schmidt and I were chasing you down. Anya took it over after he died."

"You remember any of it?"

"Ramón thought the murder sites were tampered with after the summonings. He figured that was why we couldn't find any recognizable symbols. But most of his theories he shared with Anya."

"Then we'll just have to ask her when we see her." Matt said. *If she's still alive.*

It was noon before they reached the chateau.

Malcolm turned the van into the drive. "Matt, those compasses ready?"

"Doing the second one now." Matt held an open water bottle between his thighs and pressed the plastic pricker to his finger. He pushed the button and it clicked with a short jab of pain. The van rumbled over a cattle grate, slinging a bit of water onto his leg. Matt held his finger over the bottle's mouth and squeezed four fresh drops inside. *Not too much to spare,* thinking of Susumu's transfusion. The blood swirled and mixed with the drops he'd added that morning, refreshing the compass's potency. He screwed on the bottle cap. "Ready."

Malcolm pulled the van through the arched gate and into the chateau's courtyard. The house's front doors stood open.

Matt checked the compass. "There's one inside. No, make that two."

"Could be the masks," Allan said.

Matt shook his head, eyeing the red beads. One ahead and to the left, the other further to the side. "They're moving."

"But not the masks?" Allan asked. "You should be picking them up in the entry hall."

"Not seeing them," Matt replied.

Malcolm stopped before the front steps and opened the driver's door. "Allan, you stay here with Susumu. Keep him safe. Radio if you see anything."

Allan swallowed. He eyed the open doors, obviously wishing he could go inside, but simply nodded.

Malcolm drew his machete. "Everyone on me."

Matt pulled the sliding door open and stepped out. He drew Dämoren from her holster and cocked the hammer as he scanned the chateau's windows for movement. Nothing.

He checked the compass. One of the red globs, the one toward the house, rolled quickly along the bottle's inner wall. It was moving fast, though Matt couldn't tell if it headed toward or away from them.

"All right," Malcolm said. "Our knights might still be in there. Look before you attack anything. We don't want any accidents."

Cautiously, they headed up the stone steps and through the entranceway. The giant mirror on the back wall was broken. Bits of silver glass still clung along the edges of its gilt frame around a bullet hole in the wall behind. Matt tasted the tinge of smoke. Torn clothing, shoes, and other effects littered the tile floor beside several smears of dried blood.

"The masks are gone," Luiza said. She flipped the wall switch, but the lights didn't work.

"No." Matt picked up a broken piece of green stone off the floor. It was about two inches across. One side was smooth, the other bore fine lines, like carved hair. "They broke them."

Luc motioned to a second cluster of broken jade. "The other is here, as well."

Metal glinted from the scattered debris and Matt picked up a thin, half-circle of gold. The engraved pattern along the outer side seemed drawn out, nearly invisible at the ends. He'd seen it before. Rings, stretched to the breaking point when a demon's body changed. Though if the demon was susceptible to the metal, such as a silver ring on a werewolf, the ring could cut off its expanding finger. He offered it up to Malcolm.

Malcolm flipped the crescent over in his hand and frowned. "It's Ben's ring." He turned to Luc, sifting through the second pile of tattered clothes and broken jade. "We know who that is?"

Luc checked a torn blue jean leg, split almost perfectly along the seam. "Definitely not Master Schmidt or Turgen. Mikhail, I believe."

God damn it. A cold pang stabbed Matt's chest, like an icicle sliding between his ribs. *He's just a kid.* "How?"

"Someone put the masks on them." Pocketing the broken ring, Malcolm picked up a black snub-nose from the floor and opened the cylinder. "All five shot." He looked around. "We need to find the others."

Matt checked the compass. The moving bead pointed in the direction of the left hall. He gestured the direction and stood when a roar echoed down the passageway.

A mustard-yellow animal with a shaggy, dark mane stepped into the hall. Its shoulders stood just above the silver handles of the hall doors. Curved white fangs jutted outward from the creature's mouth. It growled, and then charged.

Matt raised Dämoren and fired. The bullet hit the demon lion's shoulder, jolting it, but the beast didn't slow. He cocked and fired again, hitting the beast's head. It staggered, then roared. Blood poured from a strip of exposed bone above its brow.

Dämoren empty, Matt back-pedaled, holding the revolver ready to slash with its blade.

The devilish lion crouched, about to leap when Luc charged forward, his mace high. The demon sprung, but Luc dropped, smashing Velnepo into the creature's side. Bones cracked as the demon's body folded around the mace like a deer hit by a truck. It slammed into the wall, bringing down shards of broken mirror with the impact.

Spectral green fire ignited from the wound, quickly spreading over the monster's broken body.

Matt nodded to Luc. "Thanks."

The huge hunter looked at the burning corpse. "I always hated those masks."

"Where's the other one?" Luiza asked.

Matt checked the compass. He pointed in the bead's direction. "Back of the house somewhere."

"Then let's find it," Malcolm said. "Be careful. Whoever released them might still be here."

Weapons ready, the hunters moved deeper into the dark chateau.

"Cameras are still working," Matt said, noting the red lights still glowing from the upper corners.

"Nick had them set with backup batteries," Malcolm said, scanning through an open doorway. "Said any attackers would cut the power first and he didn't want us blind."

He was right.

They checked rooms as they passed, finding them tossed. Cabinets and cases stood open, their contents spilled out on the floors. Carpets were peeled back and paintings knocked from the walls.

"This isn't random," Matt said, working his way through the smashed dining room. "They were looking for something."

"The orphan weapons," Luiza said.

Matt's eyes widened. "We need to check on them."

Malcolm stepped over a fallen chair. "We are. They're the same direction from us as the demon."

The rear dining room door stood open, the dark wood splintered at the hinges. A mangled and bloody corpse lay on the ground. Its legs were gone, and its stomach torn open. Pink tubes of gnawed intestine splayed out from the hole like fleshy roots.

"Who is it?" Matt coughed, his stomach lurching at the stink.

Malcolm glanced at the half-eaten corpse and quickly looked away. "Colin."

"Oh God," Luiza said, closing her eyes.

Matt checked the compass and pointed past the edge of the house. "That way."

"I know where we're going," Malcolm growled, marching forward, his jaw set.

The hunters turned around the side of the building to see the long, cinderblock firing range at the base of the hill. The second lion-like demon paced back and forth before the battered and mutilated steel door. A black-clad corpse lay sprawled face down a few feet away.

"Hey!" Malcolm yelled.

The demon's head snapped around. Black lips curled back from its jagged fangs.

"Come on, you ugly fucker!"

The beast snarled and charged up the hill toward them. Matt squeezed Dämoren's ivory grip.

Malcolm stepped forward to meet the demon, but the beast dodged, circling around with incredible speed. Luiza lunged, thrusting her katana. The creature sprung to the side, then back as Luc moved in with his mace.

The demon growled, its green eyes moving over its attackers.

Matt circled around behind it, boxing it in.

The demon lunged toward Luiza. She dodged the claws, slicing a wound in the beast's shoulder. It yowled but swiped again.

Malcolm dove forward, ramming his blade deep into the monster's side. It staggered, but didn't fall. It wheeled around to face him, when Matt stepped in chopping Dämoren's blade down into the demon's exposed back. Blood sprayed and its back legs crumpled. Luiza and Luc closed in from the sides, finishing it off.

Green fire erupted from the beast's wounds, and Matt yanked Dämoren's blade free.

"Good work," Malcolm panted.

Matt checked the compass. The demons were gone. Taking a moment, he knelt and slid his fingers into the burning gash. He gasped, exhaustion and blood loss swept away in a sudden rush. He paused, suddenly realizing that he'd known the man whose blood now healed him. *It's demon blood,* he corrected, *not theirs.* It didn't comfort him.

The hunters continued down the hill toward the black clad body.

Its right leg was twisted and broken, pants torn from

where the demon had gnawed it. The rest of the body seemed undamaged, except for the three bullet wounds curling out from its back. A black polymer pistol rested on the grass beside it.

"Who is it?" Malcolm asked.

Luiza knelt and rolled the body over.

Matt found himself looking at a young man with dark hair. "That's the prisoner from the museum."

"Looks like someone else got him," Luiza said, noting a bloodied cloth cinched around his lower thigh.

"Curious they didn't burn him," Luc rumbled. "Maybe he was alone."

"Then where is Jean's car?" Malcolm asked. "Anya obviously got him here, but it wasn't out front."

Metal squeaked from the range's battered door. Matt spun to see a black rifle barrel jutting out from the opened crack, trained on him.

Luiza drew her pistol.

"Hold!" The door opened, and Max Schmidt, his sparse hair tousled and eyes ringed with dark circles, stepped out, holding a high-power hunting rifle.

"Schmidt!" Malcolm cried.

"Thank God you made it!" Schmidt slung the rifle over his shoulder.

"We could see you on the cameras, but that monster had us trapped."

The door opened further. Riku came out behind him, holding a pump shotgun. His dark eyes searched the hunters.

"What happened?" Luiza asked.

"Anya," Turgen said, pushing his way past Riku. His cane jammed into the ground with each step. "They got to her somehow."

"Got to her?" Malcolm asked. "How?"

"We don't know." Turgen eyed the hunters, his gaze focusing on the katana in Luiza's hand. "Where are the rest of you?"

Malcolm's smile vanished. "We were ambushed. Kazuo's dead." He looked at Schmidt. "And Jean."

Schmidt's face paled. He staggered back, looking as if he might fall.

"We saved Lukrasus," Malcolm continued. "She still lives."

Schmidt gave a half-hearted nod. He pressed a fist to his lips and looked away.

"I'm sorry," Malcolm muttered.

"Susumu is hurt," Luiza said.

"Hurt?" Riku blurted.

"Stabbed," Luiza answered. "Allan's been taking care of him, but we need to get him into the clinic."

Turgen frowned. He turned to Schmidt. "Max?"

Schmidt looked up, his lips tight and colorless.

"We need you right now," Turgen said, his voice calm, but pleading.

Schmidt nodded. "Take me to him."

The chateau's lights all came on at once, followed by the hum of climate control. Matt followed Allan and Luiza to the kitchen, having left Susumu in Schmidt's care as Riku paced around outside the clinic's door, unwilling to leave. Schmidt had started Susumu on an IV and antibiotics for infection. The old man's reaction to hearing that they had given him Matt's blood was surprisingly indifferent. Matt had expected anger or reprimand. Even a questioning look would have been something, but Schmidt remained composed, even robotic as he started his work. He complimented Allan's dressings, then curtly ordered everyone out.

"It doesn't make sense," Allan said to the air. "How did they get Anya?"

"If a demon bit her, it could have taken her over very fast," Matt said. "Trust me."

Allan shook his head. "But she wasn't bit."

Matt shrugged. "Not that we saw. Besides, not all demon-marks are bites."

"All right," Allan said. "Then how did she approach the demon masks?"

"Maybe they didn't work," Luiza said.

"No." Allan pushed open the dining room door and stepped inside. A platter of crackers and cheese sat on one of the tables. "There's two dozen confirmed reports that they do work.

Besides, Malcolm should have sensed it if she was possessed."

"He had no reason to check her," Luiza said. "He was a little preoccupied at the time."

"Anya wasn't possessed," Turgen said coming out from the kitchen.

He set a plate of sandwiches on the table and gestured for them to sit.

"How do you know?" Allan asked.

The old knight lowered himself into one of the chairs. "Because whatever virus crashed the computer network was done before you left. The mask cases were also unlocked and their alarms disabled before she arrived at the chateau."

"How do you know?" Matt asked.

Turgen pointed his cane at a black security camera up in one of the room's corners. "We had a few hours to watch the videos while trapped in the bunker. She simply opened them, and no alarms sounded, meaning they were done beforehand."

Matt helped himself to one of the sandwiches. "So what happened?"

Turgen sighed. "We should wait for the others. Luiza, could you help me with the coffee machine? I can never get that contraption to work."

"Of course," she said, rising from her seat.

"Thank you. I imagine everyone would need some." He turned to Allan. "How is Susumu?"

"Schmidt is optimistic," Allan said. "Time will tell."

Turgen sighed. "Time, I fear, is one thing we have too little of."

The broken back door creaked open. Malcolm and Luc walked inside.

"Everything looks clear," Malcolm said. He set his sawed-off on the table and helped himself to some of the food. "So what happened?"

"Anya called to let us know she was almost here," Turgen said. "She told Max it would be half an hour and had him start readying the clinic for Mister Varghese. I was in my office on the phone with Louis about the break-in at the time. Ten minutes later she pulled into the drive. Mikhail went out to meet her and she and her accomplice took him by surprise. They then brought Mister Varghese and Mikhail inside."

Luiza stepped into the kitchen door to listen, while the coffee machine whirred and beeped behind her.

"Once through the door," Turgen continued, "Anya put on a medallion and held it before one of the demon masks. She then removed it and placed it on Mister Varghese's face. She had started on the second mask when Mikhail unholstered a pistol at his back and fired several shots, even wounding her accomplice before Anya wrestled the mask onto him. Those shots were what alerted us." He sighed. "Unfortunately, by the time we could respond, Mikhail and Ben had transformed. With only one knight, we fled to the bunker. Colin tried to hold them off while the rest of us could get safely away. It was then we realized they'd set fire to the library."

Allan rubbed a hand across his mouth nervously, but didn't speak.

"Tom ran off to deal with the fire. Colin ordered him to the bunker, but he didn't listen. He ..." Turgen swallowed. "He was so desperate to be useful that he just charged up there with no concern for himself. He managed to get the fire out, but ..." The old man drew a breath and held it. "Colin tried to fight the demons back, but Anya shot him. The beasts took him. They started coming for us at that point. Max managed to kill her accomplice before the demons forced us inside."

"Didn't you have anything that could kill them?" Matt asked.

Turgen shook his head. "Nothing we knew of. By that time, the database was down. We thought jade might work but all the jade ammunition was gone."

Matt looked away, remembering how much of the jade he'd taken anticipating the oni. Not just him, but everyone. Not that there had been that much to begin with.

"The bunker is extremely secure and with the death of her accomplice and us trapped inside, Anya proceeded to search the house. After two hours she left with Ben and Colin's swords."

"What about the other weapons?" Luc asked.

Turgen shared a look with Malcolm and Luiza. "God's

weapons are still safe. Anya never knew we kept them in the armory."

Of course, Matt thought. *No wonder Nick was so paranoid. Always changing the combinations.* Luiza had only opened one of the safes. Matt had assumed they only held more guns.

"It still doesn't make sense," Allan said. "How could she be one of them? She's been a knight for over three years. She's bonded to Baroovda for Christ's sake."

"Has anyone ever seen her actually kill a demon?" Luc asked.

The hunters remained quiet.

"When we found her in Rome," Luc said, "there were demon sightings followed by reports of a man killed by a sword. Then the sightings stopped. That's what told us there was a hunter involved. But no one ever saw her do it."

"She shot the succubus at the museum," Malcolm said. "She did the same thing in Gothenburg last year."

"She killed an itwan in Germany," Allan said. "But none of us actually saw her do it. Just the body after."

A guilty dread wormed in Matt's gut. "Maybe she wasn't actually bonded to Baroovda," he said carefully.

"Why do you say that?" Luc asked.

Matt licked his lips. "One night I woke up. Needed to go to the bathroom, so I snuck out of my room. I took a wrong turn and found Mikhail standing outside Anya's door holding this journal. Just standing there, soaked with sweat. I guess he was sleepwalking, because he didn't hear me. I touched his shoulder and startled him. He ran away, but dropped his journal." He fidgeted with the table edge. "It was full of pictures of Anya's sword. Hundreds of them, just page after page. I think it was calling to him."

"And you didn't tell anyone?" Malcolm demanded.

"I wasn't supposed to be out of my room, remember. I didn't think it was any big deal. I bonded with Dämoren years before I inherited her."

"Yeah," Allan said. "And I told you that was unusual."

"Not for me. I figured if Mikhail had it too, then maybe I wasn't so ... *unusual.*"

"What did you do with the book?" Turgen asked. Unlike the others his manner remained calm.

"I slid it under his door. My way of telling him that I wouldn't tell anyone about him if he didn't about me."

Malcolm scowled. "You realize that if you'd told us then none of this would have fucking happened!"

"Now, Doctor Romero," Turgen said, raising a hand. "None of us can say that. We never had any reason to suspect Anya. Our knowing of Mikhail's obsession could have been explained as something else. We wouldn't have wanted to believe one of our own was a traitor. I suspect that if Mister Hollis had said something the suspicions would have been on him."

Malcolm clenched his jaw, but remained quiet.

Luiza carried in a pot of coffee and several small cups. She set them down on the table, then poured three cups. She gave one to Turgen and took a seat beside Matt, giving him the other cup.

"Spain," Allan blurted, closing his eyes. "She's the one who found the lead. Ramón was researching demon cults, so she sent him there. She set it up."

"She wanted you to go, too," Luc said, pouring a cup. "Remember, she argued with Master Schmidt that you go on the rescue mission instead of her."

Allan balled a fist. "Fucking bitch. That would have left her as the last Librarian left, except ..." He turned to Turgen. "Sonu!"

Turgen waived his hand. "I have already contacted our knights in India. They are safe, though Anya's virus disabled their computers, as well."

Allan's face went slack "The records?"

Turgen nodded.

"They're gone?" Allan asked.

"He hopes he can recover part of them," Turgen said.

Allan looked sick. "Years, centuries of research. That's why files kept going missing or never saved. It wasn't the system. She was changing them."

"She did her work well," Turgen said.

"I'll fucking kill her," Malcolm grumbled.

Luc and Luiza nodded in agreement.

Matt sipped his coffee. Luiza had remembered exactly how he liked it. Then it dawned on him. "The ifrit. It wasn't me."

The others gave him a quizzical look.

"In Spain," Matt said. "Anya was behind me. It was looking at *her.* She wasn't supposed to be there." He pointed to Luc. "They expected Allan to go. That's why they backed off. If they attacked they'd lose her as a spy. Even if she came back with some story of being the only survivor it might raise suspicion, so they retreated."

"And threw the blame on you," Malcolm said.

Matt nodded. "Yeah."

Malcolm shook his head bitterly. "I think I owe you an apology."

"Fucking hell," Allan said as he and Matt stepped into the charred and wrecked library. Toppled shelves and burned books littered the floor. Blackened and soot-stained paintings lay strewn amidst broken glass, all dusted in white powder like snow.

Matt covered his nose against the overpowering stink of smoke and acrid chemicals. Light shone through the open windows, their panes smashed away. He assumed Tom did that as a way of letting some of the rain inside to fight the fire. He picked up a red extinguisher off the floor. It felt light. He checked the CO2 gauge. Empty.

"Eight hundred years." Blackened debris crunched under Allan's shoes. "All gone."

Careful of his footing, Matt circled around a half-burned desk to see a torn and bloodied corpse on the other side. Black flies scuttled across the pink flesh. The square shaft of Tom's prosthetic leg jutted from a discarded shoe. Bite marks marred the dull aluminum. A second red extinguisher, the chemical kind, responsible for the layer of white dust, rested nearby. "He's here."

Tom's red-stained jeans were singed and speckled with burn holes.

He had succeeded in quelling the fire, but gave his life to do it.

Allan set the rolled-up stretcher on the floor beside Tom's body and picked up a leather-bound book. He brushed the gray dusty cover and opened it. "At least they're not all gone. Still …"

Matt stepped over to the open window. A cool breeze wafted in, bringing fresh air. Outside Luiza and Malcolm carried Kazuo's body to one of the stacked wooden pyres. "Can I ask you a question, Allan? Between you and me?"

"Of course."

Matt licked his lips. "If Ibenus was broken, do you think you could replace her?"

"No," Allan answered flatly. "I don't even want to think about that." Wood crunched as he stepped closer. "I could tell you weren't too comfortable with Luiza's change."

Matt turned to face him. "Then how could she do that? If Dämoren broke I'd die. I … I can't imagine how I could go on. And she just accepted another sword. How?"

Allan gave an understanding nod. "Let me ask you a question. If you died in that mine, leaving Dämoren without a protector, would you want her to find someone, or would you want her alone?"

"That's different."

"No it's not," Allan said. "You saw Luiza after it broke. She was torn to pieces. Like losing your spouse and child all at the same time. That was real grief. Do you not think Feinluna would want her to find someone?"

Matt thought about that. "I suppose," he said eventually.

"And do you think Kazuo would want his sword locked up in a safe somewhere, alone, waiting for someone to come along? No. He'd want Akumanokira bonded to a guardian. He'd want it to find someone, and it did. I was as shocked as you were about the timing, but it happened. Matt, she's still grieving. I can see it. She feels guilty because Kazuo's sword chose her, and she thinks she's betraying Feinluna. Don't be upset with her."

Matt nodded, feeling a pang of shame at Allan's words. Of course she was upset. She'd reached out to him, and he'd treated her coldly ever since she found Akumanokira. "You're right. I'm sorry."

"Don't apologize to me. She's the one who needs your support."

Matt stepped over a burned chair and found the toppled case dedicated to Dämoren. Most of the original sketched designs were too far gone. He sifted through the shattered glass and found a photograph. He picked it up. Clay and Schmidt smiled up at him, their young faces proud, seemingly frozen in a light-hearted moment. *At least they're not all gone.*

"Hey Matt?" Allan asked, his voice rising.

"Yeah?" Matt slipped the photo into his shirt pocket.

"That flash drive I gave you, do you still have it?"

"Yeah. It's in my things."

Allan let out a relieved sigh. "Oh thank God."

Matt's brow creased. "You think it's still good?"

"I copied it before Anya's *security* upgrade." Allan laughed, running his fingers through his brown hair. "You know what this means? The records are safe! Schmidt and Malcolm were so damned worried you might do something to them, and now here you are with the only copy in the world. I need to check it."

"We will." Matt motioned to the mauled body. "But first we need to take care of Tom."

EVOLVED FOLKLORE (EXCERPT)

BY SIR STEPHEN BERNIER, 1999

Modern culture has rationalized the horrors of old, forcing them into paradigms that it finds understandable. For example, Lycanthropy and Vampirism—seen today, as viruses or communicable diseases.

People, when faced with the wholly incomprehensible and alien, will naturally attempt to make sense of things by explaining them in accordance with the most current of scientific theories. While this behavior is beneficial when studying objects in our physical universe it is wholly inadequate when dealing with the truly supernatural.

Supernatural entities and powers are not of our world and therefore do not obey the laws of nature. Instead, they follow symbolism. The symbolic act of dominance in a demon's bite is where the possession occurs, not in the transference of saliva. Silver does not hold power over these demons because of its atomic structure, but because of what the metal itself represents to the demon. To understand these beings, we must study the whole rather than minutiae.

The notion that demonic possession is transferable as a disease may be an acceptable theory for people who themselves do not believe in demons. However, we, the hunters of demons, must never allow these newer mythologies to affect our judgment or ideas about the creatures we face.

CHAPTER 15

Matt awoke to a knock at the door. Instinctively, he grabbed Dämoren off the bedside table. *Demons don't knock*, he realized, his tired brain firing to life. After the lengthy service and burning of the fallen knights, one which included a lot of Latin, which Matt understood, and Valducan ceremony, which he didn't, Matt had stayed up most of the night cleaning and reloading Dämoren's shells. He'd given in to exhaustion before he could start the task of stripping and cleaning mud cake from the Ingram.

The knock came again. Luc's deep voice called from the other side of the door. "Matt?"

"Yeah," he replied, his voice a little gruffer than expected. He looked at the clock. 11:32.

The door opened and Luc leaned in. His eyes gave a moment's start seeing the black and gilt revolver trained on him.

Matt lowered the gun. "Time to get up?"

"There is a meeting," Luc said. "I came to fetch you."

Matt quickly dressed, pulled on Dämoren's shoulder rig, and followed Luc into the hall. Haphazard clumps of broken furniture, picture frames, and various curios were piled through the house. Salvageable items were stacked or packed into boxes. The citrus tang of cleaners almost masked the lingering stink of smoke. The Order had been busy.

"Why didn't you wake me?" Matt asked, feeling a little guilty for sleeping so late.

Luc led him down the stairs to the first floor. "You needed it. We tried to let everyone sleep as late as they could."

To Matt's surprise, they bypassed the dining room and continued toward the front of the house. A pile of small boxes rested beside the open front doors.

Malcolm walked up the hall toward them, carrying a green plastic tub in his tattooed arms. "He rises," his voice strained. "Grab a box. We're evacuating."

Matt picked up a cardboard box loaded with crumpled balls of brown paper. He grunted, surprised at the weight of whatever was wrapped inside, then followed Malcolm to where the van waited out front. Riku stood at the rear door loading boxes into the back. The morning breeze carried the stink of spray-paint. Matt noticed someone had painted the duct tape patches blue, blending them to the vehicle, which was a just a shade darker. Still, it looked better than tape.

"How's Susumu," he asked, sliding the box inside.

"He woke up this morning for a little while," Riku said. "He wants to thank you for helping save Shi no Kaze."

Matt caught Malcolm's eye. The hunter gave a look as if to say, "He'll thank you for the naginata, but don't expect more than that."

"I'm glad to hear he's all right," Matt said.

Riku nodded. The hint of the usual disdain seemed to be gone from the young man's eyes.

Luc heaved a box onto the top of the stack and closed the door.

Malcolm fished the keys out his pocket. "Luc, Matt, get in. Riku, keep an eye on Susumu and bring down some more boxes for when we get back. You have that phone we gave you?"

The boy tapped his front pocket. "Yes."

"Good. Keep it on you. Call us if you see or hear anything."

Riku nodded again.

"Where are we going?" Matt asked.

"Air strip."

A discomforting knot tightened in Matt's chest. *Please not that airplane again.*

Matt stared out the window, watching the French countryside as Malcolm drove. Two days ago he'd been sitting in the museum, worried about aging techniques on a counterfeit adze. So much had happened since then.

The werewolf's words still troubled him. What if Luc was right, and a sliver of the wendigo still lived within him? He'd suspected it before, of course, but what did that make him? What might happen if it took control? Matt knew the answer. He would kill everyone. Kill them and eat them. But if the demon was still alive, what kept it at bay? He touched the old bullet wound at his chest. Dämoren's slug rested about an inch below the surface. Would his humanity die if it was removed?

He closed his eyes. *Urakael.* He rolled the name around inside his head. There was a familiarity to it. He'd heard it before. A dream? No, something deeper. *Urakael,* he thought again.

"I hear you, Spencer," a voice said.

Matt's eyes sprang open, his hand reaching for Dämoren. He turned in his seat, looking around.

Buildings moved past the window outside. They were near the airport.

Matt allowed himself to relax. He'd fallen asleep. *More tired than I thought.*

"You all right back there?" Malcolm asked, watching him through the rearview.

"Yeah," Matt said. "Bad dream."

Malcolm gave an understanding nod. "To be expected after all this."

They entered the small airport and drove to where white and blue hangers stood lined like tents in some Roman army encampment. The Valducans' ancient airplane sat inside one of the larger ones near the back.

"Security shows none of Anya's friends came by," Malcolm said. "So we should be safe here." He wheeled the van around and backed in beside a small hatchback and beat up, green truck.

They found everyone in folding chairs, seated before a small flat-screen. Turgen sat in the middle, Luiza and Schmidt on either side. A leather-sheathed sword rested beside Schmidt. Jean's sword.

"That should not be a problem," said a voice, its loud volume implying it came through a speaker and not anyone in the room itself.

Luiza gave Matt a glancing smile and he took the seat beside hers. Allan sat at the table by the television, staring at Matt's black laptop, one of the last ones still working.

A dark-skinned Indian man stared out from the screen. Thin wisps of steel-gray hair circled his shiny bald head. His thick moustache seemed strangely large on his thin face. His sunken eyes and stubbled cheeks told that he'd been awake for too long. The man looked in Matt's direction, though not directly at him, as he sat down. A window in the lower corner of the screen showed the seated knights from the perspective of a gray, spherical web camera mounted beside Allan.

"Sonu, this is Mister Matthew Hollis," Turgen said to the screen. He turned to Matt. "Master Rangarajan is one of our Librarians."

And Ben's former mentor, Matt remembered.

Sonu gave a brief nod Matt's direction, then looked back at Turgen.

"We searched the databases on demonic mothers," Sonu said, his voice coming through the speakers. "Lilith being the most notable one. Unfortunately, the symbol does not resemble any of those from Lilith cults we've encountered, or at least of any files that Anya left available. That, of course, left us no choice but to consult the original records here. None of them, so far, depict any pictogram of a winged serpent."

"Any records we had on it would have been the first Anya burned," Turgen said. "If she hadn't destroyed them already."

"Did you check any old databases?" Allan asked. "Old backups or drives that had been offline for a while?"

"We did," Sonu said. "Unfortunately none of them predate Anya's time as a Librarian. We can assume any files or records concerning this cult were the first she removed or altered. Uwe's searching for some old disks he'd held on to, but ..." He shook his head. "It will take time."

Turgen rubbed his chin, massaging his own collection of stubble. "Any theories?"

"One," Sonu said. "The symbol bears a resemblance to ancient depictions of Tiamat, the Babylonian Goddess."

Turgen's brow rose.

"The myth is that Tiamat gave birth to monsters to sow

chaos and destruction," Sonu explained. "She was later slain by Marduk with an invincible spear."

Matt leaned toward Luiza. "I thought Tiamat was a dragon."

"Not so," Sonu said.

Matt sank into his seat, embarrassed the microphone had heard him.

"Tiamat gave birth to many different monsters," Sonu said. "Including dragons, though she was not one herself. Mythologies never describe Tiamat's form. Depictions of her vary from a winged lion, a beast with many animal heads, even a bearded woman. But some do portray her as a giant serpent."

"And you believe the symbol on the medallions is her?" Malcolm asked.

"That is my theory," Sonu said.

"If that is all we have then we will continue to explore it," Turgen said. "Good work."

The Librarian gave a terse smile.

"I look forward to seeing you," Turgen continued. "Let us know if you find anything more."

"I will," Sonu said.

Turgen motioned to Allan and the screen went green.

"We're going to India?" Luc asked.

"No," Turgen answered. "They should arrive here in two days. After that, we will pack whatever effects we can, and leave. The chateau is no longer safe."

"Where are we going?" Luc asked.

"Not we. *You* are going to Italy. Sonu checked the information on the man you killed, Alessio Brunelli. He was scheduled to fly into Florence yesterday."

"Florence," Matt said, searching his memory. "That's where Anya went to school."

The old man nodded. "As did Signor Brunelli. He lived in an apartment there until last year. His current address is a postal box." He smiled. "Mister Havlock, please bring up the picture."

Allan clicked on the laptop.

"Sonu searched old blog and networking sites for our friend, and found this," Turgen said, gesturing to the screen.

Matt found himself staring at an image of six people, all in their twenties, he guessed, sitting at a cafe table, holding glasses of wine. Three were men, the others women, but not sitting as couples. One of them, a much younger man in a blue and white striped button up shirt, looked familiar.

"The man from the museum," Luc said. "The prisoner."

"May he burn in Hell," Malcolm growled under his breath.

"Another classmate?" Matt asked.

"Not that we know," Turgen replied. "However, he was living in the city at the time."

"Not much of a lead," Luiza said. "Florence is a big place and there's no guarantee they'll stay there."

Turgen sighed. "It's all we have. The lunar eclipse is in two weeks and it will cover that area. The weapons might not be destroyed until then. We don't know what they plan to summon, but if it is some kind of demon mother, we must stop it. Malcolm, I want you to lead them. Luc, Luiza, Allan, and Matt will accompany you."

Malcolm nodded. "And where will you be going?"

Turgen held up a hand. "I believe it best not to say. If one of you should be corrupted, then the secret will be known to our enemies. We are too fragile at the moment to hold them back should they come for the surviving weapons. We will communicate with the new phones Luc purchased until Sonu can build a fresh network for us."

"I understand," Malcolm said.

Schmidt drew a long breath. "Alex, I wish to accompany them."

Turgen turned to Schmidt, his brows raised in a puzzled expression. "You what?"

"I would like to go to Florence with them," Schmidt said, flatly.

The knights' eyes all moved apprehensively away from the old man.

"Max," Turgen said carefully. "I don't think that is a good idea."

"We can search more effectively the more people we have. Lukrasus is still bonded to me; you know that never goes away.

Now that Jean is gone, I am her protector and she is calling me to act."

"You retired, Max," Turgen said. "Ten years ago."

"And I have regretted it every day since."

Turgen crossed his hand over his lap. "You are seventy-three years old. You are out of practice."

"That does not make me an invalid," Schmidt said, his blue eyes hard. "I can defend myself. Malcolm and the others can stay to the front line, but I can help find them."

"Max, you are my friend. Please, I need you. You have more knowledge of our needs and assets than anyone else. We need that knowledge to survive. One of our knights must stay with us in case Anya's people attack us again. If you go, then someone else stays. I need you here."

Schmidt swallowed then nodded.

After a tense, but brief silence, Turgen turned to Malcolm. "How quickly can your team leave for Florence?"

Malcolm looked at the others. "We will need to restock weapons and supplies. It's a long drive. We can leave by this evening."

FROM THE JOURNAL OF SIR ERNEST BURROWS

1873

23 June - *I have arrived in Paris and found the shop of Célestin Dumonthier. He is an agreeable man, and became very excited at my plans. I expressed my desire for all of Dämoren to be used in the pistol's creation, as well as incorporating the Boxer cartridge. Dumonthier showed me several of his pieces, as well as those of his competitors, asking me which features I wanted most. When he asked if I would leave Dämoren in his care I explained that it was not possible. I told him Dämoren was a treasured heirloom and that I would spend my entire fortune and more to see her rebuilt. He understood and has invited me to stay with him and his brother until the task is complete.*

3 July - *Dumonthier is a genius. He has designed the gun from my dreams. Seven-shot, using an attached ejecting rod, unlike his cutlass pistol. The bronze of Dämoren's quillons will be used for the cartridges. Like Watson, Dumonthier insists Dämoren's older steel is not strong enough for the barrel, but quickly ceased his protests when I told him it was not negotiable.*

7 July - *Dumonthier demonstrated today that a barrel made solely of Dämoren's steel cannot work. A barrel made from sword steel he estimated to be the same quality as hers, shattered on the second shot. With much reluctance I have agreed to have finer-quality*

metal mixed with Dämoren's to make a more suitable pistol. Still, he has agreed to use all of Dämoren's steel, using much of it in the tools required for loading. Somehow I fear that despite his insistence, much more of her blade will be used for these tools than for the gun itself.

11 July - Today has been a most trying day. Dumonthier melted much of Dämoren's blade in his shop, and while I know in my heart that this is necessary, I cannot help but wonder if I am simply desecrating her. I forced myself to watch, to be with her. I will not leave her side, no matter how much it may pain me. The Frenchman was sympathetic, seeing my reaction. I think he suspects her true importance to me.

14 July - Dumonthier bored the barrel today. Without my prompting, he gathered all the shavings for later use.

22 July - Dämoren's frame is complete. Today Dumonthier introduced me to an engraver named Cassel. Cassel is a small man, almost child-like in stature. Dumonthier insists he is the most capable man for the task.

The papers reported a most gruesome killing in Loriet. A pair of children were torn apart by some animal. It is the second killing in as many months. Once, such reports would hasten me to investigate further, but I find myself impotent to act.

30 July - Dämoren has thirty completed cartridges. Her bullet mould and press should be finished in a few days.

Cassel hides in the corner chiseling Dämoren, but refuses to let me watch. It is maddening, but Dumonthier defends him. Cassel is a religious man. This morning I overheard him singing psalms while working and it comforts me to know that a man of God is decorating her, even if he is infuriating.

6 August - Cassel has engraved the cartridges and tools. I now

understand Dumonthier's recommendation of him. His work is magnificent. He says Dämoren's gold leaf is almost complete. I yearn to touch her again.

11 August - *This morning Dumonthier presented me with Dämoren. I cannot describe the joy, her beauty. On holding her I could feel my mistress still inside. She lives!*

He honored me with the offer of her first shot. Under his guidance, I moulded the bullet of the finest silver, and while Dumonthier was not observing, I mixed several flakes of my own dried blood into her powder. This is my sacrifice, my tribute.

I thanked Dumonthier for his work, and generously paid him for his hospitality and for any documentation he had made of Dämoren. He pleaded that we test a shot before I leave, but I refused. Dämoren's first shot shall be in combat.

I suspect a werewolf is terrorizing Loiret. I ride now to meet it. Either Dämoren shall slay the beast, or I shall die as the madman who killed and defiled her remains.

CHAPTER 16

A short, orange truck raced down the narrow street, its chrome rear-view whooshing inches past Matt's ear. The raised walkways along Florence's stone streets took some getting used to. The locals navigated the ancient city's cramped thoroughfares with a confidence and speed that would make a stunt driver wince. Pedestrians and motorists never slowed for one another, but somehow moved in perfect synchronicity like gears inside some bizarre clockwork machine.

The smell of fresh pastries wafted down the canyon streets as bakeries prepared for the morning's tide of tourists. Matt jogged down the little path, Luiza a few feet ahead of him. The sidewalk was no more than eighteen inches across, building facades on one side, and hurried commuters on the other, forcing them to remain single-file. It made it inconvenient to talk for their morning jogs, but the view of the knight's tight rear inside those running shorts was at least some consolation.

Sweat ran down Matt's face and neck. Luiza was running him a lot harder than normal and keeping up was becoming a real problem. He suspected her frustration at their lack of progress was the culprit for today's chase. Matt swallowed, trying to ease the dry tickle in his throat. Pink water sloshed inside the bottle in his hand, teasing his thirst. In the dozen days since coming to Florence, Matt had lost count of how many blood compasses he'd made. Every morning he made new ones for everyone, refreshing them again in the evenings and late hours of night.

They had scoured every part of the city, Anya's school, her old apartment, and haunts, finding no signs of her people, not even a single demon. They'd searched outlying villages, and nearby cities. Twice, Matt had gone to Siena. Allan and Luc had taken the train to Bologna. Three days prior, Malcolm had gone off to Rome with a compass, though its potency once he'd arrived would have diminished to maybe thirty feet; a dangerously short distance when trying to track a demon. However, Malcolm's creepy beetle tattoo would help. Every time, they'd come back with nothing. It was like chasing shadows.

Luiza turned at the next intersection and Matt followed her around the corner. A few blocks later the street opened up into a large plaza. Reaching their cool-off spot, Luiza slowed to a brisk walk as she passed a statue of a mounted rider.

Matt caught up with her as she reached a marble fountain of Poseidon, staring down over the plaza. A pair of middle-aged women in oversized plastic sunglasses stood before it, snapping pictures.

"You running from something," Matt panted. "Or late for a date with the fish god, here?"

She swigged from her water bottle and shook her head. "Just … frustrated. We're running out of time."

Matt held out his hand for the bottle, which she gave him. He squeezed a gulp down and sighed. "We knew it was a long shot. Maybe Allan and Malcolm will find something in Pisa today."

Luiza wiped the sweat from her face and frowned. "If the cultists were going to Pisa they'd have just flown there. They came *here*. So where are they?"

"Wish I knew," Matt said, leading her past the fountain. They passed a crowd of giggling girls circled before a towering marble copy of the David. An open-air sculpture gallery rested across from it. He stopped before a green figure of Perseus, sword in one hand, severed head of Medusa in the other. Bronze blood and gore hung from the gorgon's neck.

"You know there are lots of other statues to admire," Luiza said. "You don't have to keep looking at the same one every day."

Matt shrugged. "Schmidt had told me that Perseus's sword was a holy weapon and Medusa was a demon. In a way, Perseus was one of us."

"At least *we* get to wear clothes," she said.

He grinned. "True."

"Come on." Luiza motioned her head to the side. "Let's get back."

"You go on ahead."

Luiza gave him a look. "The boys will be leaving soon and will need some of your compasses."

"Made them this morning when I did this one." Matt held up the pink-filled sports drink bottle. He offered it to her. "Here. Go on back to the hotel. I'll catch you at breakfast."

She took the bottle, hesitant, as if accepting it made her an accomplice or something. "Are you all right?"

"Yeah." He scanned the open plaza. A couple of the street vendors wheeled out their little carts of postcards and cheap trinkets. His *little purchase* should be ready by now. But he couldn't get it with Luiza around. "Just want to think about some stuff. Clear my head."

"All right," she said, her chocolate eyes still probing. "Don't take too long. You have your phone?"

Matt nodded, turning back to the bronze sculpture. Luc had picked them all up fresh disposables the day they'd left for Florence. New numbers Anya wouldn't know or be able to track. "I'll be fine. I'll see you in a bit."

He studied the statue as Luiza left. There was a time when demon hunters were heroes. Men with monuments and legends, not pseudo-criminals hiding from the world's notice. What would it have been like to be honored by kings?

Once Matt was sure Luiza was gone, he turned and left the plaza. He followed the streets, turning alongside the river that cut through the city. Ahead, a bridge spanned the canal, its deck bulging with tan and yellow buildings. Some were slung so far off the sides that Matt questioned their safety. He walked toward it.

As he drew closer he passed an ancient iron ring affixed to the riverside wall, probably used to tie up horses once, he guessed. Dozens of padlocks hung from the rusty hoop, many linked through each other into a bulbous lump. Some were engraved, others initialed in faded marker. A few feet later, he passed another, this one completely buried beneath locks. It was almost organic, as if they'd grown there like brass and silver barnacles. One tour guide Matt had eavesdropped on said lovers did that as a way to eternalize their commitment. Matt figured that it was a more tasteful expression than the American method, which was spray painting names on an overpass.

Turning onto the bridge, he passed several tiny shops, their doors and windows still shuttered. Matt stepped into an arched alcove and waited.

A herd of tourists shuffled past. Their guide, a busty woman with thick black hair and stiletto heels, led the way, carrying a slender stick with a bright green cloth tied to the end so her flock could find her. She walked in quick bursts, then stopping every thirty or so feet to allow the procession enough time too *ooh* and *aah* as they caught up.

Eventually, he spied a woman with short, graying hair work her way through the growing crowd. She unlocked one of the shop doors and slipped inside. A minute later she came back out and began lowering the dark wood shutters from the windows.

"Good morning," she said, as Matt approached.

"Good morning," he replied. "Is it done?"

The woman smiled. "Finished it last night." She led him in to the tiny store, cramped with glass cases of gold and silver jewelry.

Matt admired several of the pieces. Their hefty prices might discourage some, but there were still more than enough customers hungry for real Ponte Vecchio gold to warrant the inflation. He would know. He was one of them.

"Here we are," the jeweler said, opening a black velvet box and removing a pendant with a long chain. She held it out, as if offering a scepter to a king.

Matt took it. A diamond-shaped shard of polished steel rested in the pendant's center, framed by a border of twisted gold, reminiscent of Feinluna's ornate hilt. The broken sword's name appeared at the bottom, etched perfectly along the curving frame. It was beautiful.

"Is that how you wanted it?" the woman asked.

What the fuck am I doing? Matt thought. He'd been so sure

of himself. Spent three gold coins for it. Clay's coins. Matt had never cashed one until now. He'd thought the gesture sweet, but now, holding the pendant, he doubted his plan. What did he think Luiza would say to a gift like that? It would be like losing a child and having someone fashion their severed finger as a gift to the grieving parent.

"It's exactly as I asked for." Matt forced a smile. "Excellent work."

The jeweler woman thanked him, then coiled the chain back into its case and placed it into a shiny black paper bag. Matt walked out, trying to mask his growing dread and headed back to the hotel.

After a shower and a change of clothes, Matt found his way to the hotel's dining room. His hand rested on the black laptop bag slung over his shoulder. He could feel Dämoren through the padded leather. The Ingram was inside as well, separated by a thin dividing wall. The machinegun's giant suppressor was too long to fit if attached. Matt had cut the stitching along the side of the bag, creating a narrow gap big enough to get his hand through. He prayed he wouldn't need it, but if things got bad, he could shove his hand in, and fire Dämoren from inside the case. He could shoot the Ingram, too, if needed, but hot brass bouncing around inside the tight bag with his hand in there sounded more like punishment than a tactical advantage.

Luiza sat at a small table on the far side of the room, her back to the wall. A long, nylon bag rested beside her, "Canon" embroidered in red along its side. Matt had initially thought any attempts to carry a sword in public would be too noticeable. Of course no one would suspect a katana was inside the tripod cover. They'd suspect a gun, or at least he would have. But after seeing the amount of high-end camera equipment some tourists lugged around, he conceded Akumanokira's urban camouflage was pretty effective.

"Took you long enough." She stirred her tiny cup of coffee.

Matt took a seat. The bulge from the pendant's case suddenly felt huge in his pocket. "Sorry."

"You just missed the boys. Luc followed Malcolm and Allan

to the train station. I think he's getting restless. When he gets back, Malcolm wants us to go to Sesto."

Matt rolled his eyes. "Again?"

She shrugged. "Several of Anya's people lived there."

"Yeah, two years ago."

"Do you have any other ideas?"

"No." Matt sighed.

After a waiter came over and filled his coffee, Matt helped himself to the remnants at the buffet table. He ate quietly as Luiza fidgeted with her tablet computer, marking a map for their day's journey. A television blathered on from the wall beside him, its volume low enough it wouldn't disturb any conversations, but too low for anyone actually interested to hear much of anything.

Matt sipped his coffee, his eyes unconsciously moving to the screen's flickering colors. The image was of several reporters fighting to get their microphones before a man in a pale blue suit. Lines of forced calmness and sincerity marked the interviewee's face. The screen changed to a photograph of two green and white buses, "Tuscia Tours" blazoned on their sides in orange and gold. He couldn't read the foreign words along the side of the screen but, leaning closer, he managed to hear most of the news report over the clinks of silverware and low murmurs from the other diners.

"Owners first became concerned when the tour failed to return at nine thirty last night," said the announcer's voice over. "Neither the driver or guide responded to calls."

"You see this?" Matt asked.

"What?" Luiza asked, looking up from her screen.

"A local tour bus is missing," he said, remembering she couldn't understand Italian. "Tuscan day trip. Supposed to come back last night, but didn't."

The image changed again to a map of the Tuscan countryside. A winding path, highlighted in bright red, followed the roads from Florence to San Gimignano, Siena, and through several little villages.

"Missing?"

"Yeah." Matt leaned closer, straining to hear the announcer's voice. "Twenty-eight people, including the driver and guide. Says they made it to San Gimignano, but no one knows after that."

She snorted. "How can no one know?"

Matt nodded. "They said the buses all have GPS, but authorities are still trying to get the last coordinates." The news story ended, changing to a weather update. Matt looked at Luiza. "That might be worth checking into."

"A missing tour bus?"

"You can't just *lose a bus*. They're huge. No one on board has made a call? The GPS tracking doesn't work?"

"You said the authorities were ..." Luiza's eyes widened. "If the police don't have the GPS info already, then something's wrong."

Matt downed his coffee. "Exactly. The eclipse is tomorrow and a busload of people coincidently ups and vanishes."

"No harm in checking it out. What was the tour company's name?"

"Tuscia Tours."

Luiza typed the name into her computer. "Here we go." She tapped the screen, selecting a language. "Due to recent events, all tours are cancelled until further notice."

"Any street address for them?" Matt asked.

Her finger scrolled along the page. "Not seeing it. Places like this usually just take payment online and pick you up somewhere. We'll probably have to call them to find out where they are."

Matt's phone rang. He pulled it out, leaving the pendant case in his pocket and checked the screen. Luc.

He answered it. "Yeah?"

"I think I found something," Luc rumbled.

Matt grinned. "Let me guess. Missing tour bus."

Luc paused. "Tour bus?"

"Yeah, a tour bus went missing last night. Why? What did you find?"

"I'm standing on the street looking at that symbol right now."

Matt straightened up. "The cult symbol?"

Luiza's gaze lifted up from her screen.

"Yes," Luc said. "I found it."

"What is it?" Luiza asked.

"Luc," Matt answered, holding the receiver away from his mouth.

"He found the symbol."

CHAPTER 17

They found Luc standing on a corner beside a tightly packed row of parked scooters. Luc peered down the narrow lane. He wore an old fashioned green backpack. His heavy, flanged mace left an irregular bulge where it pressed against the pack's leather bottom.

Luc turned as Matt and Luiza approached.

"Got here as fast as we could," Matt said.

Luc returned his attention to the other street.

Matt followed his gaze. The narrow road, pressed between three-story buildings, extended a little over a block before curving out of view. Black iron bars of various styles encased all the first floor windows on either side, relics left from Tuscan house wars. Open shutters framed the upper windows. "What are you looking at?"

"Third door on the right," Luc said, subtly pointing that direction.

Squinting, Matt peered at the dark wooden door about forty feet away. Thick stone molding outlined the entrance, blackened by years of soot and exhaust. "What am *I* looking at?"

"Top middle." Luc glanced around. "I haven't seen anyone. Go. Look closer."

Matt checked his compass. Still pink.

He motioned to Luiza, and they made their way down the alley. He tried to look casual, hand resting on his bag just above the access slit. Luiza walked beside him. The street was too small for even a sidewalk.

A monstrous bronze knocker stared out from the center of the door, sculpted like a lion's head. The ring in its mouth formed two women curving down to an etched sphere in their outstretched hands. Matt's gaze moved up to the top of the door. The stone border was chipped and worn, its carved details eroded nearly away. At the center above the door, the molding blossomed into the shape of an oval shield, held up by a pair of winged creatures. An elaborate fleur-de-lis adorned the right upper section of the shield.

Matt stopped.

A long, winged serpent, its feminine head raised as if to strike, decorated the oval's bottom.

It's been here the whole damned time.

Luiza removed a gray camera from her bag and turned it on.

"What are you doing?" Matt hissed. He scanned the streets on either side. A teenage girl walked up the street a block away, her attention apparently hostage to the phone in her hands.

"If they've seen us, then we've already been seen." The camera whirred, its lens telescoping out. It beeped, snapping a picture. "Otherwise we're just another pair of tourists photographing every door in the city."

If Anya's people were inside they'd know what every one of the knights looked like. Did they know they'd followed them to Florence? Matt glanced back at the girl. She was getting closer.

The sharp click came from the door. Matt's fingers slid into the bag, finding Dämoren's ivory grip.

The door pulled open and a slender man with thinning hair stepped out. He glanced at Matt and Luiza standing just a few feet in front of him. No acknowledgement. No familiarity. He reached into his pocket.

Matt cocked Dämoren.

The man withdrew a ring of jingling keys and turned to lock the door behind him.

Matt ground his teeth. Either this man was an incredible actor, or simply a local seeing some tourists outside his house. Luiza was giving him a "What do we do" look. Matt glanced at Luc still at the end of the street, standing a bit straighter than he had a moment ago.

The full moon was a day away. There wasn't time for caution.

"Excuse me sir," Matt said in Italian, no idea where he was going with it. "Is this your home?"

The man turned, giving Matt a puzzled look. "Yes."

"My name is Walter Franks. I'm an author." Removing his hand from the bag, Matt gestured to the symbol above the door. "I noticed the crest above your door and wasn't familiar with it."

The man looked up to where Matt pointed.

Luiza shot Matt a wide-eyed look. "What are you doing?" she mouthed.

"Play along," he whispered back in English. Matt looked to the man. "I'm writing a book on Florentine heraldry and happened to see that. Do you know what family it is?"

"My mother said it was an old family. Barugni or something. I don't know."

"Your mother knows?" Matt asked. "Could we contact her? I'm very interested to know more about it."

The man's mouth opened in hesitation. He held up a hand. "I'm sorry, I don't think—"

"I will pay for your time, of course," Matt said, reaching for his wallet. "Will one hundred be enough, Mister ..."

The man's hand lowered. "Celestini."

Matt withdrew a hundred euro note. "Mister Celestini, I would very much like to add this crest to our catalog. Might we speak with your mother about it?"

The man smiled. "Yes. Please, call me Gianni. I'm sure she would love to speak with an interested author. Could she call you tomorrow?"

Matt gave an exaggerated wince. "Unfortunately my associate and I have to be in Rome tomorrow." He slid another hundred partially out from his wallet. "Could you help us now?"

Gianni's smile widened. All teeth. "Of course. Please, come inside." He turned to unlock the door.

"What did you say to him?" Luiza hissed, low and sharp.

"I told him about the book we're doing on lost heraldic symbols. He said his mother knows the history of it."

"His mother?"

"Yeah." Matt pulled the phone from his pocket and called Luc.

Gianni opened the door and gestured Matt and Luiza inside.

"Yes?" Luc answered, his tone curious.

"Hi Alexi," Matt said in French, holding a finger up to Gianni. "Look, something came up and we'll be a little late. Just stay there and listen to the presentation for me. We shouldn't be too long." Before Luc could speak, Matt turned the phone's speaker down as low as it could go and slipped it, still on, into his pocket. *Please don't hang up.* Smiling, he motioned Luiza, *After you,* and they followed Gianni inside.

"Mama?" Gianni said closing the door.

Matt swallowed, his hand resting on his bag. The house smelled vaguely of lavender and old pipe smoke. A red and white vase rested on the entry table beside them, the leaves of its artificial flowers slightly faded. A metal crucifix adorned the opposite wall. *A good sign.*

"Yes, dear?" a woman's voice called from further inside.

They followed Gianni through a tiny living room and into a creamcolored kitchen painted with yellow flowers. Matt could see a little courtyard through the window. An old woman sat at a narrow table in a side nook, hunkered over a printed word puzzle. She looked up, pencil still in her hand.

"Mama," Gianni said. "These people would like to talk to you. They're writing a book and have some questions about the markings on the door."

Matt offered his hand. "Walter Franks, ma'am. This is my partner ... Maria Estrada."

She shook his hand. Her old skin felt like tissue paper. She motioned them to sit. "Are you Tuscan?"

"Me?" Matt said, taking a seat. "No, ma'am, I'm American."

She smiled warmly. "Your accent is Tuscan. I would have guessed you local."

"Thank you, ma'am."

"Please, call me Zita. Gian," she said, to her son. "Bring something for our guests. Coffee?"

"Yes, please," Matt said.

Gianni hurried over to the coffee machine in the corner.

Matt shifted his bag onto his lap below the table. "Zita, as your son said, I am writing a book about lost family crests in

Italy. I noticed the symbol above your door and didn't recognize it. Gianni said you might know something about it."

The old woman nodded and pushed her puzzle aside. "That is the Barugnani family crest. They built the original house in 1601. Of course, it was very different back then." She smiled. "Bombings destroyed the back part during the war. The front stonework is still original."

"Barugnani?" Matt repeated loud enough to hope Luc could hear him. He didn't have any notepad in his satchel and wouldn't have risked opening it if he did. Not with Dämoren and a machine pistol inside. "Can I have your tablet?" he asked Luiza.

She removed the computer from her bag and turned it on.

"How do you spell that?" Matt asked Zita. He tapped the letters in as she did.

Gianni set a pair of tiny white cups on the table, their foamy contents dusted with cocoa.

"How long have you lived here?" Matt asked.

"I grew up in this house," Zita said. "My grandfather was the first of my family to live here."

"So you are not related to the Barugnani family?"

"Oh no," she laughed. "That family has been gone for a long time."

"Gone?" Matt asked.

She nodded. "Gian, go upstairs and bring us my family box. The gray one."

The thin man obediently hurried away.

"I have all the information on them with our genealogy records," Zita said. "A hobby I picked up from my mother." She motioned to the coffees. "Please drink, Gian will only be a minute."

Matt and Luiza shared a look. A tension in her lips told him "*no*," but he didn't want to offend the old woman, not when she could help them.

He took a sip. It tasted good. Not as good as the hotel's or even Luiza's at the chateau. He didn't notice any tang of poison, not that he really knew what to taste for. Malcolm claimed the snake tattoo on his arm could warn him of poisons, and Matt really wished he was here now. *Never thought I'd wish for that.*

"So you research your family tree?" Matt asked, hoping to distract the old woman from the fact Luiza wasn't drinking.

"Yes," she said. "At least I used to. Haven't looked at it in several years. It's a bit exciting."

"Really?" Matt asked.

"Oh yes. Lots of secrets come out." Her eyes gleamed mischievously. "Scandals your family never knew or didn't tell you."

"I can imagine." He pursed his lips. "So if you're not related to the Barugnani family, why research them?"

"Once you've found all about your own family that you can, you still need something to research." She shrugged. "My mother found a few papers during the restoration, so I added to them. The house is part of our family so … I decided to learn where it came from."

Footsteps clomped down the stairs and Gianni came in carrying a gray, plastic file box. "This one?"

"Yes," Zita said. "Bring it here."

Grunting, Gianni heaved it into an empty chair beside the old woman and opened it. Dozens of yellow folders, each labeled in crisp black writing and packed with papers, filled the box.

"Here we go," Zita said, flipping through the bent tabs. She removed a thin folder and opened it on the table. "The Barugnani family."

"What do you know about them?" Matt asked, leaning closer.

The old woman squinted over the page, running her finger along the text. "It was an old family. Merchants, but not very important. In … 1578 Guittone Barugnani gained favor with the Medici's who *encouraged* a marriage with Imalda Veronesi. Her dowry made the family very rich. In 1580 she gave birth to their only son, Marco. Guittone died of a sudden illness in 1593, leaving thirteen-year-old Marco head of the family."

Zita leaned closer. "Marco Barugnani, now there was a scoundrel. He was said to be beautiful and quite brilliant. His rivals also had a tendency of dying. They said that no woman, or man, could refuse his charm. Eventually rumors of scandal became too much and he chose to leave Florence and founded the village of San Pettiro in 1608."

"What rumors?" Matt asked.

"Oh, many," Zita said. "Some said he had seduced the Grand Duchess, even fathering one of her children. Others branded him a devil worshiper. And instead of punishment or assassination, do you know what the Grand Duke did?"

Devil worshiper? Matt shrugged.

"He gave him title and a village to rule."

Matt snorted. "That was generous."

Zita gave a small smile. "Grand Duke Fernando the First died the following year."

"So the crest?" Matt asked. "That was Marco's crest, or the family crest from before his title?"

Zita flipped through several pages, finally stopping at one, and offering it to Matt. The foreign words meant nothing to him, though the grainy photocopy of a shield blazoned with a styled fleur-de-lis was understandable.

"That crest was the family's. Marco added the basilisk," Zita said.

"So what happened to Marco?" Matt asked, sliding the page to Luiza.

"He ruled San Pettiro for several years, but eventually rumors came out that Marco was a devil worshiper and had kidnapped several local girls. Tales of his wickedness reached Rome and Inquisitors were sent."

"They tried him?" Matt asked.

Zita shook her head. "No. When they arrived at his castle, they found Marco Barugnani and his household had all been gruesomely murdered."

"Murdered? By whom?"

The old woman gave a small shrug. "No one knows. Maybe the families of the missing girls. Political rivals, perhaps."

Matt rubbed his chin. Something about Zita's story seemed familiar. He looked at Luiza, sitting quietly beside him. She watched him, her expression blank. Her understanding of Italian was rudimentary at best. She'd be lucky if she understood a third of the conversation. "What year did that happen?"

Zita checked her notes. "July of 1628."

Matt typed the date and a few notes into the computer. Maybe Allan or Malcolm might make more of it. He stared at the screen, trying to think of any more questions. "Could I make a copy of your notes on the Barugnani Family? I promise I will give you credit in my book."

The old woman's eyes widened, excited. "Oh! Of course you may. It's just … I don't have another copy to give out."

"That's all right." Matt spread the pages out and using Luiza's tablet, photographed them one at a time. *Allan's going to love this.* "Thank you, Zita. I promise I'll give you credit for all your work." Matt took her name and information. Once finished, he handed Luiza back her computer and gave the signal it was time to leave.

They stood. Gianni swooped in from across the kitchen to help clean. Matt hadn't paid the other hundred yet. Now Gianni was hovering about, making sure he was noticed.

"It was good to meet you," Zita said. "Maybe next time you are in Tuscany you can visit Marco's castle."

Matt blinked, his mouth open. "Marco's castle?"

"In San Pettiro. Someone bought it a few years ago and has been restoring it. I think it will be a bed and breakfast once it's complete."

"I'll be sure to visit it," Matt said, smiling broadly. Shouldering his satchel, he and Luiza made their way toward the door. He offered Gianni a folded hundred-euro bill. "Thank you for your time."

The balding man snatched it with his index and middle fingers, curling it into his hand like a street magician performing a trick. "Be sure you credit my mother what she's due."

"I will." Matt stepped out into the street, quickly spotting Luc at the corner, phone still pressed to his ear. He and Luiza started toward the black knight as Gianni's door closed behind them.

"What was that about?" Luc asked, pocketing the phone.

"Just a hunch," Matt said. "Did you hear us?"

Luc frowned. "Not very well."

"What did she say, Matt?" Luiza asked. "I heard Medici,

murders, something about devil worship. I can't believe you drank that coffee. What if that was poisoned?"

"Then you or Luc would have been there to save me."

She shot him a cold stare. "That's not funny. You walked into a house with that symbol on it and *drank* something a stranger gave you."

"I'm sorry," Matt said. "It was a risk."

Luiza shook her head and turned away.

"So what did you find?" Luc asked.

"I think I found our cult."

Luc and Luiza both looked at him.

"Where?" Luiza asked.

"San Pettiro. Find out where that is." Matt drew the phone from his pocket and speed dialed a number.

Malcolm answered on the second ring. "Yes?"

"It's Matt. Where are you?"

"A few minutes outside Pontedera," Malcolm said, his voice confused.

"Okay," Matt said. "Stop there and come back."

"Why?"

"I think I found them."

"What? Where?"

"San Pettiro." Matt leaned to see the map screen in Luiza's hand. "Hold that. You and Allan go back to Empoli. We'll pick you up there and drive to San Pettiro."

"All right," Malcolm said. "How do you know they're there?"

"I don't." Matt noticed San Gimignano, where the missing tour bus was last seen, was only a few miles away. "But I've got enough that we need to check it."

CHAPTER 18

They found Allan and Malcolm outside the Empoli train station. Malcolm wore a straw fedora and a tan long-sleeve shirt that covered his tattoos. He said it helped him blend in as a tourist. Matt thought the sleeves in the summer just made him stand out.

Luc pulled into the drive. Malcolm nodded and tapped Allan, engrossed in his laptop, on the shoulder.

Luc slowed to a stop as the two knights picked up their gear and hurried across the lot to the car. Clutching their instrument cases, Allan's black and Malcolm's worn and brown, they could have been in a band or maybe old-time mobsters with Malcolm's hat and all.

"Good timing," Malcolm said, sliding into the back seat beside Matt. "We just got here."

Allan squeezed in after Malcolm.

"You find anything on that info I got?" Matt asked.

"Oddly, yeah," Allan said, beaming. "Enough that I think you're right."

"Well." Luiza checked her map screen in the front seat. "We should be in San Pettiro in half an hour. What do you have?"

Allan clicked his seatbelt as Luc pulled the car out and started back onto the road. "To start, there's no record of a Marco Barugnani in any of the records."

"Not surprising," Matt said. "Anya would have deleted it."

"Precisely," Allan said, opening his laptop. "So I searched for other things that might link to him. Things she either couldn't delete or wouldn't have thought to look for. Specific years, other names, and that type of thing. One passage came up that I found particularly interesting." He clicked the keyboard.

"Sir Isidore Vidal wrote a note about a known cambion named Marco *Barugnano* who was an Italian lord, but also ..." He grinned. "Tried to summon a *black demonic goddess b*efore the Order killed him and his *demonic cult* in 1628."

Matt slapped his thigh, an important piece of the puzzle clicking into place. "I remember reading that. I thought Zita's story sounded familiar."

"So why didn't Anya delete it?" Luiza asked.

"Because the name is misspelled," Allan said. "Either Sir Vidal wrote it wrong, or the Librarian who translated it, or even whoever then transcribed it into the database. Whichever it was, Anya didn't find it. I searched the rest of the records and found no other mention of a Barugnano. No knight's journal reports, nothing. Just this one note. But that was enough to get me digging deeper. There was a lunar eclipse over Tuscany in July of that year."

"Same month the Inquisitors found Marco murdered," Matt said.

Allan nodded. "Additionally, two knights were killed about that time. No record how it happened, but one sacred weapon was catalogued in the Valducan orphan inventory the following month, and another was inherited by Sir Ignacio Perdomo, after his master's funeral. No mention how he died. Bit odd."

"What about weapons?" Malcolm asked. "Any vanish or destroyed in the preceding months?"

Allan made a face and clicked his keyboard. "Let me check."

Malcolm turned to the others. "Did you see the news on the missing bus?"

"Yeah," Matt said, a slight pang that Malcolm had mentioned it first. "Twenty-eight people vanish the night before a demonic ceremony?"

Malcolm nodded. "San Pettiro wasn't exactly on its route, but close enough."

Luc steered the car around a tight bend. "If they did kidnap them, we can stop the ceremony if we find them first. Take away their sacrifice."

"Not a bad idea," Luiza added. "Buy us enough time to the next eclipse if nothing else."

"We'd have to find them first," Malcolm said. "I'd rather take care of Anya and this cult of hers and put an end to it."

Luc eyed him through the rear-view. "But if we don't get that option …"

"I agree," Malcolm said. "If we get the chance to free them, we will, but delaying these bastards means they'll only do it again. We need to end this, not prolong it."

Luc's eyes remained on Malcolm until the road drew them away.

Matt guessed the question in the enormous hunter's gaze. Would Malcolm sacrifice twenty-eight innocent people if it meant killing Marco Barugnani's cult? Matt could guess the answer, too. Yes.

He'd watched the way Malcolm had killed those people back at the mine. No remorse. Matt understood the idea. It was Clay's only lesson that Matt had never accepted. Kill some to save many. How many innocent people would die if the demons summoned whatever dark mother they served? Hundreds? Thousands? Cold and honest math, but seeing the worlds as simple numbers wasn't human.

Clay's humanity once led him to save two people from a house fire while a vampire escaped. By the time he'd tracked it down, it had killed nine victims, two of which were children. Something in him broke that night. Died. Matt wondered what horror had killed Malcolm's humanity.

"Interesting," Allan said.

"What?" Matt asked, hoping for uplifting news.

"The Order's log of holy weapons shows no changes between 1628 and 1629."

Malcolm frowned. "Anya could have deleted the records. Hidden the discrepancy."

"Possible," Allan said. "But I checked them ten years each way. No weapons were lost in that period. I doubt she could have hidden it so well over such a spread. You have to remember, the Order only had twenty weapons at the time, twenty-one at the end. Losing any would have been difficult to hide."

Malcolm ran a hand across his stubbled chin and upper lip, his gaze set on some distant thing only he could see. "Theories?"

Allan shrugged weakly. "Either they sacrificed weapons that were not under the Order's care or they didn't sacrifice any at all."

Malcolm nodded, still staring at the invisible thing. "The Order's knights stopped the ceremony. Four hundred years later they try it again, this time set on destroying us first. Retaliation." He turned to Allan, then Matt. "Preemptive. They did it to draw us out. Kill us before we could stop them."

"Then if sacrificing the weapons isn't necessary for a summoning," Matt said. "What's to prevent them from breaking them now?"

"Let's just hope they haven't," Luc said.

It was after 2:00 when they reached San Pettiro. The bright sun beat down on the tiny village, bleaching the stucco and stone walls in shades of yellow and white. The town consisted of no more than fifty buildings, most two-story, nestled at the foot of a steep hill. Atop it, an enormous orange-roofed villa stood, looking out over the valley of vineyards and farmland.

Matt checked the blood compass in his lap as Luc guided the car down the narrow road into the village. A disappointed weight settled in his chest at seeing the still-pink water. *No. They have to be here.*

A few locals walked the streets, or sat at one of two outside cafes. No one seemed particularly interested as the hunters' car rolled past. A good sign. Matt searched their faces for Anya or any of the others from the old photograph. Unsuccessful, he scanned the old buildings for more signs of Marco Barugnani's demon cult, finding none.

Malcolm leaned over Luc's shoulder. "Try to get us closer to the castle. Maybe we'll get a hit on Matt's compass." He pointed to a cobbled street snaking behind the shops toward the hill. "There."

Luc steered the sedan around the bend, working up the hill. Matt watched the bottle, praying for a bead.

After passing a few tiny buildings precariously perched along the slope, they came to a metal gate blocking a manicured road leading further up to the villa. A blue sign with white writing stood beside the closed entrance.

"Castello di Pettiro," Allan read aloud. "Opening next spring."

Matt peered through the iron bars, up the cypress-lined path to the near-hidden villa. "Too far for the compass to pick anything up. Don't suppose they'd mind letting us in for a closer look?"

Luiza snorted. "I doubt it."

"Didn't think so."

She motioned to a blocky white camera mounted on the gate. "They've got eyes on the door."

Malcolm grumbled. "Keep driving. Don't want to draw attention."

Luc let off the brake and continued up the winding road along the hillside, eventually leading them back down to the town.

"We need to know if they're inside that place," Malcolm said, bending to get a better view of the castle above.

"We could wait until nightfall," Luiza offered. "Sneak right up there."

He shook his head. "We don't have time to wait."

They crossed through a tiny plaza, a small stone obelisk at its heart, capped with a bronze bust of a man. A pair of dark-haired boys on bicycles rode down the road toward them. They stared at the hunters' car and Matt met their eyes as they passed.

Nothing to worry about, just kids checking out the tourists. But the tingle at the back of his neck wasn't quelled. "Whatever we do." He turned. The riders continued on at their normal pace. "We need to do it soon. Driving through town over and over looks suspicious."

"Good point," Malcolm said. "Find a good place to stop. Out of the way, but with an exit."

Luc followed the curving street to the edge of the village, finally pulling the sedan into a tiny lot between an old church and another building. He steered it around and parked, facing an exit.

Matt peered around, seeing no one. "Looks good."

Malcolm nodded. "All right. Matt, I want you to make a

fresh compass. No. Two. You say they're good for a hundred yards out in the open. What's the range to see through that castle's walls?"

Matt pursed his lips. Back in the States, a thick wall was brick, maybe cinderblock. He'd never dealt with an actual castle before. "Fifty, at most. Thirty to be sure."

"Then that's how close we'll have to be," Malcolm said.

"You want us to go up to that place," Allan asked. "Right now? In the middle of the day?"

"No. Matt and I will do it. The rest of you just lay low here."

Matt opened his laptop bag with Dämoren and the Ingram inside, and removed the plastic pricker from a small, zippered pocket, and started refreshing the compasses.

"Seriously, Mal," Allan said, shaking his head. "Let's wait until nightfall."

"I agree," Luc echoed.

Malcolm smiled reassuringly. "We'll be fine."

"We can surveil it for a few hours," Allan said. "Then send you two in after dark."

"Surveil what?" Malcolm asked. "It's a big house with few exterior windows. We're not just going to see an ifrit strolling around. Everything they've done so far has been too careful for them to make a mistake now. Besides, few windows means less chance of anyone seeing us approach."

Matt screwed the cap back onto the refreshed blood compass. "I agree. Clay and I used to do this type of thing all the time." He reached over and took the compass bottle resting beside Allan and Malcolm.

"This isn't just some house," Luiza said. "You need to be careful."

"We will be." Matt handed the second compass to Malcolm, who then offered it to Luiza.

"Keep an eye on this," Malcolm said. "You see anything, call us and get out of here."

Luiza took the bottle. Worry tinged her eyes.

Matt opened the car's door and stepped out. A warm breeze rustled his hair as he adjusted Dämoren's bag over his shoulder.

"Ready?" Malcolm asked, coming out behind him. He

carried the case with Hounacier inside. He slipped on a pair of dark aviator glasses.

Matt checked the compass and nodded. "Let's do it."

Together they made their way out of the lot, past a trio of narrow shops crammed inside a building before following the narrow asphalt road out. Beads of sweat dotted Matt's brow and he found himself envying Malcolm's fedora. Keeping the castle in sight, they circled the hill around. Trees lined the road along a fence line, but the slope itself lay mostly exposed.

The sound of tires rumbled from the road ahead.

"Car," Malcolm said, lowering his head so the hat shielded his face.

Matt turned away and made as if scratching his temple as a faded red coupe came into view. It cruised past them, spinning leaves in its wake. He glanced back as it rounded a bend, then disappeared behind the trees.

A half-mile later they came to a junction in the barbed wire fence paralleling the road. Straight-trunked trees followed its path, cutting along the back of the property. Smaller trees with tiny round leaves dotted the slope, hiding the castle from view. Malcolm checked that the road was clear and pulled two of the rusty barbed wire strands apart to create a long gap. Matt squeezed through, then took the gritty wires and held them for Malcolm to follow.

They hurried along the fence line until the road was out of view, and then made their way up the rocky hill toward the castle.

Sweat ran down the back of Matt's neck, his shirt clinging against his back. The foliage opened up about sixty feet behind a rain-silvered wooden shed. The castle's stone walls loomed another hundred feet beyond it. Matt checked the compass but the bottle was unchanged. He and Malcolm hurried up through the open span, keeping low and using the shed as cover.

Malcolm reached the tiny building first. Holding up a hand for Matt to stop, he pressed his ear to the planked wall. He shook his head and motioned Matt to follow.

Crouched, Matt clutched the heavy satchel and ran up the grassy slope to the shed. He pressed his back to the wall and checked the compass again. Still pink.

Cautiously, Matt straightened up and peeked through a dusty window. Various tools and boxes lined the shed's cluttered walls. A rust-colored tractor, at least fifty years old, sat in the middle facing the wide door.

Malcolm peered around the corner toward the villa. "Check this out," he whispered.

Matt scooted behind to see. A huge stone barn or carriage house stood off to one side of the castle. A man with a brown cap leaned against one side of the closed green doors, sheltered in a wedge of shade from the sun. A blued rifle hung from the crook of his arm. Further past the barn, two rows of cars sat parked in a small paved lot, circled by slender cypress.

"Interesting," Matt said.

"You recognize any of those cars from the mine?" Malcolm asked.

"No, never got a good look at them. I thought they flew down, anyway."

"Someone would have needed to drive their guns down. Also, the demons that can't or won't change to human form. Unless they had a marked body down here waiting for them, they'd have to be driven."

Matt nodded. "True. So what's in the barn?"

Malcolm didn't answer right away. Eventually he said, "Something they either don't want or can't put inside the castle."

"Tour bus? Bet it's big enough to hold one in there."

"Just what I was thinking." Malcolm withdrew his head to the safety behind the shed.

"So what now?" Matt asked, creeping back from the edge.

"You got a hit on that compass yet?"

"No."

"Then we move closer until we do. We need to be sure this isn't some mafia gang bootlegging olive oil or something."

Matt let out a long sigh. It was like dealing with Clay, cautious to the point of obsessive. Matt couldn't argue because all the circumstantial evidence in the world still wasn't proof. He hadn't realized just how many of Clay's infuriating habits he'd forgotten over the years. *They'd have gotten along well*, he thought. *If they didn't kill each other.*

Malcolm peeked around the edge again, then moved to the other side of the shed to look from there. "Getting closer to the castle won't work. Guard will see us, but I think we can move closer to the barn."

"That's where the guard is," Matt said flatly. He crawled up and peered around to where Malcolm was looking.

"Yeah, but if we follow that line of hedge we can move around to the back side." Malcolm set his case in the grass and eased the brass latches open. Hounacier, sheathed in its wooden scabbard, lay inside, strapped down with black Velcro. Malcolm's sawed-off rested beside it, as well as a dozen shells, color-coded to denote their contents.

Matt eyed the low strip of shrubs. It wasn't much cover and bushes didn't offer any protection from bullets if the guard spotted them. "Let me do it."

"What?"

"I'll do it," Matt said. "Two of us only doubles our chances of being seen."

"Then I'll do it," Malcolm whispered. "I'm the senior knight."

"I'm not Valducan," Matt said and dashed into a crouched run before Malcolm could continue the argument. Almost crawling, he dove behind the strip of dense green hedge. The bushes were too thick to see through. He looked back to where Malcolm waited behind the shed, his lips pressed into an unhappy line.

Malcolm peeked around to see the barn and signaled Matt it was safe.

Careful not to crunch any leaves or lift his back too high, Matt followed the line thirty or so feet until it ended at a stone-paved gap. The hedgerow continued ten feet across on the other side.

Slowly, Matt peeked around the corner. The guard still leaned against the wall, not fifty feet away, the glazed look of boredom on his face.

Matt wiped a trickle of sweat from his brow, then scuttled across to the bushes on the other side. His foot caught a hook-shaped twig, rustling the bush. *Fuck!*

Pressing himself down, he turned back to Malcolm. The knight checked, then shook his hand side to side, telling him to wait. Matt rolled his head, hoping to see under the hedge, but couldn't.

Footsteps approached slowly.

Matt slid his hand into the bag, finding the Ingram's cold metal handle. He'd have to be fast.

The footsteps stopped, maybe twenty feet away.

Matt tightened his jaw. *Why did he stop? Can he see me? Is my foot visible?* He suppressed the instinct to draw the gun up. He imagined rifle rounds blasting through the shrubs any moment.

A grunt, then the footsteps moved away.

Several long seconds passed before Matt turned back to Malcolm.

Crouched, holding his sawed-off and machete, Malcolm peeked around the corner again. He bobbed a finger, signaling Matt to go on. Letting out the breath, Matt licked his lips then continued down the hedgerow.

He reached the end and looked around the edge. The gray stone barn loomed just a few yards away. He was far enough around the side that the sentry couldn't see him. The compass was still pink. Feeling brave, he leaned out further, searching the grounds for other people. Seeing none, he emerged from the hedge and hurried to the barn.

He crouched beside the wall, behind a rose bush the size of a recliner. From his angle he could still see Malcolm watching him. Matt checked the compass again.

A red bead pressed against the bottle's wall, pointed toward the building beside him. An exalted surge washed over him. *Bingo.*

Matt lifted the bottle for Malcolm to see, then gave a thumbs up. Malcolm returned the signal.

Now that they had their confirmation it was time to get the hell out of there. Matt eyed the hedgerow, readying to make the dash, then hesitated. What was inside the barn? What were they protecting? He's assumed the tour bus but didn't know that for certain.

"It's got to be important for them to be guarding it," he imagined Clay saying. *"Knowing what it is gives you the advantage."*

Cursing the old man's training, Matt eyed the giant building. No windows on this side. Careful to remain quiet, Matt made his way around to the back of the barn. A pair of giant green doors, identical to the front, faced out the rear. A thick steel chain looped through the iron ring handles, secured with a sturdy-looking padlock.

A large window stood open above the doors, too high to reach. Matt crept closer to the doors. The tight-fitted planks were devoid of any knot holes, and he didn't dare try pulling them open enough to see through. Searching the doors for any kind of spyhole, he eventually found a slender gap on the far end, just above where the lower hinge met the wall. Matt lowered to his stomach and peered through the crevice.

A huge shape filled the room, blocky and long. As his eyes adjusted to the dimness more detail melted out from the shadows. He made out chrome-capped wheels, the cocked open windows, then eventually "Tuscia Tours" written in orange and gold on the sides. *I knew it.*

Movement caught his eye and Matt looked closer at the windows. Several forms moved on the other side of the dark glass. The hostages were still alive and here. He didn't see the demon, but a werewolf or aswang in human form would blend in. Perfect plant with the hostages. Matt watched the silhouette of what appeared to be a man fanning himself with his hat. Malcolm might consider these people expendable for the greater good, but Matt didn't. And now that he knew where they were, a plan began forming in his mind. Yes, knowing this did give him an advantage, but first he needed to get out of here.

Matt rose to his feet and quietly hurried back to the hedges to escape.

"There had to be sixteen, seventeen cars in that lot," Matt said, pulling the barbed wire fence open for Malcolm to slip through. "No telling how many people we're looking at, but I'd guess thirty, maybe forty. If only half are demons that's still more than we can possibly handle."

"You're forgetting the element of surprise," Malcolm said. "Every time we've encountered this group they've had the home court. They're not expecting us this time." He started down the road back to the village.

"Maybe if we had ten people," Matt said hurrying to catch up. "Unless you've got a missile hidden up your sleeve I don't see how we can do it."

Malcolm drew a breath, long and slow. "The hard part will be getting us all up there unnoticed. We can take the same path we just did. If there are any guards we can take them out quietly, especially if we can get Luiza down-light of them to cut their shadows. Once the grounds are clear, we cut tires. Prevent any of them an easy getaway. One swing of Luc's mace will bring down any locked door. Once the doors are gone, we lay covering fire, take out Anya's cultists while holy weapons take out the demons. Allan moves fast enough with Ibenus that he can take point. If they have candles like they did in Spain, that'll give Luiza plenty of shadows to chop through. And don't think I've forgotten how well you shoot Dämoren. Between the five of us we can do it."

Matt played the scenario is his head. Malcolm had a point. It wouldn't be a random clusterfuck like Limoges, but a well-planned blitz. Maybe if they could get some lights from one side, headlights, maybe an airborne flare, Luiza's sword could decimate them without even putting her in harm's way. Malcolm's weird hand tattoo could hold back attackers long enough to—"Candles?" Matt blurted. "You want to attack during the ceremony?"

"Of course," Malcolm said. "There's no way to guarantee the weapons are even there but they will be then. Also it's the only way to be sure Anya and her cronies are all present. We'll wipe them out once and for all."

"I just said there's probably forty people there now. Tomorrow night there could be twice that. We need more people."

Malcolm shook his head. "It can't be helped."

Matt wiped the gritty sweat from his face and neck. Sixty, maybe eighty people. The rest of the team wouldn't agree to it.

How could they? It was suicide. In the end, their enemies would tear them apart and destroy their weapons. "There is another way," he said finally.

"I'm not seeing one."

"We need to cripple their plan first. Go for their balls before their throat."

Malcolm snorted. "I'm listening."

"I came across a demon summoning once a few years back," Matt said. "They kidnapped this girl, possessed her with a demon."

"Okay?"

"Well what we saw in Spain was different. They possessed Selene, but the others, they were used, too. Remember their legs? Completely stripped of skin. There was blood everywhere but inside that ring. It was like the oni used every bit of that in its creation. Like one body wasn't enough. "

Malcolm's brow creased, though he said nothing.

"So we think the weapons aren't required for this ceremony of theirs," Matt continued. "But what if multiple people are? They're not just being sacrificed, but physically needed to bring forth this demon mother of theirs?"

"That's possible," Malcolm said carefully, trying to guess where Matt was going.

"We don't stand a chance attacking sixty-plus people, not if we're all going to survive. Even if we get forty of them first we're still dead. Then our weapons are lost as well and no one left to stop them. We need an army."

"We don't have one."

They rounded a bend and the village came into view through the trees.

"But we *do*." Matt grinned. "What do you think the authorities would do if they were told a group of terrorists has a busload of people locked in a certain barn? There are already a thousand cops scouring Tuscany for them. No wreck has been found. They have to have figured out by now that something happened."

Malcolm looked at him, then laughed. "You want to call the cops?"

"Yeah. Why not?"

"What do you think will happen to them if they raid that castle? No silver, no iron, just bullets?"

"But those culties aren't immune to bullets. If we call it in like they're some militant crazy bastards with automatic weapons, the cops are going to come ready for a fight."

"What about the holy weapons?" Malcolm asked. "How, in that plan, do we save those?"

Matt thought about that. "If the police get them we'll at least know where they are and can begin recovery. Steal them, maybe say they were stolen from us. I'm sure Turgen can pull some strings. Otherwise we have ten GPS trackers in our gear. We can sneak out tonight and tag some of those cars in case any of them get away we can follow them. Maybe we can sabotage the other cars before the raid."

"Too many factors." Malcolm shook his head. "If we lost those weapons then they're gone. I can't risk that."

"Look," Matt said, his voice lowering as they neared a building. "Full lunar eclipses don't happen often. If we can stop this ceremony tomorrow, it might buy us enough time to track these people down and end this."

Malcolm sighed. "These knights they've killed are just names to you. But to us they were our family. I don't … expect you to understand this. But telling Master Turgen, or Master Schmidt, or Master Rangarajan that we let the people that murdered their … children … escape. It'd kill them."

A lump of pity formed in Matt's chest. He's always seen Malcolm as some balls-out, stone-cold demon hunter. He'd ridden Matt's ass since the minute they first met. He'd considered punching Malcolm in the mouth more times than he could count. But now … now he understood. Malcolm was grieving. He licked his lips, finding the words. "And if the five of us die?"

Malcolm didn't answer.

They entered San Pettiro again, passing the first building. A blackclad priest stood on the sidewalk ahead behind a microbus loading cardboard boxes onto a wooden wagon.

Finally Malcolm spoke, his voice low. "We'll talk to the others. Figure out the best plan."

Matt hid a smile. *A small victory.*

"Excuse me," said a man's kind voice.

Matt looked up to see the young priest looking straight at him. His face was red and dotted with sweat.

"Could one of you help me with this last box?" the priest asked, smiling. He gestured to a red, flat, plastic case loaded with brown books.

Matt looked at Malcolm.

The knight seemed unsure, his eyes narrow. He nodded reluctantly. "Of course, Father."

Malcolm took a step closer. The priest reached toward one end of the crate and drew a revolver. The antique looked like some relic from the First World War, its blued finish worn to dusty silver.

He cocked the hammer. "Hands where I can see them."

A door squeaked behind them. Matt glanced back, hoping a surprise witness might cause a distraction. A pair of gray-haired men stepped out from one of the shops. One held a pistol, the other a double-barrel shotgun. *Shit.*

"Hands where I can see them, Mister Romero," the priest said again.

Empty hand out, other still gripping the handle of Hounacier's brown case, Malcolm stepped back beside Matt.

"You too, Mister Hollis," the priest said, training the revolver on him.

Matt lifted his left hand. His right inched toward the slit in Dämoren's bag.

A shotgun pressed into his back. "Slowly," a burly voice growled.

For a brief moment Matt considered spinning, catching the man's gun and disarming him. The silver-ringed barrel of the priest's pistol changed his mind. Matt raised his hands. "Mal?" he said, not moving his lips.

"Put the case down," the other man said, prodding Malcolm in the back with his little semi-auto.

"Okay," Malcolm said, his voice calm. "All right." Slow and deliberate, he bent down, lowering Hounacier's case to the stonepaved sidewalk.

Suddenly Malcolm cocked a leg and kicked back, slamming his foot into his captor's knee. The man howled as the joint popped. He fell, his pistol firing into the air with a deafening crack.

Malcolm swung the long case back, knocking the shotgun out of Matt's back. "Matt, now!"

Matt thrust his hand into his bag, his fingers finding Dämoren's ivory grip.

Malcolm swung the case again. Shotgun Man dodged the attack and slammed the gun's steel butt-plate into Malcolm's face, sending him sprawling.

Spinning, Matt cocked Dämoren's hammer and aimed her inside the awkward satchel at Malcolm's attacker.

He fired. Thick smoke billowed as the leather exploded outward. The bullet missed, shattering one of the microbus's windows.

Shotgun Man stumbled back, bringing the double-barrels up. Matt shoved Dämoren's barrel out through the now shredded hole in his satchel and cocked the hammer again.

A cold smooth muzzle pressed hard into the side of Matt's head, just below his ear.

"Drop it."

Matt froze. He looked out the corner of his eye, down the long barrel to the priest at the other end.

The man's face was hard. Angry. "Drop it. Now!"

Shotgun Man stood a few feet away now, his weapon aimed straight at him. There was no way Matt could take them both.

Defeated, he closed his eyes and withdrew his hand from the bag.

CHAPTER 19

Matt lay face down on dirty carpet the color of wet cardboard, his wrists handcuffed behind him. The microbus jolted, smacking his face into the floor. Broken glass bounced across the carpeting. Air whistled through the bullet hole in the window above. Cold shears slid up his thigh, snipping through his jeans. The pant leg fell open, exposing him to his captors, and then the shears started up the other ankle.

From the corner of his eye, Matt glanced over to Malcolm beside him. He was naked, save the steel cuffs around his wrists. Bright tattoos of various patterns and shapes covered his upper arms and back. Some were elaborate, others simple, almost primitive. A crude, red, stick man with a head like a push broom adorned one shoulder. A knot-work face leered out between his shoulder blades. Dark blood caked his cheek.

Malcolm looked back, his swollen and purple eye just a slit. In that moment Matt could see Malcolm's rage, the hatred, the remorse. Matt couldn't tell if the death-look was meant for their captors or him.

Matt's pants split fully open. Hands pulled his shirt out from beneath his cuffed wrists.

Snip. Snip. Snip.

The vehicle turned sharply and started up a steep grade. Matt's shirt fell apart. He was naked.

"Your friends can't save you," said a voice behind him. He couldn't tell whose. There were at least three people in the back of the microbus with them. They'd left the guy whose knee Malcolm had broken on the street in the care of some woman. Was the entire village in on it?

"We got them half an hour before you," the voice continued.

A dreadful weight settled in Matt's gut as he heard the names.

"Luc, Allan, Luiza."

They weren't bluffing.

"You and your murdering order are done. Now you'll pay for your crimes."

"Fuck you," Malcolm growled.

A hard *thwack* sounded and Malcolm grunted in pain.

The vehicle slowed and turned into a stop. The back door groaned open and a breeze flowed in across Matt's bare back. Firm hands grabbed his arm, forcing him up and out the rear of the microbus. He stepped barefoot onto sun-warmed stone. Malcolm came out beside him. Three men and a woman, all with guns, surrounded them. They stood at the edge of a wide, walled courtyard paved in gray blocks. A massive three-story building wrapped two sides of the yard, its roof tiled with orange terracotta. A pair of workers maneuvered across a scaffolding frame along one of the building's faces.

One of the gunmen removed a padlock from a barred door, like a jail cell, its crisscrossing flat bars riveted at their intersections. It screeched open. Someone behind him twisted Matt's arm up, driving him forward through the door and into a small brick room. Three nude prisoners stood inside, facing the rear wall, their hands cuffed behind them. At least they didn't appear hurt.

Malcolm bumped into Matt's shoulder as his captors shoved him inside. The door clanged shut behind them. Metal rattled and the lock clicked. The room was small, no more than six by fifteen feet with a vaulted ceiling. No windows. No other exit but the single locked door.

Luiza spun around first. She looked at Matt, her chocolate eyes tinged with worried relief.

"Mal?" Allan exclaimed.

"I'm all right," Malcolm said, stepping forward. "Any of you hurt?"

"No," Luc said. "They took us by surprise."

"It's my fault." Allan's eyes downcast. "This priest approached the car. Asked if we were tourists ... needed directions … then he had a pistol and some friends."

"I think we met him," Matt said through a bitter smile.

Malcolm shook his head. "This is my fault. I wasn't thinking. I should have left Matt in the car. Taken one of you instead."

Matt's face grew hot. *This again?* "Me? What the hell did I do?"

"No," Malcolm said, shaking his head again. "You didn't do anything. When you're near me my scarab doesn't work. It senses you and as long as you're nearby I can't feel other possessed. It left me blind. If I'd left you in the car I might have sensed that priest or one of his pals before they attacked us. Maybe before we even left the village."

Matt's anger cooled. "I see."

"So you think they're possessed?" Luc asked.

"Maybe not all of them," Malcolm answered. "But they got us in the middle of the street, broad daylight, guns out, two shots fired, and no one stopped it. No worry someone might call the police? I'll bet this entire town is either cultists or familiars."

Allan frowned. "That's a real big assumption."

"Why not?" Matt asked. "Villagers spread stories that Marco Barugnani worshiped the devil, then why not preemptively align the entire community to their side? The Valducans killed Marco, but how many of his followers survived? They've had four hundred years to build up in this town. Work their way into the customs. Then, once they're ready to make their move, Anya's friends all fall off the grid, move from Florence to here. Whoever isn't a card-carrying member of their little religion finds themselves bitten and enslaved to a demon."

"And giving the demons a local body to jump back into when needed," Luiza said, finishing Matt's thought.

Matt nodded. "Exactly." He stole a glance at her dark nipples. He looked away, feeling a tinge of guilt.

"All right, I'll buy that." Allan eyed the iron-barred door, his voice lowering. "So any idea how we're going to get out of this?"

Matt twisted at the cuffs behind his back. In a life of carrying guns, fencing stolen merchandise, and killing demons, ending up in police custody had always loomed as a possibility. Since he was thirteen Clay had drilled him on blindly picking a handcuff lock. His peak time had been thirty-seven seconds. Though in that case Matt had a pick, which he didn't have now, and the cuffs weren't double locked, which this time they were.

"They took my leather bracelet," Luc mumbled. "I had a key hidden in the braid."

"Mine too," Malcolm said. "Nick made 'em."

Luiza grinned half-heartedly. "My jeans. I always stitched one in the inside near the top."

"That's a lot of keys," Allan said. "I just kept one in my back pocket."

"Your jeans aren't as tight as mine," she said. "Police aren't as likely to search your back pockets as thoroughly, either."

Matt chuckled. It wasn't real amusement. Dämoren gone, stripped naked with no means of escape, he just needed the release.

Luiza's brow arched. "So what about you?"

"Paperclip," Matt said. "Stuck to the inside of my belt with black electric tape. Clay used to say that getting caught with a handcuff key was enough probable cause to earn a police ass-beating. Said no one looks at the inside of your belt and paperclips don't leave much of an imprint."

Malcolm gave an impressed nod. He looked around, his left eye was swollen shut now. "So unless one of you got a hairpin I don't know about, they've successfully stripped us of all our keys. Any other suggestions?"

Matt cocked his head, eyeing the door through the corner of his eye. A long-legged man with a pump shotgun stood outside the gate.

The man caught Matt's gaze and stared back at him, his expression cold. Challenging.

No use hiding it. Matt turned and faced the door.

The man straightened, a little smile at the corners of his mouth.

Matt popped his hips forward, bouncing his dick a little. He puckered, giving the man a little kiss.

The guard snorted uncomfortably and looked away.

Matt checked the door. The iron hinge pins were bent on either side. *No sliding those out.* He stepped closer, trying to see more of the courtyard. Three workers moved lumber from a large stack into the back of a flat-bed truck. Nearby an older man, with hair the color and texture of steel wool, shoveled construction debris into a wheelbarrow. Metal pinged above as the two scaffolding workers broke down the pipe framework. A huge disk of polished copper adorned the wall above them, its face depicting the image of a winged serpent.

"You boys didn't have to clean up on our account," Matt said.

The guard twisted his hand around the shotgun's wooden grip. "Step back from the door."

Matt scanned the castle's windows. Too dark to see anything, save wine-colored curtains.

The guard raised the gun. "I have orders to shoot you if I so much as think you're trying to escape. Back up."

"Orders from who?" Matt asked, meeting the man's gaze.

"Agostino."

Thank you. Smiling, he stepped away from the door.

Hours passed.

Shadow crept across the courtyard until finally sunlight faded from the sky. Matt sat, leaning awkwardly against the rough brick wall, allowing enough room for his cuffed hands at the base of his back. His stomach rumbled angrily. His last meal had been a hurried sandwich on the ride to Empoli. Had he known it was going to be his last meal for the day, he'd have had one of the fruit bars probably still in the car. Maybe even killed a couple of those water bottles Luc had brought along for compasses.

Allan rested beside him quietly humming some tune that, at best, Matt could figure was a random sampling of ten-year-old pop songs. Luiza sat a few feet away, her knees up before her. Matt tried to keep eye contact whenever he looked at her, though their current situation left little room for modesty. Malcolm and Luc whispered between themselves in the corner. He had no clue what they were talking about. After three hours of huddled conversations everyone else had all come to the same conclusion: the cultists had all the cards. The next move was theirs.

Their long-legged guard had changed an hour before. The

new one, a guy with hair slicked back so tight it looked like a helmet designed for speed, was even less talkative than his predecessor. Any attempts to approach or communicate quickly resulted in staring down the barrel of a loaded twelve-gauge.

Lights flicked on around the courtyard. A gray and black werewolf strode out the castle's double-doors alongside a featureless, black rakshasa. A balding ghoul followed them. Earlier he'd seen a lamia slither out from a black sedan and into the house, her tail striped in bands of purple and black. The humans working the grounds, still cleaning the last of the construction, all stopped and bowed their heads respectfully as the monsters passed. It was like a scene from Hell.

A pair of figures approached the cell door. The first was a man, thin with a head of thick gray hair. The second—

"You fucking bitch!" Malcolm spat.

Anya smiled. "Eloquent as always, Doctor."

"How?" Luiza asked. "We took you in. You lived with us. They *trusted* you."

"Should a rancher feel guilt for his herd? No. They got what they deserved."

Luiza's lip quivered, rage boiling in her eyes. "Deserved? You killed them!"

Anya's brows rose impassively.

"So you're here to gloat?" Malcolm asked, forcing himself to his feet.

A grin crept along her lips. "I wanted to thank you for bringing your weapons. The Great Mother will appreciate your sacrifice."

Malcolm sprung across the little room, ramming into the iron door. He pressed his face through the bars. "Fuck you!"

The guard raised his gun. "Back!"

Malcolm didn't move.

"Back!" the guard repeated, his voice rising. "I'll shoot."

"He's quite serious, Doctor Romero," the gray-haired man said.

"Mal," Allan pleaded.

Malcolm backed away from the door, his jaw clenched.

"Hello, Matt," Anya said. She fingered a gold pendant at her neck. "I wanted to thank you for the necklace you gave me."

Matt's eyes narrowed, seeing the shard of sword blade trimmed with twisted gold.

"Do you like it, Luiza?" Anya asked.

Luiza glanced at the necklace, but didn't respond.

Anya flipped it in her fingers to look at it. "I think it really captures Feinluna's memory, don't you?" She let it fall, settling between her breasts.

Luiza gave a puzzled expression, then her eyes widened in horror. She looked at Anya, then to Matt.

Matt bit his lip and looked away, unable to look at her. He felt ill, his guts boiling and churning.

"Thank you, Matt," Anya said, her overly sweet voice tinged with razors. "I'll cherish it."

"Oh, Anya, stop it," the man said. "You're embarrassing him."

"And who are you?" Matt asked, looking up. "Agostino, is it?"

The man smiled, displaying a mouth of very large, very white teeth. "Very good, Mister Hollis. Agostino Molinelli, High Priest of Tiamat, descendent of Marco Barugnani."

"So, Agostino," Matt said, "when can we have some water? Or even a toilet?"

Agostino regarded him. "And did any of the angels you slaughtered get a last request?"

"Angels? They're monsters."

"They are divine beings greater than ourselves. They are to be honored."

"They kill people," Matt said, his face growing hot. "They enslave them."

"And you kill animals," the Agostino said. "You wear them. Eat their flesh. Does that make you a monster?"

A hot spike of rage erupted in Matt's throat. "That's different," he managed.

Agostino gave a slight shrug. "It is because, unlike the others, you, Mister Hollis, are a monster. You, who exploit the power of their blessing, and then destroy them so that no other can savor it." He nodded to the others. "They are ignorant, afraid of what they can't understand. You know that power and still you murder your kind."

The spike grew. Matt clenched his fists, pulling against the cuffs until his wrists felt as if they might snap.

"Your death will be celebrated above all the others. Tomorrow night Anya, our most honored sister, shall become the vessel in which Tiamat reawakens, and once she has become flesh, we will offer her you, the murderers of her children."

"And what about you?" Matt asked. "What do you think will happen to you when you unleash this monster?"

"I will serve her as she wishes," he said proudly.

"She'll kill you," Matt said, meeting the zealot's gaze. "And kill everyone you love."

"If that is her wish," Agostino said calmly. "Then who am I to question it?"

Matt's stomach gurgled hungrily. He sat near the cell door, watching workers position a large metal fire pit. A trio of men armed with sledges pounded a black iron spike into the ground. A giant ring of spikes, their heads protruding about six inches high, dominated one half of the paved courtyard. After hours of lying uncomfortably on the stone floor, his hands behind him, Matt had finally managed to fall asleep until the clangs of hammers woke him. Now he sat as a condemned man in some Western movie, watching his gallows' construction as the clock ticked away.

More followers appeared throughout the day, talking and laughing as the workers finished setting up the courtyard. Many glanced at the prisoners, locked behind the iron cage; some pointed, joking and laughing with their compatriots, though none approached. Long burgundy banners, adorned with the winged serpent, hung from the walls, rippling in the breeze. The smell of food wafted down from the villa's open doors. Matt's stomach ached as he caught the aroma of grilled meat.

"Christ," Allan groaned, wrinkling his nose. "I don't want to smell that. It smells so damned good."

Matt nodded, his dry mouth suddenly wet with hunger.

"Probably tastes like crap. No garlic, salt, rosemary." He grinned weakly. "Lot of food allergies with this crowd."

"Quiet," Luc growled. "Don't talk about food."

The others nodded in agreement, their pained expressions angry.

Matt swallowed, exchanging an apologetic look with Allan, then closed his eyes, trying to force away the hunger.

A soft shuffle and rattle of handcuffs behind him. Luiza scooted up to his side. His lips tightened. They hadn't spoken since Anya's gloating visit. He'd never wanted company less.

Clearing his throat, Allan made a sadly unsubtle exit as he inched to where Luc and Malcolm whispered just a few feet away.

"How are you doing?" she asked.

Matt suppressed a snort. *How do you think I'm doing?* He pushed it away. She didn't deserve that. "I could really go for that hotel buffet right now."

"Me, too. I wonder how the people in the bus are doing?"

"I saw them carrying food out for them this morning," Matt said.

"Big cooler of water. They probably have no idea what's in store for them."

She didn't say anything for a long time. Finally, "Matt ... the necklace Anya had."

Matt's chest tightened. It was hard to breathe.

"What was that? Why did she thank you for it?"

He licked his dry lips, trying to find the words. "When we went back to the mine, and you were so broken up over losing her, I found a piece of Feinluna's blade. I kept it. I don't know why. I just wanted to do something with it to help you ... honor her." He stared out across the yard, not really watching as workers started another spike. "Our second day in Florence I found one of the goldsmiths on the Ponte Vecchio to make it into a pendant. That's where I went yesterday morning, to pick it up. I planned to give it to you, but then we saw the news reports and Luc called about the symbol. I never got a chance." He shook his head, then turned to her.

Tears framed Luiza's dark eyes.

"It was still in my pocket when Mal and I got captured. They must have found it. I ..." He drew a breath. "I just wanted to give you something. It was stupid. I'm sorry."

Matt watched horrified as a tear ran down Luiza cheek. He'd never wanted this. He'd hurt her. With everything they now faced, torture, execution, Dämoren's destruction, in that moment, seeing that tear, the pain he had caused her, was the worst of them all.

"You made that?" She sniffed. "For me?"

Matt nodded shamefully. He was suddenly aware everyone was quietly watching him. "I don't know what I was thinking, I—"

"Thank you."

He froze. "What?"

Luiza swallowed. She tried to wipe her eye on her shoulder. "Thank you."

Matt smiled, his guilt melting away. "I'm sorry I didn't give it to you in time."

Night finally came, slow and inevitable. Scant clouds hurried across the starry skies. Matt couldn't see the moon from the doorway, but its silvery light shone over the yard. The chattering crowd had all gone inside before dark, leaving only their guard outside. He sat in a folding chair several feet away watching them, his shotgun resting in his lap.

One of the far doors opened, spilling a wedge of light across the grounds. Five robed figures stepped out, their faces hidden under pointed hoods. They each turned toward the copper disk mounted high on the building's wall and touched their foreheads. One of them broke off from the group and crossed the yard toward the cell.

The guard straightened as the figure approached.

"I'll take over," it said in a feminine voice. "Go get ready."

The guard rose, handed the hooded woman his gun, and a small ring of keys, and then hurried away.

The woman slipped the keys into a slit-like pocket. She stood, ignoring the metal chair, her eyes hidden beneath the dark round holes in her hood. The brass pendant of Tiamat glinted on her chest.

Matt watched as the other cultists lit the four caged fire pits through the courtyard, casting long shadows across the ground. Once finished, the figures brought out a large bell suspended inside a metal frame and set it on the far side of the ring. More arrived, carrying a round-bottomed drum.

A growing dread spread amongst the hunters as they quietly watched the robed cultists prepare. Once finished, they each turned back to the great disk, now cast in the flickering orange glow, touched their foreheads and retreated back into the castle. Two remained. One beside the bell, the other behind the drum.

"If one of you has a plan," Allan said, his voice low, "now's the time."

The cultist beside the bell raised a short mallet and struck it. The sharp tone echoed off the walls. Before it faded out, the other hooded cultist hit the drum.

The castle's double doors opened and a line of robed and hooded people slowly walked out. The one in the front carried a metal censer, hanging by a long chain. Trails of gray smoke wafted out as it swung with each step. Burgundy fringe tinged with gold, trimmed the second figure. It carried a twisted staff.

Agostino, Matt guessed.

Slowly the procession descended the stone steps, the drum thumping every third second. Four of them carried poles supporting a stout pedestal topped with a V-shaped anvil. Behind them, two more robed cultists carried a long plank, wide as a door, and shrouded beneath a red cloth. After the line of nearly forty hooded figures, a procession of demons marched slowly out behind them.

"Jesus," Matt muttered as eight werewolves strode out behind a rank of pale vampires. The dread only grew seeing two nude succubi, a muscled incubus, rakshasas, a lamia, two ifrit, a crimson strutter, a pack of ghouls, three wendigo, a horned frog-like beast with golden skin, a pair of giant black dogs with eyes glowing like embers and, finally, a pair of towering one-horned oni. The last one, a female with bulbous saggy tits, carried a wedge-shaped maul.

Nowhere in any of the histories Matt had read was there

ever an army as this. Forty-one demons. What had they been thinking to even pretend they could actually fight that many?

The procession circled the ring of spikes twice until finally stopping around it. Matt squinted, straining to see through the ranks.

"Tonight," Agostino's voice boomed. "The Great Mother returns to us."

"Hail the Great Mother," the congregation said in unison. *"Hail Tiamat."*

"What are they saying, Matt," Allan whispered.

Matt hadn't even noticed that he didn't recognize the language.

"Long has she slumbered," Agostino said, Matt translating it the best he could. "Fleshless, hungry, waiting for us, her devoted children, to awaken her and make her whole."

"Hail the Great Mother. Hail Tiamat."

"Tonight, beneath the blood moon, we call her forth by her true name, and offer her flesh worthy of her glory."

"Hail the Great Mother. Hail Tiamat, Icthwyn the Undying Goddess."

Icthwyn? Matt thought. The name was familiar somehow. A silhouette in the mist, like from a dream he couldn't quite remember after waking.

The bell rang five times and the circle peeled back, opening at one side. Matt spied Agostino standing within the half ring, his scepter high.

Matt recognized the heavy creak of the courtyard's outer door. The low sounds of whimpers and shuffling feet came through, growing steadily louder.

Someone screamed.

"Oh my God! Oh my God! Oh my God!" a woman wailed.

A werewolf's distinct, guttural snarl erupted and the woman went silent.

"What is it?" Luiza asked pushing her way up beside Matt to see.

"The prisoners," Luc muttered.

Matt's teeth clenched tighter as he watched a line of nude people, their faces contorted with fear as a gray, seven-foot werewolf led them into the ring of cultists and monsters. The youngest was a boy, maybe eleven, with matted curly hair. The eldest, a woman, probably in her late sixties, her plump legs purple with varicose veins.

The great doors groaned and thudded shut. The black-robed cultists closed in on the terrified mob.

Gritting his teeth, Matt forced himself to watch the hooded figures lash the weeping and pleading prisoners to the jutting spikes. The surrounding demons growled and laughed as they sobbed and pleaded for their lives.

We have got to get out of here! Their guard wasn't watching them, distracted with the unfolding ceremony. But the shotgun in her hands was still ready. Maybe when they opened the door Matt could rush her, get her gun and the keys ... *And what?* Fight off over forty demons and just as many cultists with one gun, his hands bound behind his back, and no clue where Dämoren was?

Or did he?

Matt eyed the strange anvil, barely visible behind the oni that had once been Selene. None of the other demons carried weapons. The hammer's chisel-like head looked as though it might fit perfectly inside the anvil's slot. Matt struggled to his feet, trying to get a better view.

His movement drew the guard's attention. Her hand tightened around the gun.

Squinting, Matt peered at the cloth-covered plank a few feet beside the anvil. Several shapes bulged from beneath the crimson shroud.

"I know where the weapons are," he whispered to Luiza.

Her head snapped up toward him. "Where?"

He nodded to the draped cloth. "Under there."

"Are you sure?"

Luc leaned closer to the cage door, his eyes studying the cloth. "I recognize Velnepo's shape. She's there."

"All right," Allan whispered. "So what do we do?"

Matt gnawed his lip, his hands pulling against the hard cuffs. "Wait for an opening."

Allan snorted. "Oh, yeah, of course. We're fucking dead."

"Shh," Luiza hissed. "I'm not."

Once the prisoners had been tied down, the cultists and demons enclosed the ring around them. They chanted something, low and impossible for Matt to hear clearly as the drum thumped in a slow, methodical rhythm. He licked his lips, trying to see through the wall of bodies. Wisps of smoke rose above the crowd and Matt managed to make out the incense carrier slowly circling the ring, circling the pendulum-like censer over each of the bound prisoners.

The incense carrier completed the ring and the drum sounded three quick times.

Agostino stood at the center and raised his staff high. "Bring forth the forsaken. Let them bear witness to the Great Mother's rebirth and suffer her judgment for their sins."

"We're up," Matt said.

"What?" Allan asked. His eyes widened as a robed figure and a pair of vampires peeled from the congregation and strode purposefully toward the cell. The drum pounded slowly as they approached.

The guard withdrew the keys from her robe and handed them to the cultist. She aimed her gun at the door. "Step back."

The hunters backed away as the cultist unlocked the cell. The pale-skinned demons stood behind him side by side. One a male with wavy brown hair, the other a bald female, her pointed ears almost transparently thin. Her spider-like hand hung at her side. Each finger a digit longer than a human's and tipped with a yellowish claw. Matt searched her red-ringed eyes, wondering if she had been the one that killed Clay.

The door squeaked open. "Out," ordered the cultist.

The hunters all shared a look, then Malcolm, his face bruised and gritty with dried blood, gave a resigned nod and stepped out. Matt followed, then Luiza and the others. The slow drum beat mocked his racing heart.

Malcolm stood tall, his shoulders back, as they walked, giving Matt the courage to do the same. Defiantly Matt met the eyes of their captors as the vampires led them around to the far side of the courtyard. Firelight from the metal basins lit the ring of terrified tourists bound to the ground; arms and legs spread, their touching feet formed a giant star. At its center, Agostino watched them with hateful, victorious eyes.

The female vampire stopped. She stabbed a clawed finger downward. "Kneel."

Matt grunted as his knees met the hard flagstone. One of the basins burned behind them. His eyes watered from the smoke. Thirty feet ahead, the oni stood beside the raised anvil. The red-shrouded plank rested beside it. Above, a dark shadow swallowed the moon, only a quarter of it still visible.

The vampires returned to their ranks leaving the two cultists to guard the prisoners. The woman with the gun stood a few feet off to Malcolm's right. The other, far to the left, was beside Luc.

Agostino returned his attention to the congregation. "Now that the time is upon us, I call forth our beloved sister, Anya, whose sacrifice and devotion has earned her the honor of becoming one with our mother." He raised a hand, palm up, to one of the hooded figures.

The bell rang.

The cultist stepped over the staked prisoners into the ring and stopped before Agostino.

"Do you accept this honor?" Agostino asked.

"I do," she said.

The bell chimed twice more and a pair of cultists entered the ring from either side. Anya extended her arms outward and they removed her robe with delicate reverence. They removed her hood and unclasped her two pendants, one brass, the other Feinluna's broken shard, leaving her naked. Her clothing folded in their arms, the two attendants bowed to Agostino, then to her, and quietly retreated back into the ranks.

The bell rang three times and the incense carrier stepped into the ring and circled Anya. She stood still, allowing the smoke to waft over her pale, glistening skin.

Matt glanced up at the moon. It was just a sliver, slightly orange at its edge.

Finished with his work, the carrier stepped back into the circled ranks, leaving only Agostino and Anya inside the ring. Agostino turned and began walking around the circle, bringing the base of his staff down between each of the bound prisoners' feet, a hard drum strike with each tap.

Malcolm coughed.

The moon's tiny sliver of white was almost gone. The reddish orange hue had spread more across its once black face.

Malcolm coughed again. "Matt."

Matt glanced over at him. Malcolm bobbed his nose toward the ground ahead. Matt followed his gaze but saw nothing.

"The wire," Malcolm said. No, he didn't say it. *Not exactly.* He spoke nonsense, just a light grunt and cough, but Matt understood his meaning.

Matt peered harder, trying to see what Malcolm did. There, nestled in the gap between two of the paving stones five feet away, the bent end of a wire protruded above the surface. It was short, maybe four inches. Probably some relic from the construction, fallen between the narrow channel where the sweeper's broom had missed it. Matt swallowed, excitement rising. It looked thin enough to work. He gave Malcolm a nod.

"I'll cause a distraction," Malcolm grunted in his non-language.

"Get it."

Matt nodded again.

A small grin tugged the corner of Malcolm's lips. "I knew I shouldn't have trusted you," he spat, his voice clear. "This is your fault!"

The shotgun woman's head snapped from the ceremony to Malcolm. "Quiet!"

Malcolm stared hatefully at Matt. His eyes darted quickly toward the wire. "I'll fucking kill you!" he screamed, lunging.

Matt tried to move out of the way, but the bound wrists made it awkward. Malcolm's shoulder clipped him, sending him falling to the hard stones.

"You fucking fuck!" Malcolm yelled, kicking as he struggled up.

Matt rolled, but taking one solid strike to the thigh before he escaped Malcolm's range. He scrambled across the ground, scraping his back, desperately feeling for the wire with his bound hands.

The guards rushed Malcolm, the woman jamming her shotgun into his ribs as the man drove his heel into his back.

"I'll kill you!" Malcolm howled.

Something sharp jabbed Matt's bicep. The wire! He scooted higher, his fingers desperately searching the narrow gaps between stones.

The male guard yanked Malcolm up and forced him back in line.

The woman aimed her shotgun at Matt. "Stop."

Matt inched himself a bit further. He felt the tiny wire and scooped it up as the woman took a step toward him.

"Up!" she ordered.

Lowering his eyes submissively from her and her gun, Matt palmed the wire and forced himself up. He winced, realizing he'd scraped a knee. Head down, he moved back into the row of hunters.

Malcolm watched him through the corner of his eye, hopeful.

Matt glanced back at the woman standing a few feet beside them. She snapped a finger, telling him *"eyes front."*

Malcolm's plan had worked, but the guards were watching them closely now. He couldn't risk any move yet. Matt turned back to the ceremony, giving Malcolm a quick smile as he did.

Agostino had finished his circuit, and now stood outside the ring on the far side. He raised his arms. "The time has come to call our Great Mother back into this world!"

The drum sounded.

A pair of robed cultists approached the covered plank and carefully removed the red shroud. Nine weapons lay spread out across the polished wood. Dämoren rested in the very middle. One of the cultists took Anya's sword, Baroovda, from the end and placed it on the anvil, its curved blade resting across the open V-slot.

The drum thumped again. All white from the moon was gone. It glowed red.

The robed figures began to chant. *"Take the flesh. Taste the Flesh. Rise and Destroy. Rise and Rule. Icthwyn. Icthwyn. Your children call. Your subjects call. Rise and destroy. Rise and rule."*

The drum thumped. At the same time, the oni raised her giant, pointed hammer and smashed it down into the anvil, shattering Baroovda's blade.

Shrieks erupted from the bound prisoners. They shook, fighting against their bonds as they all howled and screamed. Anya stood calmly in the center of the hysteria, her arms raised, head back.

The weapon killers picked the adze from the museum up and set it on the anvil as the congregation continued their chant.

"*Take the flesh. Taste the Flesh. Rise and Destroy. Rise and Rule. Icthwyn. Icthwyn. Your children call. Your subjects call. Rise and destroy. Rise and rule.*"

The drum thumped as the oni smashed the adze with a loud clang.

Blisters rose on the prisoners' feet and inner legs, boiling and bubbling. Skin split open. It peeled away in strips, exposing pink muscle beneath. Flesh and blood coursed through the air as if trapped in a cyclone within the ring.

Matt glanced back. The black ceremony held the guards' attention. Carefully, he took the wire in his right hand and felt for the cuff's tiny keyhole.

"*Take the flesh. Taste the Flesh.*"

Matt slid the wire's tip into the narrow hole and pressed it to the side, bending a little finger at the end.

"*Rise and Destroy. Rise and Rule. Icthwyn. Icthwyn.*"

Blindly he fiddled around the side, trying to reach the double lock's catch. Brushing away bits of splintered adze, the weapon killers placed Colin's thick-bladed sword on the block.

"*Rise and Destroy. Rise and Rule. Icthwyn. Icthwyn.*"

Matt felt the catch, he pressed against it, but the flimsy wire bent under the strain. *Shit!*

"*Your children call. Your subjects call. Rise and destroy. Rise and rule.*"

The maul came down, shattering the blade.

Anya screamed, shrill and inhuman. She fell to her knees. The skin along her spine swelled and split open, revealing a nest of fingerlength cilia, writhing like pale maggots. The prisoners' howls had ceased. Tendons and muscles unraveled from their bones, swept up into the red maelstrom.

Matt's fingers trembled. Fighting the fear and adrenaline he rebent the wire and worked it back toward the catch.

"Take the flesh. Taste the Flesh."

The hooded figures placed Ibenus on the anvil.

"Rise and Destroy."

Matt felt the tiny lever. Holding the wire as close to the keyhole as he could he pressed against it. He felt it click.

"Rise and Rule."

Sweat ran down Matt's face as he moved the wire around to the other side of the catch.

"Icthwyn."

The catch gave and the cuff popped open.

"Icthwyn!"

Matt jumped up, tossing the bent wire at Malcolm's feet and charged the woman guard. She turned in surprise just as Matt punched her in the jaw. He grabbed the shotgun, yanking it from her grip as she fell backward.

"Your children call."

Matt raised the gun at Anya, now convulsing on the ground, her legs fused into a gruesome tail. He fired. The blast caught one of the hooded cultists in the back, knocking him forward into the ring. His body blew apart as if caught in a wood chipper, joining in the bloody cyclone.

Cultists screamed, and closed in the gap, forming a human wall between the gun and their goddess. Others broke ranks and charged.

"Your subjects call."

Racking another shell, Matt ran toward Dämoren. He fired at the oni about to destroy Allan's sword. The beast jolted but the buckshot had no effect.

"Rise and destroy."

Matt was almost there. He shot one of the hooded weapon killers racing toward him. The oni raised its hammer.

"Rise and rule."

Twisting its body, the oni brought the hammer down to the

side, missing the anvil and smashing it down onto the plank. *Onto Dämoren.* The wood buckled, splitting in two as the holy revolver crushed and shattered under the maul's power.

Matt froze, his eyes wide. Bits of metal and ivory spun through the air, tinkling to the ground. *Gone.*

A dark blur flew in from the side. It slammed into him, knocking Matt to the hard stones. The shotgun fell from his hand. His arm cracked and broke, but he didn't feel it.

The bald vampire stood above him, enraged. Her long fingers wrapped around his neck and she dragged him across the unforgiving stones away from the ceremony. Matt didn't fight. He only stared at Dämoren's broken remains. She was dead.

The vampire threw him against the castle's wall. He slumped to the ground. The demon crouched over him, her fanged mouth inches from his face. "You failed, killer."

A roar came from the ring. Matt couldn't see what was happening inside it. He didn't care. He felt numb. A soothing wave rolled up him, like slipping into a warm bath. Blackness closed inward.

"No one will save you," the vampire cooed. "You're going to die."

Dämoren was dead. Clay's gun. The sword of Victor Kluge. Eight hundred years and now gone. He wanted to die. Deserved it. He felt helpless as he had all those years ago. Arm broken, his family dying. A monster glowering above him. Fitting.

"I'm going to drink you dry and feed your corpse to the ghouls," the vampire said. "Then your friends. They'll die screaming."

A searing pain stabbed into Matt's chest, hot and twisting. He gasped, trying to draw breath, but couldn't. The burning spread like molten steel through his veins. Tears welled in his eyes. He'd felt this before. Dämoren's slug.

The vampire laughed, her putrid breath cold against his cheek.

The fiery blood coursed into Matt's brain and something erupted inside him. Awakened.

The vampire's eyes widened, glee melting into confusion.

A clawed hand sprung up into Matt's vision, grasping the vampire by the throat. Muscles bulged and swelled beneath its icy blue skin, shimmering in the firelight. Silver nails dug into the vampire's neck. She screamed but the sound was squelched off as her throat crunched. Green flames erupted from the demon's mouth as the strange claw tore out the vampire's neck.

A surge of power, ecstasy and exhilaration shot through Matt's body. Fiery blood poured down the strange arm. Confused, Matt looked down to see where it had come from. Then, to his horror, he realized the clawed hand was his own.

CHAPTER 20

Blue-green fire dripped down Matt's monstrous arm as the vampire's burning corpse fell. His bones crunched, body swelling with power. The handcuff, still locked around his left wrist, tightened against his expanding arm. The shackle popped and clinked to the ground.

A supernova of foreign memories exploded inside his head. Thoughts and emotions, a seemingly endless history unfolded before his mind's eye.

Standing, though not of his own will, he looked around, seeing everything with more clarity and detail than he'd ever imagined, as if his whole life he'd only seen the world through a dusty window, now smashed away. Flecks and colored veins adorned each of the gray flagstones. The crimson moon above burned bright as any sun, rendering shadows meaningless. Seething lights of souls swirled in the cyclone of Icthwyn's invocation. The brown eyes of the hooded cultist aiming her shotgun at him were ringed prisms of color.

The blast knocked Matt's head back, lead shot shredding his skin and shattering bone. The wounds closed as fast as they opened, leaving but a tingling memory. As if watching it, not in control of his own body, Matt closed the distance between him and the shooter before she had time to rack another shell. He knocked the gun aside, grabbed the woman and threw her to the ground. Bones cracked as easily as if they were made of dried spaghetti. A greenish wisp of light fluttered from her corpse as her soul retreated this world.

Matt noticed the children, their hands still bound behind them. The eldest soul, Malcolm, whose gold-tinged purple essence reminds him so much of his own lost child, Clay, scooted across the stones toward the dead female.

What is happening? Matt wondered, realizing his own consciousness was nothing more than a shrinking island within an ever-growing sea.

Malcolm dug in the corpse's pocket.

Fighting the invader, Matt tried to tell Malcolm to get the keys and save the weapons, but his tongue wouldn't move.

Matt turned to face the blue-skinned oni. It was old, a general in the Legion. He knew its name once. It stood still, its hammer raised above Matt's brother. The oni stared at him, her mouth open in a dumfounded O.

A drum thumped. A wave of power sucked inward then exploded out from the ring at Icthwyn's returning. Now was the time to kill her, while she was weak, disoriented, unused to the flesh. But he couldn't. He had to save his brethren, those who shunned him for breaking the oath. He couldn't let them die. Just as he couldn't let the boy Spencer die. The boy's death would have destroyed the child, Clay. Love made him break his most sacred vow. Not greed. Not power. Love.

Now Matt is charging. The oni readied to meet him; its iron hammer whooshed through the air at his approach. Ducking the swing, Matt crouched below it and then sprang upward, his hand a flat blade, driving his silver-clawed fingers up beneath the demon's ribs. His arm slid deeper into the sticky wound, finding the oni's beating heart. Sweet fire erupted as he tore the demon's heart free. The dead general fell and Matt held the flaming heart high.

Humans and demons alike turned in horror, seeing Matt above the fallen oni. A great shape loomed behind them. Icthwyn had become flesh, become Tiamat. Matt opened his mouth, his jaw stretching wider than he could have ever imagined, and swallowed the oni's heart. The demon's soul tasted sweet.

A werewolf roared and charged from the ranks. It lunged, hooked claws extended. Matt twisted to the side, grabbing the werewolf as it passed. Swinging his body, he yanked and slammed the demon into the ground. Stunned, the beast looked up as Matt's foot stomped down, crushing its head like a pumpkin. Scarlet flames splattered across the ground.

Matt struggled, fighting to regain some control of his body and mind. The lines between his being and the invader's blurred and melted. He knew its name. His name. Urakael.

The blood within his veins pulled to one side, warning of a demon's coming. Spinning, he caught a ghoul's arm as its filthy claws ripped into Matt's shoulder. The pathetic creature howled and writhed, snapping at him with jagged teeth. Matt's grip tightened and the ghoul's arm broke. His other hand grabbed it by the neck and crushed it. He slung the sinewy body to the feet of its closing brethren, yellow fire igniting across its leathery skin. The cowardly ghouls scattered, their pack leader dead.

Urakael's control had grown too strong to fight, its consciousness too vast. Exhausted, Matt finally succumbed, allowing the being to take him.

They are one.

He felt the bond, the love for each of his one hundred nineteen children. The souls he touched, their hands wielding him as a sword then pistol. He knew their names. Mourned their passing. The illusion of time warps and cracks. He knows everything. The origin. The pact. The betrayal.

The blood pulls him again. Urakael turns, seeing a crimson strutter and a pair of familiars, their golden eyes peering beneath their black hoods. Short knives glisten in the familiars' hands. Steel poses no threat to his body.

The strutter's enormous tongue slithers out from behind its fangs and peels open, its nest of pink tentacles bursting out. The greasy strands wrap around him, their toxin burns, though not as horrific as before. Gritting his teeth, Urakael doesn't pull away. He thrusts his arm deeper into the writhing mass. He loops his arm around the tendrils then yanks. Strands rip and pop like piano wires. The demon lurches forward. Urakael wrenches the tendrils again, harder. The sound of tearing meat and then the tongue rips free from the strutter's throat. The demon staggers, the remaining few of its unbroken tendrils flailing wildly. Urakael throws the severed tongue aside and lunges. He drives his thumbs through the strutter's golden eyes and pulls outward. Bone rips as the creature's skull splits apart. The two familiars freeze, their enslaved souls released. Purple and orange flames coat his skin, healing the poisoned wounds.

Tiamat's enormous form rises up from behind her wall of followers, long and snake-like. Her skin glistens like beaten brass. Hundreds of squirming eels run the length of her back like wind-swept hair. Their pale noseless faces are all Anya's. Their black eyes all look at him, though Tiamat's remain closed.

A gun blasts behind him. Turning, he sees the child Malcolm free of his cuffs, firing into the cultists as he and the others charge for Urakael's brethren. Allan is the first to reach them. He takes Zhygan, Ibenus's true name, from the anvil and swings, instantly teleporting behind a blonde vampire and decapitating it with one stroke.

Many of the Legion seem unsure, hesitation in their eyes. Fear.

Luc snatches Velnepo from the ground. He strikes a wendigo with the mace. The blow knocks the demon's corpse away like a child's toy.

A dark glimmer shoots toward Malcolm, a rakshasa, its form invisible to human eyes. Urakael leaps toward it, cresting fifteen feet in the air. Malcolm spins to face him, unable to see the closing demon. Buckshot rips through Urakael's chest.

Raising his claws high, Urakael slashes down as he lands. Invisible flesh tears open. The demon takes form. A black shape, its eyes and mouth empty wells of nothingness. The demon blurs, then splits into two, four identical fiends.

They close.

Urakael swipes at one, but his hand passes through the illusion. Cold claws rip into his back, tearing muscle and tendons. Serrated teeth bite into his neck.

Screaming, Urakael reaches behind, blindly catching the frenzied rakshasa by the back of its head. Flailing claws slice him as he wrenches the demon up and over, flipping it onto the ground. Urakael punches down, crushing the rakshasa's head. Stygian fire spreads across the corpse. He scoops black flames to his lips. Sweet intoxication. His bleeding wounds mend. He rises.

Malcolm stands before him. His warding palm is open, though still at his side, ready to be raised. "Matt?"

Urakael nods to Hounacier and Khirzoor still lying beside the roken plank. Pieces of his own smashed vessel litter the ground beside them. A guttural voice resonates from Urakael's chest. "Save them."

Ten demon corpses lay burning on the ground. Using the flickering shadows of a dead vampire's light, Luiza cleaves off a werewolf's legs.

Urakael turns to the remaining Legion. They stink of fear. They were always cowards. Dozens of black-robed humans flee, those whose souls had been freed or whose fear of mortality outweighed faith.

Tiamat watches him through slitted eyes. The wife of his father, though herself not a god. The betrayer made flesh, made mortal. Her death will give him absolution.

He rushes toward her. A pair of glowing-eyed hellhounds race to meet him. One leaps, jaws open. Deflecting the beast with a forearm, Urakael spins to the side. The other hound crashes into him, knocking Urakael to the ground.

He lands on his back, the demon pressing on top of him. Snarling, it snaps its jaws just above his face. Urakael brings a knee up, wedging it between himself and the hound, and kicks. The beast flips up above his head. Urakael rolls to his feet just as the other hound comes at him again. It springs, sinking its fangs into his arm. It shakes its head, tearing the flesh.

Howling in pain, he grabs the black hound behind its skull and drives his claws in. Vertebrae snap and crunch. Blue fire erupts from the wounds, but the beast's jaws refuse to open. Urakael rips the animal free, tearing the meat from his arm. The power of the dead demon's soul heals him quickly.

Blood pulls him from behind. Urakael wheels around in time to catch the other hellhound flying toward him. He chomps into the demon's spine, tasting the sweet fire explode into his mouth. He tears a piece free and swallows it, bone and all, then hurls the burning corpse at a rushing vampire.

He turns to face Tiamat, murderer of his father. The demon mother has taken flight, her serpentine form undulating through the air. Coward.

Nearly twenty demons burn in the courtyard. His brethren's

children move as a circle, cutting their way through the yard. A ring of bound corpses lies in the center, their bodies dissolved below the ribs. The blood moon above still glows red. As long as it does, the ring holds power. Not all is lost, but he must act soon.

Their mother gone, the Legion begins to flee. A white-haired succubus flies off on leather wings. A trio of ghouls clamors over the castle's wall like cockroaches. Urakael spies a werewolf lying in the corner, its feral features melting away as the demon moves to another body on this world. The child Allan appears beside it and splits the fiend open before the transference completes.

Urakael approaches the children. A robed man with a knife charges. Urakael kills him with a backhand. Luiza is the first to see him near. Four bleeding gashes run down her arm. Luiza's eyes narrow with fear, fear of what he has become. The others notice him as well.

"Go," Urakael says. "Tiamat will return. My brethren must survive."

"Who?" Luc asks. Blood oozes from a cut in his thigh.

Red tinges the mace's glow. Anger. Animosity. He is the betrayer. They don't trust him, neither do their children.

"The weapons," Urakael says. "You must take them from here before she returns."

"Matt?" Luiza asks. "Is it you?"

"He is with me."

"Wha ... who are you?" she asks.

Urakael looks at the sky. The eclipse nears completion. "I am Urakael." *The Fallen.* He meets her gaze. "You called me Dämoren."

Her eyes widen. "How?"

"Go. Now." Urakael turns back toward the ring. Though weak, it still pulses with Icthwyn's power. She is still bound to it. He remembers his father. How could he have loved such a creature? Urakael steps over black-robed bodies. Would his father have loved them as well? Was it wrong that he did not? His father was virtuous. Hatred was no virtue. Tonight Urakael's hatred would die, either with Icthwyn or with himself.

He stops at the edge of the ring. It stinks of death.

"Mother!" he cries to the moon in the First Tongue, the language spoken at Creation. "I call you, Icthwyn. I invoke your name. Come. Come before me. I, Urakael, Seventeenth Son of Dythn, challenge you. Face me!"

Faint light swirls within the ring.

He looks about. The children have left. "Icthwyn, come before me! Icthwyn, face me!"

His consciousness barely intact, Matt remembered Kazuo's words.

"When the laws of the universe are called and powers are invoked or bound by their true names, waves are felt everywhere. That's when prophecies come true. All worlds feel the ripples."

All worlds.

"Icthwyn!" Urakael screams. "I call you!"

The swirling colors surge and spin, consuming the last of the ring's power. A howling wail shrieks down from the heavens as Tiamat flies down toward him, connected to the circle by an almost invisible thread of light.

The earth shudders as she lands. Lips curl from ivory fangs.

"Urakael," the eels utter as one.

He attacks.

She darts to the side, smearing corpses beneath her. Claws splayed, Urakael wheels around to face her. Tiamat swipes a scythe-like talon. He ducks. They whoosh over him, nearly taking his head. Seizing the opening he springs. His claws rake across her wide ventral scales, but they are too hard.

Tiamat lashes to the side, knocking Urakael to the ground. Her reared head shoots down, jaws open. He rolls away as the demon mother snaps. She strikes again, but Urakael jumps out of her path.

He leaps, digging his claws into the flesh behind her forearm. The tiny scales of her shark-like skin peel open, chipping his claws as he tears into her.

Roaring, she buckles and thrashes, trying to knock him free. Urakael holds tight, his toes and left hand dug deep. He slashes her again. Tiamat's serpentine head strikes. Urakael springs out of the way and lands in a crouch.

The agile demon whips around and attacks. He barely escapes, her talons ripping through the flagstones behind him. He leaps for her tail and digs in. He needs to weaken her. Slow her down.

The human-faced eels along her back hiss and strike. One bites his calf. Its long fangs pierce deep, striking bone. Poison burns his veins.

He howls. The venom is quick. It cuts through his veins like broken glass.

He swipes, severing the rubbery eel's neck, then falls, crashing into the hard stone.

Tiamat rears above him. The headless eel along her back detaches and drops to the ground with a wet thud. The hole it occupied closes and a new maggot-sized worm sprouts.

Urakael tries to stand, but falls. Dark blood seeps out from around the claws in his poisoned leg.

The demon mother's thin lips twist into a smile. "Did you really think you could best me?" the eels ask.

He meets her cold gaze.

One of the longer eels slithers out from her neck and flies off into the night.

Tiamat ignores the pale hatchling. "Pathetic." Her jaws open, wide enough to swallow Urakael whole. She strikes.

Urakael leaps away. His father had blessed all his children with a gift. Few understood his. He can't teleport, or attack shadows. He can't wield fire or ice. Father gave him fortitude. The blessing that allowed him to survive being broken as a sword, allowed him to inhabit a pistol, its bullets, pieces of him, constantly replenished. The blessing enables him to survive a toxin that would have slain most of his kin.

Tiamat's diving maw strikes the empty ground. Stone buckles. He springs onto her snout, safely away from the writhing eels. He slashes through one of her giant eyes, shredding it like pudding.

She screams, lashing her head like a whip. Blood and ooze slings through the air. Urakael holds tight. He tries to blind the other eye. His weakened toe claws break under the strain, ripping free. She snaps her head to the side, sending Urakael flying into the castle's wall.

He falls to the ground, beside the body of a dead cultist.

The shrieking demon continues to thrash. Black blood pours from beneath her closed eyelid. Three more eels wriggle free and escape.

Urakael stumbles to his feet. His injured leg wobbles beneath him. Blood runs from the empty sockets at his toes. Dark pinheads begin seeping around the claws at his hands. He tastes it in his mouth. One fang begins to loosen.

With a roar she charges, slithering across the yard like a rampaging train, her taloned hands raised. Favoring his left leg, Urakael springs and rolls out of the way. He swipes at the passing demon, but hits her hard belly scales. Tiamat's long tail wraps to the side, boxing him in. The ring of eels along her back leer down at him. He's too weak to safely jump them.

The demon's one eye glares hatefully down at him. Her jaws open.

An engine roars and a green, flat-faced bus bursts through the castle's gate. Tiamat and her eels turn to face the newcomer. Seizing the opening, Urakael hobbles and leaps over the tail, taking one of the brood out with a passing swipe. He staggers away, leaving bloody footprints in his wake.

Brilliant light shoots from the bus's lamps. Tiamat's pupil shrinks to a narrow slit.

Allan and Luiza race through the open gate door and cut to either side around the yard. Luc and Malcolm step out from the bus.

Tiamat grins wickedly. She strikes at Allan. The child swings Ibenus and teleports out of the demon's path. He brings the sword up, slicing her behind the jaw. She rears high, blood staining her long neck. Another eel detaches and wriggles away.

"I told you to go," Urakael says to Allan.

"We did," the child replies, his eyes on the swaying demon. "We're back."

Tiamat's jaws shoot down at them. Urakael rolls away. Allan blinks to the side, but the demon lashes her head, knocking him to the ground. She snaps at the fallen human, but Urakael leaps onto her neck and bites through the rough skin.

She whips her head, but Urakael holds tight, ripping a mouthful free. She swipes a talon, splitting his side open and knocks him loose. He hits the ground with a thump. Two of his claws are gone, still lodged into the demon's neck.

Malcolm races past, Hounacier high. Tiamat raises a talon to strike him, but a long slice opens along her back, severing four of the eels. She bellows in pain. Another opens, showing white bone beneath. The child Luiza stands against the far side of the yard, hacking at the great shadow cast by the bus's light. She stabs, driving Ausva into the darkness, then pulls it out and to the side.

Tiamat wheels about to face her. Luiza opens a three-foot gash along her belly. The monstrous demon flounders. Luiza swipes again, but Tiamat moves her shadow out of the blade's path. She turns back to the bus. She starts toward it, but Malcolm steps in and hacks Hounacier into her side. Luc and Allan close in. Allan chops deep into Tiamat's flesh. Luc bashes her with Velnepo, sending a visible shockwave through her body.

She falls.

Limping, Urakael runs and jumps onto the back of Tiamat's head.

More weakened claws crack and break free but he holds tight. He bites deep into the base of her skull. Blood explodes into his mouth and Urakael rips in deeper, tearing through bony scales.

Tiamat wails, trying to rise, but Luc, Allan, and Malcolm tear into her. Three pale eels wriggle free to escape, but Luiza hacks their shadows, and the spawn fall writhing to the ground, encased in amber flame.

Urakael rips a scale plate free from Tiamat's neck. He spits it out and punches down into the exposed bone. It cracks and gives way. He drives his arm deeper into her skull, plunging through the fibrous sludge. He twists his remaining claws.

Tiamat's body seizes, then collapses, nearly crushing the child Luc. Power surges and swirls around Urakael's arm. He pulls it free, unleashing a geyser of gold and silver fire. Flames erupt from her other wounds, quickly spreading over the slain demon's body. They wash over Urakael, straddling her neck.

He licks the fiery blood from his hands, tasting power unlike anything he's ever fathomed.

The burning poison in his veins subsides and his wounds mend.

Absolution. Revenge. He has won.

Urakael closes his eyes, savoring the victory, then releases his control on the child Spencer.

Matt slumped, his strange body numb. Brilliant demon fire burned all around him. He slid, then fell off the great demon's corpse.

He watched his hands, coated in flaming blood, shrink down to human size. The glinting claws retracted and smoothed out into his normal fingernails. Bones and ligaments popped and shifted. Shadows invaded the dark recesses of the courtyard and colors dimmed as the dusty window of humanity fell back into place.

"Matt!" Allan ran toward him. Tiamat's fiery blood blazed along Ibenus's blade.

Matt scrunched his eyes, trying to force himself to sit up. His cheeks were wet. Tears.

Hands rolled him onto his back. He opened his eyes. Luc and Allan crouched above him.

"Is he okay?" Malcolm yelled pushing his way between them.

"Matt?" Allan repeated. "Matt, are you all right?"

Matt blinked at them. Their halos of color were gone.

Footsteps raced across the yard toward them. Matt rolled his head to see Luiza, Akumanokira in her hand. Ausva. Its true name was Ausva.

"Matt?" Luc said. "Say something."

Matt's lips quivered. The memory of Tiamat's taste still on his tongue. "I … I'm fine." He glanced up at the moon. A white sliver shone at the edge. The redness faded. Had it only been just a few minutes? He'd seen lifetimes, eons. Memories like an endless ocean. He could spend the rest of his life exploring their—

His eyes widened. The memories were vanishing, receding

as quickly as they'd come. "No!"

"What?" Allan asked.

Matt shook his head, trying to form the words. "I need you to listen to me. I know everything. The origin, where they come from."

The Englishman's brow creased.

"Remember saying you couldn't understand why someone would want to be possessed?"

Allan nodded.

"Then listen. Help me remember before I forget."

Reaching them, Luiza dropped to her knees taking Matt's head into her hands. "Are you all right?"

Matt met her eyes and smiled. She was beautiful. "Yeah," he said, pressing his hand against hers. "Yeah, I'm good."

THE ORIGINS OF DEMONS AND HOLY WEAPONS

BY SIR MATTHEW HOLLIS

Introduction:

In the brief time that I shared the mind of the entity Urakael, I learned the answers to what Valducans have questioned and theorized for centuries. What I can tell is only a small glimpse of that revelation, which, in many ways, leaves only more questions.

However, I will answer them to the best of my ability.

The root of all the answers lies in the origin.

Demons, as we've understood them, are otherworldly entities that can possess the bodies of living creatures. To sustain themselves these demons feed on humans and animals, either physically eating their bodies, or their life-energy. The physical bodies a demon inhabits can be killed, but killing the demon itself requires a holy weapon. This theory is true.

Holy weapons, as we've understood, are physical weapons that can kill a demon. Whether that power comes from a divine blessing or by being possessed by an angelic entity has been the subject of much debate. The truth is that holy weapons are possessed by a living entity. Though calling that entity an angel might not be entirely correct. They are closer to demons than anyone had suspected, more akin to "Higher Demons" or a more evolved demon. These entities do not sustain themselves by consuming the bodies or essence of organic life, but instead feed on demonic souls.

The process of creating a holy weapon, or possessing a weapon with a divine being as we now understand it, has always been a mystery. No successful combination of ceremony and precious materials has ever been duplicated. The reason for this is simple. Every angelic being is unique and requires different ceremony. Demons, for the most part, are not unique. There are many werewolves, rakshasas, and other demonic breeds, and a ceremony to summon a species will always work, providing the summoner is not attempting to invoke a specific entity. For that reason, priests and Valducans were never able to successfully repeat the same method. Furthermore, like demons, possession can occur spontaneously if the perfect combination of factors exists. A soldier taking his officer's sword, holding absolute faith that the power of his Emperor will save him, is how Akumanokira, a nondescript army katana, came to be blessed.

While it is within their power, these "angels" do not possess living things. There is a sacred oath that they will never dominate or inhabit a living creature. Instead, they choose to possess inanimate objects, imbuing them with their essence, and feeding on demons through them. Urakael is the only one of these entities, that I know of, to break this oath. An act that it very much regretted and was shunned for.

There are many reasons for this oath. First, destruction of a holy weapon does not kill the entity itself, only severs its physical tie to our world. Mortality, as we know it, is only achieved through Dämoren inhabiting a mortal creature. Second, these entities consider demons as inferior, and therefore will not demean themselves by lowering to their level. Most importantly, their refusal to possess living creatures is based on an oath given to their father, Dythn. Dythn, for the lack of a better word, was a god. I do not believe he was a god in the sense that we normally use the term, but merely an evolved entity like themselves but far more powerful. Dythn taught his children that humans are their children, and must be protected. Dythn was killed and consumed by his wife, Icthwyn.

As I have said, I do not know all of the answers. However, in the following pages, I do hope to answer many of our greatest questions.

CHAPTER 21

Matt stared at a blinking cursor, his mind blank. The top of the page read "Chapter 1: The Creation of Demons." Below that, empty whiteness.

A warm breeze drifted through the open window, rustling his notes, now suddenly useless, pinned beneath a half-geode serving as his paperweight. Outside, across the green hills, towering white wind turbines stood like a field of mechanical flowers. There were thirty-six in operation, five more by the end of the month. A small brass plaque adorned each of their towers, every one engraved with the name of a fallen Valducan knight. For most, it was their first monument.

Matt clicked the keyboard, typing out the first sentence.

"To understand demons and angels, one must accept that worlds exist outside our own universe."

Frowning, he deleted it. Matt licked his lips, watching the cursor, his fingers poised above the keys.

A bird began singing furiously from the bush outside his window. Another replied.

Matt glanced at his notes. They contained everything he remembered, or what Allan had hastily transcribed as Urakael's memories dissolved, leaving nothing but vague residue, like the high-water mark after a flood, a tell-tale sign of how much was no longer there. Matt had outlined everything he needed to say. Except where to begin.

He looked back at the screen. The dueling birds outside had somehow become louder.

Sighing, Matt opened his email. Sergio still hadn't responded to his last message.

Disappointed, Matt opened the last file the gunsmith had

sent. A teal image of a trigger mechanism, its tip smoothly hooked, filled the screen, seemingly floating before a slate-gray background. He scrolled down to the next picture, a 3D image of a revolver cylinder. Sergio said the new design would easily handle the pressure from modern powder. A more powerful round would be nice, but not dealing with a wall of smoke after each shot was what really made Matt tingle. *Just five more weeks.*

The door behind him opened.

"Aren't you supposed to be writing?" Luiza asked.

"I am," Matt said. "Just taking a break."

"Uh huh." She bent and kissed him on the cheek. "New pictures from Sergio?"

Matt breathed in her sweet perfume, vanilla and mango. He kissed her back. "No. Same ones from Thursday." He scrolled down past images of tiny parts at various angles until reaching the bottom. A full-color picture of a large, gold-etched revolver. A thick blade extended below the barrel, seeming to melt out from the bottom. A pair of bronze wolf heads capped the angled grip. *Five weeks.*

"Looks good," Luiza said. "Still say you should have gone with a swing-out loader."

"Not as structurally sound," Matt said.

"And? With all the high-grade steel and titanium you're using, it won't matter. Reloading will be faster."

"Too modern," Matt said. "I can't pass her off as an antique if the cylinder swings out." Master Turgen had already found a curator to *authenticate* the new revolver as an original Scholberg from 1874.

"Baby," Luiza said, her voice calm like a mother's. "Most countries won't care if it's antique or not. A gun is a gun. Akumanokira has to slip past customs, Dämoren can, too. Why not an uzi?"

Matt gave her a look.

Luiza smiled, obviously pleased with her needling. Feinluna's gold-framed shard glinted on her chest.

"No."

"Aw, come on. You know you want it." She mimed firing a

machinegun, her finger bouncing with imaginary recoil.

"No."

She pouted her lip. "You're no fun."

Matt raised his hands in mock surrender. "I think it's a great idea."

He tapped his chest, above the silver slug beneath. "Urakael, however, wants to be a revolver. I'm just following orders."

Luiza gave an exaggerated sigh. "His loss."

A green pop-up appeared in the corner of the screen with a loud *bloop*.

Matt glanced at it. "Allan's calling."

"I swear he has a crush on you."

Matt snorted. "He just likes talking to another Librarian and Sonu isn't much of a conversationalist." He clicked the screen.

"Crush."

A window opened, showing Allan's smiling face. "Hi, Matt. How are you doing?"

"Good, Allan. You?"

"Fine. How's the missus?"

Luiza hunched down, level to the camera atop the monitor. "Hi, Allan."

"Ah." Allan smiled. "Speak of the devil. How are you doing, Luiza? Chile treating you well?"

"It's all right." She shrugged. "Getting a little antsy. Need some field time."

"I understand," Allan said. "Master Turgen is sending me up to Scotland. We think Glasgow might have itself a vampire."

Luiza grinned. "Sounds fun."

Allan gave a sullen shrug. "It's Glasgow."

"So what's up, Allan?" Matt asked.

"Nothing much. Mal and Schmidt should be arriving there in a couple hours, so I figured I'd catch you first, see how the report was coming."

"It's coming." A slight pang of guilt prodded Matt's gut.

"Great! Look forward to seeing it."

Matt smiled, praying Allan wouldn't ask how far into it he was. The question might hang in the air too long. "I'll send it to you the minute it's done. Don't worry about it."

"Good to hear. Have you done the section on their relation to humans, yet?"

"Not yet."

"What about Tiamat?"

Swallowing, Matt rubbed his chin. "Working on that right now."

Luiza cleared her throat. "I don't mean to spoil your little reunion here, but Matt and I have to head to the airport in about an hour, and I have a few things I need him to finish up first."

"Oh," Allan said, his voice a few octaves higher. "All right, then."

"Sorry, Allan." Matt wondered what chores Luiza had in mind. He'd already done everything they needed.

Allan nodded. "Well, I'll talk with you later. Give Schmidt and Mal my regards."

"We will."

"Good luck in Scotland," Luiza said. "Be safe."

"Thanks." Allan gave a small salute. "Talk to you soon."

Matt clicked the window closed and turned toward her. "So what do you need me to do?"

"Nothing. I just couldn't stand watching you twist uncomfortably like that."

He chuckled. "Thanks."

She kissed him. "We're leaving for the airport in an hour. I suggest you use that time to have something ready before Malcolm and Master Schmidt land. You know they'll want to read it."

Matt nodded.

"Hey." She kissed him again. "I love you."

He met her chocolate eyes. "I love you, too."

To: Alexander Turgen; Margaret Lennox; Sonu Rangarajan
CC: Max Schmidt
From: Clay Mercer
Subject: My Resignation

Gentlemen,

It has been one of my greatest honors to have served as a Valducan knight for the last 22 years. However, due to recent events it has become clear to me that I can no longer continue in the Order. I have listened to each of your concerns, your threats, your bribes, but I do not feel that I am the one being listened to.

Dämoren has chosen Matt to live. At first I did not understand why, but now I do. I've put off taking an apprentice because doing so was an admission that one day I would have to surrender Dämoren to another. So Dämoren has done it for me.

Matt is a brave and brilliant child and Dämoren saw that. He's bonded to her. I don't know how, but I see it. This child is Dämoren's, and in that, he is mine. If we are sworn to protect these holy instruments and honor their wishes, then I am sworn to do this. I will defend him with my life. All I ask in return is that you honor my choice.

If my decision means that Dämoren will not be reunited with her lost shell that Alex located, then so be it. I know that it will be safe with the Order and one day they will be reunited. But I find it very petty that the family I have belonged to for 22 years would hold a piece of Dämoren as leverage against me.

I am sorry it has come to this, but this is not my decision. I do not hold any grudge against you and hope nothing but the best for you all, but if any attempt is made against this child, I swear on Dämoren that I will kill whoever tries to harm him. He is my son.

Respectfully,

Clay Mercer

.

ABOUT THE AUTHOR

Raised in the swamps and pine forests of East Texas, Seth Skorkowsky gravitated to the darker sides of fantasy, preferring horror and pulp heroes over knights in shining armor.

His debut novel, *Dämoren*, was published in 2014 as book #1 in the Valducan series; it was followed by *Hounacier* in 2015, and Ibenus in 2016. Seth has also released two sword-and-sorcery rogue collections with his Tales of the Black Raven series.

When not writing, Seth enjoys cheesy movies, tabletop role-playing games, and traveling the world with his wife .

Visit Seth's website: http://skorkowsky.com/

Curious about other Crossroad Press books?
Stop by our site:
http://store.crossroadpress.com
We offer quality writing
in digital, audio, and print formats.

Enter the code FIRSTBOOK
to get 20% off your first order from our store!
Stop by today!